Acknowledgements

To my wife Jane, for her continued support, as always. Thank you, I love you.

To Nick Berriman, my faithful test-pilot. Three down many more to go. Thanks again, my friend.

To Lucy James and Kenny Andrew, of The Studio Tettenhall. Thank you for yet another stunning book cover design.

To David Berriman, for sharing his wealth of experience and giving his valuable time so freely. Thank you, David.

Also by Robert J Marsters:

The Ascension of Karrak

The Bane of Karrak

Robert J Marsters

THE CESSATION OF KARRAK

ASCENSION THREE

A CIP catalogue record for this title is available from the British Library.

ISBN 978-1-9996518-8-6 (Paperback)
ISBN 978-1-9996518-4-8 (EBook)

CHAPTER 1

Plumes of thick, black smoke billowed high into the starless night sky, the fires from whence they came engulfing structure and flesh alike.

Agonising screams ripped through the air as yet another body was incinerated, eviscerated, decapitated or crushed by falling masonry.

There had been no warning before their attackers struck.

Believing the gates to be secure, many were slaughtered, oblivious to the onslaught that would soon ensue.

The enemy poured through the parting gates, destroying everyone and everything in their path.

Many attempted to stand their ground in a futile attempt to repel the unknown assailants.

Emnor stood defiant, his magnificent staff raised high above him. He bellowed orders for his fellow wizards to band together. He was unheard, it seemed, his voice drowned out by the numerous explosions around him. Instinctively, he blocked a fire spell that had been launched in his direction by one of the mystery assassins. He reversed it and it flew toward its caster who was immediately turned to nothing but a charred skeleton that hovered momentarily, before collapsing in a heap. Emnor barely had time to witness this as he was already defending himself against another attack. He launched spell after spell, finding it difficult to move forward as his foes fell before him. His heart sank. For each adversary he defeated he saw at least one of his fellow wizards fall, but they did not fall alone, each taking the lives of many enemies before their own imminent demise.

It had all happened so quickly that he had not realised how ghastly their enemies appeared. Some were ghostly in appearance, floating in mid-air, clouds of black smoke that had a will of their own. Others appeared to be no more than walking corpses that wielded heavy swords, hacking mindlessly at any within reach. Worst of all were the beasts. They darted between ally and enemy alike, their huge, fanged jaws tearing at limbs indiscriminately.

Amidst the mayhem, Emnor caught sight of his oldest and most trusted friend, Yellodius Tarrock. He seemed to revel in the carnage. Waving a staff of his own and casting spells with his left hand, he slashed wildly at the walking corpses that now surrounded him with a sword clutched in his right. Emnor desperately wanted to reach his position but as the body-pile before him increased, he found it more and more difficult to move. The expression on his face was a mixture of rage and anguish as, trapped and unable to reach them, his friends and colleagues fell in greater numbers.

Still he battled on. How many enemies had he felled? Why were their numbers not decreasing? Emnor's strength was failing, how could he or any of his kind possibly survive such a mindless, cruel assault? The noise, combined with the billowing dust created by the exploding walls around him, only added to his confused state as he tried to fathom why this was happening.

Suddenly there was a loud screeching from many of his enemies as scores of them turned to face the wide-open gates. They halted their onslaught momentarily, in awe it seemed, at the entity that had appeared between them. Twenty-feet tall, it hovered inches from the ground, surveying the battle-ground of the inevitable victory that was about to be his. His black robes billowed around him as if fluttering in a non-existent breeze. Turning to face Emnor, buried deep within shadow-like features, his red eyes flashed brightly. Emnor stood petrified. The entity slowly stretched out its arm. The old wizard tried to retaliate but was too late. Instantly clutched in an invisible grasp, he was unable to move. The battle continued before him. Tears streamed down his cheeks as, one by one, he watched his friends fall to sword, spell or beast.

Yello was the last man standing. Roaring at the top of his voice he continued to bring down his enemies in droves until, with a wave of the enemy leader's hand, he was thrown the full length of the courtyard and crashed into the damaged wall. Falling heavily to the ground, he lay motionless. His wounds were severe. As powerful as the old wizard was, he could defend himself no more. The enemy fell silent. A blood-curdling laugh came from the gargantuan entity as it once again faced Emnor. The new terror seemed to sense how much Yello meant to him as he heard its voice inside his head.

"I am the Shadow Lord Karrak. All shall bow down to me. All shall fear me."

With a wave of Karrak's hand the wall above Yello began to crumble, huge pieces falling, to both crush and entomb his battered body.

***

"NO!" Emnor suddenly yelled, sitting bolt upright.

"Bad dreams?"

Emnor wiped the sweat from his brow and looked across at Yello, "You could say that," he said rubbing his eyes.

"Understandable, with all you've been through."

"I suppose so," Emnor sighed. "It's just that it seemed so real, so vivid."

"Care to share?" asked Yello, peering over the top of his book.

Emnor could recall every intricacy from his nightmare but, glancing across at his friend, decided not to reveal its details, "Oh, you know how it is," he replied. "Ghosts, ghouls, monsters, all that nonsense."

"I think the only thing that's vivid is your imagination," scoffed Yello. "Ghosts indeed, as if!"

"What do you mean, as if?"

"Don't tell me you actually believe in them?" laughed Yello.

"I don't have to believe in them. I've seen them."

"Oh really! You've seen them? Are you sure you hadn't just been at the wine again?" Yello sniggered.

"No, I hadn't! If you'd have spent a bit more time in Reiggan instead of galivanting halfway around the world, you'd have probably seen them as well!"

"Why would I want to be cooped up in that place? Look what it's done to you!"

"And what exactly, do you think it's done to me?" asked Emnor.

"Well, look at you. You wouldn't have been having nightmares, for a start," replied Yello, pointing at him. "And then there's your attitude," he added.

"What's wrong with my attitude?" exclaimed Emnor. "I'll have you know I have the patience of a saint."

"Exactly!" replied Yello. "You're like an old mother hen the way you pamper this lot. And don't get me started on the subject of Jared."

"What's this got to do with him?"

"Everything, you daft old git!" said Yello. "You mollycoddle him," he mumbled.

"Preposterous!" retorted Emnor, "I do not mollycoddle him!"

"Yes, you do. I'm surprised you don't tuck him in at night! There was a time when you'd have blasted the crap out of him. You used to believe that harsh lessons were the only way a wizard could learn to defend himself. Not your beloved Prince Jared though. Oh no, teach him all the nice stuff to keep him safe. 'When in danger, scarper' seems to be your new motto."

"I'll have you know that Jared is one of the most gifted students it has ever been my honour to instruct!"

insisted Emnor. "Look at the time he faced the boys, four on one."

"Cobblers!" replied Yello. "They're just a bunch of kids. What's he going to do when he comes up against one of Karrak's lot, eh? They won't be polite enough to hang back in case the teacher tells them off for hurting the new boy."

"So, I take it that you believe you can do better?" asked Emnor.

"I never said that. I would never undermine the instruction you have given him," replied Yello, reassuringly. "However, if I were instructing him, I wouldn't be scared to set his arse on fire during training either!"

Emnor paused, contemplating Yello's last statement. "What would you do different, if you had the chance?" he asked. "Considering that he is of royal blood, of course."

"Royal blood or no, Emnor. It's only when you feel pain that you truly realise how much you want to protect yourself against it. If you ask my opinion, and I know you haven't, Jared needs to take a few knocks to bring him into the real world."

"I'm not convinced, old chap. What if he takes offence and decides it's too much for him?"

"It's for his own good, Emnor. Whether he likes the idea or not it's only a matter of time before Karrak comes looking for him. He must be prepared. It's going to be survival of the fittest, I'm afraid. Look at young Drake for instance, he's a prime example."

"What have I done now!?" asked Drake, appearing unexpectedly.

"Ah, Maddleton!" said Yello with a beaming smile. "What fortuitous timing. I wonder if you'd mind helping me out with a little experiment?" he asked.

Drake flinched, "This is going to hurt, isn't it?" he asked sheepishly. "And why are you using my first name?" he continued, becoming increasingly nervous.

"Ha ha, I love your sense of humour. Don't worry, it'll only take a second. Now, Emnor, as I was saying…"

Without warning, Yello took a swipe at Drake's head. Drake was too fast for him and quickly dodged out of the way.

"Hang on a minute!" yelped Drake. "What the bloody hell was that for? I didn't do anything! As a matter of fact, I didn't even say anything!"

Yello smiled at Emnor, "See what I mean?" he said. "Basic survival instinct."

***

Only the distant lightning flashes broke the gloom of the evening sky. The thunder was in stark contrast to the silence that had ensued between the two strangers. Neither moved a muscle as they stared at one another, both pairs of eyes hidden beneath heavy cowls.

"Tell me, did you honestly believe that such an obvious falsehood would delay my decision to destroy you?" asked Karrak.

"Well, I'm still standing here, aren't I? Although you are very much mistaken about it being a falsehood."

"The person once known as Karrak Dunbar no longer exists."

"Oh, I think you know that that's a lie. He's in there, trapped and suppressed admittedly, but he still exists."

"You seem very confident for one who is about to die. Perhaps you would be better off if you were to beg for mercy."

"I think the confidence comes from my father's side of the family. And I'm sure you're the merciful type! Forgive and forget? Somehow, I don't think so."

"You may have survived this encounter if you had copied the actions of your friend and remained silent."

"If you don't mind me saying, you're not very good at this intimidation lark. And as for him, you have no idea. Remain silent? That'll be the day! It was a relief to control his mind just to shut him up. Do you realise how annoying it can be when circumstances dictate your actions to the point that you have to pretend to be something you're not? I've been wanting to fry this little creep for years. I have enjoyed our little games together at times, I'll admit. I kept implanting false memories whenever I put him in a trance. He believes that he killed his brother when he was a child, accidentally of course, a brother whose ghost now haunts him. Honestly, it's hilarious to watch, he never even had a brother, he's an only child. First time I saw him he'd been trapped in an alley by a gang of street kids. If I hadn't intervened when I did they'd have cut him to pieces. Naturally, I erased all memory of what actually happened to him, who would want to remember passing out at the mere sight of a knife anyway? It was infuriating the amount of times I had to virtually spell out answers to the simplest of questions, that's when I'd arrange a meeting with his ghostly brother. It worked perfectly, all eyes were on the 'looney in the room', as it were. Nobody even gave me a second glance. I was reading scrolls that were hundreds of years old right under their noses and they never even noticed. I did whatever I needed, and they watched him, Alexander Hardman, the most annoying, self-righteous git it has ever been my misfortune to meet. I had to 'play nice' so that the old cronies wouldn't become suspicious. They thought I was being a friend and taking care of him. But you can learn a lot when you live in a wizard's fortress."

"You know of Reiggan Fortress?" asked Karrak.

"Yes. I also know all there is to know about the Elixian Soul, that pretty little gem you wear so proudly in your breastplate." Karrak moved forward. Whether as the shadow lord or as Prince Karrak Dunbar, never had he been spoken to with so much disdain. "I'd calm down if I were you, or I may decide not to share my secrets with you, secrets revealed by the Peneriphus Scroll!" sneered the stranger.

Karrak backed away, "What do you know of the scroll?" he asked. It was a subject he desperately wanted to learn more about, but he could stand no more. Storming forward, he raised his hands. He would destroy this impudent upstart. If it was a show of strength his enemies wanted, a show he would give them.

The stranger began to laugh, "What's wrong, Daddy? Can't light the fuse?"

Karrak twisted and jerked. What was happening? The Elixian Soul was his to command but even as he had attempted to destroy his enemy, it had denied him. "What have you done? What is happening to me?" he bellowed.

"There's been a slight change of plan, Father dear. You never did your homework, did you? Well, I did. It seems that for your little trinket to 'work its magic', if you'll pardon the pun, we both have to be present. I'm afraid you've been demoted. You see, you have the strength to bear the Elixian Soul whereas I, sadly, do not. The downside for you unfortunately is that, when you and I are together, it will only obey my commands. I'm sure we can work out our differences, but let's not worry about that now, there'll be plenty of time later. We've got some catching up to do. I'm known as Xarran, Xarran Althor. Perhaps you could tell me my real name?"

***

"Come on, come on! Hurry up, it's time to leave!"

"Lodren!" shouted Faylore, suddenly. "Will you please calm down? We are not going anywhere until I find out what this is all about."

"But Faylore! Thelwynn… he's waiting. He said we have to go now! Jared and the others are in danger. Come on!"

"Lodren," she sighed, placing her hands on his shoulders. "How many dragons have you met? Before you came here, of course."

"Well," he replied, "there was the time when I thought I'd seen one, but that turned out to be a glamoch that had been rolling in the moss by the river. Then… no, that was another glamoch, I think. Ooh, a friend of mine told me that…"

"So, that would be a grand total of…?" she asked, almost singing the words.

Lodren began wringing his hands, "None," he mumbled.

"Sorry?" said Faylore, to emphasise her point, "How many?"

"None," repeated Lodren, even quieter than the first time.

"Ah, well in that case, I'll let you into a little secret," she whispered. "You've probably figured out, by yourself, how nice they are, and I completely agree with you on that. The thing you don't know is this, they do tend to over-exaggerate things somewhat."

Lodren frowned at her, "You're just saying that because you think it would be rude to ride on a dragon's back," he chuntered.

"You should know me well enough by now, Lodren. I do not tell lies. It's the truth. For instance, Thelwynn sent one of the dragons to us for some ointment once because Fireweigh had a splinter in his hand that had become infected. By the time the messenger reached us, the story was that Fireweigh had managed to impale his arm on a tree limb, and they needed one of us to amputate it in order to free him!"

"Wow! They wanted you to cut his arm off just because he had a splinter?"

"No, Lodren, that's not what they wanted. They wanted us to attend immediately. The reason that they exaggerate so is because they're also very impatient."

"Alright, I understand that, but why now? Why us?" asked Lodren, a little confused.

"It's obvious ain't it?" said Grubb, roaring with laughter.

Lodren looked blankly at him, "Erm… No!"

"'e's bored. 'e wants us to take 'im on a jolly with us!" said Grubb, wiping his eyes. "The crafty sod!"

Even Faylore hadn't worked it out so quickly. She smiled at Grubb, "Do you honestly think he wants to come with us?"

"Well work it out. 'ow long's it been since 'e left that place for more than an hour or two?" asked Grubb.

Faylore tried to recall, "I don't think he ever has," she replied. "He's been there since he was an egg."

"An' is that 'ow dragons 've always behaved? I'm sure they didn't grow wings just for flyin' around the frozen wastelands."

"You know what that means then, don't you?" asked Lodren as he started getting excited again. "He likes us. He really, really likes us."

"That's all very well," said Faylore. "But that does not mean that we should take advantage simply because you want to ride through the clouds. It's positively obscene. Riding on a dragon indeed!"

"So, what do we do?" asked Lodren. "He'll be terribly disappointed if you say he can't come with us."

"Wait here, I'll talk to him," said Faylore, "I'm sure he'll understand."

"But I don't want him to understand," said the frustrated Nibby, "I want him to come with us!"

Faylore began to walk away. Turning slightly, she pointed at Lodren, "Stay there, Lodren. I mean it," she added seriously.

"Ah, Your Majesty," said Thelwynn as Faylore approached him. "Is all going well with your preparations?"

"Not exactly, my lord," replied Faylore. "I have to admit that I am not altogether comfortable with your suggestion."

"Oh dear," said Thelwynn. He paused for a moment before leaning down and whispering, "Scared of heights?"

"Not in the slightest, Lord Thelwynn. That is not the issue and I'm sure you're quite aware of it!"

"Why are you so concerned, Faylore? All I offered to do was to help you reach your friends in a more timely manner. What could be wrong with that? We are friends after all."

"And you are the high lord of all dragons! You should set an example. You wouldn't expect me to carry someone on my back, why should you?"

"So, it's a question of etiquette? You sound more like your mother with every day that passes, Your Majesty."

"And what's that supposed to mean?" she asked.

"Merely that it seems the adventurer inside you is beginning to fade, and the monarch emerging. Comes to us all, I suppose. We can't stay young forever."

"Well I.... Listen you, I'm as adventurous as I ever was. I'm not that old yet. I've seen and done more than the last three Thedarian kings combined, and broken plenty of rules along the way, to boot."

"Yet you shy away from taking one simple flight on a dragon's back?" asked Thelwynn, obviously taunting her.

"There is more to consider than merely what I am prepared to do," she replied.

"Please, Your Majesty, enlighten me."

"Well look at the other two who will be along for this jaunt of yours. One is a shapeshifter who can and has become a hawk, so he knows how to fly. He can be the most obnoxious person you've ever met and would probably criticise your technique all the way. At least you could tip him off and tell him to follow. Then there's Lodren," she continued, "have you seen him since you made your suggestion? No? What a sight that is, he can't keep still. Jumping around like a spoilt child telling Grubb and I to 'hurry up' every five seconds."

"Well, what do you expect?" asked Thelwynn, quietly. "With a bloodline like his, it's quite natural."

Faylore paused, "What do you mean?" she asked, "A bloodline like his?"

"Well, he is Drakeborn. Isn't it obvious?"

She had no idea what Thelwynn was talking about, "Sorry. He's what?"

Thelwynn laughed, "Drakeborn. You must have had an inkling at least? His arms, the big eyes, the hammer?"

Faylore looked at him blankly, "No… still have no idea what you're talking about."

"He's Drakeborn, a dragon hunter. So are all his kin, have been for generations, actually."

"Dragon hunter!" exclaimed Faylore. "He nearly got himself squashed by a glamoch the first day I met him. I hardly think he'd be a match for a dragon if he were to face one."

"Perhaps 'hunter' was not the right word," said Thelwynn. "His people never hunted dragons to harm them, they hunted them to protect them."

"That doesn't make any sense. Dragons are peaceful, why would you need protection and from whom for goodness sake?"

"The ones who were doing us the most harm, Faylore. We needed protection from ourselves."

"Oh," said Faylore, realisation dawning on her face. "Can you tell me more?"

Thelwynn sighed, his warm breath causing Faylore's hair to flutter gently. She smiled at him.

"Well," he said, "it began many millennia ago. Dragons were primitive beasts, much the same as any other. They roamed the lands and skies unaware of the existence of others. So large and terrible were they that the merest whisper of one within ten leagues would cause decent folk to hide. No sensible person would venture outside, for they were quite certain that if the dragon saw them, they would undoubtedly be eaten. The situation remained unchanged for centuries until, one day, a stranger entered the lands. His kind had never been seen before and conversations were rife with the rumour of an enigmatic hero who had sworn to capture and tame all dragons. The villagers and cave dwellers he encountered on his quest implored him to rethink his plans. Why risk his life capturing such monstrous beasts when killing them would be far easier? The stranger replied that he would never take the life of a dragon. He explained that, although ferocious, they were also intelligent and that he had spoken to many in his time. Whenever he tracked a new dragon he would be forced to face it in combat as dragons knew no other way. He had defeated all that he had faced and once the battle was done he would tend the dragon's wounds, remove his armour and lay down his giant hammer. He would invite them to eat him if they felt the need but asked for a little time in which to explain why they should not. Not one, having listened to him ever posed a problem to anyone again. He had discovered a labyrinth of caverns hidden deep within the frozen wastelands. The lava flow was a natural heating system that would ensure they would never be cold again and a mythical gem buried deeper than any could possibly reach would calm their aggressive nature. The legend of The Nibrilsiem has been told by my kin ever since. The legend of the one who united our species with kind words, determination, love, and a giant hammer. Well, that's how the story goes, anyway."

Faylore jumped, without realising, she had become mesmerised, "Oh, my word. So you believe Lodren to be one of the Nibrilsiem?"

"Without a shadow of a doubt, Your Majesty. He's a dragon rider if ever I saw one. Which I haven't by the way, but the description in the tales…"

"So why refer to him as Drakeborn?"

"I have no idea if you want the truth. We just do. The name got changed ages ago and I can't understand why. The old term was so much better. 'BOGGUMS' we used to call them, has such a noble ring to it, don't you think?"

Faylore was agog. To think that she had known Lodren for years, and never once suspected him of being anything more than the polite, amiable Nibby that she had grown to love dearly, simply astounded her. She turned and stared at him, open-mouthed.

***

"Ooh 'eck," mumbled Grubb. "Somethin' ain't right. They're lookin' over 'ere. No, don't look! Pretend you 'aven't seen 'em!" he whispered.

"If I don't look I won't have to, because I haven't seen them, have I?"

"Oh, 'ang on a minute, it's not as bad as I thought. They're not lookin' at me. They're lookin'at you."

"How's that 'not so bad'!" exclaimed Lodren.

"'cause they like you more than they like me. Trust me, I'll be in the firin' line for somethin' shortly."

"What absolute nonsense! They like me more than you. Whatever gave you that idea?"

"Not sure, somethin' in the eyes. You've gotta be careful, Lodren."

"I think you're losing it, Grubb. I haven't heard ravings like that since…" he lowered his voice, "… since Koloss, and we all know he was mental."

Grubb lowered his gaze to the floor, "Mmm Koloss," he repeated.

Lodren seemed a little concerned and tilted his head to one side to catch his friend's eye, "Grubb?" he said, "We are friends, aren't we?" he asked, tentatively.

"Depends," said Grubb, eyeing him carefully, "What ye done?"

"I haven't done anything, stupid!" exclaimed Lodren. "But we are, aren't we? Best friends, I mean."

"Course we are! I wouldn't be sittin' with ye if we weren't," Grubb's suspicion returned as he once again stared at his friend. "Come on," he said, "out with it. What's goin' on in that big bonce o' yours?"

"I need to ask you a question, but I don't want you to feel insulted," Lodren lost his nerve. "On second thoughts, forget it. It's none of my business. I should be ashamed of myself for probing around in people's private affairs. Please accept my apologies, Grubb," he pleaded.

"FOR WHAT!" exclaimed Grubb at the top of his voice, "You didn't even ask me anythin'!"

"Shhh, calm down! I'm sorry, I promise it won't happen again!"

"What won't?" continued Grubb, now in more of a fluster than Lodren. "How can it happen again? It didn't 'appen that time! Now will ye stop messin' about and just ask me what ye wanted to and get it over with, ye stupid Nibby."

"I shouldn't pry, Grubb. As I said, it really is none of my business."

Grubb transformed into Wilf in a flash. Grabbing Lodren by his tunic with two of his huge hands, he hoisted him into the air until they were nose to nose, "Ask… me… the blasted… question!" he growled.

Lodren gulped, "Well, so long as you're sure," he whimpered. Wilf lowered him gently to the ground and began to shrink. Lodren was still procrastinating and began smoothing his tunic down, "Oh dear, this will definitely need pressing before I can wear it again. Look at the collar, it's all…"

Grubb was sitting directly in front of him. Leaning forward, he fixed his gaze on him and asked his own question for the last time, "The question?" he said, quietly.

"Yes, of course, the question. I was thinking, and please stop me if you think I'm overstepping the mark," he looked at Grubb, who was now glaring at him. "Hmm, well, do you remember the time right before we went into the hall of history with Jendilomin and Faylore?" he asked nervously.

"What about it?" asked Grubb, frowning.

"Just before Faylore and I found you by the cart, you said that Koloss had insulted you… because you were different. You said that he said you should be ashamed. It really hurt me to see you so upset, Grubb. What would make him say such a thing if he knew it would hurt you so much? What did he believe that you should feel ashamed about, and who are you different to anyway?"

Grubb took a deep breath, "I can see this 'as been playin' on yer mind a bit. Why didn't ye ask me sooner, ye puddin'?"

"I didn't like to," replied Lodren, "I couldn't get the look on your face out of my mind, still can't to be honest. What's the big secret?"

"You've never met any other Vikkery 'ave ye, Lodren?"

"No, you're the only one. Actually, now that I think about it, are you the only one?"

"My word, no," laughed Grubb. "Might 'ave been a lot easier if I was. No, I 'ave family and kin, same as everyone else. We just... never got along, I suppose. That, o' course, was down to me bein' different."

"How are you so different to the other Vikkery? Are they taller or broader, more intelligent, no offence," he added, raising his hand to affirm it.

Grubb laughed again, "Intelligent? Don't make me laugh! 'alf of 'em wouldn't know the difference between an apple and the tree it fell off! No, they're different, or should I say I am because they can transform themselves into all kinds of 'real' animals, not made up ones like I 'ave to. I'm a squelch!"

"A squelch! What's a squelch?" exclaimed Lodren

"Alright, alright! Keep yer voice down," urged Grubb. "There's no need for all of 'em to know. It's kind of a nickname they give Vikkery like me. It's the noise we make when we transform, see? Fer years and years, I tried me best to get it right, but I just can't do it. Ye all seem to love Wilf, but it ain't what he's really supposed to look like."

"What is he supposed to look like then?" asked Lodren, slightly unsure of whether he wanted to hear the answer.

"A bear. Simple and straightforward ye'd 'ave thought, but I can't even get that right. Closest I ever got was the eagle, and that was supposed to be a pigeon.

Closest I ever got to transforming into a real beast," Grubb replied.

"Well, if you ask me, Wilf's ten times better than a mangy old bear. He's bigger for a start and with twice as many arms. How much of a bonus is that!"

"That's not the way the other people in our village saw it, they mocked me every day for years, I couldn't take it any longer."

"Is that why you left? To get away from all the horrible comments?" asked Lodren.

"It wasn't that simple, I'm afraid. The taunting was what started it all though."

"Started what?" asked Lodren.

"The war," replied Grubb, solemnly.

"The war!" exclaimed Lodren. "What war?"

"The civil war between the Vikkery. My family on one side and my cousins and their families on the other."

"Oh, so it was a small family dispute then?" asked Lodren, hopefully.

"Not, exactly," replied Grubb. "There were about seven hundred of us and more than six hundred of them, so I'd hardly call it 'small'. And if you think that the way to settle a family dispute is to tear one o' yer cousins in half, then aye, ye could call it a dispute."

"My word!" exclaimed Lodren, "How did you manage to resolve your differences?" He gulped, "Don't tell me your entire family were wiped out!"

"O' course not! None of the elders would 'ave let it go that far. No, it was settled with single combat between the leaders of the two sides."

Lodren knew what the answer to his next question would be, but he asked it anyway. “Who were the two leaders?”

“Me an’ me cousin, Crump.”

Lodren sighed, “I should’ve known,” he said. “So, what happened?”

“Well, our abilities being what they are, we very rarely use weapons. We always battle beast-style, as it were. Ye face off in a circle and try to time it right for when ye change, too soon an’ ye’ll give yer opponent the upper hand of knowing what ‘e’s up against. Too slow and ye could lose an arm, or worse.” Lodren never commented as Grubb continued with his story, “Now, I knew that Crump’s favourite thing was to change into a wolf, and he’d always go for the throat, so all I had to do was bide my time. Sure enough, he leapt at me, transforming in mid-air. He wasn’t fast enough. Turning into Wilf I caught him with one ‘and, crushed ‘is skull. If I ‘adn’t killed ‘im, ‘e would’ve killed me. His family got all funny about it, said it weren’t fair ‘cause it weren’t a real animal as I’d turned into.”

“So, the war carried on?” asked Lodren, totally engrossed.

“The village elders ‘ad a meetin’. Decided that they’d let the result stand on one condition,” replied Grubb.

“And that was?”

Grubb gave a huge sigh and dropped his head, “That I was banished for life,” he replied.

“But that’s not fair!” exclaimed Lodren, “All you were doing was defending yourself and your family. Surely they can’t be allowed to banish you for that?”

"Would ye prefer the alternative? Keep fighting each other until a few 'undred more are dead. It was the best solution in the end. Me leaving meant that all me family were safe and that's all I wanted, especially as the reason it all began was because of something so petty. Pride, Lodren, the most dangerous emotion you'll ever encounter. And now you've met the biggest idiot who has ever fallen victim to it."

CHAPTER 2

Jared sat cross-legged on the ground, quietly reflecting on all that had taken place. Tucked into a corner of the gibbonite's cave, he drew patterns in the dirt with his dagger. His thoughts were of Karrak and, what he felt to be, his own weakness when dealing with him in the past. It was as if destiny itself had spoken to him so many times. He had been presented with countless opportunities to end his brother's life but had been too weak or simply too delusional to seize them. Jared could have easily nudged him, sending him plunging to his death from the ramparts of Borell Castle during one of his drunken rants. Seeing the rage in Karrak's eyes revealed his hatred of all he felt were beneath him when he launched his unprovoked attack on Jared during their impromptu training session. Hannock had saved him, it was true, but why not end it there? Why not simply cut Karrak's throat as he lay unconscious? It may have seemed callous at the time, but still, it would have brought about the same inevitable result they now sought. If he had been stronger, if only he could have set aside his pathetic sentimentality for a split second they would not now be facing a tyrannical shadow lord, and so many lives would have been saved. He glanced at the wizards, young and old. Would they be the next to be sacrificed? Was this an unwinnable war? Jared had inadvertently begun to thrust his dagger into the dirt.

"I think I'd better take that, Your Highness."

Jared looked up. The sun was streaming through the open roof of the cave and was sitting directly behind the silhouetted Hannock.

"Don't worry, Hannock. I'm not suicidal, yet," he said, smiling up at his friend.

"It's not that I'm worried about," replied Hannock. "You've made an awful mess of that blade. Give it here, I'll sharpen it for you." He stretched out his hand and helped Jared to his feet.

Jared looked at his friend in admiration, "Why, Hannock?" he asked.

"Because you've blunted it," replied Hannock.

"No. I'm not talking about the dagger, you idiot. I'm talking about you. Why are you here? Borell has fallen, there is no king, yet still you hold your sense of duty toward a house that no longer exists. It's all gone, Hannock. There is nothing that binds you to your service of it anymore."

Hannock straightened his tunic, as shabby as it was looking, he attempted to maintain an elegant appearance, "There's you, Your Highness," he replied. "You are heir to the throne, Jared. I swore to protect all members of House Dunbar and I will never break my vow."

"The throne of Borell!" exclaimed Jared, "There is no throne, Hannock. There is nothing left! All that remains is a king whose mind is in shreds and a prince who has no subjects, a prince who has no idea what to do next. I'm as lost as the rest of you! It all ended, Hannock. It ended when my brother destroyed everything that you and I hold dear. We were so proud, so foolish. It was a dream! Borell, the safe haven where all citizens would be protected from harm. They were unaware that the worst threat of all lay within the very walls that were set to protect them!" Jared sank to his knees, "Why did I not end this long ago? Why did I not kill Karrak when I had the chance?"

Hannock squatted down in front of his friend. Placing his hand beneath Jared's jaw, he gently raised his head and looked deeply into his eyes. "Because you're not him," he whispered. "Because your heart is not as hard and cold as ice, because you are an honourable man who wants desperately to believe that there is good in all of us. That's why, Jared."

Jared nodded.

"But!" exclaimed Hannock, realising how sombre the mood had become, "We all make mistakes. Man or boy, Karrak was always a git! Now get up, we've got things to do."

Smiling, Jared rose from the ground once more. Following his friend, he glanced around the cave. The gibbonites were as relaxed as ever and as he passed them the one that Lawton and Poom had followed gave him the familiar 'thumbs up' and smiled at him. Jared wondered if it would be so carefree if it knew the possible fate that the future had in store.

***

"I do not need to lose weight! I got through the entrance, didn't I?"

"Yes you did, Lawton. But only after you cut your way through," laughed Poom.

"I might not have had to if there hadn't been so much of your fur caught on the branches, hang on a minute I need to cover my eyes, the sun's shining off your bald patches."

"Oh ha, ha. How original."

"Have you two quite finished?" asked Yello, frowning. "You behave like a couple of spoilt children some days."

The two Gerrowliens looked at one another and sniggered. "Every day," whispered Poom, nudging Lawton.

"So, what's the plan?" asked Drake.

"I've calculated that we can reach Mellanthion before nightfall, providing we are all in agreement, of course," said Emnor.

"I don't mean to be rude, Emnor, but have you gone off your rocker?" laughed Hannock, "You do realise how far it is, don't you?"

"No, I haven't and yes, I do," replied Emnor. "It's simple really. We use relocation spells. We have plenty of water now."

"Unlike Alex and Xarran…" said Harley, his voice tailing off.

"Why the long faces?" exclaimed Yello. "Don't you dare give up on them! I've had dealings with some of the greatest wizards that have ever lived and those two will be fine, they probably just got a little sidetracked."

"You actually believe that they would allow themselves to be sidetracked, knowing that there was a possibility that we were still out here, dying of thirst?" asked Harley, pointedly.

"I never said 'allow', now did I? Of course, they wouldn't allow themselves to be sidetracked. What I meant was that they probably ran into an unforeseen obstacle that delayed them slightly."

"Or they've fallen off a cliff; or have been eaten by wolves; or have met up with some of Karrak's lot and been burnt alive." The group turned and faced Poom in disbelief. "Just saying! Come on now, you were all thinking it."

"Perhaps!" said Emnor, "But we would never be so indelicate as to say it, you stupid Gerrowlien."

"Bit harsh isn't it?" sniggered Poom.

"Can we please get back to the plan," urged Drake. "If we intend to reach Mellanthion by nightfall, we'd better get a move on!"

Emnor smiled at him, "Well said, Drake. Everybody gather round."

***

"You've done alright, so far, I suppose. But what's it all for? You must have some sense of purpose? And before you start, don't give me all the usual crap about dominating the world and everyone fearing and bowing down to you. It's so boring." Xarran turned to face Karrak, "Nothing to say? Thought as much. None of this makes any sense. Love what you've done with the castle by the way, you've really captured the derelict, crappy look perfectly. Wanting to rule the world, I understand that part. Wanting people to fear and bow down to you, I get that too. But it's never going to happen is it, Father?

Do you know why? Because you kill everyone in sight or turn them into a beast or a part of your undead army!" he bellowed.

The chapel in which they stood was damp and dimly lit. Half-stocked candelabras set on the altar caused the shadows of the statues about them to perform a macabre dance on the walls behind them. The occasional groans from the ghoulish guards echoed around the cavernous room, resounding like an undead chorus to the highs and lows of Xarran's voice.

"You should beware, boy," Karrak said slowly. "The Elixian Soul has its own agenda. Do not be fooled for a single moment that you have any control over its power."

"I have no delusions of that, Father. What I do believe is that, you do have control over its power, and I have control over you. That is all I need."

"You are deluded, boy. Walk away now and I shall allow you to live. Refuse my offer and the price you will pay later is one that you can ill afford."

"Oh, please!" exclaimed Xarran, "More threats? You can't touch me, old man. You've tried, and failed, or hadn't you realised that the Soul wants me around for a reason?"

"Tell me, boy, for what reason does it want you? Do you have any idea at all?"

"Stop calling me 'boy'," roared Xarran. "Do not provoke me, Karrak, or you may find yourself joining your own ranks."

"Forgive me," said Karrak in a mocking tone. "You feel that you are safe, and from a direct attack from myself it appears that you are. What if I were to force my will upon another and compel them to do you harm?"

"Ifs, buts and maybes, Karrak. Be quiet, I've heard enough. Time to arrange a little test of strength, I think." Xarran strolled across to Alex. Still in a trance, he stood eyes wide as Xarran stroked his cheek, "Would you like that, Alex? Shall we send some of the nasty dead men to attack the little wizards and Uncle Jared? Shall we have them tear the flesh from your little friends?" Without realising, Xarran was beginning to sound more like Karrak by the hour. His voice was deep and rasping, his eyes were tinged red and his thoughts were becoming warped and twisted.

***

"What if they've had to leave Reiggan? How will we know where to find them?" asked Lodren.

"Don't ye think we should get there first? Trust you to start worryin' about things that 'aven't 'appened yet."

"There's nothing wrong with being prepared for the worst."

"S'pose not. But there's nothin' wrong with a bit of optimism now and again either," snorted Grubb.

"Ooh, Grubb. This is going to be so much fun!"

"I'm glad you're lookin' forward to it. I'm crappin' meself!"

"Oh, Grubb, REALLY! Do you always have to be so crude?"

Grubb spun round and stuck his nose against Lodren's "It could've been worse, stumpy. I was bein' polite!"

Although still excited, Lodren had managed to calm himself slightly and he, Grubb and Faylore were now gathering provisions, preparing properly for the next chapter of their adventure. Lodren, as usual, was paying particular attention to his pots and pans as he sat on the ground cramming anything he could think of into his trusty backpack, "I think it'll be a bit colder up there, Grubb, make sure you wear something warm," he advised.

"Yes Mum!" replied Grubb."

"Are you ready, Lodren?" called Thelwynn.

"We'll be with you in just a moment," replied Faylore.

"No, Your Majesty, not you. Someone will collect you presently. For now, I need only the Nibrilsiem."

"The what?" exclaimed Grubb. "What did he call him, Faylore? A nibrillillosummat."

"That's not what he called him, Grubb," Faylore hissed, glaring at him and shaking her head vehemently.

"What did he call me then? I wasn't listening," mumbled Lodren, not even looking up from his packing.

"I'm not really sure," lied Faylore. "Probably just a dragon word, a term of endearment, I suppose."

"Oh, that's nice," said Lodren, still only half paying attention.

Grubb was staring in amazement at Faylore, "You lyin'…" he mouthed. The piercing look that Faylore gave him was enough to make him realise that now would be a good time for him to shut up.

Faylore swept away, "My lord, Thelwynn. I do not understand. I thought that we agreed that you would carry us?"

"No, Your Majesty. We agreed that it would be much quicker for you and the rest of your party to be carried by dragon to reach your friends. I never said that I was capable of carrying all of you. Then there is the Nibrilsiem to consider. He is the true dragon rider. Surely you would not expect him to share his saddle with another?"

"In the past, we have always shared whatever we have. Food, shelter, we have… Saddle!" she suddenly yelled, "What do you mean, saddle?"

"You don't expect a Nibrilsiem to ride a dragon without it? We are very proud of it, my kin and I. We have taken care of it for centuries in the hope that one day, the Nibrilsiem would return." Thelwynn actually seemed more excited than Lodren at the thought of being ridden like a pony.

Faylore was exasperated. She pointed at Lodren, "He's a five foot Nibby," she said slowly. "He's a nomad who wouldn't harm a fly."

"No, madam. That's only what he appears to be. His heart is that of a sky warrior." Raising his voice slightly, he called politely to Lodren, "Lodren, would you care to join me for a little walk?"

Lodren looked across at him and then down at his trusty backpack.

"Yes, you can bring that with you," said Thelwynn, "you're going to need that." He watched as the Nibby, once again, seemed unsure of his next move, “The hammer as well,” he added.

Lodren picked up his belongings and, after briefly shrugging his shoulders at Grubb, followed the dragon lord. “Where are we going?” he asked.

“Not far,” replied Thelwynn, “I’ll need a bit more room in which to spread my wings than is afforded to me here, I’m afraid. Oh, and I have a gift for you.”

“What sort of gift?” Lodren asked suspiciously. “It’s not dart-shaped with green feathers on it, is it? I don’t want to wake up in a strange place with no memory of how I got there again, thank you.”

“Not at all. Whatever gave you that idea?”

“Never mind,” sighed Lodren. “As long as you promise that’s not what’s going to happen?”

“You have my word, Lodren. This is a gift with which you will be delighted, I’m sure.”

“What is it then?”

They were at the edge of the glade where they had first encountered Jendilomin after arriving in Thedar. Thelwynn was delighted with being able to move without the fear of treading on something, or someone, by accident and unfurled his wings to their fullest extent. Lodren’s mouth fell open. He had witnessed the dragons stretch themselves before but not until now did he realise just how gigantic they were. Thelwynn gave a huge yawn and smacked his lips together a few times before turning to face Lodren. The Nibby sucked in his cheeks. For a dragon lord to pull a face like the one that Thelwynn now wore was far from flattering. He looked positively gormless. His eyes were half-closed, and the ends of his lips curled upwards showing what could only be described as a 'silly grin', "It's hidden beneath that bush," he sighed, pointing one of his huge claws.

Lodren stooped and shuffled into the foliage beside him. His hand fell on something smooth and he grabbed it tightly and pulled. Staring at the shiny black surface, he smiled up at Thelwynn, "It's lovely!" he exclaimed, enthusiastically, "What is it?"

"You don't know?" asked Thelwynn, genuinely surprised.

"It could be a pillow," replied Lodren. "But it would have to be for someone with a head that's even bigger than mine!"

"It is not a pillow!" said Thelwynn, slowly, "It is the saddle of a dragon rider."

"Oooh!" exclaimed Lodren, "Am I going to meet a dragon rider?"

Thelwynn sighed, "No, Lodren you are not going to meet a dragon rider," he replied.

"That's a shame. I'd bet they have loads of tales about heroic deeds and all the adventures they…"

"You are the dragon rider!"

Lodren looked at him blankly, and then burst out laughing, "Do you know?" he said, "For a second there, I thought you said that I was the dragon rider."

Thelwynn lay down in front of Lodren, placing his head flat on the ground and fixing his gaze on the Nibby.

Lodren stopped laughing, "Me?"

Thelwynn nodded.

"No! Not me. I'm a Nibby, a traveller. I camp outdoors and watch the stars. I make campfires and do my catering. I've never been on a dragon's back in my life! It wouldn't be right. You don't ride dragons!"

"Have you finished?" asked Thelwynn. "Only, the sooner we get started, the sooner you'll understand."

"Understand? Understand what? There is nothing to understand!" rambled Lodren. "I'm just a Nibby, plain and simple. I may have been a little over-excited when you first suggested it, and I'm sorry for that. Not that I wouldn't still love to be able to go into the clouds with you, but a saddle? That can't be right! Can it?"

"Calm down, Lodren. After all, it's what you wanted anyway."

"I know that. I don't know much about them but it looks as if this saddle is only made for one person. Who's going to hold on to me when we're up there?" he asked, gesturing toward the clouds with his thumb.

"You won't need anyone else, Lodren. The moment you sit in that saddle you'll understand. It's where you belong. If you have the slightest concern, I won't even attempt to fly with you on my back."

The next few minutes were quite stressful for both parties. Lodren had never dreamt of, let alone tried to saddle a dragon. Thelwynn unfortunately, was proving to be of little help. His clawed hands were far too big for him to be able to offer any practical aid and not being able to turn his head far enough to see what Lodren was doing limited any helpful advice he may have had to offer. All that the poor dragon could do was try to offer the frustrated Nibby encouragement, "Now Lodren, take that strap, no not that one, the other one. That's right, now thread that underneath that one, no, the one in front of that one, oh dear now you've got it twisted. How did those two end up knotted together? Perhaps we should start again!"

"NO! I'VE HAD ENOUGH!" roared Lodren, "Stupid flipping thing! See, now I'm using bad language. This was a bad idea from the start!"

They heard the laughter from behind them and turned to see Grubb and Faylore who were in hysterics at their antics.

"Ye should see the pair of ye, IT'S BLOODY HILARIOUS! Talk about the left 'and not knowin' what the right one's doin'? I could watch this all day."

"If you think it's that funny, WHY DON'T YOU HAVE A GO!" bellowed Lodren, launching the saddle at Grubb.

It fell in front of the Vikkery who, transforming into Wilf in order to be able to lift it, picked it up and walked toward them. "S'pose I'd better or we'll be 'ere all day, ye moron. Look, it's just a bigger version o' Buster's saddle. Got to be honest though, 'avin' four arms don't 'urt none either." His hands, all four of them, were almost a blur as he set about his task. With a slight grunt he pulled the last strap snugly into place. "Told ye it was easy," he said, smugly. "'ow's it feel, Thelwynn? Not too tight, is it?"

Thelwynn shook his head, "No, not at all," he replied. "It feels surprisingly comfortable actually. Wish I'd tried it on years ago," he held his hands up in front of him and studied them, "Then again," he added.

"Come on then, stumpy. Up ye go," laughed Grubb, having dwindled back to his normal self.

“Alright, alright! Don’t rush me, I’m doing it, okay? No I don’t need any help, thank you. Grubb, will you stop trying to… now look what you’ve done. Just take a step back and…” Lodren was becoming frustrated with the unwanted aid being offered by his friend. “Now all I need is my hammer. Grubb, you’re standing on it. I don’t care if it helps you see without changing, get off it!”

Eventually, Lodren gripped the edge of the saddle and hauled himself into it. He was a little nervous, but only for a second. Thelwynn stood up allowing Lodren a completely new experience, the landscape viewed from a dragon rider’s perspective. The Nibby suddenly felt powerful, an unexpected exhilaration swelling his chest. Gripping his hammer tightly, he held it aloft, “For the Nibrilsiem, YAAARRGHHH!” he roared.

Faylore and Grubb were shocked by his sudden battle cry. They had never seen him behave this way before and would never have believed it possible if they hadn’t witnessed it first-hand.

“Know what?” muttered Grubb, “I think ‘e likes it.”

Faylore gave a gentle laugh, “I think you’re right, Grubb. He definitely seems to.”

As Lodren gave another exalted, thundering roar, Thelwynn launched them into the air. The sudden downdraught from his wings created an unexpected loud ‘boom’ and a blast that caused bushes and trees to bend precariously. They watched the magnificent spectacle of the dragon rider’s flight. The early morning sunlight glinted across the golden scales that covered Thelwynn’s wings, but they also noticed something that made them a little nervous. The flash of ruby-red close to Thelwynn reminded them that they were to be the next to be privileged enough to ride upon a dragon’s back, as Fireweigh came into view.

CHAPTER 3

Emnor's plan had worked perfectly. With very little effort, and many hugs from the gibbonites before their departure, he and the others had arrived on the very outskirts of Mellanthion. Hidden in the treeline, they watched the villagers going about their daily business.

"Don't you think something feels a little… off?"

"What exactly do you mean by off, Hannock?"

"Well look at them, scurrying around like rats when the cat appears. How can you be too afraid to walk outside in broad daylight?"

"No idea, Hannock," replied Jared. "What say we go and find out?" Jared turned to the others, "Wait here, we'll go and have a scout around and see what we can find out. We'll signal you when it's safe to come out."

"Oh, my hero," mocked Drake. "No thanks, I think I'll do some digging of my own, and before you start, we've had this conversation already."

Jared shrugged his shoulders, "If you insist," he said grinning at Drake. "But not all of us. Let us err on the side of caution, at least for now."

The three ventured slowly into the village. They had not gone far before they were noticed. "Just a minute you three. Where d'you think you're going?"

Hannock glanced at Jared and Drake, "Leave this to me," he mumbled. "To the tavern," he replied, turning to face the inquisitive guard who now approached.

"We don't like strangers coming into our village. We've 'ad a lot of strange goings-on of late. Guards disappearin' an' the like. What's your business in Mellanthion?" he asked, now flanked by at least a dozen of his men.

"Nothing much," replied Hannock. "We were hoping to purchase some horses, if there are any for sale, of course."

"Buy some 'orses? Buy 'em, or steal 'em?" sneered the guard.

Hannock felt insulted at the unwarranted accusation, but remained calm, "No, we mean to buy them," he repeated, "I am Captain Hannock of Borell and this is Prince Jared Dunbar, heir to its throne."

The guard burst out laughing, "Yeah, of course you are, and I'm a fairy princess."

"You certainly look like one," muttered Drake, under his breath.

The guard took a step toward him.

"We mean no harm, we simply need to buy a few things and then we can be on our way," said Hannock, stepping in front of him.

"So, you reckon he's a prince and you're a captain? Well your armour says somethin' different, or at least the rust on it does, anyway."

Hannock ran his hand across his chest, embarrassed that the guard had noticed his slightly dishevelled appearance, “It has been a hard road but I assure you that I speak the truth.”

“Look,” began the guard, “I don’t care where you got your armour to be honest, providing you can pay the toll, that is. I don’t care if you cut a prince’s throat or chopped his head off completely. I don’t care if you pulled his arms and legs off, but I do care that there are taxes to be paid here in Mellanthion. Now, ordinarily, we collect ‘em once a month but as you say you’re not going to be here, I think I should collect yours personally, now!”

Hannock stepped back and cast another glance at Jared.

The prince shrugged his shoulders, “I think you should give the man what he’s asking for, Captain,” he said. “He has made his position quite clear, after all.”

Drake hadn’t understood Jared’s meaning and suddenly blurted out, “Or you can tell him to ‘piss off’ before you run him through!”

Jared sighed, “Nice one, Drake. There goes the element of surprise.”

The guard suddenly became interested in Drake again, “You two I get,” he said, frowning. “But him? What’s his story?”

“Mind your own bloody business, half pint,” Drake snapped. “Get out of our way before I fry you and all the other little piglets you’ve got with you. Go on, sod off while you’ve still got the chance!”

The guard became agitated and pointed at him nervously, “H-h-he’s one o’ them wizards like the ones before. He’s even the right age. Kill ‘em all!” he suddenly yelled.

He had hardly taken a step when he felt the cold steel of Hannock's dagger at his throat. "You die first, understand? Tell your men to back off, or there will be some throat-cutting taking place today, namely yours."

The guard instinctively raised his chin, a terrified look in his eyes, the realisation of his peril dawning on him. He raised his hand, a signal for his men to hold their positions.

Another guard attempted to sneak up on Hannock, thinking that he had not been seen but he too felt a tap tap on his shoulder. Frozen in fear he moved his eyes to see the tip of a Gerrowlien spear resting on it, "I wouldn't do that, if I were you. He's had a very hard day and he may take it personally, you backstabbing little creep."

The second guard turned his head a little, his panic-stricken eyes being met with the sight of razor-sharp fangs. Lawton's razor-sharp fangs to be precise.

Each member of the guard, having followed the order of their commander, had drawn their weapon. But all quickly released them, allowing them to fall unceremoniously to the ground as they realised that they were now the ones who were surrounded. The Gerrowlien's spears were trained upon them, as were the staffs of Emnor and Yello. However, the one thing that seemed to facilitate their immediate surrender was the sight of the two wands wielded by Drake and Harley. It seemed that they had seen something similar before and made it quite clear that they wanted no part of a defiance to one who held its like again.

Keeping his dagger at the commander's throat, Hannock leaned closer to him, "I think you and I can have that little chat now, don't you?"

Despite his interrogation of the fort commander and his men, Hannock learned very little. None of them had actually seen anything. They had heard rumours of wizards and war hounds but had witnessed nothing first-hand. The only thing that linked any of the stories, it seemed, was the tavern. Emnor stepped in when it appeared they could extract nothing useful from their captives and, with a wave of his hand, sent them all into a deep sleep, "That'll stop them interfering for a while," he announced.

"At last!" exclaimed Hannock, "A breakthrough."

"What are you talking about, Hannock?" grumbled Yello. "We know no more now than when we entered this grotty village. What's the breakthrough?"

Hannock grabbed Yello gently by the front of his robes, "Don't you see?" he said in a pleading manner. "A tavern! All that wine and ale, just begging for me to drink it. I may even feel like a Borellian again, if I drink enough, that is."

"Oh, for goodness sake, Hannock!" exclaimed Jared, "Everything we've got to contend with and all you want to do is get drunk?"

"Ah well, that's the beauty of it see, Jared. I can do both, question the patrons of the tavern and drink myself into oblivion at the same time."

"Drink yourself into oblivion? Why would you want to do that, Hannock?" asked Drake.

Hannock grinned at him, "You wouldn't understand, Maddleton, you're far too young."

Drake ducked and looked around him nervously, "I wish people would stop using my first name, it usually ends up hurting."

“We’ll split up for a while,” suggested Emnor. “Yello and I shall make enquiries around the village. The rest of you can head for the tavern, we’ll join you presently.”

“Master Emnor, perhaps I should accompany you? I am your apprentice, after all.”

“If you’d prefer, Harley. But I doubt we shall learn much,” replied Emnor as he turned and headed toward the centre of the village. “See you later,” he called.

Jared, Hannock and Drake entered the tavern. As usual, the Gerrowliens chose not to join them, “We’ll be in those trees over there if you need us,” said Poom.

“Just get him to blow something up as a signal and we’ll come to the rescue,” laughed Lawton, slapping Drake gently on the shoulder.

***

Emnor, Yello and Harley ambled across the village square. They were in no rush and, understandably, slightly unsure of who might be a reliable source of information.

Yello scanned the market stalls. Various vendors plying their wares called out in a half-hearted attempt to attract passers-by, but it seemed that they had as little enthusiasm toward their goods as their potential customers. Only one stood out from the rest, the blacksmith. He was swinging his hammer with an enthusiasm the likes of which Yello had never seen before. Sparks flew into the air with every strike he made, his clothes were sopping wet and the sweat from his brow had formed a sooty line that ran down and dripped from his, rather bulbous, broken nose. Yello nudged Emnor gently, "I think we may have found our man," he said quietly.

"Why him in particular?" asked Emnor.

"Well for one thing, do you think that anyone in this village could afford new armour? And even if they could, why would they need it?" replied Yello.

"And it's completely different to what the guards wear. There's no detailing or crest of any kind. That armour is made for a single purpose, to protect expendable soldiers who are to be sent into battle very soon," noted Harley.

Emnor raised his eyebrows, "My, my, Harley. We have been paying attention, haven't we?"

"Yes, Master Emnor, far more than you would believe, if you were to so much as glance in my direction occasionally," Harley replied, testily.

"Listen to me, my young apprentice," Emnor began quietly, "if I thought that I would have to keep my eye on you in everything you do, you would not be my apprentice. Do you understand what I am saying to you, Harley?"

Harley lowered his head, "Yes, Master Emnor, my apologies. It's just…"

"Just nothing!" interrupted Yello. "Do you think you're the first apprentice to ever feel left out? Now be quiet, let's get on."

Emnor made his way through the sparse crowd and stood facing the smith. Fixing his gaze upon him, he waited for his response.

"Unless it's something trivial sir, I'm afraid I can't help you today. I have an important order to complete, so unless it's a horse you want shod quickly or a small crack in your armour..." he glanced up at them, "... perhaps not. Come back tomorrow gentlemen, I'll give you a special price for your patience, good-day."

"It is not your skills as a smith we require, good sir. We need information," said Emnor, raising his voice over the clanging of the smith's hammer on the anvil.

The smith stopped almost immediately and stood stretching his aching back, "Ah, that's a different kettle o' fish, isn't it? Sorry, old-timer, but it doesn't pay to gossip about other people's business in these parts."

"We're not enquiring about anyone in particular, my dear sir. We simply wondered if there have been any strange goings-on of late."

The smith placed his hands on his hips, "Not that I can recall," he said. "Mind you, I'm finding it difficult to focus on anything at all lately, what with all the rising prices. I've only got this one order to complete and who knows where the next one'll come from. Looks like my poor wife and young 'uns will be going hungry again if I don't get some coin from somewhere."

Yello stood aghast at what he was hearing. The smith was a stout fellow and his pronounced paunch was testament to the fact that he had not struggled to afford food of late. Yello also doubted the fact that he even had a family, let alone one that was destined to starve to death.

Emnor searched in his robes before handing the smith a few gold coins, "Perhaps these will help your focus, sir?" he asked politely.

The smith took the coins and raised one to his mouth, biting it to prove its authenticity. "Thank you, sir," he said in mock gratitude. "Well now, what can I tell you?" he stood tilting his head and stroking his unshaven chin. "No!" he announced suddenly. "Nothing strange at all, good-day gentlemen."

Surprisingly, it was Harley who was next to act. As the smith turned to face his forge, a pair of tongs, glowing red hot, shot into the air and hovered in front of his face. He attempted to dodge from side to side but they matched his every movement, getting closer and closer. "Not good enough!" said Harley. "We've tried this the nice way, smith, but my colleagues have far more patience than I. You've been paid, and you think you can fleece us? Do you realise what any one of us could do to you if we were of a mind?" The smith never replied. Arching his back as much as was possible to avoid the floating tongs, he was too terrified to speak. "I think it'll suffice to remove just the one eye for now. If you deign to speak, you'll still have one left, that will allow you to work your forge. You see I'm not completely without compassion. But unless you say something interesting, well then, I'm afraid I'll have to take both. Then you and your fictional family will starve to death, won't they?"

"Alright, sir, you've made your point. Just my little joke!" he gave a nervous laugh. "Strange, you say? Well the fella who ordered the armour I'm making, he was a bit different. Big, dark-skinned fella with long black robes."

"Dark-skinned you say?" asked Emnor with a sudden, urgent interest.

"Yes sir. Great big bloke he is. Much taller than any of us."

"And you saw his face? It wasn't hidden in any way?"

"Well he had a hood on, sir and it was pulled forward a bit but no, not hidden," replied the smith, looking completely confused.

"Can you describe him to us? Tell us what he looked like?"

By now, the smith had no idea what was happening as he faced his interrogators, "Like I said, sir, he had dark skin…" he paused and took a breath, "… and two eyes, a nose, a mouth and a chin with a little fluffy beard. That's all I know, honest!"

Harley waved the tongs into the middle of the forge, "Did his face… move?" he asked.

"Only when he was talking," whimpered the smith. "Please, I don't know no more, have your coins back and let me carry on with my work, I meant no offence."

"Shortly!" snapped Emnor. "This armour, how much of it did the stranger order?"

"A hundred sets and a sword to go with each. I've got two more forges burning on the edge of the village. I've got blokes heating the metal and then bringing it to me, so I can shape it. I'm just trying to earn a bit of coin, sir. There ain't no harm in that."

"So, you've only just started?" asked Yello.

"No, sir. This is my second day. I'm nearly half way through the order, I haven't slept since I started."

"Where was it to be delivered?" asked Emnor.

"He didn't say. Just said he'd be back and headed off toward the tavern. I think he was looking for a fight, sir."

"A fight? With whom?"

"I don't think he cared, but I warned him to watch out for the guards. Not long after he went in there, loads of screams could be heard. Mind you, one sight o' that dog of his would be enough to make anybody scream."

Emnor grabbed him, "Dog, what dog?"

"Ooh, 'orrible thing it is, sir. Twisted face, huge uneven teeth and just little patches of hair on its wrinkled skin." The smith shuddered. The three wizards looked at one another knowingly. "Mind you, I ain't seen him or his mutt since yesterday, and we've got a new looney who's appeared. Mad old bloke who's scared of his own shadow."

"I think it's time we re-joined the others," whispered Emnor, releasing the smith.

***

The barkeep looked up nervously. He nodded toward Jared and Hannock but as he saw Drake behind them, his attitude changed drastically. "GET OUT!" he yelled suddenly, "I don't want any more of his kind in here! I've had enough! Kill me if you like, you might as well, seems like you've already murdered all my customers. Go on, GET OUT!" he bellowed, grabbing a cosh from under the bar.

Hannock turned and looked at Drake, "Do you have to start trouble everywhere you go? Can't you behave yourself, just once?"

"What are you on about!" exclaimed Drake, "I've only just walked through the bloody door, how could I have done anything? Hang on, what does he mean, his kind?"

Jared held his hands out in front of him and approached the barkeep slowly, "We're not here for trouble, my friend. We'd just like to have a drink, that's all. Obviously you've been having a few problems, but I can assure you that they have nothing to do with us."

"At least, not that we know of," Hannock mumbled under his breath.

Still clutching his cosh, the barkeep backed away slightly, "What do you want?" he asked abrasively.

"I'll have an ale and a bottle of your finest brandy, a lemonade for my nephew and, Jared, what would you like?" chirped Hannock.

"I meant in the village. What do you want in the village?" repeated the barkeep.

"We heard about a tavern that has such a welcoming atmosphere that it's the talk of the land. The innkeeper's an absolute sweetheart, apparently," smirked Drake.

Jared smiled at the barkeep, "We want a drink, plain and simple."

Placing his cosh beneath the bar, their host sighed, "My apologies, gentlemen. There have been so many awful things happening of late, and for some reason, always inside my tavern. A whole troupe of guards killed by a sorcerer and then in turn him and his horrible hound attacked by two others and tortured before my very eyes. It's a wonder I've kept my sanity after all that I've seen over the last few days. Makes me wish I was back to the times when all I had to contend with was a gang of homicidal, bullying guards."

Hannock took a large gulp of his ale, "Oh crap!"

"This sorcerer," said Jared, slowly, "what did he look like?"

"Big," replied the innkeeper. "Bigger than you, much bigger. Dark-skinned fella. Polite enough with me but you could tell he was looking for trouble as soon as he walked through that door. Those guards didn't stand a chance, especially once his horrible beast started ripping into 'em."

"And here we go again," sighed Hannock. "We can't even have a quiet drink without your brother coming into the conversation. I'll be so happy once I've killed him. Just a minute, did you say he was attacked by two others?"

"Yes, astonishing really, they were so much younger than him but far stronger somehow. When I say they, it was only the one that attacked him. The other one never said a word, just stood there looking gormless."

"Can you describe them?" asked Jared.

"Not really, just a couple of young lads at first appearance, they'd be about his age I suppose," replied the barkeep, nodding toward Drake.

"Why did the sorcerer attack the guards, and why did the young men attack the sorcerer?" asked Hannock.

"The sorcerer came in with his mangy animal and the guards weren't too happy that I'd allowed it. I tried to tell him to leave it outside but the look in his eyes scared the living daylights out of me, far more than being pushed around by the guards. They started taunting him and he didn't like that. One of 'em made a move for his sword and before you know it there was blood everywhere and all of 'em were dead."

"Did the young men know him? Were they acquainted in some way?" asked Jared, probingly.

"Not from what I could tell. The one who attacked him kept on about some lord or other. A shadow lord, yes that was it, a shadow lord."

"What did they want to know?" Jared continued.

"I'm sorry, sir. I have no idea," replied the innkeeper becoming slightly agitated as he started to wipe the tankards with a less-than-spotless rag, "I'm not a brave man, you see. First chance I got, I dodged down through the cellar hatch. I hid behind some barrels and stuck my fingers in my ears so I couldn't hear anything. I was down there so long that I must have dozed off. When I woke up it was all quiet up here. I crept back up through the hatch to find they were all gone, thankfully."

"Any idea where they may have gone?" asked Hannock.

"No, sir. I'd got my fingers in my ears. I just told you that!"

"Oh yes, of course you did. How silly of me," said Hannock. "Anyway, don't let us keep you from your duties, we can see that you're busy," he added, glancing briefly around the deserted inn.

Moving as far away from the bar as possible, the three sat huddled around a large table, eagerly awaiting the arrival of the others.

"Well you have to give him his due," said Hannock, "he's done a remarkable job of cleaning the bloodstains off everything."

"Give it a rest, will you!" hissed Drake. "This is serious. Don't you realise? The two young men he's on about can only be Alex and Xarran!"

"I think your imagination is running away with you a little, Drake. They attacked a sorcerer and defeated him with ease, apparently. That doesn't sound like our friends to me."

"You're wrong, Jared. It sounds exactly like them. One attacking and the other looking gormless. It describes Xarran and Alex perfectly. Somehow they've decided to go after Karrak by themselves!"

"As eager as Xarran is to prove himself to his father, and as strange as Alex can be on occasion, I seriously doubt that either of them would be stupid enough to face Karrak without the rest of us," replied Jared.

Hannock slapped Drake gently on the back, "Perhaps you're not the only wizards that survived," he said. "Perhaps we have allies we know nothing about."

"We can hope, I suppose," agreed Drake. "Does seem a bit coincidental though, doesn't it?"

***

Suddenly, the door to the inn flew open. There was a lot of bustle in the doorway as Emnor, Yello and Harley struggled to control a very dirty, seemingly uncontrollable, peasant. Try as they might, it was quite apparent that he had no intention of entering the premises without a fight.

"Here!" yelled the innkeeper, "You can't bring that scruffy herbert in my nice clean premises, throw him back outside, he stinks."

"Hold your tongue, barkeep," bellowed Emnor. "Or would you like to see what I can do with this?" he asked, brandishing his staff.

"Why me? Why do you all have to come in here? Why can't I get some nice customers who just pay the tab and smile as they leave?" whimpered the poor innkeeper.

Jared had the mother of all looks of confusion on his face, "Emnor, what are you doing? He doesn't want to come in, let him go. He's obviously used to the outdoor life, just give him some coin and send him on his way. Some people are happy being well, smelly and covered in… oh my word that smells disgusting."

"Let me go!" protested the old vagrant, "I need to leave. Who are you? I sleep in that hedge all the time. Leave me alone, please," he implored.

"This is ridiculous," sighed Emnor. With a wave of his staff the old man closed his eyes and sank to the floor.

The mixture of the ale and the brandy were now beginning to take their effect on Hannock, who found the scene most amusing, "If I'd have known you wanted a pet, Emnor, I'd have bought you a dog, or a goat, or something," he sniggered.

Emnor glared at him, "Thank you, Captain!" he snapped. "But this is no pet. Not any more anyway! Don't you recognise him, Jared?"

Jared shook his head, "No! Is he the winner of this year's village idiot contest, perchance?"

"Don't be flippant, Jared. Take a closer look, are you sure he doesn't look familiar?" asked Yello, sweeping the bedraggled old man's matted hair from his face.

Jared stood, held his nose and leaned forward to get a better look at the old man's features. He peered at him for a few seconds shaking his head as Emnor attempted to wipe some of the filth from the stranger's face with his sleeve. He was about to speak when, as he realised who he was looking at, his mouth fell open and he simply stood there agape, "Barden Oldman!" he breathed in realisation.

"Yes, Jared. Barden Oldman," replied Emnor, "We were talking to the blacksmith a short while ago when there was an almighty fuss behind us. Apparently, Barden had tried to steal a loaf of bread from one of the market stalls and the baker was none too pleased. Of course, we never realised who he was, but decided to intervene when the butcher got involved and threatened to chop his hands off. Imagine our surprise when we recognised him. The smith said that he appeared here just after some sort of incident that happened here in the inn, but the innkeeper refused to speak about it with anyone in the village."

All eyes turned to the poor innkeeper, who now looked decidedly nervous, "What you all looking at me for? I don't know anything about it," he said, unconvincingly.

Yello ambled toward the innkeeper, his staff raised, "My friend here…" he said, gesturing toward Emnor, "… is far more polite than I, of that I can assure you. He threatens people all the time but would never actually harm anyone. I, on the other hand, threaten very few people, but when I do I am always prepared to do them harm should the need arise. I warn you, dullard, that need is arising right now."

"More threats!" exclaimed the innkeeper, "I've had enough, do your worst! Go on, roast me alive, turn me inside out, spread my innards up the wall if you like! I don't care anymore!"

Emnor and Yello suddenly felt terribly guilty. Their actions were not far removed from the actions of those whom they condemned on a regular basis. How could anyone differentiate between a sorcerer and a wizard if their behaviour was so similar? How could they believe that threatening an innocent, for that was exactly what the innkeeper was, would ever be comprehended as acceptable? The innkeeper fell backwards and slid down the wall sobbing.

Lowering his head in shame, Yello handed his staff to Emnor before venturing behind the bar. Leaning down, he took the man gently by the arm, "Forgive me," he said, gently. "These are trying times for us all. We mean you no harm, my friend. The horrors you have witnessed must have taken a great strain on you. But, I must inform you that worse is yet to come, unless a few brave souls are willing to stand with us in the hope that we may prevent it." He helped him to his feet and looked into his eyes, "Tell us your name."

"Douglas, sir. Douglas Torran."

"Well, Douglas, is there any way in which you could find it in your heart to forgive us? Would you be willing to help? Any information may prove useful, however trivial it may appear to you."

“I’ll tell you everything I know, but first I want that thing out of my tavern,” he said, pointing at Barden.

“Don’t worry about him,” said Drake, quickly. “I’ll clean him up so he doesn’t stink the place out. All I need is a couple of buckets of water and a good stiff brush,” he added, a menacing grin spreading across his face.

“No, you don’t understand,” replied Douglas. “He’s the beast. He’s the one that was with the dark-skinned fella. He’s the one who ripped the throats out of the guards. That young lad turned him into an old man before he left. Burst out laughing when he saw his face, kept making fun of him. It was as if he knew him.”

Emnor and Yello turned to face Jared.

“Gentlemen, take a seat,” said Hannock. “I think we may be here some time.”

CHAPTER 4

To Lodren, riding a dragon seemed to come as second nature. As they soared high in the clouds he was able to re-direct Thelwynn with the slightest movement. Leaning gently to one side would cause the dragon lord to turn and leaning forward, to descend gently. It had not taken long for the excitement to take hold of the Nibby as he rode upon the winged behemoth's back. Within minutes he was charging upwards through the cloud before tilting forward and plummeting rapidly toward the ground. Faylore held her breath more than once, fearing that the over-exuberant novice would make a fatal mistake and cause both he and Thelwynn to crash into the trees or rock faces far below them. Throughout, there were the exalted roars of the newly-discovered Nibrilsiem. Grubb was not impressed and wasted no time in telling Faylore exactly how he felt about Lodren's new, larger-than life persona.

"Look at 'im. What a pillock! He's gonna smash into the floor next time 'e tries that, you mark my words."

"He knows what he's doing," said Fireweigh, unexpectedly. "It's in his nature. You don't think that Thelwynn would allow them to fall do you? There's a synergy between them that can only exist between a dragon and a Nibrilsiem. They feel one another's movements, hear one another's thoughts. The only reason Lodren moves is for balance."

"Cobblers!" snapped Grubb, "'e's just showin' off. All that shoutin's gettin' on my bloody nerves, to be honest."

"He can't help it, Grubb. He's just excited. I'm sure he'll calm down once he gets used to it. The same as you may stop using that kind of language in front of me, when you do," said Faylore.

"I hate to interrupt, Your Majesty," said Fireweigh, "but if anything, it will probably get worse. At the moment he's only experiencing being airborne for the first time. Once Thelwynn allows him to access his mind fully he'll learn how to ride a dragon into battle. I'm afraid that's when he'll begin to learn the war songs of his, and our, ancestors."

"Songs!" exclaimed Grubb. "That's all we need! Not only will 'e be full of 'imself for ridin' dragons, 'e'll be bloody singin' while 'e's doin'it!"

"Do not worry, Grubb," chuckled Fireweigh, "that won't come for some time yet, if at all."

"Could we possibly land for a while, Fireweigh?" asked Faylore, politely. "We Thedarians much prefer to walk and I need to stretch my legs, as it were."

"Of course, Your Majesty," replied Fireweigh. "Give me a moment to inform Thelwynn. Hold tight." He began to dive in order to catch up with Thelwynn who, at Lodren's request, was skimming only inches above the ground.

Grubb glanced behind him, the sight of Faylore made him smile. She appeared very different to the Faylore he knew. Her glittering white skin, reflecting the ruby red of Fireweigh's scales gave her a crimson hue and her hair, whipped back in the billowing wind, resembled the bellows-induced flames of a smith's forge. But one thing remained constant in Grubb's mind. Crimson red or pale white, Faylore was the most beautiful creature he had ever seen. Leaning back into her arms, he gave a contented sigh.

Moments later they were strolling through the long grass that had resembled a plush green carpet from high above. Faylore breathed deeply, savouring the scent of the morning dew as she allowed it to brush between her fingers. This was where she, and her kin, belonged. Grubb had transformed and now, as Wilf, lumbered along behind her. The only reason he had changed was because he couldn't see where he was going in the tall grass!

Lodren had not been so eager to land as they and was now becoming a little annoying. At least once, every minute, he would swoop past them still mounted on Thelwynn's back and bawl something barely audible.

It took Thelwynn himself to explain to Lodren that he, as the rider, could probably stay in the air indefinitely but that he, as the one doing the flying, could not.

They landed directly in front of Fireweigh and Lodren dismounted, "My word!" he shouted, "That gets the blood pumping."

"Lodren, if ye don't sit down and shut it, I swear your blood is gonna be pumpin' all over the floor!" snapped Grubb.

"What's wrong with you?" asked Lodren, completely unaware of how obnoxious he had been over the last few hours. "Didn't you enjoy it? Do you not like heights? Did it make you nauseous?"

Faylore hurriedly stepped between them, "Let us say, he's had better days, Lodren and leave it at that, shall we?"

"Righty-ho then, if you think it best," Lodren replied, cheerily. "Think I'm going to dig into my backpack, I'm starving. Fancy a bit of lunch, Faylore? I've still got some honey cakes."

Grubb watched Lodren as he rummaged through the provisions he had stored before they left. He hummed to himself for a while but every so often he would utter a random word subconsciously. Dum dum dum, strike, dum dum dum, hack, dum dum dum, burn. There was no tune at first, but one definitely began to form as the Nibby went on.

Grubb dragged his hand across his face as he studied his friend with dread, "There'll be no living with 'im if we don't put the mockers on this fast," he mumbled to Faylore.

"If we don't, what?" asked Faylore.

"This dragon-rider nonsense. We've got to nip it in the bud before we lose 'im altogether."

"Ah, so that's the problem. You're scared of losing your friend!"

"Course I am, an' 'e's me best friend at that! When I say 'e's me best friend, I don't mean that you an' Jared an' the rest of 'em ain't, but…"

"It's alright, Grubb, I understand," said Faylore, smiling.

"Could ye have a talk to 'im? It'd sound better comin' from you."

Faylore sighed and, rubbing Grubb's horned head roughly, she wandered over to Lodren.

He smiled up at her as she approached, "Is there anything in particular you'd like?" he asked politely, "I managed to pack a fair bit before we left."

"Oh, anything will be fine, I'll trust your judgment as always."

"Is this about the dragons then?" he asked.

Faylore tried not to look too surprised at the question and pretended to brush her hair from her face to hide the smile that had appeared on it.

"I'm polite, Faylore, not daft," said Lodren without looking up from his backpack.

Faylore began to pace slowly, "They cannot accompany us, Lodren. Once we reach Reiggan Fortress, we must send them home."

"But why? Imagine how easy it would be to beat Karrak if we had two dragons fighting beside us."

"Imagine how you would feel if one of them were severely injured, or killed? This is not their fight, Lodren. It would be unfair to ask them to join something that could ultimately set them as a target for Karrak should we fail."

"You're the first one to say that, and mean it. If we fail. Jared and Emnor and the others seem to think that, if we all stick together, we'll beat this 'shadow lord' easily. Not once has it entered their heads that Karrak could win. They seem to be ignoring the idea, but I think there's a very good chance of him killing all of us no matter what we do. I've never told anyone this, Faylore, but that day he attacked us at the castle… well, I was terrified. You couldn't see it but my hands were shaking so badly, I could barely grip my hammer. But when I climbed into that saddle today I felt strong and unafraid. I felt like I could take on the whole world."

"All the more reason for you to stop before you become addicted to that feeling, Lodren," Faylore said, stroking the Nibby's cheek. "The person riding that dragon is not you, it is a memory, a shadow of days long passed. Dragon riders existed when the dragons themselves were little more than mindless beasts. To expect a dragon to bear a rider now is an insult. Would you expect someone to place a saddle on one of us as if we were a beast of burden?"

"But, Thelwynn was the one who suggested it," pleaded Lodren, "I would never dream of insulting anyone… maybe Grubb, but nobody who would take real offence, and most assuredly not a dragon."

"They… must… return… to… their… home, Lodren," said Faylore, emphasising each word.

Lodren sighed, "You're right," he said. "It was just nice to not be afraid for once."

"We are all afraid, Lodren. It is the truly brave ones that keep it to themselves. The brave ones such as you," she said, comforting him. "Now let's have that lunch you promised us."

***

Returning to the skies, Lodren did his best to curb his enthusiasm, but failed… dismally. He roared and sang at the top of his voice, pausing occasionally as

Faylore told him to shush, but the pauses lasted no longer than a few minutes before he resumed with his battle cries and war songs. It was with great relief that, many hours later, they spied Reiggan Fortress far off in the distance.

"We'll be there within the hour," Fireweigh informed them, raising his voice slightly for fear of it being drowned out by the raucous chanting of Lodren.

Grubb tugged at Faylore's sleeve to get her attention, "When we land, can I punch him?" he pleaded. "Go on, just once, just a little tap. I won't hurt 'im… much, honest."

Faylore sighed and rolled her eyes.

They landed in the deserted courtyard of Reiggan. It was a large area, or at least it had always seemed to be. Now, housing two fully-grown dragons, it appeared far less spacious than it once had.

"It seems that our friends had a pressing engagement," noted Faylore.

"Does that mean they didn't want to wait an' buggered off without us?" asked Grubb, his brow furrowed.

"It means that they could not wait for us, not that they never wanted to," said Faylore, correcting him.

"That's alright, whichever way they went, it won't take long for us to catch up with them now we have our dragon friends with us," announced Lodren, his chest puffed up like a peacock.

Faylore peered at him, "But our friends are not coming with us are they, Lodren? Our friends are returning to their home."

"Maybe they could take us just a little further. You wouldn't mind, would you, Thelwynn?"

Lord Thelwynn looked down at the Nibby. Faylore was dreading his response, he seemed as intoxicated by their synergy as Lodren was, but he was also no fool. Dragons have exceptional hearing and, unintentionally of course, he had listened to the conversation between them earlier that day.

"I am afraid I must leave you, Lodren. Our journey together was one that I shall not soon forget, but I fear that we must part company. We shall meet again I'm sure, for now, I bid you a fond farewell."

Thelwynn launched himself into the air, followed closely by Fireweigh and the pair disappeared into the clouds within seconds.

"Now them pair 'ave buggered off 'an all. Looks like it's just the three of us again. Are we goin' after Jared straightaway? I got to be honest, I could do with a bit of a kip first, but if you say we leave right away, Faylore, that's fine by me."

Faylore hardly heard him, she was too busy staring intently at Lodren.

"They've gone. Just like that. He never even took the saddle off, he just… left me behind," said the Nibby, agog at what had happened.

"Don't you worry, Lodren. If ye want to fuss over a pet, I'll let ye take care 'o Buster. Or 'ad ye forgotten 'e was with us?"

Lodren never answered, he simply stood there staring into the clouds, a faint hope that the dragons may return, stirring in his mind.

"Ye can brush 'im and feed 'im if ye like," added Grubb.

"Yeah… if you like," said Lodren, dreamily, "I'll build a fire and cook it for you."

Grubb recoiled in horror.

"I'm sure he didn't mean that," Faylore laughed. "Lodren. LODREN," she shouted to get him to pay attention.

He turned to face her, still only half listening, "Yes?" he replied.

"Go and have a quick look around inside to make sure no-one was left behind, will you?"

Lodren nodded and strolled off, following Faylore's instruction reluctantly.

"Are we leaving right away then?" asked Grubb.

"There seems no reason for us to remain. I know you are fatigued but you can sleep on your pony for a while, the route is quite flat for a distance," she replied.

"And dry, remember?"

"We managed well enough. Pack a few more water skins if you feel we may need them. We must travel the route much faster than last time."

Lodren returned and shook his head, "Nobody here," he muttered.

They set off, making much better time than their friends had. Faylore, with her long legs, strode ahead; Buster carrying Grubb, had no problem keeping up with her; and Lodren, although a little forlorn, simply lowered his head and ploughed onward. He was, after all, of a nomadic breed that was used to rough terrain.

But, unbeknownst to them, they were being watched.

"I was correct, as usual. This is the only route open to them. All we need to do is follow them, Korbah. They will lead us straight to Karrak and when our opportunity arises, we shall kill them all."

"Great idea, Ramah," hissed Korbah. "Last time we tried that we ended up tied up in a dungeon."

"Do I detect a little doubt in your tone, my friend?"

"I ain't your friend! All my real friends are dead, 'cause of followin' you!"

"I see," said Ramah. "Firstly, we were not in a dungeon and secondly, your friends followed me willingly. I am not your enemy, Korbah. Every ill deed that has been done to us and our kind can be laid firmly at the feet of the sorcerer Karrak and his brother. It is the Dunbar name that is responsible for our downfall, that is why we must take our revenge."

"You'd better be right this time," growled Korbah. "If you're not, I'll kill you meself."

***

"I can't believe it! It's ridiculous, I mean, Alex wouldn't have the guts to torture someone, it's not like him at all."

"Harley, I know you don't want to accept it, but the overwhelming evidence cannot be argued with," said Yello.

"What evidence? A vague description and the fact that they were wizards? Hardly damning, is it?"

"You seem to be overlooking the obvious, my young friend," said Emnor. "He was using his wand. You four are the only wizards that I have met who use them."

"So, in conclusion, it had to be them," sighed Yello.

"Not necessarily," Jared said suddenly. "They're not the only ones who use them."

"What!" exclaimed Yello. "How do you know?"

"See, I told you it couldn't have been Alex and Xarran!" protested Harley.

"It was a few years ago," continued Jared, "Hannock, you remember, don't you? There were reports around the local villages of a young man terrorising the villagers and attacking anyone who refused to meet his demands. When we caught up with him, he tried to kill us, wounded me quite badly actually. If it hadn't been for Grubb, who knows what might have happened. He was armed with a wand."

"Was it like ours?" asked Harley.

"Oh no, nothing as elaborate as the ones you forged. It was just a carved wooden stick that he used to cast poison spells, made a real mess of the one chap as memory serves."

"Do you remember when we first arrived? Those guards were up for a fight until they saw our wands," noted Drake. "They'd seen something like them before. I suggest we question them, they may have the answers we need."

"Before we do, shouldn't we see if we can get anything out of him?" They were still in the deserted tavern and Yello pointed toward the back of the room where Barden lay outstretched on one of the tables.

"I'm afraid that would be pointless," said Emnor. "Despite all that he once was, his mind has gone. The most we could expect would be insane ramblings. We don't have time to waste attempting to unravel hysterical rantings that would eventually lead to nothing. No, his body lives, but the Barden Oldman we knew is no more."

"No time like the present," said Jared, "Hannock, care to tag along?"

Hannock clutched his pewter mug to his chest, "No, not at the moment," he replied, his eyes half closed, "I'm going to catch up with an old friend of mine." He took another swig of ale, "A very close and dear friend," he added with a stupid grin.

Shaking his head, Jared made for the door, followed by everyone but Hannock. They worked out their strategy before facing the guards and, reaching the fort, Drake led the way. Venturing into the dungeon, they paused as Yello fumbled through a large bunch of iron keys he had removed from a hook in the room above. It took three attempts before he finally found the key that opened the first gaol cell. The door creaked open. The guard inside scurried back to the wall as he saw Drake enter. The young wizard smiled at him. Tapping his wand against his thigh so that the guard could see it, he stooped down to face him, "We have questions for you."

The guard began to shake, his eyes transfixed by Drake's wand, "I'll t-t-tell you anything, anything you want to know, ju-just don't use that thing on me. I don't know much, honest, only what I saw. It's G-Ginger you should be talking to, he knows a lot more than me."

"How do you know? I haven't even asked you anything yet," whispered Drake, menacingly. He was enjoying this far too much.

"Y-Yeah, I know, but he's the captain, h-he's bound to know more than me about everything."

Drake held up his wand. He pointed it toward the ceiling and began slowly moving it from side to side, the guard's eyes following it intently. "So, you've seen one of these before?" he asked.

The guard nodded nervously, "One of the young lads, he had one. B-but h-his was more like a gold colour," he replied, shakily.

Drake's brow furrowed, "Are you sure?"

The guard nodded frantically. "Yeah, I saw it clearly when he was pointing it at the beast, or I-I thought it was a beast 'til it got up and ran off. It was an old man. Filthy he was, but when he was on the floor I would've sworn it was some kind of hairless dog."

"This, Ginger. Why would he know any more than you?"

"He was talking to the two young lads when they first came into town. He tried to get them to hand over some coin like he did with you. Next thing, he's told us to sod off and dropped his sword on the floor. That's all I know, honest. Please sir, can I go now? I was just following orders, I'm not a bad bloke."

"You extort money from travellers and villagers alike, and you're 'not a bad bloke'! If it were up to me, you'd be left to rot in here for the rest of your life," bellowed Drake.

Jared stepped forward and placed his hand gently on Drake's arm. Without realising, he had raised it and now held his wand inches from the guard's face. The guard was shaking violently, tears streaming down his cheeks. "I'm not going to stop you, Drake, but if you do this you must live with it for the rest of your life. His face will haunt your dreams forever."

Drake lowered his wand and stormed out of the cell. Locking the door behind them, they followed him upstairs.

"I thought you were going to kill him!" exclaimed Harley, "What was that all about?"

Drake glanced at them, finding it difficult to make eye contact, "You heard what he said about the wand?" he paused, expecting an enquiry, but his friends remained silent, "He said it was a golden colour. We all thought it was Alex who had gone mad, but it isn't. Alex's wand is almost entirely platinum, it's Xarran's wand that is mostly gold, I should know, I tested them all, remember?"

Emnor sank slowly onto a chair, "So it's worse than we feared. Not only have we confirmed that it is two of our own who are guilty of these heinous atrocities, we have discovered that the one we least suspected is the ringleader in this mystery."

"He could only have one motive," announced Yello. All eyes were now on him, "He intends to join forces with Karrak."

"Cobblers!" exclaimed Drake, "Why would he do that? There's no logic to it."

"Unfortunately, Drake, there is a definite logic to it," began Emnor. "He believes we have no hope of defeating Karrak and thinks that joining with our enemy may ensure his safety."

"What about Alex? He would never go along with a plan like that," insisted Drake.

"Who knows what goes through the minds of others when they are placed in mortal peril?" asked Emnor, "I think we should have a little chat with this other fellow downstairs."

"I'll talk to him," said Drake, but the rage in his eyes prompted Jared's response.

"That won't be necessary, Drake. I'll take care of this one," he said, heading toward the stairs.

"There he goes again, the hero. You can't stand the thought of someone else making a piece of the puzzle fit, can you?" sneered Drake.

"Hold your tongue," snapped Yello.

Jared held up his hand, "It's alright, Yello. I'll handle this," He pulled up a chair and spun it around in front of Drake. Straddling it, he looked up at the young man, "Do you believe that this is some sort of game, Drake? Do you think that it matters how the puzzle is pieced together? Do you think that any one of us bears a lesser importance than the others? We are a unit, Drake. Do not forget that. Now, if you want an explanation as to why I won't allow you to do this, then I shall give it to you. The man we must question is the captain of the so-called guard here. I doubt very much that he will be prepared to offer any information without a little… persuasion. A very strong incentive may be our only way of extracting anything useful from him."

"I'll make him talk, don't worry," growled Drake.

"Will you?" asked Jared, "What if he doesn't, what then? He knows that we have already questioned one of his men, he'll have heard. He knows that no harm came to him, why would he answer any of our questions? I know what guard captains are like, I have one as a best friend. They are stubborn and proud. Although the one downstairs is not in the same league as Hannock, he will not break easily."

"He will when he sees this," said Drake, holding up his wand.

"No, he won't," sighed Jared. "There is a good chance that he must be tortured. Could you do that to another man, Drake? Could you wound and inflict pain upon a soul that cannot defend itself? You're not cut out for that, we saw it just now. You could have killed that man downstairs, but you didn't. Leave this to me, Drake. This is a puzzle that you should leave in its box."

Pushing past Jared, Drake stormed through the doorway and headed for the tavern.

Jared turned to face Emnor and raised his eyebrows.

"He'll be alright," said the old wizard, "once he's calmed down."

"Perhaps it might have been an idea to at least let him try," suggested Harley.

"That would have been the worst idea, Harley. Things like this change a man. There is no going back once it is done. One day he may have to venture down such a dark path," said Jared. "But I intend to keep you all in the light for as long as is possible."

"Come on then, let's get on with this," said Yello. Reaching the top of the staircase he raised his voice.

"Ginger, you'd better have some answers for us," he bellowed, winking at Harley.

They descended the staircase.

***

Drake threw the tavern door wide open, "Give me a drink!" he yelled at the innkeeper. "Anything that will numb my brain quickly," he added. He slumped onto the bench opposite a very tipsy, Charles Hannock. "Why do I even bother?" he shouted, "Nobody listens to a bloody word I say and, if I offer to help, Prince Perfect jumps in to steal the glory. No wonder Alex and Xarran buggered off!"

The bleary-eyed Hannock leaned forward, placing his elbows on the table to steady himself, "You shouldn't say things like that about Jared. He's my best friend, you know. He's lovely when you get to know him, he's a lovely fellow, lovely, lovely, lovely…"

Drake grimaced at Hannock's statement, "How many of those have you had?" he asked, pointing at the flagon still clutched tightly in Hannock's fist.

"Oh… a couple… maybe a few, I haven't been counting," replied Hannock, grinning inanely.

"Too many, if you ask me," muttered the innkeeper.

"Well nobody did ask you, Fatty. So, shut yer face and just bring me another one," giggled Hannock.

Drake shook his head in disbelief, "You're absolutely slaughtered!" he exclaimed.

“Good choice of word,” said Hannock, waggling his finger. “And if you don’t listen to Jared, that’s what you’ll be… slaughtered, literally,” he sniggered. “What was I saying? Oh yes… slaughtered. I know Jared can be a bit of a pompous prig at times, but his heart is in the right place. Did I tell you he’s lovely?”

“Yes, you did, you drunken prat!” snapped Drake.

Hannock frowned, “Bit harsh, isn’t it? Anyway, all I’m trying to say is that Jared, as annoying as he can be, wants to keep you safe, wants to protect you, that’s all. What you do in life defines who you are, defines what you are. Look at me for instance. I’m a soldier, it’s all I ever wanted to be, so when Jared gives me an order, I obey. You should do the same, Drake.”

“Why? I’m not one of his soldiers he can order about. I’m a magician, I can defend myself. I don’t need his protection, anyone who messes with me will get blown to pieces!”

Hannock hiccoughed, “He’s not trying to protect you from others, you stupid man. He’s trying to protect you from yourself.”

“You really are sozzled, aren’t you? That makes no sense at all.”

Hannock’s eyes were now almost closed as he waved his hand in front of Drake’s face, “What if he allows you to do exactly what you want? Allows you to attack and kill anyone who disagrees with something you say? Worse still, what if you start to enjoy it? You could be the next Karrak in no time, then you would be the target of us and our allies.”

Drake felt insulted at Hannock’s comparison between he and Karrak, “I’m nothing like that psycho!”

he growled. "He roasts people alive, tears them apart or changes them into beasts, I could never do anything like that."

"Neither could Karrak," mumbled Hannock, his eyes now closed. "I've known him since he was a child. Whinging little git, he was. Treated the servants in the castle like dirt, and enjoyed every moment of it. Tamor never saw it, of course and the more the brat got away with, the worse he became. Did you know, he murdered one of the royal guard well before... he… learned magic…" he began to snore loudly.

***

Ginger had been shackled to a chair in the centre of the room. His captors stood around him as Jared approached, a familiar slender blue flame nestled in his hand. He brandished it in his prisoner's face. "I could remove your head without spilling one drop of blood," he whispered. "Or I could be merciful and simply take your sword arm."

"Up yours!" bawled Ginger. "Go on do it, I've got nothin' to say to you, ya ponce!"

Jared suddenly slapped his hand against Ginger's forehead and rammed the back of his skull into the chair. "I'm so glad you said that," he hissed. Placing the tip of the flame blade against Ginger's cheek, he drew it slowly down. His victim's lips parted to release the scream produced by the pain, but Jared was too quick for him. Re-positioning his hand, he clamped it firmly across Ginger's mouth. His muffled cries barely audible, Jared continued, the hissing sound of burning flesh now louder than the victim's gurgling cries. A faint wisp of smoke could be seen as Jared took his time with the completion of the blade's journey, an acrid smell filling the air.

Jared released him, allowing his head to flop forwards, "Do you feel like talking now, or shall we continue with our little game?" he whispered.

Ginger was breathing heavily, sweat rolling down his face, "I told you once, get stuffed! I don't know anythin'."

Jared consulted the two senior wizards loudly, "Gentlemen," he began, "what say you, left… or right?"

Yello was the first to reply, "Right," he said, honestly not knowing what Jared had meant by the question.

Jared glanced at Emnor, "As my learned friend suggests, definitely right," he replied.

Turning to face Harley, Jared spoke again, "I'll leave this one to you," he said. Then spinning around to face Ginger, "The boy has to learn some time." He smiled, "My, my, look at the panic in your eyes, Ginger. Don't worry, we're about to halve your panic. Harley, gouge out his right eye for me, there's a good fellow."

Harley suspected that it was an elaborate bluff. Surely Jared didn't expect him to gouge the man's eye from its socket? Unsure of what to do, Harley walked slowly toward the chair. Drawing his wand from his cloak he produced sparks that flashed in the gloom. He ran his hand across Ginger's brow as the sparks became a slender, bright blue flame, which he began to lower toward the terrified man's face. Ginger shook his head free of Harley's grip, only to have Jared grab it with both hands. Jared nodded at Harley and the flame grew ever closer to Ginger's right eye.

"ALRIGHT!" he screamed, "Alright, I'll tell you anything. Just don't take my eye."

***

After locking Ginger back in his cell, they returned to the tavern. As they reached the door they could hear the most horrible noise coming from within. Pushing the door open slowly, they were aghast at the scene before them. Drake was standing on one of the tables, dancing. Well, it was obvious that he thought he was dancing; Hannock, still in the same seat, had woken up and was banging his fists on the table; and the innkeeper was stamping his feet and slapping the bar and, the worst part was, they were all singing like a bunch of baying hounds.

Yello smiled, "At last!" he cried, "A party. Where's the brandy?"

Hannock suddenly noticed them, "Hoorah," he cried. "The gang's all here. Jared, do you know the words to… what was it called?" he said looking confused.

"We have news, Hannock, but by the look of things, it'll have to wait until tomorrow."

CHAPTER 5

"Can you explain to me exactly what it is that you are waiting for? For one who believes he is destined to rule the world, you seem quite content to sit here and do nothing."

Karrak drifted swiftly across the room until his shadowy face was merely inches away from Xarran's, "I could ask you the same. You claim to be the offspring of Karrak Dunbar, you seem to have an immunity to my control and consistently mock me. You feel that you are safe from harm, but mark my words boy, sooner or later I will destroy you."

"It amuses me, you know," Karrak inched away from Xarran, "this inherent need that sorcerers possess. The need to constantly threaten the lives of those around them. Doesn't seem to have the desired effect, does it? Why won't you accept that all I want is to offer you my help?"

Karrak offered no reply.

"Alright, if you're not going to do anything, I will." Xarran walked over to Alex who, still in a trance, stood stock-still at the far end of the great hall. "I've seen your effects at transformation, Father. If you don't mind me saying, for one so powerful, they are pitiful. Those beasts you created, for instance, what are they supposed to be?"

Karrak's eyes flashed red. He desperately wanted to slay the sarcastic child that plagued him. He wanted to tear the flesh from his bones, to hear his screams of pain until his death throes eventually halted them.

"Shall I show you how it should be done?" Xarran asked with a cursory glance over his shoulder. He raised his hand and stroked Alex's cheek gently. "There doesn't have to be all the screaming and crunching of bones when one changes one's subject. It's simply a question of application." He smiled to himself as the air around Alex began to shimmer. Xarran began to laugh as Alex grew taller. His skin bubbled and his features shifted, his whole body convulsing as if someone had hold of his shoulders and was shaking him. His skin began to darken, a faint grey mist appearing to cover his whole face. He had stopped growing and was far taller than before, and his features had completely disappeared. Only a shadow remained. Xarran paced slowly around his victim. Placing his hand behind Alex, he drew his hood over his head. "What do you think, Father? Remind you of anyone?"

If Karrak's face had had any discernible features, his expression would have been one of confusion. What was the boy's intent? Karrak glared at his doppelganger.

Xarran, still smiling, faced Karrak, "Handsome chap, don't you think? Oh, stop looking so apprehensive, Father."

Karrak tilted his head to one side, "Why?" he asked.

"Misdirection," replied Xarran. "Illusion. A decoy, Father."

"Why?" Karrak repeated.

"You've upset quite a few people with your shenanigans, Father. They mean to destroy you and any who follow you."

"Let them come, they are of no significance. I could slaughter them all with a wave of one hand."

"I'm not referring to simple villagers, Father. When you attacked Reiggan, you thought you had ended the threat of any wizard that might stand in your way, so how do you account for me? Not once have you questioned how I managed to escape your genocide of wizards. I'll tell you, blind luck. As you can see…" he added, pointing at the transformed Alex, "… I was not alone."

"There are others?"

"Oh, yes," laughed Xarran. "There are others. They are an enemy you should not take lightly. And before you start with the 'I'll smite them' speech, I'll tell you who they are. The new head of Reiggan, Emnor and his close friend, Yello. But the one that you should fear most is your own brother, Jared Dunbar. Dear old Uncle Jared."

"I fear no-one," said Karrak, confidently.

***

The dust was not much of a problem to Faylore, Lodren and Grubb as they, once again, followed the route that had proven difficult for Jared's party. Faylore took the lead, remembering to avoid certain areas that had proved troublesome the first time they had followed it, with Lodren close at her heel. Buster plodded contentedly behind, the clip-clop of his hooves breaking the silence as they covered the rocky terrain. Grubb had it the easiest. He was reclined on Buster's back. The only thing disturbing his slumber was the occasional fly that would buzz around his face, which he would lazily attempt to swat away without opening his eyes, or a jolt as Buster negotiated a slightly bumpier part of the track.

"We could have avoided all this nonsense, Faylore," grumbled Lodren. "We could have been there by now if we'd have asked the dragons to take us."

"And where is there, Master Nibby?"

"Wherever we wanted to be, of course!" exclaimed Lodren. "We could have scanned for miles while we were up there."

"An' we'd 'ave seen nothin," muttered Grubb, much to the surprise of Faylore who thought he was sound asleep.

"How do you work that out?" exclaimed Lodren. "We'd have seen a heck of a lot more than we will stuck between two mountains."

"I'll give ye that," said Grubb. "But we never would've found anythin' that might 'elp us find Jared an' the others."

"Really!" said Lodren, amazed. "There aren't that many people travelling the direction we're headed in, Grubb. Anyone we met could have told us if they'd seen our friends."

"Oh yeah, o' course they could. If you 'adn't scared 'em away before we got to 'em, what with all yer bawlin' an' shoutin'. Anyone within a mile would've hidden under the nearest bush once they heard you."

"What's that supposed to mean? Why would anyone be scared of me?"

"Imagine it, Lodren. Travellers minding their own business suddenly hear the battle cry of a stranger in the clouds and look up to see a dragon swooping down on them. How would it make you feel?" giggled Faylore.

"I wasn't that bad… was I?" asked Lodren, innocently.

"No… you were ten times bloody worse!"

Lodren looked sheepishly at Faylore, "Was I really that bad?" he asked.

"Maybe a little over-exuberant, Lodren, but it doesn't matter now. You're back to your old self again, the thoughtful, polite Nibby we love so much," she replied, smiling at him.

"How're we doin, is it much farther?"

"Try opening your eyes occasionally, Grubb. It might give you a hint," said Lodren.

"Why would I want to do that? I've seen rocks an' dust before. Anyway, I've got meself in a really comfortable position now, it'd be a shame to waste it just for that."

"Oh, I'm terribly sorry, Grubb!" snorted Lodren. "You make yourself comfortable. Don't worry about us, we'll be fine. How awful of us to disturb your nap!"

"Get stuffed!"

"Will you two stop bickering?" sighed Faylore. "We'll be clear of the valley shortly and we don't want to draw any unnecessary attention to ourselves."

“And whose attention are we goin’ to draw, Faylore? Last time we came this way we never saw a soul ‘til we got to that village, and we passed that without being seen.”

“That was some time ago, Grubb. Who knows what could be lurking around the next corner? As for the village we passed, we won’t be passing it this time, we’ll be entering it,” replied Faylore.

“I don’t think there’s goin’ to be anythin’ to be afraid of in a grotty village in the middle o’ nowhere, a load o’ merchants an’ farmers is all we’ll find there.”

“Unless our old friend Karrak has visited it,” said Lodren. “We might find a load of those horrible hound things roaming around, or even worse, he might have slaughtered them all.”

“Good grief!” exclaimed Grubb. “One mention of his name and your imagination just runs wild, doesn’t it? It’s a thousand to one chance that he’s ever been anywhere near the place but oh no, Mr doom an’ gloom ‘ere ‘as to paint the most gruesome picture ‘e can before we even get there.”

“Unfortunately, Grubb we cannot rule out the possibility that Karrak could be anywhere. We must not lower our guard.”

“Lower it!” exclaimed Lodren. “Look at him, Faylore. He can’t raise himself, let alone his guard.”

Faylore laughed, “He does seem very relaxed.”

“I’m right here, ye know. Ye shouldn’t talk about someone when they can hear what you’re sayin, it’s rude!”

"Hah! That's rich coming from you. You're the king of rude. In fact, I wouldn't be surprised if you invented it!"

"Up yours, Lodren. I can be polite if I want to, but it ain't easy when you're surrounded by annoying prats like you."

"Me! How am I annoying?"

"YAAARGGHHH! I'M A DRAGON RIDER. YAAARGGHHH! I'M THE KING O' THE SKIES. YAAARGGHHH! I'M GONNA SMASH YE TO BITS WITH ME TRUSTY HAMMER."

Lodren blushed, "I never said any of that, you're just making it up," he muttered.

Faylore shook her head, "No, Lodren," she laughed, "he's not."

"Faylore, stop!" Grubb blurted out, suddenly. "Don't move. Somethin' 'appened 'ere."

Faylore studied the ground ahead. She could see nothing different to the last time they had been there, but Grubb obviously could. "What are you seeing?" she asked, in a whisper.

"When we were 'ere before, this ground was as flat as water in a bucket. Look at it now."

"It still looks flat to me," whispered Lodren.

"It's flat alright, but only because someone wanted it to look like it did before. Look around the edges o' the clearin', see the brush marks. Someone is tryin' to hide somethin'." Jumping down from Buster's back, Grubb skirted around the edge of the clearing, treading carefully so as not to disturb the loose dirt beneath his feet. He disappeared behind a rock, "Aha!" his friends heard him say, moments before he re-appeared, clutching a large branch.

"What's that doing there?" said the amazed Lodren. "There are no trees for miles yet."

"Whoever it was, used this to cover their tracks," said Grubb. "An' the only way you'd get a tree branch out here is if ye brought it from somewhere else."

"Who would carry the branch of a tree with them?"

"Nobody, that's who. This still has the leaves on it, well almost, and ye wouldn't be able to get it here with the leaves still on it unless ye used some kind o' magic."

"Maybe it was Jared and our friends?" suggested Lodren, optimistically.

"I'm gonna scout about a bit more, see if I can find any more clues. You two stay there with Buster, I'll only be a minute." It wasn't long before he returned, holding up a large bone with fur still connected to it. He grimaced, "I'm not sure what this came from, but there was more than one of 'em," he uttered, holding his nose.

Lodren approached him and sniffed the air gently, "Oh dear, what a stench." His eyes widened, "Oh dear, my goodness. I know what it was, or should I say, what they were: zingaard!"

"How could you possibly know that by smelling a rotting bone?" asked Faylore.

"I've been cooking for longer than I can remember, Your Majesty. I can tell you when an onion was picked or a ham was cured. I never forget a smell, and the last time I caught that scent was when you were almost killed by one of those… things," replied Lodren, pulling his waistcoat up over his nose.

"Grubb, where did you find that?" asked Faylore.

"Buried amongst the rocks over there. Whoever killed 'em did a damn fine job, burnt 'em first then buried what was left."

"But there is no scorching on the bone, were there ashes from a fire?"

"None. Magic fire doesn't leave ashes though, does it?"

"So, it was Jared," suggested Lodren.

"We cannot be sure of that. All we can be sure of is that magic was used. I'm afraid this is a mystery we cannot unravel unless we find the perpetrator or a witness."

"I don't think it would be a good idea to start searching for a wizard, or sorcerer out here," said Lodren. "I think we should be on our way. What good would it do us to find out who's responsible anyway?"

"Grubb, put that back where you found it, let us make haste," instructed Faylore.

Grubb did as he was bid and quickly returned the remains to their original resting place. "Done," he said, hurrying back toward them.

"If we hurry we can clear the gulley before nightfall," said Faylore. "I think it may be a little unwise to be here after dark."

"Can't argue with you there," agreed Lodren, boosting Grubb back onto Buster's back. "Let's go," he added with a shudder.

The trail was clear, allowing them to make good progress and, as planned, they cleared the gulley well before the light began to fail. As they crossed the first patch of grass they came to, Lodren gave a huge sigh, "Ah, that's better," he said, shuffling his feet, "so much kinder on the feet than the hard rock."

"Can't beat a nice bit o' springy turf under yer aching bones," added Grubb.

"How would you know!" exclaimed Lodren. "You were on Buster's back most of the way, you lazy Vikkery."

"I am not lazy. I was savin' my energy in case we was attacked. I'd be pretty useless at defendin' you two if I was exhausted, wouldn't I!"

"You? Defend us?" the exasperated Lodren blurted out. "With your eyes closed?"

"Don't you be fooled, Lodren. It might've looked like I was sound asleep, but I was ready to pounce at any threat," replied Grubb in a whisper.

Lodren was bewildered by Grubb's attempts to offer ridiculous excuses and shook his head in disbelief, "I… forget it. I'm not even going to try, just forget it."

Faylore, as wise as she was, decided not to get involved. "I think we should set camp here for tonight. Lodren, would you be a dear and set a fire?"

Lodren scowled at Grubb, but as he turned to face the Thedarian queen his expression changed to a pleasant smile, "Of course, Your Majesty. A little hungry, are we?"

"Starvin'. I could eat a whole glamoch by meself."

Lodren glared at Grubb, "I wasn't asking you, greedy guts. I was talking to Faylore."

Grubb shrugged his shoulders and began to unload some of Buster's burdens. "There ye go, fella. Time to 'ave a good rest," he cooed. "You've earned it."

"More than can be said for some of us."

"Lodren," said Faylore, gently. The Nibby looked back at her, his smile returning immediately. "The campfire?" she asked.

Lodren dashed off to find some kindling.

***

Jared raised his head from the table and peered around the room with bleary eyes. Hannock was lying on the floor, his arm across his face to shield him from the early sunlight that streamed through the dirty windows. Yello was slumped in a chair, his head tipped back, still dead to the world and snoring loudly. Harley and Drake were on the floor, their arms wrapped around one another as if each were trying to comfort the other. It only took a second for Jared to scan the room, but then the pain came. He raised his hands to his head, it felt as if someone was banging the largest drum ever made inside his brain.

Then, he saw Emnor. Leaning against the bar, he shook his head as he studied the state the prince was in, "So," he said quietly, "it seems that even a prince of the realm is not immune to a hangover."

Jared held up his hand in submission, "I may have overdone it slightly, Emnor but there's no need to shout. The drink has not affected my hearing."

“Perhaps not,” replied Emnor. “Let’s hope it has not addled your senses either.”

“I’ll be fine, just give me a couple of minutes,” pleaded Jared, lowering his head back down onto the table.”

“Oh, no you don’t!” exclaimed Emnor. “It’s almost ten o clock. Get your lazy backside off that chair, we have work to do.” He suddenly bellowed at the top of his voice, “And that goes for the rest of you. UP, UP, do you hear me?” Somehow, he managed to keep a straight face, despite the debacle that ensued over the next few seconds. Hannock shot to his feet, grabbing for the hilt of his sword, a pointless exercise as he had removed it and placed it on the bar the night before. In his confusion, he looked for it whilst groping at his belt, lost his balance and fell sideways. Yello attempted to rise from his chair, but his efforts were thwarted as the toppling Hannock crashed into him, driving him back into, and over the back of, his seat. The two younger men woke with a start and somehow figured that the best form of defence was to clutch one another even tighter than they did in their slumbering embrace.

Emnor sighed as he wiped his brow, “May the powers save me,” he mumbled. “If it’s left to you lot, I’ll be surprised if I last another day.”

It took a while, but eventually they managed to pull themselves together. There were moans and groans from all, but it was clear that they would receive no sympathy from the head of Reiggan. “I warned you all that you’d had enough, but oh no, you knew best. Now look at the state of you. You were like children with sweets, you wouldn’t listen.”

“You’d begrudge a trail-weary warrior a well-earned flagon of ale, Emnor? Don’t you think that a little harsh?” asked Hannock in a vain attempt at defending their actions of the previous night.

“Absolutely not, Captain. I would, however, draw the line at three bottles of wine and an entire bottle of brandy.”

“That’s hardly excessive!” protested Hannock, “There are four of us, after all.”

“Yes. Yes, there are, but I wasn’t counting what the others drank. That was what you put away by yourself!”

Hannock suddenly looked a little sheepish, “Oh,” was all he could offer as a reply.

“Alright, Emnor, we get it. We went a little over the top, but what’s done is done and Hannock is right for a change, we did need to blow off a little steam.”

Hannock stood upright tugging at his somewhat-shabby tunic. “Thank you, Your Highness, very good of you to, hang on a minute. What do you mean ‘for a change’?”

Jared cleared his throat, “A figure of speech, Captain, that’s all,” he replied, avoiding Hannock’s gaze. “See if you can find the barkeep, would you? I could do with some breakfast.”

They were finishing their meal, for it can hardly be referred to as breakfast when the hour has almost reached noon, when they heard a commotion outside. People weren’t screaming and shouting so they realised that there was no immediate danger, but from the droning buzz of voices outside, they knew that something had riled the villagers. Striding across the room, Hannock threw the door open. There was a throng of people in the village square and each one seemed to be engrossed by whatever was in the middle of the gathering.

"What do you make of this, Jared?" he called over his shoulder.

Jared joined him in the doorway, "No idea, but something's definitely got their attention."

Nodding at one another, they ventured outside. As they approached the crowd they picked up on one or two things that were being said. 'It is him, you know,' 'He looks different somehow,' 'Why's he smiling like that?' 'Has he gone simple?' They reached the edge and began to part the crowd, edging their way closer to the centre. Looking down, they saw a man sitting cross-legged with his back to them. He was broad-shouldered and if standing, looked to be a mountain of a man. Stripped to the waist and wearing only a tattered pair of breeches, his dark skin was splattered with grey, dried mud. Hannock and Jared moved around in order to see his face. He looked up at them, a huge inane grin on his face. Jared crouched down and spoke, "Who are you?" he asked. The man did not reply and his grin never wavered. "Did something happen to you?" Jared continued. But the man still offered no reply and began rocking back and forth, the permanent grin still showing his perfect, pure-white teeth.

There were mumbles in the crowd behind them and, turning, Jared and Hannock saw the innkeeper pushing his way through, "What's going on?" he asked, tetchily. "You're all blocking the front of my business, nobody can get in or out with you lot standing here." Then he caught sight of the man squatting on the ground. He let out a terrified scream and began charging back through the crowd, "Run. Run for your lives, he'll kill us all."

The crowd were becoming restless. Their mood had changed as a murmuring of hostile voices came from individuals that were unseen amongst them. Jared and Hannock caught the comments that were being uttered. 'String him up,' 'He's the one that slaughtered the guards,' 'We're defenceless now 'cause of him,' 'Let's burn him before any others arrive to help him'.

They were gradually closing in. Hannock reached to his side, he was unarmed, as was Jared. He glanced at his friend, "What do we do? We can't hold them all back."

They were being jostled, the crowd baying for the blood of the mindless victim who sat helpless on the ground, but not one of them had the courage to make the first move.

Suddenly, there was a loud roar. Jared saw two men at the edge of the crowd fly into the air and within seconds they were joined by Poom and Lawton who now stood at their side, teeth bared and spears brandished.

The crowd backed away, warily. Jared thought this a good time to address them. "Friends," he called, "we know not what this man has done to raise your ire, but if he is guilty of a crime, he will be punished. It is not, however, your right to pass judgement. Please, disperse peacefully that we may resolve this issue."

One old man started shouting, "Who are you? What gives you the right to decide what happens in our village? He killed the guards with his sorcery! We demand justice, hang him!"

Lawton took a step forward and pointed his spear, "We, are the ones with the weapons, old man, that's what gives us the right," he said calmly.

"Why don't you all just leave! Can't we just be left in peace? First him," said the old man, pointing at the man on the floor, "then those two young blokes and now you lot. Scaring people with your magic and your weapons. It ain't right I tell you, not right!"

"But it is fair for you to murder a mindless fool, old man?" asked Poom.

The old man did not reply and looked more than a little uneasy at the suggestion.

The crowd began to disperse as Hannock turned to face the Gerrowliens, "Thank you friends, your intervention was much needed."

Lawton nodded but his eyes were fixed on another, "What's his story then?" he asked, gesturing toward a man who remained before them.

Hannock looked across, it was the blacksmith, "Something we can do for you, smith?" he enquired.

"They were right, you know. He does deserve to be hanged."

Jared took over, "Is he…?"

"He's the one who ordered the weapons and armour from me. I thought those two young sorcerers had done him in. Obviously, I was wrong. Darooq is his name, more than that I can't tell you, I'm afraid. Mind you, he was in much better shape the last time I saw him."

More out of instinct than anything else, the Gerrowliens turned their spears toward Darooq.

"Put them down," urged Hannock. "Look at him. He's a complete jelly-brain, he's no threat."

"This makes no sense!" exclaimed Jared, "First Barden and now... him."

"Makes perfect sense to me," called Emnor as he crossed the town square.

"Why weren't they killed?" asked Hannock, "Karrak and his followers have never hesitated before."

"This is not Karrak's doing though, is it? Another party is guilty of this. Two guilty parties, to be precise," replied Emnor.

"You're not suggesting...?" Jared began.

"It's exactly what I'm suggesting, Jared. This is the work of a new enemy. This is the work of Alex and Xarran, and it troubles me that they are far cleverer than I gave them credit for."

"In what way? Turning men into jabbering wrecks," snorted Hannock.

"Exactly so, Captain. They know that we will not simply abandon or execute their victims. It is a delay tactic. Whilst we tend to the walking wounded, they are allowed more time abroad, leaving chaos in their midst."

The blacksmith spoke again, "As I've been so helpful to you, gentlemen, would there be any chance of some sort of.... gratuity?" he asked with a slight bow.

Poom was nose to nose with him in a split second, "Your people suffer, and you expect to be paid for helping them? Here's your reward for today, smith, I'll let you live. Pray that I don't have a change of heart. Now get out of my sight, you repulse me."

The fear in the smith's eyes was plain for all to see. Hurriedly, he lowered his eyes to the ground and backed away, bowing again before turning and fleeing for his life.

"Well done, Poom," said Lawton. "Tact and diplomacy… tact and diplomacy."

Poom did not reply but watched as the terrified smith disappeared from view, "Piece of filth," he mumbled.

They helped Darooq to his feet and steered him into the tavern. The barkeep shook his head, "Oh, come on," he pleaded, "not another one!"

"Oh, shut up, you stupid man!" snapped Yello. "He can't do you any harm. He doesn't know his own name or what day it is."

"But you never saw what he did to those gua…"

"I've been witnessing things like that for more than a thousand years, you imbecile. Now be quiet and get this man some food."

Knowing when he was beaten, Douglas did as he was instructed. Grabbing a platter, he slapped cheese, meat on bread on it, crossed the room and all but threw it on the table."

"There," said Yello, "that didn't hurt, did it?" He grinned as Douglas scurried away, chuntering under his breath.

"So, now we have Barden and his master. What are we going to do with them?" asked Hannock.

"It would be useful if we could get some information from them. Alas, I think that avenue is closed to us," replied Emnor.

Yello had a mischievous glint in his eye as he stroked his long grey beard. “Erm, not necessarily,” he said slowly. “There is one way we could get the answers that we need.”

Emnor shot him a look, “Surely you’re not suggesting?”

“We know it works, Emmy old boy. We’ve seen it done, remember?”

“But it’s barbaric. We were barely out of our teenage years when last we saw it. It’s been over a thousand years. No, no, definitely not, I cannot condone its use.”

Yello was grinning from ear to ear, “Come on, Emmy, you’ve got to live a little,” he added, twitching his eyebrows.

“Impossible,” protested Emnor. “Anyway, you’d never find the ingredients. Where would you find pollum in this climate? It’s far too dry.”

Yello’s grin grew larger, “Funny you should say that.”

CHAPTER 6

It was a simple enough task for Lodren to prepare a meal for himself, Faylore and Grubb. With everything cleaned and packed away, he lay against his backpack, staring at the pale green moons above.

"Wonder what it's like up there?" he sighed.

"'ard to breathe," mumbled Grubb.

"There must be someone living on them though. I mean, look at how green they are. That must mean that there are lots of trees and grassland on them and animals that graze on it."

"Why don't ye pop up there and 'ave a look then, it'll give me an' Faylore a bit o' peace and quiet," replied Grubb without moving.

"Don't be spiteful, Grubb," said Faylore. "He could be right. And even if he's not, having a vivid imagination doesn't harm anyone."

"No, I'll give ye that, Majesty. But they don't need to share it! I don't need to hear Lodren's fanciful ideas about things that live on distant moons."

"Fanciful ideas!" exclaimed Lodren. "That's rich coming from you! I'm not the one who turns into Wilf. Four arms, covered in hair, huge teeth and claws! You should study your own imagination before you start picking on mine, Grubb."

"I didn't think 'im up though, did I? It just kind of... 'appened."

"Will the endless bickering between you two never end?" snapped Faylore. "Why can't you have a conversation without it becoming a barrage of insults and petty disagreements?" She rose quickly to her feet. "I'm going for a walk!"

"But, Your Majesty, it's not safe out there by yourself. There could be anything lurking in the darkness," protested Lodren.

"Well if there is, it had better hope that it doesn't have to tangle with me. I've had enough of foolish creatures for one day!" she turned and marched away. She had only taken a few steps when her silhouette began to shimmer, and she vanished in the darkness.

"Now look what you've done," Grubb hissed quietly, "you've upset Faylore."

Lodren's eyes widened and his mouth fell open momentarily. Turning to Grubb, he stammered, "I- I- I've... me? I've upset...?" He was shaking with anger. "You inconsiderate, foul-mouthed moaning swine! If you were anyone else, I'd flatten you. I'd take my hammer and I'd... I think I'd better go for a walk as well, if I don't, I won't be held responsible for my actions! But, when I come back, I don't want to hear a word out of you! Do you understand? Not a solitary word," snatching up his hammer, he stormed off in the opposite direction to Faylore.

"Are ye sure ye should be going back amongst the rocks?" Grubb called after him. But Lodren didn't hear, he was far too angry.

In his temper, Lodren hadn't realised how far he had travelled and now, as he paused, he noticed that he was surrounded by the rocks at the foot of the mountain they had been so glad to escape from earlier that day. Unsure of himself, he slowed his pace and kicked at the dusty ground beneath him. Small plumes appeared around his feet and he marvelled at how pretty they looked when bathed in the pale green light from the moons. He had gone far enough. All he wanted was time by himself, with a sigh, he sat on a huge boulder to collect his thoughts. Was it him? Was Grubb right in his assessment? Placing his hands behind his head, he leaned back, suddenly feeling quite weary. Perhaps the rigours of the day were taking their toll. Perhaps his disagreement with Grubb had been the final straw. All Lodren knew for sure was that he was exhausted. Fatigue getting the better of him, he closed his eyes and fell into a deep sleep. But it would be far longer than he had intended before he opened them again.

He woke with a start. How long had he slumbered? Seconds? Minutes, or perhaps hours? Glancing at the moons, he realised that they had moved considerably. Lodren, having travelled far and wide for many years, estimated that he had been away from the camp for at least four hours. Why had his companions not come to search for him? Perhaps they didn't want him to come back. It seemed Grubb may have been correct when he accused him of talking too much. Lodren was allowing his thoughts to run wild. This was a time when a vivid imagination was, perhaps, not such a good thing.

Wanted or not, he had to return to the camp. His backpack was there and, if indeed he was to resume his solitary nomadic life, it was something he could not be without. The foodstuffs within it could be replaced, but he had a few personal possessions from his childhood that he could not bear to be parted from. He had to face his former friends and be brave, although he knew it would break his heart to be separated from them. A large tear welled up in his eye and he wiped it away roughly with his huge fist. "Come on, Lodren," he said to himself, "don't be such a big baby. You were by yourself long enough before. It'll just be like old times." But although he spoke the words, he never truly believed them.

What was that noise? It sounded like rasping breath. Lodren strained his ears, tipping his head to one side as he listened carefully. A few seconds passed but he heard nothing more. Glancing around he got his bearings, took a deep breath, and headed back toward the camp. As he rounded the first massive rock, he got the shock of his life… wolves!

His heart began to pound as he realised his peril. There were five, no six, no… eight. His heart sank. Gripping the handle firmly with both hands, he clutched his hammer tightly to his chest. What to do, what to do?

"STAY BACK!" he suddenly bellowed, "I'll crush your skulls, you nasty beasts! I'll crush your skulls and break your bones! I am Lodren! Nibrilsiem. Dragon rider. Lord of the skies. Any closer and you will meet your doom!" he shouted.

Unfortunately, it was a bluff. Lodren was, in fact, terrified. He had the strength of ten men, admittedly, but he was no warrior. The wolves crept forward, snarling, their jaws dripping with saliva as they stalked, what they hoped would be their next meal.

"Last warning!" yelled Lodren. "You won't live to regret it!... Oh dear," he whimpered, "they're not taking a blind bit of notice." Apparently, he would have to fight for his life. Raising his hammer aloft, he planted his feet firmly into the ground. Then, a glimmer of hope, the wolves paused, they looked nervous. The snarling and gnashing of their jaws became louder, but it was through fear not aggression, it seemed. Lodren's confidence grew, "Having second thoughts, are we? I would too if I were you. Dragon rider, see. Best be on your way whilst I'm giving you the chance."

But Lodren was unaware of the scene directly behind him. He had backed up to the massive rock to prevent the wolves from surrounding him. Little did he know that it was that very 'rock' that was his real protection.

As the wolves had approached, the 'rock' shivered. Tiny pieces of shale and dust fell from it silently as Lodren bawled at the top of his voice. The eyes opened, the huge jaws beneath smoking nostrils were agape, revealing rows of razor-sharp teeth. It was no wonder that the wolves were more than a little unnerved by this, it would appear they were not about to dine after all. To take down the small being and devour him would be easy, to contend with a dragon however, was something a pack twice their size would not attempt. With many yelps and whispers the wolves turned tail and fled.

"And don't come back," yelled Lodren. He turned his hammer and placed it, head first, onto the ground. "You won't mess with a dragon rider, will you?" he muttered, rubbing his hands together.

Thelwynn closed his jaws and eyes and lowered his head back onto the ground. Lodren looked around, feeling very pleased with himself. Slapping the 'rock', he began to dance a little jig. "Now," he said, "time to deal with Grubb."

He was half way back to camp when he noticed Grubb, mounted on Buster, heading toward him. Right, he thought, you're going to get a piece of my mind, you nasty little Vikkery.

But his plan was thwarted as Grubb called out first, "Where 'ave ye been? I've been worried sick."

"Of course you have," Lodren replied. "That's obviously why it took you so long to come and look for me!"

"You stormed off! What was I supposed to do, grab 'old of ye and drag ye back? I'm not your babysitter. If you decide ye want to go off into the night, that's your business. Don't blame me for you being on your own!"

"I don't need babysitting by you or anyone else, thank you! But a bit of help to drive off a pack of stinking wolves wouldn't have gone amiss!"

"What!" exclaimed Grubb, "Ye saw a pack o' wolves?"

"Yes, I did. Unfortunately, they saw me as well. I thought I was a goner!"

"So ye hid where they couldn't get at ye until they went away then?"

"No, Grubb, I did not hide!" snapped Lodren, "I raised my hammer and faced them down, told them I was the dragon rider and they should think twice before attacking me. They ran away!"

"These wolves?" asked Grubb, sceptically, "'ow many were there?"

"Ooh, at least a dozen," replied Lodren, embellishing slightly. "They surrounded me, huge they were, massive teeth, slobbering and snarling. But once they saw how fearless I was, they knew better than to mess with me."

"Yeesss, I can imagine," said Grubb, slowly. "But it doesn't explain why you've been gone all this time."

"Well, erm," Lodren squirmed as he tried to think of an excuse. He didn't want to admit to dozing off as he knew this would only give Grubb another reason to ridicule him. Moments before, he had been ready to confront Grubb. Alas, all too quickly his bravado had escaped him. "I needed some time to gather my thoughts," he announced, confidently. "Nothing wrong with that is there?"

"Nothin' at all," replied Grubb. "There must be a heck of a lot of 'em runnin' through that big skull o' yours for ye to be gone that long though."

"There are, and you don't help when you start…"

"I know, and I'm sorry, Lodren. I was only teasin' ye. If I'd known you'd get that upset, I would've kept me big mouth shut." He smiled at Lodren, "For a change," he added.

Lodren relaxed and smiled back, "I know I prattle on at times, but it's only because I care. I want us all to be back together in Borell, safe inside the castle walls. It seems like it was only a dream, chasing around in that huge kitchen with all the pots and pans simmering and bubbling. I miss it so much. Sorry about the shouting and roaring about being a dragon rider, it must have been really annoying."

"No need to apologise, Lodren. As a matter of fact, I think ye did me a favour."

"How could my shouting my mouth off do you a favour?" asked Lodren, looking a little confused.

Grubb glanced furtively around him, "I've got something I want to show ye," he whispered.

"Well?" said Lodren, warily, "Go on then, show me."

"Not 'ere. Let's go behind that rock. I don't want just anyone seein' it."

"Seeing what?"

"Behind the rock, come on," urged Grubb.

Perplexed by the secretive Vikkery's actions, Lodren followed him as he scurried behind the cover of the rock.

Grubb suddenly turned and pointed at him, "Now I don't want ye makin' fun of it," he warned, "I know it's not as big as a normal one, but I think the shape's perfect. I can't see it myself, so I'll let you be the judge. I mean, if you can't tell, who can?"

"What are you blathering on about? Get on with it!"

"Right," said Grubb, "here goes." He held his breath and strained. He started to go red in the face, but other than that, there was no change.

"So, you've learned how to hold your breath until you turn purple, wonderful! Can we go now?"

Grubb was panting, "Give me… a minute… I've only done this… once… before."

Lodren folded his arms as he looked on at Grubb's antics.

Grubb held his breath once more. His facial features began to stretch, his nose becoming a snout and his mouth growing wider and baring pointed teeth. His bottom stretched, becoming pointed as it grew. His skin was turning a deep, emerald colour and appeared to be quite scaly. With a sharp exhalation of breath, he suddenly fell backward, there was a noise like a wobbling jelly and everything returned to its normal shape, well as much as normal as a Vikkery is.

Lodren never said a word. He gazed at the exhausted Vikkery, watching as he lay on the ground, panting and mopping the sweat from his brow.

"Bless me horns, this one ain't easy," he puffed. "I nearly 'ad it there," Looking up at the expression on Lodren's face, he wagged his finger. "Don't look at me like that, it's coming. I'll get it this time, trust me. Bear with me, it'll be worth the wait, I promise."

Scrambling back to his feet, he closed his eyes. Taking a deep breath, he stretched his arms out to his sides. As he exhaled, the transformation began. He quadrupled in size, his face stretched, as did his 'tail'. His legs grew thicker and huge claws appeared. His back arched and sprouted massive wings and his skin, now scaled, glistened like lustrous jade, glowing in the moonlight. Grubb had transformed into the perfect replica… of a dragon.

Lodren could not speak. He stepped forward and stroked the scales of his friend's transformation. The texture was identical to the real thing and he marvelled at the perfection of Grubb's facsimile. He paced slowly around him, finding the desire to touch his creation's wings, claws and face irresistible.

"Grubb," he sighed, "you're beautiful."

Grubb snorted, "Don't say it if it ain't true, Lodren. Are ye sure? I ain't missed anythin' 'ave I?"

"Not a thing," whispered Lodren. "It's absolutely perfect." He looked away, a burning question had entered his mind and he tried to act as innocent as possible before he posed it. “Can you fly?” he asked, tentatively.

Grubb quickly lowered his head and went nose to nose with Lodren, his warm breath causing the Nibby to blink. “Oh, no ye don’t!” he snapped. “Ye can get that idea out o’ that big head o’ yours! Ain’t no saddle goin’ on this Vikkery’s back.”

***

Emnor, sat on a chair in the tavern, rested his elbows on his knees, “I’m still not sure about this, Yello. You could end up a raving lunatic.”

“He already is!” exclaimed Hannock.

Yello laughed, “I’ll be fine,” he assured his friend. “They can’t hurt me.”

“Famous last words! Dellurim said that and look how he ended up! He never spoke again, just sat dribbling down his front for the rest of his days.”

“Very true, but you’re forgetting something,” said Yello, confidently, “Dellurim was a blithering idiot.”

“And so are you for even contemplating this. There has to be another way.”

“You can babble all day, Emnor. I’m doing this and that’s settled. Anyway, I’ve already administered the potion to them both so there’s no going back now. I’m going into their minds, and I’m bringing them both back with me when I return.”

“If you return!” warned Emnor.

"How does this work, exactly?" asked Jared.

"You'll see," replied Yello. "But I warn you, it can look a little… gruesome. It's not something that should be witnessed by the fainthearted."

"Is that why you sent the boys out?" asked Hannock.

"On the contrary," laughed Yello. "They wouldn't turn a hair at something like this. No, I sent them away because this is as close as you can get to dark magic. The enticement of its power can seduce any who harbour any hatred or resentment in their heart."

"How would that pertain to Drake or Harley?" asked Jared.

Yello's tone changed. A shadow seemed to descend on the room as he spoke. "Do you not think that witnessing the carnage at Reiggan would affect them? That seeing the mutilated and charred bodies of their friends and colleagues would cause them to feel ill will toward Karrak and his followers? Do you not think that, given the chance, they would not exact their revenge upon any one of them? It is as close to hatred as one could be. I would not expose them to the lure of dark magic, for as strong as they are, it would be beyond their power to resist it."

"Quite so," said Emnor, loudly. The two Borellians seemed startled, which had been Emnor's intention, "Get on with it then, Yello. It's obvious that you cannot be dissuaded, so let's get it over with. Don't worry, old friend, if it all goes horribly wrong, I'll always be there to wipe your chin."

"Thanks for the vote of confidence," laughed Yello, "you really are too kind."

Suddenly the door flew open. Drake stood, breathing heavily, a timid Harley shadowing him, "We were right outside the door. Did you think we wouldn't hear what you were saying? We're part of this, like it or not. You can't cover our eyes or ears as if we were children, so get on with what you were about to do, because we're staying."

Darooq and Barden had been laid on tables beside one another at the far end of the room. Emnor had dressed them both in robes after washing the mud from their motionless bodies and Yello now positioned himself at their heads. Placing his hands on their foreheads, he glanced over his shoulder, "Wish me luck," he muttered.

He closed his eyes. It was a few moments before anything happened, but suddenly Yello's body jerked as if someone had pushed him. He sighed as tiny sparks began to arc across his fingers as they slowly began to sink, moulding into the brows they rested upon. Hannock grimaced at the sight of Yello's fingers penetrating the skulls of the dormant men before him. Yello's head fell forward.

Emnor spoke quietly, "He's in," he announced, "Yello has now entered their minds."

"Will he be alright?" whispered Jared.

"Only time will tell," replied Emnor with a look of concern. "All we can do now… is wait."

***

Yello opened his eyes. It took a while for his sight to become accustomed to the gloom, but he appeared to be standing in a huge cave. “How predictable,” he mumbled aloud, his breath visible in the cold air. Thick clumps of ice clung to the walls, and frozen pools on the ground crackled as he peered through the mist that surrounded him. He ventured forth, taking tentative steps on the uneven cave floor. This was the construct of someone’s mind, admittedly, but the risk of a turned ankle or broken leg was still very real. Numerous narrow passageways sprouted in all directions, not one looking any different to the others. Oh well, he thought, each is as good as the next. This in mind, he headed toward the nearest. Yello was undaunted by the appearance of his surroundings, the sounds however, were something he had not expected. The unclear whispers of countless voices, the sound of sinister laughter from one far louder than all others and the faint screams in the distance were enough to put anyone’s nerves on edge. He shuddered slightly, “Come on, Yellodius,” he muttered to himself, “pull yourself together.” The one thing he was glad about was the fact that, although there was the danger of injury, his leg was completely devoid of pain. Carefully, he picked his way through passage after passage before eventually making a discovery. He noticed a strange shape against the rocks, it appeared to be someone huddled in an attempt to remain hidden. Cautiously, he edged forward, squinting to get a better look, “Hello,” he called. “Is someone there?”

“Shhh, keep your voice down,” came the anxious reply. “He’ll hear you.”

Yello tilted his head to one side, “Barden?” he asked, “Is that you?”

“Be quiet, you fool. He’ll find us,” replied Barden.

“Who, Barden? Who will find us?”

Barden’s eyes flashed as he looked about him wildly, “Lord Karrak,” he replied in a whisper.

“No, Barden. He cannot find us here,” said Yello, reassuringly. “You are safe, old friend.” The one thing that Yello did not think of Barden as was a friend, but this was not the pompous, self-absorbed man he had known for many centuries. Keeping his tone gentle would, he was sure, be far more advisable than a more hostile approach.

“Let him find us!” a voice announced from the mist. “He is our master, we should be at his side, not cowering in the darkness.”

Yello turned quickly, “Who’s there?” he demanded.

A figure emerged slowly from the mist. Dressed in grey robes, the stranger’s features were hidden. Confidently, he drew closer to Yello until, just a few yards away, he pulled down his hood to reveal himself. “You don’t remember me?” he asked.

Yello’s lips moved but he stammered slightly in disbelief, “Barden? But…”

“A thousand years old and you still cannot comprehend the obvious, Yellodius,” he sneered. “You always were pathetic. Too busy roaming the wilds and making friends, soaking your brain with cheap wine and seeking approval from worthless creatures!”

“Keep quiet, both of you,” urged the panic-stricken Barden.

“Be quiet yourself,” bellowed the confident Barden, “I’d end you now if I could.”

Yello stepped between them, "How, Barden? How did this happen?"

Before either Barden could speak again, yet another voice joined the conversation, "He did it to himself," it announced. "So ashamed of his cowardice, that he severed it as one would amputate a festering limb." The silhouette of a large man could be seen faintly through the mist.

"Darooq, I presume?" said Yello, loudly.

"You have me at a disadvantage, old man. You know my name, but yours is unknown to me."

"Who I am is unimportant," replied Yello. "Why I am here, however, is not."

"So, you believe that we are important? Why would you think such a thing?" asked Darooq.

"Do you know where you are?" asked Yello. "This is not real. You are both unconscious, lying on tables in a tavern. In reality, you are gibbering wrecks, the pair of you, your minds scrambled by the very sorcery you hold so dear."

"And you've come to free us from our bonds, have you?" asked Barden, insincerely. "You think that we will be so grateful to you that we would turn on our master to aid you?"

"Be quiet, I beg of you."

"That," said Darooq, pointing at the terrified Barden, "is what will become of you all if you stand in Karrak's way."

"He is but one man, powerful admittedly, but still only one man," said Yello. "We are many and we shall defeat him. Stand with us if you fear him so."

"Is that what you believe?" Darooq laughed loudly, his voice echoing about them. "You think that I fear Karrak?"

"Is it that you do not fear him, or is it that you are still loyal to him, despite what has become of you?" asked Yello. "For your loyalty is misguided if that is the case. I don't see him here attempting to save you."

"He'll come for us when he is ready!" snapped Barden. "He knows we are devoted to him, he'll come!"

"No, he won't," said Darooq, smiling. "We are as important to him as an insect that he would crush beneath his boot. If he did come for us it would be so that he could torture us a little longer. You see, old man," he said, still addressing Yello, "the reason I no longer fear him is simply because I have no cause to. I have done his bidding and am now useless to him… as is this arrogant fool." He nodded toward Barden. "Our part is played. Karrak will not waste his time looking for us."

Yello was becoming agitated, "Karrak has used you and now leaves you to perish. Join us, at least you'll have a chance of revenge."

"Join you?" bellowed Barden. Raising his arm, he chanted and flung his arms forward.

Yello raised one eyebrow as he folded his arms, "Feel better now, Barden?" he asked. "Just a tip… magic won't work in here."

***

Lodren and Grubb were discussing their time spent in Borell as they sat by the campfire. They both jumped slightly as, with a slight shimmer, Faylore appeared before them.

“You frightened the life out me!” exclaimed Lodren. “Can’t you stamp your feet as you’re approaching to give us a bit of a warning?”

Faylore looked down her nose at him, “I am the Queen of Thedar, Lodren,” she said haughtily, “I would never stamp my feet.”

“Rustle the grass or somethin’ then,” said Grubb. “We could’ve attacked ye, not knowin’ who ye were.”

Faylore gave him a wry smile, “I’ll take my chances,” she said.

“Did you see anything interesting on your travels, Faylore? Anybody about?”

“No, Lodren,” she replied, “I even climbed the tallest tree I could find. Nothing is moving, not even the beasts.”

“That’s not good,” said Lodren, pursing his lips. “There are always animals mooching about after dark. Something’s scared them if you ask me.”

“Do ye think it could be a dragon?” asked Grubb, smirking.

“Don’t be silly, Grubb,” replied Faylore, frowning. “You know perfectly well that there aren’t any dragons around here.”

“If you say so, Your Majesty,” said Grubb, still smiling.

“You two are acting very strange,” said Faylore, “I mean, more strangely than usual, but at least you’ve stopped bickering.”

“Well, a pack o’ wolves tryin’ to ‘ave ye for dinner kinda takes the edge off a good argument,” sighed Grubb.

“Oh, my word!” exclaimed Faylore, “Grubb, you poor thing. Are you alright? They didn’t hurt you, did they?”

“Not a scratch, Majesty. I’m fine,” laughed Grubb.

“That’s because it was me they came after,” said Lodren, taking a playful swipe at Grubb.

“Oh, Lodren! I’m so sorry. I should not have left you by yourself. You could have been killed!”

“Are you kiddin’?” spluttered Grubb, spilling the fruit juice he was drinking. “You’ve seen ‘im swing that ‘ammer! It’s the wolves I feel sorry for. Stumpy ‘ere bawlin’ at ‘em and swingin his anvil on a stick!”

“Don’t be horrible, Grubb! What if he’d stumbled, or one of them had sneaked around behind him?” suggested Faylore, suddenly grabbing Lodren’s head and pulling it into her chest.

“’e squashed a zingaard’s ‘ead with one bash! What chance do ye think wolves would ‘ave against ‘im?” protested Grubb.

Lodren never spoke. He just sat there with a dreamy grin on his face as Faylore held him in a vice-like embrace.

“Look at ‘im!” exclaimed Grubb, “e’s lovin’ the attention!”

“Don’t be silly,” cooed Faylore, “he’s probably in shock, the poor dear.”

"He wandered the wilds for years by 'imself and survived, do ye think one mangy pack o' wolves could get the better of 'im?"

"That's beside the point, Grubb. They were different times. The world is a far more dangerous place now. Well neither of you shall be left alone from now on, you must have an escort at all times."

"It's nice of ye to offer to hold our hand every time we need to be alone, Faylore, but there's only one of you, even you can't be in two places at once."

"I know that, Grubb, but I wasn't suggesting that I accompany you."

"I don't see anyone else here, Your Majesty. Or do ye have an invisible friend?"

Faylore smiled, "Not invisible exactly," she replied, "more… hidden." She raised her arm and gave a small gesture toward the darkness. One by one, six Thedarians appeared with a shimmer.

"Oh, Faylore!" exclaimed Lodren, "You've found your friends."

"Well, to be honest, they found me," replied Faylore.

Lodren jumped up and ran over to the newly-arrived Thedarians, "Hello, hello," he said excitedly, shaking each one by the hand. They all had the same puzzled expression on their faces and were as aloof as Faylore had been when they had met her for the first time, many years before. "Can I get you all something?" asked Lodren. "You must be hungry," he added as he raced over to his pots and pans.

They graciously declined, insisting that they were fine and needed no repast. Faylore did her best to calm the Nibby but his yearning to start catering for their guests had overwhelmed him and it took some time before he would accept that they were in no need of any refreshment.

"Well if you need anything, anything, no matter what or the lateness of the hour, you just ask," he urged.

"'ave ye finished?" asked Grubb, staring at Lodren. "Only I was just wonderin', what are they doin' all the way out 'ere? Why are they so far away from home?"

"You can thank my mother for that, Grubb," replied Faylore. "She worries about me constantly and has sent scouts far and wide to locate me."

"Why?" asked Grubb, "I mean, I know she's your mom an' all that, but why now? Yer not in any danger, well no more than usual and she's well aware that ye can take care o' yerself."

"She's also aware of what is contained in the Peneriphus Scroll, Grubb."

"But she doesn't have the scroll anymore," Lodren said, "I thought Emnor had it."

"But she has read it, or had before it disappeared from the hall of history," replied Faylore.

"So why is she so concerned? She can't have seen it for centuries," suggested Grubb.

"That is true," said Faylore, "but unlike my father in his final years, there is nothing wrong with her memory. Being Thedarian, she can remember the slightest detail of any written work once she has read it, regardless of the passage of time."

"So, she knows all about Karrak and his shenanigans?" said Grubb, quietly.

"Precisely, hence the scouting parties."

Lodren was becoming a little nervous, but questions were racing through his head and he simply had to ask, "Your friends, Faylore. Have they seen anything on their travels? Anything bad, I mean."

Faylore took a deep breath, "Not seen, but there are terrible rumours. Rumours of countless dead, men and women."

"So Karrak has been killing indiscriminately again!" exclaimed Lodren. "I bet he didn't even have the decency to build a pyre and give them an honourable send off, probably just left them to rot where they lay!"

"It is far worse than that, my dear. The dead are not at peace, they still walk. He has created an entire undead army, animated by necromancy."

"What!" exclaimed Grubb, "Why would he do somethin' like that? Surely 'e doesn't need soldiers, not with the amount o' black magic 'e's got runnin' through 'im!"

"No, I agree, Grubb. He doesn't need them, but he enjoys striking terror into the hearts of innocents and what better way than to put the walking corpse of a loved one against their own kin?"

"I wish Jared and the others were with us, we could set off right now!" roared Lodren. "When I see Karrak I'm going to crush him with my hammer. I'll break every bone in his body and show him what it's like to be scared."

Grubb stared across at Faylore, a slight smirk on his face, "Wolves?"

***

“Tell me, boy. What happened to the first?”

Xarran glanced across at Karrak, “The first?” he asked.

“The first-born son. You are the second or you would not be here.”

“Oh, him. Bad news, I’m afraid, Father. He’s no longer with us. Passed away suddenly, didn’t even show any signs of being ill beforehand. Very strange, if you ask me,” he laughed.

“You murdered your own brother?”

“Brother?” replied Xarran, curling his lip. “He was a stranger to me. Just another one of your illegitmate offspring whose mother was paid off to protect the precious name of Dunbar.”

“Regardless of his origins, he was still your brother.”

“As Jared is yours,” snapped Xarran, “but that didn’t stop you trying to kill him. Oh, yes, you failed, didn’t you? Twice.”

“The man who was Karrak Dunbar failed, but I am not he. I am Lord Karrak, keeper of the Elixian Soul. No mere mortal can hinder me.”

“Is that so? Go on then, Lord Karrak, show me your power. Strike me down, try setting your pet ghouls against me. No? Why not? Because you can’t,” bellowed Xarran. “Pay heed, sorcerer. The Elixian Soul is destined to be mine, and be mine it shall. Whether by my hand or that of another, you will perish, and the future you envisage will be yours no longer. The future belongs to me."

Karrak's eyes flashed red as he charged toward Xarran. Raising his arms, he towered above his intended victim but as he tried to strike Xarran, a force not conjured by Xarran himself, blew him backwards across the room. An ordinary man, or wizard, would have been felled by the blast, but Karrak remained upright, his breath rasping as if he had suffered an immense blow to the chest.

"Impressive boy, most impressive," he rasped, "But mark my words boy, you will regret what has taken place this day."

Xarran laughed, mockingly, "More threats? What way is that to speak to your only son?" Backing away, he pointed at Karrak with both hands before spinning on his heel and walking away, his laughter still echoing through the chamber.

CHAPTER 7

"What are we doing here?"

"Same as always, we're waiting for them to decide what their next move will be."

The Gerrowliens were on the roof of the tavern, Poom swinging his legs over the edge, showing his boredom. "No, Lawton, that's not what I meant. I meant, what are we doing here?"

"Isn't it obvious? We're helping our friends."

"But they don't need our help!" exclaimed Poom. "With Emnor and Yello alone, they have all they need to defeat Karrak and his cronies."

"Is that what you honestly believe, Poom? That we are somehow surplus to requirements?"

"They're wizards, Lawton. They have unlimited magic at their disposal. We have to use a flint if we need to start a fire, they conjure a flame out of thin air."

"But they cannot produce water in an arid environment, or had you forgotten that? If not for us, they all would have died of thirst."

"Oh, yes, I had forgotten that," admitted Poom.

"Neither can they detect a foe by their body heat through trees and bushes. When the hissthaar attacked in

Cheadleford things could have gone terribly wrong but for our keen eyesight and reflexes."

Poom stroked his cheek, "Yeesss," he said slowly, "I'd forgotten about that as well."

"So, do you still think that our friends will not benefit from our involvement in this adventure of theirs?"

"Yes, alright, we've helped a couple of times, I'll admit," began Poom, "but our skills didn't stop us being turned into trees by Jendilomin, did they? We weren't much help then."

"The others were transformed as well, Poom. Even Faylore and that four-armed beast that Grubb turns into were taken unaware. There was no way we could have prepared for such a thing," Lawton assured him.

"Exactly my point!"

"What is?" asked Lawton, looking a little confused.

"Coping with tough terrain and beasts is one thing, Lawton. But it won't be that simple from now on, I fear," replied Poom. "Soon we'll be facing Karrak, and if he has all his sorcerer sidekicks with him, what help can we be?"

Lawton chuckled as he looked at Poom, "I've never seen you concerned about an impending battle before, Poom. It makes quite a pleasant change. What's the matter, worried that the nasty man will burn a bit more of your fur off?"

"This is no time for jokes, Lawton, I'm serious! And don't think that I'm afraid either. If it came down to just me and Karrak, I'd still tear him apart before he could even think of casting a spell, let alone perform one!"

"Now that's the Gerrowlien I know, fearless and stupid to the last," laughed Lawton.

"Exactly, and if I… oh, thanks very much!"

"Trust me, Poom," said Lawton, the tone of his voice becoming deadly serious, "if it does come down to just you and Karrak… run. Run as fast as your legs will carry you and don't look back. Go home, gather the rest of the tribe and get as far away as possible."

"You know me better than anyone, Lawton. I could never flee from battle!"

"This will be a battle like no other, Poom. This is no skirmish over lands or wealth, Karrak has no interest in such trivial matters. He means to extinguish all life from our world!"

"But why destroy everyone? What would he have to show for it? Surely, he'd want slaves, or at least a few survivors to lord over and torment?"

"You'd think so, wouldn't you? If it were Karrak then perhaps, but it is no longer his will that calls the tune, this is the will of that… Elixian… thingy. The man that was Karrak has long since been consumed by it."

"You've really bought into this magical mumbo-jumbo, haven't you, Lawton?"

"More than you would believe, my friend. The one thing that worries me more than any other, is Jared."

"Jared!" exclaimed Poom, "Why would you be concerned about him?"

"He's changed, Poom. A change that I see manifesting itself more as time goes on. I watched his face as he tortured that zingaard, there wasn't the slightest hint of emotion, not even as he thrust his hand into its guts. I fear that, when faced with his brother, he may feel that they are more alike than he could possibly have imagined. That pause would give Karrak an advantage. If Jared hesitates or is unable to bring himself to destroy his brother, it could spell his doom. The thought that haunts my mind more than any other however, is that if he feels an empathy toward his sibling, he may join him."

"Never!" growled Poom. "Jared is nothing like his brother! He'd willingly lay down his life before being a part of Karrak's insanity."

Lawton lowered his head and peered up at his friend, "I hope you're right, Poom. I sincerely hope you're right."

***

"This isn't looking good, Emnor. His skin's going grey. You should give him a slap and bring him round if you ask me."

Emnor peered at Hannock, "Advice like that is precisely why nobody asks you, Captain. One does not 'slap' the wizard who is linked to another's mind! It could cause irreparable harm. Yello has joined two minds and that is far more dangerous, to force him out could kill him," he sighed.

"He is looking a bit peaky, Master Emnor," said Drake. "We have to do something."

"Indeed," replied Emnor thoughtfully. "Only one thing for it," he announced, "I must join him."

“No!” exclaimed Harley, “You’re far too important! I’ll do it, I’ve read how it works.”

“You can both forget it!” announced Drake, “If anyone’s going in, it’ll be me. I don’t do anything else lately, so if it goes wrong, I won’t be missed.”

Hannock sidled behind the two younger wizards, “Neither of you will do anything, unless you are instructed to,” he snapped, grabbing each by the nape of the neck. “And we’ll hear no more about anyone being expendable,” he added, releasing Drake long enough to slap him in the back of his head.

“You were obviously determined that someone got slapped around the head then?” laughed Jared.

“What can I say?” replied Hannock, grinning, “I just got lucky.”

Taking Emnor gently by the arm, Jared steered him away to the corner of the room, “This joining thing, how does it work, exactly?”

“Now is not the time for lessons, Jared. I’ll explain it to you later, for now I must help Yello.”

“That’s my point,” said Jared. “You see…” he whispered, “… I agree with the boys. Therefore, I’ll be the one joining with Yello, not you.”

“But you’ve never done anything like this before,” protested Emnor. “It’s far too dangerous for, if you’ll forgive my bluntness, a mere novice.”

Jared smiled, “So I’m capable of facing the most powerful sorcerer in existence, but not of learning enough to converse with someone in a dream?”

“It’s not the same, Jared!” replied Emnor in a pleading tone. “To face a real danger is one thing and you've proven on more than one occasion that you can easily defend yourself. But what you may see in there is not real and can be most confusing, who knows what you would be facing."

"But it's only a construct of someone's mind, Emnor, a dream! Surely nothing can harm me in there?"

"In most cases I'd say not," replied Emnor. "However, Yello is joined with two of Karrak's most loyal followers and they are powerful sorcerers in their own right."

"You'd better make your instruction clear then," said Jared placing his hand on Emnor's shoulder reassuringly. "Don't worry, Emnor, I'll bring our friend back. I can't make any promises regarding our enemies though," he added, gesturing toward the prostrate figures of Barden and Darooq.

Reluctantly, Emnor began instructing Jared on the secrets of joining with the minds of others. Jared understood the dangers, but it seemed straightforward enough and he had no concerns regarding its execution. He questioned Emnor on a few intricacies, making sure that he could follow his mentor's advice to the letter and, within the hour, insisted that he was ready. Standing directly behind Yello, he raised his hands.

"Now remember, Jared," Emnor warned him, "you will have little control over what takes place in there. Empty your mind, stay calm and most of all, watch your back."

"Hang on just a minute," said Hannock. "How is he supposed to get back? Can't he take a sword with him or something?"

"No, Captain, he can't take a sword with him. Jared isn't going anywhere physically, therefore he cannot carry anything with him."

Jared paused, "Hold on, Hannock might have something there."

"That's me," chirped Hannock. "Full of good ideas."

"You're full of something," mumbled Drake.

"I can't carry anything, but if I imagine I'm carrying something won't it appear in the dream realm?" suggested Jared.

"What good do you think a sword will be!" exclaimed Emnor.

"I wasn't thinking of a sword," said Jared, reaching out, "I was thinking of this," he added, carefully taking Emnor's staff.

"It'll be of no use to you, Jared. That staff belongs to Master Emnor, it will only respond to him," said Harley.

Jared's eyes flashed as he raised Emnor's staff. As magnificent as it was, surely its power would lie dormant unless wielded by Emnor himself. Gazing at the runes that had been so lovingly engraved along its shaft, Jared smiled as it began to hum! Tiny sparks were seen to dance along its length, spreading to Jared's hand as if fusing them together. Jared shivered as the front of his tunic began to twitch as if some small beast was trying to escape its cage. Suddenly the fabric was ripped apart as the medallion he so proudly wore tore through and protruded horizontally as if being pulled by an invisible hand. The chain which held it became more and more taut, its links cutting into the back of Jared's neck and drawing blood. Hannock rushed forward and thrust his dagger upward without thinking. He was shocked at how strong the chain was, but with a surge of strength he managed to eventually break it. As it travelled the short distance, the delicately crafted setting that housed the Heart of Ziniphar shattered, before the gem itself slammed into the head of the staff.

None present would witness what was about to happen. They shielded their eyes from the blinding light that was suddenly emitted by the staff. The humming ceased, the room fell silent, and all was calm once more.

It was a few moments before any of them spoke, the silence broken by Drake, "STUFF ME!" he yelled, "What was that all about?"

Reaching to the floor, Emnor picked up a part of the setting that had housed the Heart of Ziniphar, "I think my staff has a new adornment," he said quietly.

"Are you alright, Jared?" asked Hannock, concerned by the blood on the prince's collar, "Let me see."

"I'm fine, Hannock," replied Jared, seeming slightly dazed. "It's only a graze."

"I'll be the judge of that, Your Highness, if you don't mind. Producing a clean cloth, Hannock began dabbing at Jared's neck. A look of bemusement swept across his face. Wiping harder at the blood, he shook his head, "Nothing!" he announced, "There's no wound, not so much as a scratch. How…?"

Jared shooed him away, "I'm fine," he repeated. "Stop fussing!"

"May I take a look?" asked Emnor, gesturing toward the staff.

Jared seemed unnerved by Emnor's request, "It's fine," he replied. "No harm done. You know what it's like? There are always little surprises when you're dealing with magic," he added with a fake laugh.

"Nonetheless, may I?" repeated Emnor.

All eyes were now on Jared, he actually seemed reluctant to hand the staff to Emnor. Realising the attention that was upon him, he stepped forward, "Of course," he replied shakily, "it is yours after all."

Emnor took his staff warily and placed it on a table, scrutinising every inch of its length until he reached the head. The Heart of Ziniphar had not simply fused itself to the staff, it seemed that the staff had actually parted and allowed it into its core. The jewel had always possessed a shifting centre, but now was completely different. It seemed alive, a swirling torrent that was mesmerising. Now, it was time for the test that would prove to Emnor what he believed had taken place. Raising the staff as he had so many times before, he pointed it at Hannock. He chanted a few words and pushed his hand forward slowly.

"What are you doing?" yelled Hannock, "Don't point the blasted thing at me, I've seen what it can do."

But his fears were unwarranted, nothing happened.

"Mm," Emnor didn't seem surprised. Beckoning Jared to join him, he handed him the staff. "Do me a favour would you, Jared?" Jared slowly took the staff and waited for Emnor to finish. "Destroy that chair over there. Try using the staff."

Moments before, Jared had not wanted to hand the staff back to its owner. However, now handed it freely, Jared felt a little uncomfortable, "Why?" he asked innocently.

“A test, Your Highness, merely a test,” replied Emnor, smiling.

Jared shrugged his shoulders. He pointed the staff at the chair but before he uttered a single word, the chair was incinerated. It barely had time to produce a flame before it was nothing but a fine smattering of soot.

“Is that what you were trying to do to me?” bawled Hannock, “You were weren’t you? You were trying to fry me, you mad old sod!”

“Of course not, Captain. I would never do such a thing,” replied Emnor, feigning innocence, but with an amused smirk on his face.

“You’re as mental as his brother!” Hannock continued, “I don’t know who’s more dangerous, you or him. At least I’d know to be on my guard if he were around, but you lot…” he paused, staring at the floor momentarily, “I need a drink, a large drink. You lot stay away from me, I’ve had enough of your insanity for one day.” True to his word, he marched across to the bar. Uncorking the nearest bottle, he scowled at them before flopping into a chair.

Drake sniggered as he leaned across to whisper in Harley’s ear, “I think he’s a bit upset.”

Harley sighed, “Master Emnor, what’s this all about? What happened?”

“It seems the Heart of Ziniphar wants to protect our prince.”

“So, it decided to join with the staff to enhance its power?” suggested Jared.

“But the staff belongs to you, Master Emnor. It cannot be wielded by anyone else,” said Harley.

"It seems that the staff's allegiance has changed, Harley. The staff is no longer mine." Turning to face Jared, he wagged his finger at him, "No, it seems the staff now belongs, to you."

"That makes no sense! Surely it could protect me easily enough housed in the setting the boys made?" said Jared.

"It seems that defence alone will not be enough. The Heart has realised that you will not only need to defend yourself against attack but be able to mount one of your own," advised Emnor.

"Makes sense, Jared," Drake suddenly blurted out. "You can only get slapped in the head so many times before you do something to retaliate," he added, glaring at Hannock.

"Why now, Emnor? Do you think the Heart suspects that my joining with Yello could hold some danger?"

"I have no idea I'm afraid," replied Emnor. "It holds ancient powers that we may never understand."

"What if it has its own agenda?" suggested Harley. "Look at what the Elixian Soul has done to Karrak."

"I already have," said Emnor with a smile. "But the two are as different to one another as Jared and Karrak. One is inherently good, the Heart; the other evil and dark, the Soul."

"Let's not go into this now, eh? I think we should concentrate on the dangers that Yello could be facing as we speak. You said time is of the essence, so let's get on with it!"

Emnor nodded, he knew Jared was right, procrastinating would only add to the difficulties that he may face. “Stand behind Yello and place your palms against his temples,” he instructed. Now, clear your mind. Think only of Yello, anything that enters your thoughts could manifest itself once you imagine it. Are you comfortable? Now, close your eyes…”

***

A split second later Jared opened his eyes. Emnor and the others were gone. He was standing in a large cavern, quite unlike the one that Yello had encountered. The orange walls glowed and scattered flames spouted from the floor. I think I should tread carefully, Jared thought grinning. He wasn’t unnerved by the appearance of the cavern, it was rock and fire, nothing more. He took his first step, using the staff to test the ground ahead of him. The staff, he hadn’t been holding it when he joined with Yello, he couldn’t, both of his hands were holding Yello’s head. He tilted his head, staring in disbelief. The staff hadn’t even crossed his mind, he had no intention of bringing it with him. It appeared, however, that the staff had a will of its own. Jared tightened his grip and marched forward, a confidence in his step that he could not explain. As had Yello, he searched the dark tunnels leading from the cavern, taking care to avoid the sudden explosions of flame that appeared. It may not have been real, but he wasn’t about to test the theory that, what’s not real, can’t harm you. He paused momentarily, wiping his brow with his sleeve. He laughed quietly, why he had done that was a mystery, he wasn’t even sweating. Obviously my mind thinking that I should be, amongst this, he thought, glancing around him.

His thoughts were interrupted, had he heard a voice? He stood, stock still. It was difficult to hear anything other than the roar of the flames and the explosions around him. Heading toward where he thought the sound had come from, he heard it again. It was incoherent, sounding more like the buzzing of an insect than actual speech but as he grew nearer, he recognised Yello's voice. He crept forward, the staff raised before him. This place was not real, what he encountered may look like Yello, but he had to be careful. Things may not be what they appear in here, he thought.

He craned his neck around the bend of the tunnel. He could see three figures, no wait, four. One was crouched against a wall, flames spewing from both sides of him. Yello was amongst them and seemed to be pleading with the others. He appeared to be in no danger but from what Jared could hear, he was imploring them to follow him.

Jared stepped tentatively into view, "Yello," he called, "we need to leave this place."

Barden immediately went into a rage, "See!" he roared, "You ask us to trust you and then reveal yourself to be a deceiver. You secrete others in an attempt to ambush us. Gain our trust and attack us from behind once our guard is lowered, was that your plan?"

Yello held up his hands, "No Barden, no," he assured him, "I came alone. I had no idea that anyone else would enter."

"LIAR!" yelled Barden. "See, I said he could not be trusted," he warned Darooq.

Darooq did not seem alarmed as he stared at Jared. He walked forward slowly as he began to speak, "Why are you here, Dunbar?"

Jared was taken aback slightly, but managed to maintain his composure, “Not for any reason that involves you,” he replied. “Joining with you is harming Yello. In here he seems fine whereas, in reality, he is becoming dreadfully weak. Choose what fate you will for yourself, sorcerer, but I will not allow you to endanger my friend.”

“I have chosen no path for the old man,” Darooq said, calmly. “He is neither bound, shackled or incarcerated. He has chosen to remain here.”

“Jared, you must leave,” urged Yello. “They were about to leave this place, now you’ve only complicated things. Go! Now!”

“Sorry, Yello, I cannot. If you choose not to follow me immediately, you’ll die in here!”

“So, I die, so what? I’m an old man, surely my destiny should be of my own choosing?”

“We can argue about that later. Right now, however, I’m leaving, and I’m taking you all with me.”

“And if we refuse to leave?” laughed Darooq. “You can perform no magic in here, Dunbar. Even a man as large as you would not be able to drag both of us…” he looked behind him, “… apologies, all three of us if we are unwilling to accompany you.”

Jared pursed his lips, “No magic?” he said slowly. Holding out the staff, he smiled at Darooq. Turning his gaze to Barden, he blinked slowly. Barden fell to his knees, he seemed confused, looking about him wildly. His manic self, still huddled against the wall, began screaming, “Leave me, let me stay!” it shrieked. It faded, and disappeared. The arrogant Barden fell forward and closed his eyes.

Darooq glanced at Barden, "Dead?" he asked.

"No," replied Jared, "just asleep. We do not murder as indiscriminately as you do, sorcerer."

"Jared?" said Yello, "How? Why do you have Emnor's staff? This is impossible."

"No, not impossible, Yellodius. Complicated yes, but not impossible," Jared raised the staff once more. "Will you join us willingly, sorcerer, or perhaps you would prefer the alternative?"

Darooq looked down at the slumbering body of Barden. Gesturing with his hand, he bowed his head, "Lead on," he sighed.

***

Grubb drummed his fingers lightly against his thigh. He had discovered a particularly spongy, moss-covered mound to lean against and couldn't remember the last time he had been so comfortable. The smaller twigs on the campfire crackled quietly and he glanced across dreamily to see Lodren, fast asleep, on the other side of it. His gentle snoring seemed quite soothing and Grubb smiled as he recalled the Nibby's disastrous efforts to convince the Thedarians to allow him to cook them a meal. He seemed most offended and his chuntering had continued right up until he dozed off, although, he was polite enough to keep his feelings hidden from their unexpected guests.

The Thedarians had chosen to set up their own camp a short distance from their hosts and Faylore had joined them, eager to hear any news that they may have.

Grubb looked up at the moons. Ordinarily they would have shone brightly, huge lanterns hanging by invisible threads. Their brilliance however, was now diminished by the ever-present mist. "Bloody Karrak!" he growled to himself.

He studied the Thedarians in the distance, still fascinated by their glistening skin. He raised his hand and pinched it gently. They can't turn it into something different though, he thought. Unless, of course, you count becoming invisible.

He listened carefully, trying his best to eavesdrop on the Thedarian's conversation. They were speaking in whispers, so he couldn't catch a word. I wonder, he thought. With a mischievous grin, he shook his head slightly. His ear began to grow, stretching like a tentacle from the side of his head. It slithered like a deformed snake through the grass toward Faylore, and Grubb had to stifle a snigger as it wound its way toward her. Now I'll 'ear what yer up to. He covered his mouth, amused by his last thought. His tentacular appendage grew closer to its target, stopping merely inches behind Faylore.

Unbeknownst to him, his spying mission was about to go slightly awry.

Faylore spun around so quickly that he was unable to retract his ear in time. She grabbed it in her left hand and slapped it with her right, "This is a private conversation, Grubb!" she said sternly as Grubb gave out a yelp.

"Alright, alright, I'm sorry!" he yelled, "Now let go of me ear."

His ear shrank away as Faylore released her vice-like grip.

Grubb danced up and down rubbing the side of his head, “That bloody ‘urt that did!” he protested. “What d’ye do that for?”

“You know quite well why I did it, you little sneak!” She scowled at him. “In future, just ask if you want to know something. Behaving like one of Karrak’s spies. Really!”

Grubb suddenly felt ashamed, “I wasn’t spyin’. Well, not really. I just wondered what was going on is all.”

“If there is something you need to know, I’ll tell you. Don’t do that again, Grubb, it’s rude!”

Grubb looked at the ground, shuffling his feet like a naughty schoolboy, “Sorry,” he mumbled.

The noise had woken Lodren, who was most alarmed by Faylore’s terse tone. Looking straight into Grubb’s eyes, he frowned, “What have you done now?” he asked, slowly.

“Nothin’!” snapped Grubb, “Mind yer own business, go back to sleep.”

“Probably won’t be able to now,” sighed Lodren. “Shame really. I was having a marvellous dream about bashing this huge glamoch on the head and then cooking loads of steaks for the whole of Borell Castle. They were all telling me what a brilliant cook I was and giving me presents and all sorts.”

Grubb scrunched up his nose, “What sort o’ presents?” he asked.

“I’ll never know!” replied Lodren with another sigh. “Some idiot woke me up!”

Faylore joined them, "I suggest you both get some rest," she advised. "Tomorrow is going to be a busy day."

"Why?" asked Grubb, suspiciously, "What ye got planned?"

"We'll discuss it in the morning, Grubb. Now get some sleep." Without another word, she lay down and closed her eyes.

"Ye not gonna find a tree to sleep in?" asked Grubb, tentatively.

Faylore never replied.

***

The following morning Lodren, as always, was up and about well before the others. He had added more wood to the fire and was busy trying to present as comprehensive a breakfast as he could, in a vain hope of catering for everyone's individual tastes. The honey cakes were, he felt, the most important. After all, if they were good enough for Faylore, surely the rest of the Thedarians wouldn't dare refuse them. He gave a cheery 'good morning' to each Thedarian as they arose from their slumber, receiving a nod as acknowledgement. "So rude!" he muttered under his breath. Faylore was the only one polite enough to repeat his words. Then, of course, there was Grubb. He lay there, mouth open, snoring loudly. The air was chill and the vapour from his breath could be seen as he lay there.

"Look at him!" said the exasperated Nibby. "If it wasn't for the noise, you'd think he was dead." Kicking

Grubb's boot, he raised his voice, "Get up, you lazy thing!"

Grubb snorted and opened his eyes, "I'm already awake, stupid. I was only pretending to be asleep in case we were attacked."

"But of course you were, Grubb. That's why you know I took your boots off and put them on the fire."

Grubb jumped up and, grabbing at his foot, yelled, "What did ye do that for?" His hand touched the soul of his boot. "Oh, very funny," he said.

"Already awake!" laughed Lodren, "You big fibber."

Faylore smiled, "Now that you're awake, Grubb, we can start making plans."

"To do what?" Grubb asked.

"To get back to Jared and the others, of course," she replied.

"But we're already doing that!" exclaimed Grubb.

"And we would have found them by now if we hadn't refused Thelwynn's help," added Lodren.

"Whether in the clouds or on the ground, Lodren, we still had no idea in which direction they had travelled," Faylore said. "There were no guarantees that we would ever find them."

"So, what's so different now?" asked Grubb.

"Now," replied Faylore, grabbing his horns and shaking his little head gently, "we know where they are."

"What!" exclaimed Lodren, "Where… how?"

"It's a bit obvious ain't it, ye plum? Faylore's folk 'ave seen 'em."

"Oh yes!" said the Nibby, a little surprised at his own lack of deduction. "There couldn't be any other way of finding out could there?"

"No, ye pillock!"

"Grubb, please," implored Faylore, "do shut up." Grubb opened his mouth, and then closed it again. "My people have reported that they witnessed strange goings-on in a village not too far from here. Admittedly, they never entered the village, but they are adamant that there were wizards there."

"Oh, in that case, it's got to be Jared and the others, hasn't it? It couldn't possibly be Karrak and his cronies! Why don't we save ourselves the journey and roast ourselves alive now? Who's first? Lodren, do ye want to go basted or not?"

Faylore pushed her bottom lip out with her tongue. She adored the Vikkery but, at times, would happily choose to leave him behind if it were put to a vote. "It's a real shame that you do not use your ears for anything other than eavesdropping, Grubb. If you had listened to what I said you would have heard the word wizards, not sorcerers."

"Oh, and your lot can tell the difference, can they? I'm sure they could see everythin' as clear as day, lurkin' outside the village in the bushes."

"They were not lurkin'! I mean, lurking, Grubb," protested Faylore. "Have you forgotten our ability to blend? They were close enough to identify two elderly wizards, one with a pronounced limp, one carrying an elegant staff made of precious metals."

"Oh," said Grubb, quietly, "well I suppose it could be them."

"Of course it's them. How many wizards do you know who carry a golden staff?" blurted Lodren.

Grubb tried to mount a defence. Raising his finger, he pointed first at Faylore and then Lodren, "It's not all gold."

Faylore had heard enough, "It is them, Grubb," she said. "Now stop being awkward. Eat your breakfast and feed Buster, we must depart as soon as possible."

"Faylore," said Lodren, tentatively, "where exactly is this village?"

"Still some way off," replied Faylore. "Three or four days at the very least."

"Well… in that case," said Lodren, "why don't we see if we can contact the dragons? We'd get there much faster with their help."

"This again?" sighed Faylore. "They are not servants that one can beckon on a whim, Lodren. Yes, they are our friends, but we cannot abuse that friendship."

"But friends are supposed to help each other," argued Lodren. "That's what makes them friends."

"Not forgetting the fact that it gives ye another chance to scream at the top 'o yer lungs an' show off."

"Exactly," replied Lodren as he turned to face Grubb. He paused, the realisation dawning on his face, "That's not what I meant!" he snapped. "But riding them would be much faster and far less dangerous than travelling cross-country! There could be all sorts of monsters along the way."

"There are no monsters, Lodren. You're just looking for excuses to call the dragons."

"It's alright for you, Faylore! You're a warrior queen who can camouflage herself. Grubb can turn into Wilf and tear through enemies with his huge claws. Jared and Emnor, Yello and the others have their magic and what do I have? This," said Lodren, holding his hammer aloft.

Faylore knelt before him, "Do you think that we do not value you as an ally, Lodren? If so, you are dreadfully mistaken. Have you forgotten that I still owe you a life debt? You are one of the most courageous people it has ever been my honour to encounter."

Lodren would not look her in the eye, "But I'm nothing special," he mumbled. "If we end up facing Karrak again, what use will I be? I can't do anything against him."

"Do you not see that every one of us feels the same way? Karrak's strength has grown immensely, Lodren, we are all unsure of our effectiveness against him. But to give in to such doubt and fear is to surrender prematurely. We shall face him and battle to our last breath if needed, that is all we can do. If you feel that you are unable to join us, go your own way. We will think no less of you, you will remain in our hearts always."

Lodren suddenly glared at her, "You think I'm afraid!" he shouted. "You think I'm scared that Karrak will kill me or turn me into something horrible! Well I'm not! If he gets in front of me or tries to hurt any of my friends, I'll smash him flat!" Whirling around, he raised his hammer before bringing it down full force. The ground split causing Grubb and the Thedarians to lose their footing. Within seconds six arrows were trained on Lodren, but Faylore had already raised her hand and they were lowered almost as quickly.

Lodren stood with his back to Faylore, breathing heavily. She placed her hand on his shoulder, “Look before you, Lodren. That is why I would feel far safer if you were with me in battle.”

Lodren stared at the fissure that his tantrum had just created. Dust floated in the air and Grubb was attempting to waft it away from his face. “Gotta do somethin’ about that temper o’ yours, Lodren,” he said laughing. “I wouldn’t want to be Karrak if you end up facin’ ‘im.”

CHAPTER 8

Jared stepped back. He shook his head a few times and rubbed his eyes. It seemed that, other than appearing a little woozy, he had suffered no lasting ill effects from the joining. He looked across to Emnor, "It may take a few minutes before the others return."

"What happened, Jared?" asked Hannock, "Is Yello alright?"

"He's fine, Hannock." Smiling at his friend, he pointed, "I don't think you'll be needing that."

Hannock glanced down at the golden crossbow. His grip tightened as he held it even closer, "Please forgive me, sire, but my duty is still to protect you, I'm not taking any chances. We've witnessed first-hand how quickly these things can turn nasty."

Jared shrugged his shoulders, "If you insist," he said. "Any chance of a drink?"

Harley poured some water and handed it to Jared. Jared immediately poured the contents of the goblet onto the floor, "No, a proper drink."

Hannock sloshed some brandy into a glass and passed it to Jared, who downed it in one. "Another?" asked Hannock, holding up the bottle.

"Perhaps later," replied Jared. "They'll be coming out of their trance any minute."

"Who do you think will wake first?" asked Drake.

"Yello," replied Emnor, and he was correct.

Overall, the years had been good to Yello. He had been in many battles and survived countless brushes with death, walking away mostly unscathed. But now, having lived for over a millennium, he could not shake off his fatigue as easily as he once would have. He staggered as he woke, his fall broken by Drake and Harley.

He smiled weakly in gratitude as they escorted him across the room and lowered him into a chair.

Emnor sat beside him, "Drink this," he said quietly. "You'll be fine in a few minutes. It's simply the effects of the joining."

"So why wasn't Jared effected?" asked Drake.

"He would have been if he'd have remained in there as long as Yello," replied Emnor, not taking his eyes off his lifelong friend.

Yello was blinking and raised his hands to his face, rubbing his eyes and cheeks vigorously. "I say!" he exclaimed, "Who hit me?"

The others breathed a sigh of relief, it seemed the wizard was becoming his old self again. He curled his lip as he looked at the tankard, "Is that what I think it is?" he asked with disdain.

"Water," replied Emnor.

"Stuff that!" coughed Yello, "After what I've just been through! Dealing with that cantankerous old crock Barden and his smug sidekick only affords me water as a reward? Some thanks that is!" He thrust the tankard toward Drake.

It wasn't long before Barden and Darooq began to stir. Each groaned as they regained consciousness, stretching themselves as they woke. Darooq was the first to open his eyes. It took a few moments for him to focus, but as he did, he began to survey his surroundings. They were vaguely familiar to him, brief memories flashing through his mind as he became more aware. Pushing himself up on his elbows, he saw, firstly Jared, and then the others. Feeling more intrigue than fear, he tilted his head, "I know you," he said, half recognising the prince. His throat was dry, his voice not much more than a rasp.

Emnor, leaving his friend's side, approached Darooq. Supporting his head with one hand, he raised a glass of water to their enemy's lips. Darooq drank heavily, grateful for the old man's kindness. He nodded in gratitude as Emnor stepped away.

Barden began to twitch. It seemed that his awakening was going to be far less peaceful than Darooq's. Even before his eyes opened, he began to curse. His threats were apparent but directed at no-one in particular. Even semi-conscious, his hatred and bile were obvious. He was calling to his master, Lord Karrak, to save him, begging his forgiveness at having forsaken him. Hannock raised the crossbow.

Emnor offered the same kindness to Barden that he had offered Darooq, placing the glass against his lips. He allowed the water to trickle into his mouth. Barden's eyes opened. He immediately went into a rage, thrashing out and sweeping the glass from Emnor's grasp. "You coward!" he spat, "You would poison me in my sleep?"

"There is no poison, Barden. It is water, fresh water, nothing else," Emnor assured him.

“You would say that, wouldn’t you? Now that your plan has failed!”

“We mean you no harm, Barden. We merely wish to help.”

As Barden’s ravings, insults and threats continued, Jared retreated to the back of the room. The staff had begun to glow gently. Jared gazed into it, mesmerized as brief flashes of colour, fleeting but vivid, added to his awe. The light grew brighter and brighter until it could no longer go unnoticed by the others. In turn, they covered their eyes, blinded by its intensity. Jared however, continued to gaze directly into the centre. He could hear a whisper deep within its core and stroked the heart as if understanding its message. He nodded and turned his head, looking directly at Barden, whose ravings had continued. Jared smiled. His eyes flashed, resembling the purest of white pearls. A pulse of energy blasted across the room, avoiding his friends and striking Barden full force. He was thrown from the table and slammed into the wall behind him. He fell heavily to the floor and was silent. Jared’s friends stared, wide eyed at what they had just witnessed. The light dimmed, and Jared’s eyes began to revert to their normal piercing blue, but not completely. A faint pale light could still be seen deep within them, but what could have been causing it?

Emnor was the first to move. He rushed across to the limp body of Barden. It was only a moment before he spoke. “He’s dead,” he announced shakily. “Jared, you killed him!”

***

"What was that?" asked Poom, leaping to his feet.

"Not sure," replied Lawton, "but it definitely came from the tavern."

"Do we go and investigate?"

"No, Poom. I think it best to stay out of things, for now at least. They've been in there playing with magic for ages. I don't think they'll need any help from us."

"You see," replied Poom, "we aren't needed any more. We may as well be on our way home!"

"Why don't you go for a run, Poom? You always say how it helps to clear your mind, not that there's a lot to clear," sniggered Lawton.

"Oh, shut your face, Lawton. What's the use of being here if we can't offer a little advice occasionally?"

"And what advice would you give, Poom?"

"Well I'd need to know a few facts first, wouldn't I!"

"Of course you would. But your advice would be exactly the same as always, grab a spear and charge at the enemy. Look around, Poom. There is no enemy to charge toward."

"You think I've got a one-track mind, don't you? No matter the scenario, you think I just charge into battle without a single thought in my head."

"It's what you've always done before," snorted Lawton.

"Not true, see. There was that time when…" he paused for a moment, "... maybe that's not a good example. Ah yes, when we were facing… oh my days, you're right. I've never done anything differently, have

I? Just charge in blindly and to hell with the consequences!"

Lawton leaned forward, agog at Poom's last statement, "Are you alright, Poom?" he asked. "Only you do realise that you just admitted that I was right?"

"Perhaps, yes," said Poom, slightly flustered by his own admission. "But it always worked! I'm still fast, faster than Hannock and everyone else!"

"Hannock is a man, you are a Gerrowlien. If you were a thousand years old and could barely walk, you'd still be faster than a man."

Poom sat quietly for a moment. Turning to his friend, he lowered his voice, "What about a wizard?" he asked. "Am I faster than a wizard?"

Lawton patted him gently on the shoulder, "Come on," he said calmly, "let's both go for a run. The wind in your fur will do you good and," he looked down at his portly build, "it won't do me any harm to get a little exercise. We've been sitting around here far too long as it is."

"Should we tell them where we're going?"

Lawton wrinkled his nose, "Nah," he replied, "we'll be back before they even notice we're gone. Come on, I'll race you to the edge of that field over there. Ready?"

***

Lodren had a new spring in his step. His smile had returned and his annoying positive attitude along with it. Within the first few hours Grubb was pleading with him to be quiet. But, undeterred, the Nibby continued prattling, "It's nice to have some company for a change, don't you agree, Faylore?"

"I do indeed, Lodren. But I cannot see why you are so happy that we have been joined by my kin," she lowered her voice and leaned down to him. "After all, they're hardly a chatty bunch, are they? Not with you and Grubb anyway."

"You used to be like that, Faylore," mumbled Grubb. As usual, he was reclined on Buster's back with his eyes closed. "Ye hardly used to say two words unless it was to be sarcastic. Ye used to walk about with yer nose stuck in the air as if ye were better than everybody."

Lodren whirled around, causing Buster to stop abruptly, "Grubb!" he said sharply, "Faylore is a queen, she is better than everybody else, so show some respect!"

"I meant no offence, Your Majesty," replied Grubb. "But ye were a bit toffee-nosed."

Faylore raised her hand to her face. Why would anyone put toffee on their nose? she thought.

Lodren, realising her confusion, attempted to explain.

Faylore raised her hand to stop him blabbering, "It's alright, Lodren, I understand. Grubb means that I was a little aloof."

"That's the posh way of puttin' it," Grubb said quietly, "I'd just say ye were bein' a bit of a…"

Before he could finish, Lodren swiped him from Buster's back with one arm. The poor Vikkery sailed through the air before he knew what had hit him and landed on the hard ground. Devoid of any plant life, a plume of dust enveloped him and he sat there coughing and spluttering. Lodren glared at him.

"QUEEN!" roared Grubb. "All I was gonna say was queen."

"Don't you fib, Grubb. You were going to say something rude and horrible like you always do and I won't stand for it any longer! I warned you before so don't start complaining. You deserved that."

"No, I did not, Lodren!" moaned Grubb, climbing to his feet and rubbing his nether regions, "Bugger! That stings! Well, yes I did, maybe fer all the other times, but this time I'm tellin' the truth! I wasn't gonna say anythin' nasty!"

***

"Why, Jared?" asked Emnor, still supporting Barden's head. "He did not have to die, we could have saved him."

Jared looked unconcerned, "No, we couldn't," he replied calmly. "He was evil, Emnor. One such as he would never seek nor accept redemption."

Emnor peered at him. Jared was somehow different, his voice distant. Emnor had been in his company almost his entire life, but not once had he ever witnessed him so devoid of emotion.

"Jared was right!" announced Hannock, "He was a traitor to king and country. His treachery alone was enough to condemn him. He freed Karrak and murdered innocents, he deserved to die."

“But, at the very least, we should have waited until he was fully conscious! He was confused, rambling… we should have waited,” repeated Emnor.

“There was no need,” Jared assured him. “He was evil, I could sense it. Any and all evil must be destroyed without hesitation, there can be no other way.”

“In that case, what do we do with him?” asked Hannock, pointing at Darooq.

Jared tilted his head, “He has done many ill deeds, that cannot be denied, but I sense that he is not inherently evil,” he replied. “He may yet be of some use to us. Place him in chains until I decide what must be done, I will speak with him later. For now, we must prepare ourselves for what comes next.”

Yello had noticed the light in Jared’s eyes. The voice he heard was not that of Borell’s heir apparent, it was the voice of something far more powerful, and dangerous. “And what is it that comes next, Jared? Could you enlighten us?”

“When the time is right. For now, just know that you are safe,” replied Jared. His reply seemed genuinely caring, but also dismissive. “I think I’ll take a little air,” he continued, “Hannock, would you care to join me?”

Hannock immediately stood and followed his friend out into the square, closing the door behind him.

Yello glanced across at Emnor, “I do believe we’ve just been told to mind our own business.”

Emnor nodded, “The Heart?” he suggested.

“Without a shadow of a doubt, old friend,” replied Yello. “Did you notice his eyes?”

Emnor nodded once more, “I’m sure that we need not fear him,” he said confidently. “But I’d be careful what you say from now on. If the Heart is indeed controlling his actions, it may view the slightest sympathy toward our enemy, as a betrayal.”

“What? You mean he could turn on us as well?” Drake asked.

“Most unlikely,” Emnor assured him, “but if he feels that we are a hindrance, he may be inclined to… how do I put this? Brush us aside.”

“Like he did with Barden?” suggested Harley.

“No!” snapped Yello. “Not like Barden! He was rotten to the core. It wouldn’t take a relic like the Heart of Ziniphar to tell you that. You could hear it in the venomous spite that spewed from him every time he opened his foul mouth.”

“Alright, I’ll say it as you lot keep dancing around the issue! Can we trust him?” Harley, Yello and Emnor looked across at Drake. His question was a simple one. The answer however, was not.

“Of course we can,” replied Yello, feigning laughter that fooled no-one.

“We’ll just keep an eye on him,” suggested Emnor. “If he shows any signs of ill will toward us, removing the staff would break his connection with the Heart and allow his mind to clear.”

“And what if the Heart doesn’t want to be parted from Jared?” asked Drake, warily.

“Stop looking on the bleak side of everything, Maddleton. The Heart of Ziniphar is pure, its only purpose to do good. Let’s leave it at that.”

Yello sniffed and raised his eyebrows. He, for one, was not convinced.

***

Karrak stumbled. He felt weak and his vision was blurred as he leaned on the altar in the great hall. What was happening to him? Even before he had acquired the Elixian Soul, he had never been affected by fatigue. Regaining his balance, he looked around him, he was alone. In his mind, he could see a brilliant light. What was it? Where had it come from? Why did it fill him with dread? Sweeping from the hall, he began to search for the boy who claimed to be the son of Dunbar. A rage began to burn inside him. Two of the undead guards were set ablaze with a wave of his hand, unaware of how or why. Sensing that the boy was near, he turned, heading down the darkened passageways until, with a loud crash, he smashed through a door to face him, "What have you done?" he roared.

Xarran was sitting behind a desk, peeling an apple with his dagger. He glanced up, unconcerned by the presence of the shadow lord, "You really should work on that temper of yours, you know. You'll give yourself a heart attack carrying on like that."

With a wave of his hand, Karrak threw the desk across the room, splintering it against the wall, "Do not play games with me, boy!" he bellowed, "What have you done?"

"How rude!" snorted Xarran, "That was my favourite desk, just the right height to rest my feet on."

Karrak charged toward him. Xarran held up his hands, “Alright,” he said quickly, “I can see you’re upset, but honestly, I’ve been here most of the day. I haven’t done anything.”

“No… magic? No… sorcery of any kind?” Karrak asked, menacingly.

“No. And no necromancy either. Speaking of which, when are you going to do something about those… things? They’re starting to stink the place up a bit now they’re beginning to decay.”

Karrak turned away, his featureless face not revealing his true concern.

“Oh, I peeled an apple. Well, I was in the process of peeling an apple…” Xarran paused realising that this was not one of Karrak’s usual rants. This was something far more serious, “Tell me what happened.”

“A blinding light, something that holds great power,” Karrak replied. “Nothing should be able to harm me now that I possess the Soul.”

“Ah… yes,” sighed Xarran, “I was meaning to mention that to you. Silly me, how did I forget? Oh I know! Possibly because you’re an annoying despot who never listens to a word I say.”

Karrak turned to face him, “Do not try my patience, boy…”

“Yes, I know. Peel the skin from me, roast me alive, string me up for the crows, blah blah blah. Give it a rest! I’m trying to help you!”

Xarran’s words peaked Karrak’s interest, “What makes you think that I, the shadow lord, could need your help?” he sneered.

"Shall I have a guess?" smiled Xarran. Not waiting for a reply, he continued, "You were going about your normal stuff, whatever that is, and you suddenly went wonky. Confusion, loss of balance, and strange visions you don't understand. Am I getting close?"

Karrak's eyes flashed red, "How would you know if you were not part of it?" he asked quietly.

"That's easy," replied Xarran, cockily, "It was all in the scroll." Leaning forward, he pointed at Karrak, "You've been found, mate. You've been rumbled."

"I remain hidden, boy. If anyone had approached this place, I would have sensed them."

"It's not a someone that's found you though, it's a something. You see, that pretty little bauble you have embedded in your breastplate has a sister, the Heart of Ziniphar. Problem is, it's the opposite of the Soul. It was created for good, created to quell the evil of its twin. It wants to find the Elixian Soul, and it's coming to get whoever possesses it. Trust me, Father, it will find you."

***

Lawton crept through the tall grass as stealthily as he could. He and Poom had spotted their quarry well before they had begun their approach. Lawton was now within a few yards, ready to pounce on his unsuspecting victims. Planting his feet firmly he sprang forward and roared. Buster reared into the air, throwing Grubb to the ground. Even as he stood, he was beginning to transform. Lodren raised his hammer and screamed at the top of his lungs. Poor Buster charged off into the distance as Lawton, staring at his friends, began to roar with snarling laughter. Until, that was, the Thedarians let themselves be seen. They had completely surrounded him, arrows trained and ready to fire.

Slipping between them, Faylore appeared, “You could get yourself killed pulling stunts like that, Lawton,” she said dryly. “Where’s the other one?”

“Right here,” Poom replied. Turning, she could see the points of two spears pressed firmly against the back of two of the Thedarian archer’s necks. “You don’t think we’re that daft, do you?” he asked with a grin.

Faylore waved her hand, instructing the bows be lowered, “What were you thinking?”

“Thought it’d be a laugh,” replied Poom. “No harm done.”

“No harm done!” bellowed Grubb. “Ye stupid pillock, ye could’ve been killed. And look at my Buster, he’s already a mile away.”

“He’ll be fine, he’s going the right way,” laughed Lawton.

“Right way, my arse! He’s not safe on ‘is own! You can go an’ fetch ‘im back! I swear, if anythin’ ‘appens to ‘im, I’ll pull yer ‘ead off.”

“I’m sorry, Grubb,” said Lawton, still trying to stifle his laughter, “but your face when I…”

“Fetch Buster, NOW!”

Lawton dashed off.

“Sorry, Faylore,” said Poom, smiling. “We’ve been bored out of our minds in the village and when we saw you out here we just thought…”

"No, Poom, you didn't think! You never think! This is no longer a game, it's time you grew up."

Poom became angry, "Now you listen to me, your queenship! We're here because we chose to be! We're not in your debt and we're definitely not under your bloody command! You should remember that next time you feel that you want to start throwing your weight around. You may command these soulless things that follow you everywhere, but you don't command Lawton and you don't command me. Is that clear enough for you?" Turning, he grabbed Grubb and threw him onto his shoulders. "I'll take you to Buster," he muttered. Looking down to Lodren, he pointed, "The village is that way, you should make it by nightfall," he advised him, and sprinted away.

Out of earshot within seconds, Grubb spoke, "Bit strong, wasn't it?"

"No! It's about time you all realised that we aren't a couple of idiots who can be ordered around. We've been in more battles than you lot put together but nobody ever chooses to ask our opinion. You just expect us to follow orders blindly and, quite frankly, I'm sick of it."

"It's only 'cause they care, Poom."

"No, it's because they don't have enough soldiers to dictate to, so they think that Lawton and I can fill that void."

"Know what? I used to think the same way as you until I got used to 'em."

"I don't think I'll be sticking around long enough to get used to them," said Poom, tersely. "Not after this."

"Okay, if that's what ye want. But imagine if one o' them Thedarians 'ad been a bit quicker, or if Lawton 'ad been a bit slower. It could've ended up with 'im 'avin an arrow sticking out of 'im. Wouldn't be so funny then, would it?"

"It still doesn't give Faylore the right to speak to me like that. I'm a grown Gerrowlien, not a cub."

"All the more reason why ye should understand 'ow Faylore feels about the two of ye."

"I know exactly how she feels, Grubb! She thinks we're idiots."

"No, she doesn't" laughed Grubb. "She only thinks you're an idiot. She likes Lawton just the way he is."

CHAPTER 9

As the tavern door closed, Hannock placed his hand gently on Jared's arm, "Are you alright?" he asked.

"I'm fine. Why?" replied Jared, somewhat surprised by Hannock's enquiry.

"Why? You just killed a man in cold blood, Jared. Don't you feel anything at all?"

"Not really. Why would I? I have removed a symptom of the evil that surrounds us, Hannock. Do you expect me to feel regret or guilt? That man proved himself to be our enemy a long time ago. Who knows what acts he may have performed during his deluded servitude? Who knows how many lives he has taken or victims he has tortured, by order of Karrak?"

"I don't want you to think that I'm coming to his defence, Jared, but as you asked yourself, who knows? He may have been nothing more than a lunatic, nothing more than a doomsayer, and you slaughtered him without even allowing him to defend himself."

"Not so, my friend. I had witnessed both sides of Barden. When I entered Yello's mind, there were two apparitions of him; one cold and menacing, issuing threats and singing Karrak's praises; the other, completely insane, terrified for his life and begging to be left in peace. I merely destroyed the one and allowed the other the peace for which he yearned."

"But, be honest, Jared. Does that give you the right to condemn and execute him? We may have been able to cure him, perhaps even turned him against Karrak and learned something that would have aided us."

"You do not understand, Hannock," said Jared. As he turned, Hannock noticed the change in his eyes. "He was evil, there was no way he could have been saved, we could see that."

Hannock gazed at his friend. He had said we. Why would he use that term? he thought. He had heard it used by Tamor in many of his royal speeches, but Jared had always hated the pomposity of its use and vowed he would never use it in that context. This was something else… something more. Something… unnatural.

Jared smiled, "Don't look so worried, Hannock. I promise not to start setting fire to innocent villagers or destroying buildings simply because they are there. Go back inside and have a drink, I'll take the air by myself. You can discuss your concerns with the others."

"No, I…" began Hannock.

"It's alright," said Jared, interrupting him, "I can see inside your heart, Hannock. I understand your reticence. It will take time for you to understand the purity of what we must do. But be assured, the pure of heart have no reason to fear us."

Hannock watched as Jared strolled away. We… us. What was going on? He re-entered the tavern.

"That was quick," said Drake. "Where's Jared?"

"He preferred to walk alone," replied Hannock, quietly.

Furtive glances passed between the four wizards, unnoticed by Hannock as he stared at the floor, frowning.

"Something the matter?" asked Emnor, attempting to feign ignorance.

"Erm… not sure, to be honest," replied Hannock. He shook his head, "No, it's nothing. Just seeing things that aren't there," he smiled weakly. "Being around magic, I suppose. There's a simple explanation I'm sure."

"Explanation for what?" asked Yello, scrutinizing Hannock, who hadn't looked up from the ground once. "The pale glow in Jared's eyes, perhaps?"

Hannock raised his head, "You saw it too then?"

"We did indeed," replied Yello.

"We?" said Hannock, suspiciously, "Why did you say we?"

"Because I witnessed it as well," replied Emnor. "Hannock what's wrong? You have to tell us."

Hannock rushed to the bar. Grabbing a brandy bottle, he sloshed some carelessly into a glass. "He was talking to me, Jared, that is. But instead of saying I or me, he was saying we, and us. He also told me that when he entered your mind, Yello, that he saw two separate versions of Barden. Does it mean that the same is happening with him?"

Harley grinned as he volunteered to help. "Should I explain?" he asked.

Emnor folded his arms, scowling at their younger member. "Got this all figured out have you, Harley?" Harley nodded confidently. "In that case, please continue," he said, gesturing for Harley to 'take the floor'.

Harley stood and walked to the centre of the room. He looked deep into Hannock's eyes before he spoke, "You weren't speaking to Jared," he said calmly.

Hannock laughed, "Of course I was talking to Jared, you idiot. He was right in front of me. There was nobody else there."

"Precisely," replied Harley, looking a little smug. "The only body that was there was Jared's. One body, yes, containing two consciousnesses."

"Two what?" blurted out Hannock. "What's a consinessness, a connisens, what's one of those?" he asked, struggling to pronounce the word.

Harley closed his eyes and sighed, "Two consciousnesses," he repeated. "Two essences, two souls."

"Thank you, Harley. Allow me," said Emnor, quietly. "What Harley is trying to explain, Hannock, is that the Heart of Ziniphar now dwells within Jared. It was not Jared that decided the fate of Barden, the Heart did."

Hannock looked shocked, "Well we must remove it!" he exclaimed. "What if it does to him, what the Elixian Soul did to Karrak?"

"But that is exactly what we need to happen, Hannock. Do you not see? The Heart of Ziniphar is pure, it can only do good."

"It made Jared slaughter a defenceless old man! How can that be purity?" shouted Hannock.

Emnor stroked his beard, he needed to word his next statement very carefully. "What would you do, Hannock," he began, "if you knew, without a shadow of a doubt, that at some point in the future a child or man that you faced now, would be responsible for the deaths of tens of thousands of innocents? Would you kill that person to prevent those deaths? I do not mean suspect, I mean that you know it as a cast iron fact."

"How am I supposed to answer a question like that?" bawled Hannock. "If it were a warlord or someone who had proven himself to be a blight, of course I would."

"We are talking about a person who is destined to be such but, as yet, has done no wrong. What then would be your decision?" asked Emnor, pressing the issue.

"No, why would I murder someone who has done nothing wrong?"

"But you know that they will. What would you do? Think, Hannock! Jared, all of us, massacred, when if you had had the courage you could have prevented it. Would you be able to take that life?"

Hannock threw the glass against the wall, "YES!" he screamed, "Yes I would! Satisfied now? I'm a killer, it's what I do! It's all I know how to do! I'm a soldier, nothing more! So, judge me, wizard! Am I next to die? Bring in my lifelong friend and have him destroy me, surely I have as much blood on my hands as that pathetic old man!"

There was a faint whistling sound. Hannock raised his hand to his neck and pulled out the tiny, green-feathered dart, before collapsing in a heap.

***

"I wonder if someone will let me use their kitchen when we get to the village. It would be so nice to use all my pots and pans at the same time again."

"We ain't seen Jared an' the others for months, an' all ye care about is findin' a poxy kitchen ye can use," snorted Grubb.

"Well, obviously!" groaned Lodren, "I'll bet they haven't had a decent meal since we last saw them. Trust me, they'll need feeding up!"

"They're in a village! There'll be loads o' food. They ain't gonna starve to death just 'cause you ain't around to mollycoddle 'em."

"They may be eating," replied Lodren, haughtily, "but they won't be eating properly."

"What do ye mean, properly? Ye get hungry, ye eat, simple as that!"

"No, that's where you're wrong! You need a balanced diet. Plenty of vegetables and fruit, that's what you need, not just meat and beer, like some people think."

"Know somethin' Lodren?" laughed Grubb, "You'll make a good mum someday."

Lodren scowled at him, "You won't be so flippant when I put your dinner in front of you tonight, will you? You'll just wolf it down like you always do. That is, of course, if I decide to feed you."

Faylore smiled as she listened to them. She was strolling behind Buster, quelling her excitement at being re-united with the rest of the companions. Knowing that they were expected was a relief and, unseen by the others, she was gently patting Buster's flanks to hurry him along.

They approached the village. Faylore could see Jared and Hannock stood outside what seemed to be a tavern. Typical, she thought, Hannock as near to wine or beer as he could be. As they entered the village, Hannock turned and walked into the tavern. Jared had not seen them and began to stroll in the other direction. Strange, thought Faylore. It seemed that the Gerrowliens had not informed them of their meeting.

It was at this point that Lawton suddenly appeared. He had leapt from a nearby tree, a look of deep concern on his furry face, "They don't know you're here yet, Faylore," he said quietly. "Something's going on and we're not sure what. Jared's acting very strange and there's a heck of a racket coming from the tavern. Hannock's going crazy about something."

"Thank you, Lawton," she said. "Don't worry, we'll get to the bottom of it," she added stroking his shoulder. Glancing up she saw Poom lying in the tree from which Lawton had descended. Taking a few paces, she leapt to the lower boughs. "I believe I owe you an apology, sir."

Poom looked sideways at her, "Forget it," he murmured.

"Want a fight?" she asked.

Poom was amazed at her question and reeled backwards, "What!" he exclaimed.

"I thought it might clear the air and allow you to let off some steam," she smiled, "or are you scared of losing?"

Poom stared at her, was she serious? "I don't fight women," he said with a curl of his lip, "It wouldn't be fair."

"Ah, so you are scared," she giggled.

"Terrified," sighed Poom.

She flung her arms around his neck, "Get out of this tree and stop sulking, you stupid cat." Pulling as hard as she could, she dragged him from the branch. They both fell, Poom landing first and catching Faylore. Placing her gently on the ground, he stuck his tongue out, "Your Majesty," he said dryly, "you lose."

Approaching the tavern, they could hear Hannock's rantings from within. They had no idea where Jared had gone but never gave it much thought, knowing that he would return soon enough. Faylore climbed the steps to the tavern and opened the door. All inside had their backs to her and she stood for a few moments, listening to Hannock as he raged on.

"… have him destroy me. Surely I have as much blood on my hands as that pathetic old man!"

Faylore raised her blowpipe to her lips.

***

"So, you know where they are?"

"They've settled in a village by the name of Mellanthion, and they've been there for some time as far as we can gather."

"Perfect! This is what you must do, boy."

"Will you stop referring to me as boy? I have a name, use it!"

Karrak stared at him momentarily, "Very well, Xarran, this is what you must do."

"That's another thing, Karrak. I don't have to do anything! You seem to forget that I am here of my own free will. You can't control me like I'm one of your grotesque creations! If you need me to do something, ask. You're in no position to give me orders!" It seemed that Xarran was more like his father than he realised as he raged at the shadow lord.

Karrak yearned to tear Xarran apart, but he knew that he could not. Something was protecting him, the only explanation was his blood, and ultimately, the Elixian Soul. For now, he must bide his time, "Very well, Xarran. Would you be kind enough to embark upon a mission that would be mutually beneficial to us both?"

"See, didn't hurt, did it?" sneered Xarran.

Karrak stood motionless, "What is your answer?" he hissed.

"That depends," replied Xarran. "What does this mission entail?"

"I will not lie to you, Xarran," he replied, emphasising his name. "It will be treacherous, at best. If you are unsuccessful, it could prove to be fatal."

"If it is as dangerous as you say, why not go yourself?"

"And you wonder why I refer to you as 'boy'?" replied Karrak, deliberately goading Xarran. He knew that manipulation of the mind did not necessarily have to be done with the use of magic. "You are correct, of course," he continued. "A mission such as this could never work if entrusted to someone who doubts his own abilities. Remain here, boy, I shall attend to this myself."

"I doubt nothing!" Xarran screamed, "I'm every bit as powerful as you! I don't need to float or look like a spectre from a nightmare to accomplish my goals! Tell me your plan, shadow lord. When it is completed, without your aid, I will take great pleasure in rubbing your nose in it."

Karrak swept forward until he was face to face with his son, "So there is a fire in there!" he hissed, "Good... very good. You may surprise me yet."

"Tell... me... the... plan."

Karrak retreated, "I need the scroll, Xarran. You are going to obtain it for me, at any cost."

***

Hannock's eyelids flickered.

"Master Emnor, I think he's waking up," called Drake.

"So he is," replied Emnor, "I thought he'd be asleep for a lot longer than that, it's barely been an hour," he looked questioningly at Faylore.

"Oh, I only used a small dose," she confessed. "He's not sick, I just wanted to calm him down."

Yello chuckled, "You did that alright. It's been ages since I've seen that done. I love your anaesthetics, Faylore. I wish my Abigails Mercy worked that fast on my leg."

"Would you like me to see if I can help?" she replied.

"Oh, no, no, no. There's nothing you can do, I'm afraid. It's down to old age more than anything. No, you save your herbs for someone who really needs them," he smirked, nodding toward Hannock.

"How ye doin', Captain?" asked Grubb, nudging him gently.

"I'm alright," sighed Hannock, pushing himself up on his elbows. "What happened? I feel like a house fell on me."

"Been mixing yer drinks again 'ave ye?"

"No, Grubb, I have not been… GRUBB!" exclaimed Hannock. "Where did you come from?" he sat up quickly, "Faylore! Lodren! You're all here! Is everything alright? It's so good to see you! Where have you been? We've all been worried…"

Faylore held up her hand, "All in good time, Charles. Take a breath, calm down. We're all fine."

Drake sniggered, "Yes, calm down, Charles."

"That's enough out of you, Maddleton," warned Faylore.

Hannock surveyed the room, "Where's Jared?" he asked slowly.

"No idea," replied Emnor. "We haven't seen him since he left with you."

"How long was I asleep? How did I fall asleep?" he asked, suspiciously.

"Could have something to do with all the booze you've been swilling down lately," Drake, of course, hadn't meant to say it aloud, but as usual his mouth had worked far faster than his brain. "And you haven't had much sleep either, you must have been exhausted," he added quickly, patting Hannock on the shoulder in mock sympathy.

Hannock frowned, "How long… was I… asleep?" he repeated.

"Less than an hour," announced Yello. "So, stop fretting about Jared. He probably fancied a little time alone."

"Have you forgotten what he did?" asked Hannock, his ire beginning to rise again.

"We haven't forgotten," replied Emnor, solemnly. "But no amount of speculation or accusation can change that. We've been over it and, unfortunately, we'll simply have to wait and see how this pans out."

"But, Emnor! He k…!"

"Yes, yes, we are quite aware of what happened, Captain," interrupted Yello.

Hannock glanced at Faylore, unsure of how much she knew of recent events.

"It's alright, Charles," she said with a gentle smile, "Master Emnor has informed me of what has occurred here."

"Nobody has mentioned the fact that Jared doesn't seem to want to go anywhere without Emnor's staff," said Drake, staring at the floor, "Grabs it before he takes his first step."

"Sorry, Drake, but you're wrong," said Harley, confidently, "He doesn't reach for the staff, the staff goes to him. It just seems to appear in his hand, like a pet that cannot bear to be parted from its master."

Yello laughed, "Nothing escapes your watchful eye, does it!" he said, looking directly at Emnor.

Emnor smiled, "No," he replied. "However, there is one point on which you are mistaken, Master Harley. The staff no longer belongs to me. It belongs to Jared."

"But, how can that be?" asked Harley, looking puzzled. "We made it for you! It is bound to you, Drake and I witnessed that."

"It seems that magical extensions, not unlike people, can have a change of heart. The staff's allegiance is now to Jared, it's irrefutable."

"Could its allegiance change again?" asked Lodren, looking concerned. "What if we get in front of Karrak and it decides it wants to be on his side?"

"Dear oh dear," sighed Emnor, "You really are a worry-monger, aren't you? But, in answer to your question, that could never happen."

"But you don't know that for sure, do you?"

"Yes, I do, Lodren," Emnor assured him, "Karrak has the Soul, which is evil. In order to contend with its evil, Jared now has the Heart. One cannot command both simultaneously."

"Oh, that's alright then," chirped Lodren. "It's getting late. Anyone hungry?"

"Not for me thanks," said Hannock, rising. "I'm off to look for Jared. Faylore, would you care to join me?"

"I think that Her Majesty should remain here for the time being, there are many things we need to discuss," Emnor suggested. A point on which Faylore agreed.

"Don't worry," laughed Drake, "I'll come with you and hold your hand."

Hannock's face fell, "Wonderful," he groaned.

CHAPTER 10

Drake shadowed Hannock as he scoured the village. The locals seldom remained outside lately and Hannock's questioning of the few that did brought no information. Drake, understanding Hannock's concern, remained silent. He knew that this was no time to be making jokes or poking fun.

"Do you think he's left the village, Hannock?"

"That's the one thing I'm trying not to think about."

"Well, I can't see him wandering off across the plains. That leaves the road, or the forest. Which way shall we try first?"

"You seem awfully keen to find Jared."

"Yeah, well, he's a friend, same as you are," replied Drake, not wanting to make eye contact. "And friends take care of each other."

Hannock smiled. Drake was growing up at last. He placed his arm around the young man's shoulders.

"Sod off!" exclaimed Drake, shrugging him off. "This is no time for male bonding, you pillock! Which way are we going?"

"We'll take the road for a while," Hannock chuckled. "We'll track for a couple of miles and, if we can't find any trace, we'll make our way back through the forest."

"Come on then," urged Drake, setting off at a brisk pace. Hannock drew level with him, studying the ground as they walked. "I'm sure there's nothing to worry about, Hannock. Jared obviously has a lot on his mind at the moment. He probably just needed a break, you know, blow some of the cobwebs from his brain."

"It's not his brain I'm worried about, Drake. It's that bloody staff. When Jared and I left the tavern earlier today, I could hardly believe my ears. It was as if I was talking to a complete stranger. The things he said, it wasn't Jared. Well it was Jared, but his voice seemed different, distant."

"Magic does that occasionally," said Drake, "you think you're in full control of your actions but the magic takes over. It's happened to me loads of times, usually when I was testing a new wand. It was as if the power itself knew that I was in danger and acted to protect me."

"Is that what you think the staff is doing, protecting Jared?"

"I can't say for certain, but I'm sure it won't allow him to come to any harm if his intentions are pure."

"How do you mean pure?"

"Think about today. Jared, or the staff, whichever way you want to look at it, destroyed Barden without the slightest hesitation, agreed?" Hannock nodded. "But it allowed the other one to live. What's his name… Darooq. If he was as nasty as Barden, surely he too would have been executed?"

"So, you're saying that, because there was a chance that he could somehow find redemption, the staff spared him?"

"Certainly seems that way. And if the staff refused to do harm to one that had already performed many unspeakable deeds, it seems only logical to believe that it would protect someone who is guilty of none."

Hannock stopped dead in his tracks and studied the young wizard momentarily. He ran his hand through his hair, "Why aren't you like this all the time?" he asked, confused.

"Like what?" asked Drake, even more confused than Hannock.

"You're a brilliant wizard, you've proven that, but you're so much more. You're insightful, intelligent, empathetic, understanding and caring. Why do you always act like such a prat?"

Drake laughed, "Oh that!" he said. "Because I'm bloody good at it! Now come on, we haven't got all day. Let's find Jared."

They could find no tracks as they searched the road and headed off into the woods as the light began to fail. Stepping into the treeline, they had not realised just how dark it would be once the sun began to set.

"Just a minute," Drake said suddenly. Stooping down, he fumbled on the ground until he found two sizeable branches. Stripping the smaller twigs from them, he withdrew his wand and mumbled a few words. The branches erupted in flame, creating torches that would allow them to see where they were going. "That's better," he said, sounding rather pleased with himself.

"Better than walking into a tree," laughed Hannock, taking one of the torches.

After a while, Hannock had to admit defeat, "This was a stupid idea," he sighed. "I can't track him in the dark! It's not as if I know the layout of the place. If we were closer to home I'd be able to get my bearings but, in here, I have no idea which way to head."

"I've got an idea," Drake said quietly, "why don't we head toward that light over there?"

"What?" asked Hannock, who was a little distracted and hadn't heard him. Looking up, he saw the look of dread on Drake's face as he stood, posed like a gormless scarecrow with his arm outstretched. In the distance Hannock could see a pale light between the trees. "That is odd!" he said. "That's not the light from a campfire, it's far too bright."

"No. No it's not," gulped Drake. "That's magic, that is. I just hope it is Jared, I don't feel up to a battle in the woods at night."

"Where's your sense of adventure, Drake? Come on, let's investigate."

Hannock hurried ahead, followed by the not-so-enthusiastic Drake.

As they drew closer, they extinguished the torches. Crouching low, Hannock continued to lead. Making as little noise as possible, he parted the bushes as they neared a clearing. Reaching behind, he grabbed Drake's shoulder and pulled him alongside. Leaning across, he whispered in his ear, "What do you make of that then?"

Jared, sat on the ground cross-legged, had his eyes closed. But it was quite apparent that he was not merely sleeping.

"What's he doing?" whispered Hannock.

"How the bloody hell should I know?" hissed Drake.

"Well it is magic, isn't it? I thought you might know."

"Well I don't. Do you think I know everything about magic?"

"You always act like you do."

"Oh, shut up, Hannock. It doesn't matter what he's doing, let's just wake him up and you can ask him yourself."

"But what if we startle him? He might, you know, blow us up or something."

"He's our friend, he's not going to attack us!" sighed Drake. "And you say I sound like a prat!"

Jared was encompassed by a huge sphere of light that pulsed gently. It was this that bathed the area with a surrealistic glow. Hannock studied his friend. It did not seem that he was trapped, quite the contrary, he could not recall having seen Jared looking so serene.

Hannock approached the sphere cautiously. The pale light it emitted was hypnotic, but Hannock was wary, fully aware that it may also pose hidden dangers. He paused, looking for clues that may reveal how best to proceed. Drake however, despite his vast knowledge, could not resist the attraction of the sphere. He reached out to it.

There was a loud crack and a flash and before they could react both he and Hannock found themselves hurtling through the air. The sound of them crashing through the undergrowth seemed magnified by the stillness of the night. They lay there, convulsing as sparks travelled the length of their entire bodies. It only lasted a few seconds, although they were sure they would feel the effects for some time yet.

Drake groaned, “Hannock, are you alright?” he asked, struggling to his feet.

Hannock shook his head vigorously, “I told you! Didn’t I tell you? I said he’d blow us up! Either that or he’s decided that it’s about time we learned how to fly!”

“Stop messing about! Are you alright?”

“I’m fine, Drake. Just give me a minute.” He shook his head again, “This must be how the guard in the courtyard felt,” he added.

“What guard?” asked Drake, confused, “What courtyard?”

Hannock looked up at him, “A long time ago, dear boy. Maybe I’ll tell you about it sometime.”

“Did you bang your head? Only, you’re not making much sense.”

“Shut up, Drake. Here, help me up, would you?”

Drake helped him scramble to his feet and they both limped back into the clearing, not too much the worse for wear by their experience. Jared hadn’t moved. The bubble was intact and he remained in the centre, seemingly oblivious to what had just happened.

“Do you think he’ll hear us if we call to him?” suggested Drake.

Hannock raised his eyebrows, “If a noise as loud as a clap of thunder and you screaming profanities at the top of your voice didn’t disturb him, do you honestly think he’ll respond to us calling his name?”

“It was just an idea! We can’t leave him out here by himself, what if something happens to him?”

"Like what?" asked Hannock, cynically. "What do you think could happen to him whilst he's stuck in there? Look what happened to us, do you think there's something in these woods that could get through that?" he added, gesturing toward the sphere.

"YES! Karrak!" Drake replied loudly.

"He's nowhere near here! And what's more, why would he be ferreting around in the woods in the middle of the night?"

"Well, I'd like to think that we aren't the only idiots who'd be doing something as stupid as that," snapped Drake.

Hannock laughed, "Come on," he said, "let's head back to the village. Jared's quite safe, I wouldn't leave if I didn't think he were. Grab those torches, there's a good chap."

***

The following morning, nobody questioned how their search had gone and they, in turn, offered no explanation nor information. Jared had not yet returned, but not one of them seemed overly concerned by his absence. They breakfasted quietly, none making the effort to strike up a conversation. However, their peaceful start to the day would not last long.

The door to the inn flew open.

"I want a word with you lot!" It was the blacksmith.

"And a good morning to you too!" said Yello, sternly.

"Never mind good morning. Where's it gone?" he asked, angrily.

"My good man, we have no idea to what you are referring," said Emnor, sincerely.

"Don't give me that claptrap you old codger. You know exactly what I'm talking about. I want it back, or I want paying."

"My friend just told you," said Yello, raising his voice, "we have no idea what it is, or where it has gone. However, I suggest you keep a civil tongue in your head because I do know what this is," he continued, placing his booted foot on the table, "and I know exactly where it will be going if you don't change your tone."

Emnor waved his hand in order to calm his friend down, "Please, Yello, you're not helping matters."

"See, there you go, threats as usual. You magic types are all the same! Go on then, turn me into a toad, you might as well now you've put me out of business."

"A toad?" said Yello, suddenly sounding interested. He reached for his staff, "What a wonderful idea."

Emnor shook his head as he saw the startled look on the smith's face, "What is it that you have lost?" he asked, "Would you like us to help you find it?"

"I ain't lost anything and you know it! It was stolen!"

Emnor rested his head in his hands in frustration, "What was stolen? he sighed.

"Ninety-five chestplates with gauntlets, greaves and helmets to match," answered the smith. "The ones he ordered," he added, pointing at Darooq.

All eyes turned to Karrak's former henchman. Calmly, Darooq held his hands in the air, "I admit I commissioned it to be made, and you all know who for. But as you know, I have not left the inn for a single moment since you rescued me."

"Why would Karrak need armour?" Hannock shouted, his tone demanding an answer from Darooq. "Does he have an army, men whose minds he has twisted somehow?"

"No, not men," replied Darooq, quietly. "They were… once. Now they are something completely different."

"I don't care who's wearing it!" shouted the smith, "I just want paying for it. You only gave me half up front, and it's cost a lot more than that to complete the order!"

Faylore glared at him, "Then you are a fool!" she exclaimed. "Surely you realised something was terribly wrong? Guards were murdered, although it sounds to me as if they deserved it; wizards were travelling through the village and then disappearing without a trace, yet you blindly continued to fulfil an order for which it was highly unlikely you would ever receive the full remuneration?"

"That's because I'm an honest businessman, miss. My word is my bond. I took the order, I made the stuff," replied the smith, smugly.

"I don't know you well enough to know whether you are honest or dishonest, my good man. However, I am known to be a good judge of character, and yours seems a little… lacking. And by the way, it's Your Majesty, not miss."

The smith was unused to being spoken down to by anyone. He was quite wealthy compared to the other villagers and commanded a certain amount of respect from them. This was something totally alien to him, therefore he was uncertain of what his response, if any, should be. This became apparent as he ran his finger around the inside of his collar whilst giving a pleading look to Hannock, who pursed his lips and nodded a few times.

"Well… erm, sorry… Your Majesty," continued the smith, "but he's the one who ordered it and he should pay up."

"We found him naked and covered in mud!" shouted Yello. "Unless he was concealing a bag of gold up his a…" It was his turn to be glared at by Faylore. "Ahem… he has no coin, you see," he continued. "So, what are you going to do? Does it look as if we have an armoury here?"

Emnor did not allow the smith to answer, "Tell me…" he began, "… where exactly were you storing this supposed armour? I've seen your forge and, if you'll forgive my bluntness, there is no way that you could store a tenth of the amount you purport to have lost."

"Of course there ain't!" sighed the smith, "That's just my workshop, I keep all the big orders in my warehouse."

Faylore curled her lip, "What's a warehouse?" she asked.

"I just told you, it's where I keep all the big orders until my customers collect them. I found an old empty barn just outside the village a few years back. It needed a bit of work I'll admit, but now I've tarted it up, it's perfect for storing things. It don't let the rain in or nothing, no risk of anything going rusty."

Faylore frowned, "So it's a barn then?"

"No. It was a barn, now it's a warehouse, 'cause I keep my wares in it. Well I did until last night."

"Alright, alright, it's a bloody warehouse!" exclaimed Yello, "Where is it? I might be able to shed some light on your disappearing armour."

Drake cast a furtive glance at Hannock. Hannock raised his eyebrows. Checking to see that they had not been noticed, he shook his head slightly. Folding his arms so that his hand was clearly visible to Drake, he pointed toward the door.

"Do you actually think I believe that you're going to help me find my stuff?" scoffed the smith.

"Whether you believe it or not is beside the point," replied Yello. "But the truth of the matter is, that we are. Come back late this afternoon and we shall go there together."

"But it'll be dark by the time we get there! You won't be able to see a thing."

"No need to concern yourself, my good man. Let me worry about that, I am a wizard after all."

The smith grunted and shuffled toward the door, shaking his head and mumbling under his breath as he went.

"Right!" announced Hannock, "I'm off to have a scout about, see if I can figure out where our missing prince has disappeared to. Drake, fancy tagging along?"

The young wizard nodded and followed him through the door. Once they were outside, Drake could barely contain himself, "Do you think Jared pinched all that armour?" he hissed.

"That's the question, my friend. He may not have anything to do with its disappearance at all, it could merely be a coincidence."

"Yeah, I suppose you're right. Jared being out in the woods in the middle of the night with a ball of light surrounding him, and it happening to be the night all the armour that was made for one of Karrak's servants vanishing into thin air. Yeah, must be a coincidence."

Hannock frowned at him, "Don't try sarcasm with me, Maddleton. You're dealing with a master of it, remember?"

They were interrupted as the door opened behind them. It was Lodren and Grubb. "What you pair up to?" asked Grubb, suspiciously.

Hannock glared down at him, "We're not up to anything," he snapped. "And anyway, what business is it of yours?"

"Just seemed a bit odd, that's all. The blacksmith comes in all hot and bothered about some of his stuff going missing, Jared's nowhere to be found, and you and 'im couldn't wait to get out here an' 'ave a chinwag. I presume that's what all the finger pointin' was about?"

"My, my, Grubb. What a vivid imagination you have," chuckled Hannock.

"Yeah, I know," smiled Grubb, "and there's nothing wrong with me bloody eyesight neither! What's goin' on?"

“Mr Captain, sir,” said Lodren, “just because we’re smaller than you, doesn’t mean we’re stupider than you.” He suddenly looked at little uncomfortable as his face began to redden, “When I say stupider, I didn’t mean to say that you’re stupid and you think we’re even more stupid. What I meant was…”

“Alright, Lodren. I get the idea,” sighed Hannock.

“What’s on the tray?” asked Drake, noticing it for the first time.

Lodren glanced down at it, “Breakfast,” he replied, “for the guards you’ve got locked up.”

“Good grief!” exclaimed Hannock. “You’ll be reading them bedtime stories and tucking them in next!”

“It gives me something to do,” snapped Lodren, “until such time as you lot decide what we are going to do,” he added, storming off across the village square, tray in one hand, trusty hammer in the other.

“I’d better go with ‘im,” sighed Grubb. “But don’t, for one minute, think I’ve finished with you,” he added, pointing at Hannock, before scampering after his friend.

Hannock and Drake simply stared at one another in disbelief.

***

The steel door clanged loudly against the wall as Lodren stormed through it. “Wake up!” he bellowed, “Got some breakfast for you.” Pulling the large bunch of keys from his belt, he unlocked the first cell door.

“There you go,” he said, “can’t accuse us of trying to starve you, can you?”

The guard said nothing as he stared, open-mouthed at the Nibby, “What are you?” he asked quietly.

“Me? I’m the one who cooked your breakfast,” snapped Lodren. “So keep a civil tongue in your head or I’ll feed it to the pigs instead.”

Grubb slipped quietly through the open door and studied Lodren as he spoke to the guard. It seemed so long since he had seen his trademark smile or heard his chirpy, upbeat tones. He was quiet, moping around and looking more miserable as each day passed. As annoying as it could be, Grubb missed his friend’s normal enthusiasm for life.

Lodren approached the next cell and opened the door in the same way as the first, but the response he got from the man inside was completely different. Lodren offered him his meal.

“What? Do you think I’d eat anything that’s been cooked by a freak like you?” the man yelled. “Look at you. How do I know what sort of filth you’ve put in it? I might catch what you’ve got and become deformed. I’ve seen some horrible sights, but you’re disgusting. What are you, half man, half pig?”

Lodren began breathing heavily. In the past, he would have ignored the insults, but that was the past. Grubb was right, he had changed. He felt angry, enraged that, not only would someone think of him that way, but that they would actually say it to his face. He glared at the man and lowered his arm, the tray spilling from his hand and crashing to the ground. “What am I?” he whispered, his grip tightening around the handle of his hammer. “I’m your jailer. I’m the one who decides your fate. Your life is in my hands," he continued, allowing his hammer to hang like a pendulum before him. "I am Lodren, Nibrilsiem, dragon rider of this world. Remember me prisoner, for next time I visit, it may be to escort you to the gallows." With all his might, he drove the head of his hammer into the stone floor, shattering it into a shale-filled crater, six inches deep.

The man was sweating, his hands shaking uncontrollably, for behind his jailer a dragon had appeared. It tilted its head, its black tongue licking its lips. The dragon moved slowly closer, resting its head on the jailer's shoulder, the grey smoke from its nostrils masking them both. The door closed almost silently, and they were gone.

Outside, Lodren and Grubb roared with laughter, "Did you see his face?" asked Grubb, struggling to breathe, "I think he crapped 'imself."

Lodren wiped the tears from his face, "I've never laughed so hard," he admitted. "Do you think we went a bit too far?"

"No! Not at all. Not with a git like him. Maybe I should've bitten 'im a couple o' times, just to show 'im ye were serious."

"Oh no, you couldn't bite him!" He looked across at Grubb, "Well, maybe just the once," he laughed.

"So that's what's botherin' ye then, ye miss the dragons?"

"I just felt so alive when I was up there, Grubb. It's difficult to explain."

"No, Lodren. No, it's not. Are ye forgettin' that I actually fly quite a bit? It's so peaceful up there. No people, no noise, and nobody tryin' to feed ye every five minutes."

"Exactly Grubb. That's what I think… hey hang on a minute, every five minutes?"

CHAPTER 11

The day passed quickly, so it came as a surprise when Faylore informed them that the blacksmith was waiting impatiently for them outside.

"Good afternoon," said Emnor as he stepped through the doorway, followed by Yello, Harley, Drake and Hannock. Faylore had no intention of accompanying them on their little trip. She could not abide the blacksmith and even referred to him as 'ghastly'.

"Even on horseback, it'll be nigh on dark when we get there," the smith announced.

"Why would we need horses, you stupid man?" asked Emnor, scowling. "We are all wizards, we'll get there in an instant if we use our arts."

"Now, hang on," protested the blacksmith, nervously, "you never said anything about using magic to get there."

"Neither did I say that we would not," Emnor added. "Trust me, the blink of an eye and no harm done. Ask Captain Hannock. He travels with us regularly like this and nothing untoward has ever happened to him."

"What do you mean, nothing's happened to him? Half his face is missing!" exclaimed the smith.

"Well, there is that I suppose. But that was none of our doing, I assure you."

"Maybe not!" exclaimed the smith. "But it was magic, wasn't it? If it wasn't magic, that's what you would've said."

"Oh alright, calm down. We can't force you to go if you don't want to. Harley, he looks a little shaken. Give him a glass of water, there's a good chap."

Facing away from the blacksmith, Harley smiled as he poured the water. Yello positioned himself behind the smith as Harley handed him the glass. Placing his hand on the man's shoulder, Yello reassured him that he would be fine once he had taken a drink. Then, with a gust of wind, they all vanished.

Moments later they re-appeared. The first reaction from the blacksmith, other than the look of shock on his face, was to throw up. It was a reaction that Hannock remembered only too well. The dizziness and sense of confusion were still fresh in his mind as he remembered the first time he had been transported. However, he felt quite smug, as he had not given in to the nauseous feeling and gloated aloud, "Oh dear, not a good traveller then?"

The smith wiped his mouth on his sleeve as he staggered backwards, pointing at Yello, "You! You tricked me! I could have been killed, you lunatic!"

"Oh come now," sighed Yello, "don't be such a big baby. Nobody has ever died from a transportation spell… well, not for a very long time anyway."

The smith leaned forward and began retching once more, holding his stomach as if he had just been punched.

"You'll be fine in a moment," Emnor assured him. "Come on, let's have a look around your, erm… thingy house." He went ahead, followed quickly by the others, well, all but the smith who was far too busy feeling sorry for himself.

They approached the barn.

"There are a lot of scorch marks on the walls," Harley noted. "But the ground is untouched. This was not a natural fire, Master Emnor."

Emnor nodded, "I'm inclined to agree, Harley. This was the work of someone who is highly skilled."

"What makes you think that?" asked Hannock.

"Because a novice would have burned the whole thing to the ground," snorted Yello. "These marks are barely six inches across! It'd take at least a decade of practice to localise a spell with that kind of precision."

"So why do it at all?" asked Drake.

"That's what we need to find out," replied Yello.

"It could have been a duel," suggested Harley. "These could be evidence of someone who had missed their mark."

"If there had been a duel, trust me, there would be a corpse somewhere nearby. Hannock, have a scout around could you? See if you can find any tracks that may lead us to the caster."

Hannock nodded at Emnor and headed toward the back of the barn, studying the ground as he went. Drake followed, seizing the opportunity to discuss the situation with Hannock in private, "Whoever did this was bloody mustard, Hannock. I'd struggle to produce a spell with such accuracy, and I use a wand!"

Hannock's eyes stayed focused on the ground, "And what if you were older? Could you do it if you used, oh I don't know… a staff, perhaps?"

Drake tilted his head, a questioning look on his face, "What makes you ask that?"

"Because, whoever it was either had a staff, or a walking cane. And I doubt very much that it was the latter."

"So, you do think it was Jared!" exclaimed Drake.

"I never said that," replied Hannock. "All I said was that they were using a staff."

"How do you know, anyway? You don't even use magic."

"See these tracks on the ground, Drake? Two footprints and with every second print, a print from the right foot I'll add, a slight dent beside it, obviously made by a stick of some kind,"

"So, you don't think it was Jared?"

"No, it wasn't Jared, I can guarantee that."

"How can you guarantee that? It's just footprints."

"I can guarantee it, Drake, because I know who it was."

Drake stood agog, "Who?" he asked, nervously.

"Never you mind. Don't say a word of this to anyone, understand?"

Drake shook his head, "I don't understand. Why not?"

"Because I asked nicely. Now shut your face, let's re-join the others before they start wondering what's taking so long."

"Ah, there you are, Captain. Anything interesting?" asked Emnor.

"Well there are plenty of tracks, but nothing out of the ordinary. I wouldn't be surprised if they were all his," replied Hannock, gesturing toward the smith.

"What? You think I staged all this? You think I'm lying, don't you?" protested the smith.

"No, I don't think you're lying, idiot. You said that you had to fix up the place when you first found it, didn't you? They're old prints from when you were obviously repairing the barn. Stop being so bloody paranoid!"

They spent a few minutes inspecting the doors to see if they had been forced open, but they were perfectly intact. There were no holes or damage to any of the walls either, so, without anything conclusive to go on, they abandoned their investigation and decided to return to the village.

Emnor approached the smith, "Come on then, we'll get you back home," he smiled. "You can sod off!" exclaimed the smith. "I'll walk, you're not doing that to me again. I'm lucky I wasn't turned inside out the first time!"

"But as you rightly said, it will be dark soon," advised Emnor. "Surely you don't want to be alone in the woodlands at night. There are wolves and bears out here, you know."

"I know that, but at least I can hide from them. It's you lot I'm fearful of, bunch o' loonies performing magic on people without their consent. You should all be locked away or dropped in a pit you can't get out of. And I still haven't been paid!"

Hannock approached the smith. Drawing his sword, he slowed his pace.

"Don't kill me!" shrieked the smith, "I have a family, murder me and they'll starve!"

Hannock shook his head and sighed, "I have no intention of killing anyone," he said, turning his sword and offering it, hilt first to the smith. "If you insist on being out here alone you should at least be able to defend yourself. Give it back to me when you get back," he paused, "of course, if you don't get back, at least I'll know where to come and look for it tomorrow."

Moments later, they were crossing the village square. Entering the tavern that had become their temporary home for far too long, Emnor leaned against a table and lowered himself wearily into a chair nearby, "Well that was a glorious waste of time," he grumbled.

"I suppose it's one of the great mysteries we'll simply have to chalk up to experience," chuckled Yello.

"Very rarely do we wizards not find the answers we seek. It's frustrating to say the least," smiled Emnor.

"Well, we searched the entire area and found nothing. What more could we do?" asked Yello. "It seems that our culprit must remain anonymous."

"I wouldn't say that," said Hannock, slowly.

"Really?" said Yello, sounding surprised. "Is there something you're not telling us, Captain? It seems you have a suspect in mind?"

"Well it's obvious really, isn't it?" sighed Hannock, rubbing his hand across his face as he smiled at Yello, "It was you."

Emnor sat upright and stared at Hannock in disbelief, "Now see here, my dear Captain," he began, "you can't start throwing accusations around without any proof."

"Oh, don't sound so surprised, Emnor! I understand he's a friend, but he's a crafty old sod and you know it!"

"Thank you, I think," said Yello. "At least you still class me amongst friends whilst accusing me of… what is it you're accusing me of, by the way?"

"I'm not accusing you of anything," replied Hannock. "I have no idea why you visited the smith's barn. All I know is that you were there before today, and you were alone."

"Yello, what is he talking about?" asked Emnor.

"Forgive my interruption, Emnor," said Faylore, quietly. "But if Charles says Yello has been there before, then he has."

"Charles!" laughed Emnor, "I love it when people call you that. It reminds me of you as a boy, Tamor always called you that when you were in trouble!"

"I'm so glad my name is such a source of amusement for you, Emnor!" said Hannock indignantly.

"I meant no offence, Hannock, but…"

"Enough! It doesn't matter!" exclaimed Hannock. "Maybe you should be talking to your old pal about why he visited the barn!"

"Yello, surely you could explain?" pleaded Emnor.

"I'd love to," replied Yello, "but I have no idea what the captain is talking about."

Hannock banged his fist on the bar, "Listen!" he growled, "I may not know anything about magic or wands, or why our lives have been destroyed by a maniac who wants to rule the world, but do not question my ability as a soldier. I can track any man! Every footprint is different to the next, yours moreso than most," he said, pointing at Yello. "How's the leg? Still giving you grief? You try your best, but it still doesn't work properly, does it? Drags a little when you put weight on it? There was one set of footprints around that barn, and they were yours. Although you try to hide it, your right leg drags a little as you take each step, leaves a little scuff mark as you raise it. However hard you try, it just won't cooperate, will it? No, Yello, I'm not accusing you of anything, but you were there."

Yello smiled, "Very good, Captain. Very good indeed."

"This has gone far enough…"

"Hold on, Emnor," said Yello, holding up his hand to stop his friend's protestations. "Leave Hannock alone," he smiled. "After all, he is quite correct."

Hannock folded his arms and leaned against the bar, "I know I am," he agreed. "Now, would you care to tell us why you went out there alone? What were you up to?"

"I'm more interested in why you kept it a secret," sighed Emnor.

"The reason for the secrecy is obvious," chuckled Yello. "To save you from fretting. You're like a mother hen. You would have tried to talk me out of it."

"Talk you out of what?" asked Emnor.

"Destroying that blasted armour to prevent Karrak from getting his hands on it!"

"So that's what this is all about," gasped Drake. "I thought you'd become one of Karrak's loonies!"

"No, Drake. A loony I may be, but I'm all my own."

"How did you know where to find it, the location of the armour, I mean?" asked Hannock.

"The blacksmith told me where he had it stored," replied Yello.

"As easily as that?" asked Emnor, suspiciously. "We know he has a high regard for coin. Yet, although still unpaid, he told you where it was hidden?"

"Yes, surprising isn't it!" replied Yello, avoiding Emnor's inquisitive gaze.

"Yello, what did you do?"

"Well, I asked nicely, but he wouldn't tell me. So, I may have… drifted him a little."

"What!" exclaimed Harley, "You're not supposed to do that! Not without the express permission of the elders."

"In my defence, I did consider that. But I thought it may be a little time consuming, what with us being so far from Reiggan. Oh, and of course the fact that they're all dead."

"Then you should have at least spoken to Master Emnor. He is still the head of Reiggan!" shouted Harley.

"Nothing but a ruin," roared Yello. "Destroyed by a tyrannical maniac, who snuffed out the lives of everyone who resided there. Do not think to question me, boy! Do you think I care about manipulating the mind of a money-grabbing half-witted blacksmith who values coin more than life? A man who, as long as his pockets are lined with gold, would sell arms to our enemy without a moment's hesitation."

"He does have a point," Hannock said calmly. "It doesn't seem as if the smith has suffered any ill effects from whatever he did, so what's the harm?"

"What did you do with the armour?" asked Drake, returning to their original conversation.

"I took it a few miles out into the wilds and destroyed it," sighed Yello.

"Destroyed it, how?" asked Emnor.

"Green flame," replied Yello.

"Why not destroy it whilst it was still in the barn?" asked Hannock.

"As much as I would have liked to, the blacksmith would have had proof that it had been destroyed by magical means, and we don't want to upset the villagers unnecessarily. Then there was the chance that, if I had lingered for too long, I may have met up with some of Karrak's followers. As Hannock has already observed, I am not at my best at the moment and may not have fared too well if overwhelmed."

"You should have told me, old friend. I would have sided with you… eventually," said Emnor, patting his friend's arm.

"We do not have time for eventually, Emnor. Time moves on and Karrak becomes more powerful with each passing day!"

"It's about time we moved on," said Drake. "Let's find Karrak and finish this."

"We aren't strong enough," said Emnor. "We need Jared. Until he is ready, we must stay where we are, without him we would have as much effect on Karrak as children would have facing a zingaard."

"I wonder where he's gone? Surely he knows we don't have the time to waste."

"He's not wasting time, Harley. Just the opposite in fact, he's preparing himself for the final confrontation." All eyes turned to Drake. "Well, it's the truth," he said, sounding very mature.

***

Lodren and Grubb had joined the Gerrowliens. The four were now perched on the edge of the tavern roof, staring down into the village square as the sun set behind them.

"Why are we never included in anything any more? Don't they want us with them?"

"They need all of us, Lodren," replied Lawton. "But there are things we do not need to know. Yello has been up to something, but I feel that his escapades have been discovered."

"Best to keep our noses out," muttered Grubb. "If there's somethin' we need to know, they'll tell us."

"We could be a scout group. Head out before them and clear the way of enemies to ensure their safety. I could bring down countless enemies with my spear, tear them to shreds with my claws and…"

"POOM! We're having a peaceful afternoon, so let's not spoil it with your one Gerrowlien army battle scenarios, shall we?"

Poom snorted, "I'm not used to sitting around doing nothing!"

"You'll get all the fighting you need soon. When we go up against Jared's brother, he's bound to have others with him. Then you can gouge, bite and stab…"

"Shhh, what's that?" whispered Lodren, pointing into the treeline to their left.

"Where?" asked Grubb.

"Something moved in the trees," replied Lodren. "I didn't get a clear look, but I think it was a man."

"It could be Jared," noted Poom. "We've seen him milling about a few times over the last couple of days."

"Go and have a look, Poom. But be quiet," suggested Lawton.

"No, Poom. You stay here, I'll investigate this one." Grubb began to shiver, his transformation into a hawk almost instantaneous. With one surge, he was airborne.

"There's not a lot in this world that impresses me, but I love it when he does that," Poom growled with admiration, "If I could fly, no army would be safe."

Lawton sighed and shook his head, "When you get like this, no army's safe anyway."

"If you think that's impressive, you should see his new one," Lodren clamped his hand over his mouth. He had not meant to say it, it just… slipped out.

The Gerrowliens looked at him, "What new one?" Lawton asked.

"Yeah, what else can he do?" added Poom.

"Forget I said anything!" Lodren exclaimed hurriedly, "I promised I wouldn't say anything! As a matter of fact, I didn't, you're hearing things."

Poom frowned, "What, both of us?"

"Promise you won't say anything," pleaded Lodren, "I told Grubb I'd keep it a secret."

"So why are you panicking? You haven't told us, you daft Nibby," said Lawton.

"Hasn't told us what?" Poom was getting confused.

"That Grubb can transform into a dragon… oh dear, now I've done it!" Lodren was agitated and nervous, he hadn't meant to let slip the secret with which he had been entrusted. His eyes widened and his mouth fell open.

"Well, well," grinned Poom, "isn't he the dark horse? Or should I say, dark dragon?"

"Best not to say either, Poom. Look at Lodren's face. He obviously wasn't supposed to tell anyone."

"Oh. What, a bit wobbly is it? Not the right shape?" sniggered Poom.

"No, it is not a bit wobbly!" exclaimed Lodren. "I'll have you know, it's perfect. Even the feel of his scales is identical to the real thing!"

"So why keep it a secret?"

"Because of people like you, Poom!" snapped Lodren. "Always mocking him and laughing behind his back."

"Lodren, we mock everyone. Why should he be excused?" asked Lawton, smiling.

"He's a lot more sensitive than he lets on, you know. He takes it all to heart."

The Gerrowliens glanced at one other momentarily. "Well he won't be taking it to heart this time," Lawton assured him. "We won't even mention it, you have our word as Gerrowliens. Agreed, Poom?"

"Word of honour," replied Poom, nodding his head vigorously.

Lodren peered at them, "Not one word, not even as a joke. If you say anything, I'll never trust you again, understand?"

"Solemn promise," Lawton whispered.

A few minutes later, Grubb returned. He transformed and his friends could immediately see the look of concern on his face.

"Anyone we know?" asked Poom.

Grubb frowned and shook his head, "Not sure who it was," he said quietly. "Not even sure what it was."

"So, it wasn't a man then?" asked Lodren.

"I'm not really sure," replied Grubb. "At first I thought it was, 'cause it was walking on two legs. But when I looked closer it seemed old, very old. Almost draggin' its feet it was. And then there was the sound of its breath, rasping and dry, as if it hadn't taken water for weeks."

“Did you get a look at its face?” asked Poom.

“No, the sun’s too low and it was hidden amongst the shadows in the forest.”

“I should’ve gone,” said Poom, “I would have had a better view of it at ground level.”

“Trust me, Poom, you wouldn’t want to get any closer than I did. I could smell it from above the treetops, it was rancid. Musty and dank… decayed almost.”

They all came to the same conclusion simultaneously.

“Come on,” said Lawton, “we should inform the others.”

***

All eyes were on Drake as Lodren, ahead of his friends, gently opened the tavern door. “Well, it’s the truth,” he was heard to say as they entered.

“Ah, here they are,” smiled Emnor, “I thought you had all grown tired of our company.”

Lodren managed a feeble smile, “Don’t be silly, we’re not like that,” he said quietly.

“What’s wrong?” Faylore asked, a genuine concern in her voice.

“I think our situation is worse than we feared, Your Majesty,” Lodren replied.

Hannock marched forward and steered the Nibby to a chair, “Sit down,” he urged, “I’ll get you a drink. You look like you’ve seen a ghost.”

“Funny ye should say that,” said Grubb, gruffly.

“They’ve come at last,” Darooq sighed. “It was only a matter of time.”

Yello scowled at him, “Be quiet you, we don’t need any of your nonsense.”

Emnor leaned forward, “Lawton, do you know what Lodren is talking about?”

“We are only guessing, I’ll admit,” Lawton began. “But it seems the enemy has reached our doorstep.”

Hannock grabbed his crossbow, “Karrak? You’ve seen him? Where is he, I’ll end this now!” he growled.

“No, Hannock, we have not seen Karrak,” said Grubb, speaking quickly to stop Hannock bolting for the door, “I might have seen one of his victims, out in the woods, stumbling about as if it were lost.”

“What do you mean, you might have. You did or you didn’t, which is it?” Hannock snapped angrily.

“It could have been a man, I mean originally it could have been a man. But I’ll thank ye to keep a civil tongue, Captain. I’m not one of your soldiers to be ordered around and shouted at.”

“No, you’re not! But did it cross your mind that whatever is wandering around in the woods might once have been exactly that?”

Grubb lowered his head, “As a matter of fact, Captain, yes it did. But what or who it was before is no longer something we should concern ourselves with.

What matters is what it has become, and the threat it now poses to us all."

"It's alone! Point me in the right direction and I'll take care of it myself," said Hannock, becoming agitated.

"That would be an ill-advised course of action," muttered Darooq.

Hannock whirled around, raising the crossbow and pointing it at Darooq. "Maybe I should start with you!" he bellowed. "You're probably still serving your maniacal master!"

Darooq stared at Hannock through half-closed eyes, "I can assure you that I am not, but if you feel that it is my time to die, please, continue. However, one thing I do know is this. The creature that lurks in the shadows, as mindless as it is, undoubtedly still serves Karrak. What it sees, he sees. What it hears, he hears. It is an extension of his own soul and should you reveal yourself to it, the shadow lord will follow closely behind. Are you prepared to face him?"

Hannock tightened his grip.

"Put it down, Hannock. Surely you would not condemn a man for telling the truth?"

"You're right, Emnor, I wouldn't. But I would condemn him for the torture and murder of innocents, and we are all without doubt that he is guilty of that."

Hannock's finger feathered the trigger of the crossbow. His mind raced, images of townsfolk ablaze, heads driven onto stakes as trophies and the graves of children flashing through it. He could hear the terrified screams they would have made as they were butchered in the streets. He began to squeeze the trigger. The room was silent, every member of the companions holding their breath.

Slowly, Drake walked in front of Hannock, looking him straight in the eye. He blinked slowly and shook his head, "No, Charles," he whispered, "you're better than this. Don't become the thing you hate, my friend. You taught me about honour and respect, time for you to lead by example."

Hannock was shaking, the beads of sweat on his brow had become heavier and began streaming into his eye. He wiped it with his sleeve, his gaze falling on one after another of his companions. Lowering the crossbow, he handed it to Drake. "Quite right," he said shakily. "I need a drink. Care to join me, my young friend?"

CHAPTER 12

The night passed slowly with none of them able to rest. They knew the day would come when they would face Karrak. In their own way, each member of the party was prepared to do battle, but none held the firm belief that they were ready for it. The Gerrowliens were once more on the rooftops scanning the horizon for any movement, but there was nothing to see. Grubb paced nervously in the village square, his every move watched by Lodren. The rest remained within the tavern. Hannock, slumped forward in a chair, stared into a half-empty tankard that he had held for at least an hour without raising it to his lips. The four wizards were around a table in the centre of the room, and Faylore gazed upon them all as she honed the blade of her silver sword.

"Is no-one going to ask the most obvious question?" she asked.

"By that you mean where is Jared, I presume?" replied Emnor.

"You presume correctly, Emnor. After all, as you have said frequently, he is the only one who has the power to defeat his brother."

"He won't come alone," Yello grunted. "He may have become more knowledgeable in the ways of sorcery and necromancy, but do not underestimate him. He has learnt many other things over the years, patience being one them. He will send his beasts and other foul creatures ahead in order to weaken us before he comes to claim victory."

"Let him send them," mumbled Hannock. "When I've finished with them, he'll have to face me himself. I will make him beg for mercy before I end his sorry existence."

Faylore pitied Hannock. She knew that he was a good man, but his suffering and humiliation at the hands of Karrak had affected him more than he realised. She longed for there to be a way that she could put an end to his torment, his and everyone else's. Many times she had considered going ahead by herself, to destroy Karrak before he could do more harm. But any such attempt would probably end in her death, only leaving her friends even more vulnerable than they already were. "You didn't answer my question, Emnor," she said softly.

"That, my lady, is because I have no answer to give," replied Emnor, smiling.

"He's preparing himself," said Drake. "It must be far more difficult for him than the rest of us. I mean, how does one prepare oneself to kill their own brother?"

"Easier than you'd think," replied Harley. "Jared knows that the man he knew as his brother no longer exists. He'll be facing the shadow lord Karrak, not the man he grew up with."

Hannock bolted out of his chair, "What do you know of the man he grew up with, boy?" he growled. "He was a cruel, sadistic bully from the day he was born. He half-blinded an innkeeper for suggesting that he'd had enough to drink! Not satisfied with that, he murdered the guard who prevented him from killing that innkeeper! He's evil, I've known him all his life, and not once has he done anything good. And as I have already said, if Jared doesn't kill him, I will." His piece said, Hannock stormed out.

"You should take care of your friend," said Darooq, quietly. "He'd be dead before he got within a hundred yards of Karrak."

"Don't you worry, Faylore," said Yello, trying to sound positive, "Jared will be back soon. He will not allow us to face Karrak alone."

***

The night passed without incident and they were relieved when the pale dawn light eventually peered through the tavern windows. Drake and Harley had succumbed to their fatigue in the early hours, but their seniors had remained alert throughout.

Random villagers drifted into the square outside, ready to begin their mundane daily routine. This prompted Lodren and Grubb to abandon their own sell-imposed vigil and they entered the tavern looking damp, dishevelled and tired.

"Well that was all for nothin'," grumbled Grubb. "I'd forgotten 'ow soggy ye can get outside at night."

"We should be grateful that that's all we got," sighed Lodren as he began to fiddle with his pots and pans. "I'm sure we'll all feel better after a good breakfast."

It was not long before Hannock joined them, looking a little the worse for wear as he placed an empty brandy bottle on the bar.

"Did you manage to get a bit of sleep, Mr Captain, sir?" Lodren asked cheerily.

"After half a bottle o' brandy? I should say 'e did. Snorin' like a drain 'e was," laughed Grubb.

"Grubb!" said Faylore sharply, "We all have to deal with our stresses in our own way."

"Only sayin'," muttered Grubb.

"Any sign of Jared yet?" asked Hannock.

"Nothing so far," replied Emnor. "He'll probably turn up this afternoon."

They made small talk as best they could as the morning passed, when suddenly, they heard a bloodcurdling scream.

Hannock was first through the door, sword in hand. The Gerrowliens, not surprisingly, had beaten him to the doorstep. "What's going on?" he asked them.

In the square, a woman was being comforted by some of the other villagers. Without warning she suddenly pushed her way through the crowd, determined to confront the companions, "This is your fault!" she shrieked. "None of this would be happening if you hadn't come here."

Faylore edged forward to face the woman, "Tell me, dear lady, what has happened?"

"Don't you dear lady me, witch. They're dead. They're all dead and it's because of you and your kind."

"Who is dead, has something happened?" Faylore asked, sympathetically. "Just a moment, did you just call me a witch?"

“Never mind that,” Yello said impatiently, “Who has been killed, woman?”

“I never said they’d been killed!” sobbed the woman, “I said they were dead!”

Yello scratched his head, “Yes, but surely to be dead, one has to be killed? Well, not everyone, obviously. I suppose one could have been killed in an accident or died of old age…”

“They’re dead!” yelled the woman. “But they’re standing up and walking about like normal people! And that poor boy they have prisoner… beaten and shackled, crawling on the ground and begging for mercy. It’s your magic what’s done it! You’re all mad in the head!” Her tone changed, “I have to find my husband. We must leave this place, it’s cursed. You lot have put a curse on our whole village!” Pleading with others to follow, she hurried away. The villagers who remained huddled together, mumbling and casting furtive glances in the direction of the companions.

“I think we should discuss this inside,” suggested Emnor.

Each member had a particular part of the woman’s speech lodged in their mind as the door closed behind them, but it was Drake who spoke first, “She said they have a prisoner. It could be Alex or Xarran!”

“Or any one of a thousand young men,” replied Yello. “Now is not the time to allow our imaginations to run wild, Maddleton.”

“What we need to know is, who they are,” noted Faylore.

"Well, there's only one way to find that out, Your Majesty," replied Hannock, "and standing around here isn't it."

Faylore slung her quiver across her back, tightened the thick belt that held her sword and reached for her bow, "No time like the present," she said.

Yello took up his staff.

Emnor glanced around the room, looking briefly like an absent-minded old man. He started to chuckle to himself, "Silly old fool! I no longer have a staff, do I? I never realised how attached I had become to it." He followed Yello toward the door, "Drake, Harley, you wait here in case Jared comes back," he ordered. "He'll need to know what has transpired."

"In your dreams," Drake laughed. "You heard him, Harley, you wait here in case Jared comes back."

Harley sighed, "Yeah… not going to happen, I'm afraid."

Emnor placed his hand on Harley's shoulder, "I need you to stay here, Harley. This could be dangerous."

"I know! That's why I'm going with you!" he replied. "I'm your apprentice and one of my duties is to protect you whenever possible, the danger just adds to the fun."

Emnor smiled at Harley and Drake, "Alright," he said, "Pointless arguing with either of you. You're determined, I can see that. But, should anything happen that puts us in harm's way, at least keep your heads down."

"I'll lead," said Hannock, "I can follow the woman's tracks."

“She came from that direction,” Poom advised him. “Don’t worry, if you lose the trail, I’ll find it again for you,” he added, grinning.

Hannock gave him a dirty look, “The day I need you to help me track, Poom, I’ll probably hang myself.”

“Oooh exciting!” exclaimed Poom, “Can I watch?”

On the outskirts of the village, Hannock found the woman’s footprints easily.

“How do you know those are hers?” asked Harley.

“She’s on the large side,” replied Hannock, politely referencing the woman’s heavy build, “She shuffles when she walks, these drag marks are a tell-tale sign.”

They set off at a brisk pace.

***

Now far from the village the companions had slowed their pace, partly because they had reached the point where the footprints ended and partly because, as usual, Yello was struggling to keep up with them. The dusty road, no longer showing signs of recent use, lead Hannock to suggest that they venture into the dense forest that surrounded it.

The Gerrowliens, naturally, headed into the trees, slightly ahead of the rest. They would pause occasionally to signal that there was nothing to be seen, much to the annoyance of Hannock. “Where could they have gone?” he moaned, quietly. “They can’t have just disappeared!”

"On the contrary, Captain. They quite possibly could have. We are dealing with sorcerers after all," whispered Emnor.

"If they try to hurt any of you, I'll bash them with my hammer!" Lodren said to Grubb.

"That's the way, Lodren," laughed Grubb, "get yourself worked up, then when we find 'em, start swingin'."

"I'm not joking, Grubb," said the Nibby, "I'll flatten them, you see if I don't."

Their conversation was brought to an end as the procession ahead of them came to an abrupt halt. Poom held up his hand as a warning to the others. Unable to see properly, Grubb transformed, grabbing Lodren as he did so and hoisting him onto his shoulder. The trees had become sparse and they could clearly see that the ground began to rise steeply, large rocks protruding from the hillside they were undoubtedly about to ascend.

Poom and Lawton lowered themselves silently from the trees above to report their observations, "The hill levels out at about fifty feet," said Lawton. "There are two of those things about half way up standing guard. The problem is there's no way of knowing what it is that they're protecting. We couldn't see over the brow of the hill."

"If they manage to sound the alarm, we could be facing hundreds of them," added Poom. "It wouldn't be a problem for me, but..."

"Shut up, Poom!" hissed Lawton, "Now is not the time."

"They can't sound the alarm if they don't have heads." They all turned to face Lodren, "I'm just saying," he continued, "you can't shout for help if you don't have a mouth and you can't take that off. Take off their heads somehow."

Wilf looked up at his friend, frowning, "You know something?" he growled, "You've changed, Lodren. You've changed."

Lodren shrugged his shoulders.

"Okay. Anyone have any other ideas?" asked Hannock. Nobody did. "Right," he continued, "Your Majesty, what say we have our own little archery contest?"

Now perched in the topmost branches of a tree, Faylore prepared herself, waiting for Hannock's signal. Her climbing of the tree was graceful and swift. Getting Hannock to her level, however, was a little more time consuming and far clumsier. Needing to be stealthy had negated the idea of Wilf simply carrying him up, the size of the four-armed beast would undoubtedly result in many twigs and branches being broken. With Wilf giving him a boost by launching him into the lower branches and the Gerrowliens aiding his ascent, he eventually reached a suitable vantage point. Looking down, he closed his eyes for a few moments, and swallowed hard.

"Are you alright, Hannock?" asked Lawton, who was standing on one leg on a branch nearby.

"I... erm... I don't like heights," Hannock whispered.

"Oh, that's no good, is it?" replied Lawton. "Tell you what, fasten your tunic."

"What good will that do? Stop me splattering too much when I hit the ground?"

"Just do it!" urged Lawton.

As Hannock fastened his buttons Lawton extended the claws from his right hand. Reaching forward, he drove them through the epaulette on Hannock's tunic. "There you go, I've got you now," he smiled. "There's no way you can fall."

Hannock glared in disbelief. Admittedly, his uniform was far from its best, but he still wore it with pride and was somewhat shocked to have it treated in such a way. "Thank you," he said, smiling through gritted teeth.

He took aim. Faylore, with Poom directly behind her, did the same. Lawton held up his free hand and counted down with his fingers. The archer and the bowman released simultaneously. Faylore's arrow struck a split second before Hannock's bolt but both hit their mark perfectly, striking their targets between the eyes. Each victim released a breath that would have been inaudible to anyone mere inches away and fell, rolling down the hill silently until they reached the foot. The companions waited with bated breath.

Luck, it seemed, was with them. No alarm was raised.

They dragged the bodies of their fallen foe into the cover of the trees and concealed them with loose leaves. As they began to climb, Wilf placed Yello on his free shoulder, his leg would not support him enough to climb.

"Very kind of you, Grubb," Yello sighed.

Reaching the point where the guards had been posted, they were caught by surprise, horrified at what had suddenly appeared above them.

Xarran was being dangled over the precipice like a grotesque marionette, held by the scruff of his neck by another of the undead guards. “Wait!” he begged. “Don’t come any closer! He has Alex, he’ll kill him if any one of you resist! He orders that you drop your weapons and he’ll let him live.”

Xarran’s face was covered with blood. A deep gash on his forehead bled profusely, streaming into his eyes and dripping from his jaw. A patch on the side of his head was raw, evidence that part of his scalp had been torn from his skull, each wound smeared with mud. He had been tortured and brutalised yet, despite his injuries, his greatest concern was for the safety of his friend. “I tried to fool him, tried to trick him into lowering his guard. He’s too powerful! We have to surrender, if we do not, he will destroy us all!” Xarran lowered his voice, “He’s here!” he whispered. “He wants Jared,” he added, his eyes searching for the prince. “He is the key, if he swears to serve Karrak, all of this will end!”

Hannock’s grip tightened once more on his crossbow, “Where is he?” he growled. “Where is Karrak? This will end, but not in the way he had planned.”

“Hannock, you can’t. He’ll kill Alex,” pleaded Xarran.

“Where… is… he?” Hannock repeated slowly.

Xarran’s undead captor wrapped its bony fingers tightly around Xarran’s neck.

“He’ll kill me,” Xarran begged, barely able to squeeze the words out as he held up his hand. “You must lay down your weapons.”

Emnor leaned forward and tapped Hannock’s arm, “I’m afraid he has us at a disadvantage, Captain. Let us do as he asks. If anything happens up there, stay clear.

We wizards need no weapons." He turned to the others and nodded.

It began to rain as each of the companions disarmed themselves. Lodren was the first, laying down his huge hammer as a makeshift table for the others to use, "No sense in putting them down in the mud," he whispered, "I have a feeling we'll be needing them shortly."

They resumed their ascent.

"Wait!" rasped Xarran. The companions paused. "Drake, Harley, your wands. You must leave them too, Lord Karrak knows about them."

Drake frowned, "How would he know about our wands?" he whispered to Emnor, his suspicion aroused by Xarran's instruction.

"Look at him, Drake. He's terrified. He's been tortured, goodness only knows for how long. I'm sure that not a single detail of our exploits remains a secret to Karrak. Do as he says, place your wands on the weapons pile. You'll have to use your gifts in the traditional manner should the need arise, I'm afraid."

"Bloody hours I spent testing these!" Drake chuntered as he took Harley's wand and placed it with his own on Lodren's hammer, "And the first time it seems we may really need them, we have to leave them behind!"

Emnor raised his voice, "We are unarmed, may we approach?" he shouted up the hill. Xarran was dragged away from the edge unceremoniously by the ghoulish guard. The companions exchanged brief glances and followed, Yello, once again being carried by Wilf.

As they cleared the ridge they were surprised to find themselves on a large plateau. Flat and sparsely covered by dried grass, they were relieved to have firm footing. A treeline lay at the far end, silent flashes of lightning illuminating the scene before them as the rain grew heavier. Half way, Xarran was prone on the ground, his kidnapper cruelly grinding his face into the mud with the heel of his heavy boot.

"Call off your dog, Karrak!" roared Hannock. "Or I'll do it for you! Come on, show yourself, or are you too much of a coward to face an unarmed man?"

There was a movement amongst the trees. Slowly, a shadowy figure emerged, flanked by a hoard of undead minions. Hannock began to march toward them.

"Hannock, no!" pleaded Xarran. "Don't antagonise him!"

The monstrous figure removed its foot from Xarran's head and began to lurch toward Hannock. As it grew closer, it unsheathed its black broadsword and held it aloft. Facing Hannock, it swung it full force, but the captain was far too experienced to fall for such a crude attack. Arching back, he watched as the blade passed above him, and grabbed the assailant's arm. Ducking under its armpit, he twisted with all his might, relieving the monster of both its sword, and its decaying arm. Placing his heel against his opponent's side, he kicked it away and spun around, cleaving its head cleanly from its neck. Hannock glared at Karrak.

"If this…" he screamed, pointing at his fallen foe, "… is all you have, I suggest you start running NOW."

The hoard of ghouls surrounded Karrak. Hannock raised the sword with both hands, touching the blade against his nose. He closed his eyes momentarily, preparing himself for battle as he took his stance. But his enemy did not approach.

Unexpectedly, Karrak raised his arm above his head. There was a bright flash and an explosion that made the ground shake, but it had not come from Karrak. Hannock was confused, was it thunder? Then, he heard a second blast, and the sound of Emnor's voice screaming, "… NO!"

Hannock turned, a look of horror appearing on his face. Yello lay on the ground, his robes smouldering as Emnor attempted to douse the small flames that licked around his friend's body. Just behind them, lay another victim, but Hannock could not make out who it was. From what he could see, all were accounted for, so who was the stranger? Hannock began to panic… Jared. Dropping the sword, he ran back to his friends, dread in his heart at the thought of losing his lifelong friend. "Jared!" he called as he reached them.

Drake grabbed his shoulders, "Calm down, Hannock," he said hurriedly. "It's not Jared. It was Darooq!"

No-one had noticed Darooq as he had followed them from the village. He had tailed them every step of the way, watching and waiting for events to unfold. At last, it seemed he had chosen his moment to strike.

"Is Yello dead?" asked Hannock.

"No, he's still alive," Drake replied, shakily. "But it doesn't look good. I don't think he'll survive!"

Emnor clutched his friend's hand, tears in his eyes, "Come on now, you old coot. It's only a scratch, you're going to be fine."

Yello reached up, wiping a solitary tear from Emnor's cheek. He smiled weakly, "Not this time, old friend," he whispered. "You must act quickly, I must be drawn."

Emnor recoiled, "No!" he exclaimed, "I could never… Yello, you would surely die."

"I'm not going to survive anyway," smiled Yello, "but a thousand years of knowledge cannot be lost, my friend. Someone must draw it before I take the eternal sleep."

"This makes no sense, why would Darooq wait until now to attack? He had countless opportunities whilst we were in the village." Emnor sneered at the body of the sorcerer, "Well, he's dead now, I made sure of that. I should have finished him when we first discovered him."

"That's not very gracious of you, Emnor."

The companions turned to see who had spoken. It was Jared.

"You always taught me that all life is sacred, yet you seem to feel no remorse at killing the man who saved your life."

"What!" exclaimed Emnor. "What do you mean, saved my life?"

"Yello was going to kill you. Darooq saw what he was about to do and stepped in, so to speak."

"Nonsense!" yelled Emnor. "Why would Yello want me dead?"

"He didn't, but Karrak does," Jared replied, softly.

"I know you all think I'm a bit thick," Drake announced. "Sorry, but could you please tell me what the bloody hell you're talking about, Jared."

"Don't you think it strange that the only person to survive the attack on Reiggan just happened to be the best friend of the head?"

"Pure coincidence," snorted Emnor.

"I'm afraid not, Emnor," replied Jared. "He was left there deliberately by Karrak. He knew that he'd be accepted into the fold without question. A puppet in the enemy camp, with him pulling the strings."

Emnor gazed into his friend's eyes as he cradled his head, "Yello, is this true?"

"It wasn't me, I… I tried to resist him but he took control! Forgive me, I never even remembered doing it until Jared mentioned it."

"We all know how good Karrak is at controlling the minds of others, Yello cannot be blamed for his actions," Jared stooped down and patted the old man's hand.

"Jared," whispered Yello, "I have a final request. I must be drawn, you must take my powers. It will help you defeat Karrak."

"Speaking of which…" uttered Hannock, clearing his throat and pointing across the plateau.

"Oh, him!" laughed Jared. "Don't worry about him. That's not Karrak."

"Not Karrak!" exclaimed Drake. "Well who is it then?"

"Not really sure," replied Jared. "But we'll know in a few minutes."

"How?" asked Harley. "Are you going to face him?"

"No need," said Jared, calmly. "Our allies will discover his identity soon enough."

“Allies? What allies?”

“You’ll see them shortly, Drake. Subtlety is not one of their strong points.”

Yello was becoming agitated, “Jared, you must… you must perform the drawing ritual, before it is too late.”

“I already have,” replied Jared. “Joined to the Heart of Ziniphar as I am, I can take the powers of any witch or wizard with the slightest touch. Only if it is for the purpose of using it for good, I should add.”

“So, you took Yello’s power just by touching his hand?” gasped Drake.

“Yes, and it is far less painful than it would have been if performed in the ancient, traditional way.”

Emnor smiled, “There you are, old friend, you have your last wish, now, let’s see about getting you healed.” Emnor looked upon his friend’s face. His eyes were closed and he looked more peaceful than Emnor had seen him in years. “Yello... Yello?” Emnor took his hand, and wept.

The trees behind Karrak quivered. Two luminous green-skinned bodies appeared, one directly behind Karrak. Ramah roared as he thrust two swords through the shadowy figure, both running clean through and steaming as if just removed from the forge. Karrak looked down in shock, his body shaking, his arms reaching out in disbelief and confusion. Black smoke poured from his form, flakes of ash drifting from its features, floating fleetingly in the breeze before dissipating. His mouth fell open, but instead of crumbling completely, normal, smooth skin could be seen beneath the disguise. Jared was correct, the figure that stood before them was not Karrak… it was Alex.

Xarran rose to his feet. Looking back at Alex, he let out a piercing scream, “He was mine!” he bellowed. “He belonged to me and you took him away!” The rain had become torrential, washing away the blood from Xarran’s face. The gash in his forehead healed miraculously and the raw patch on his skull vanished. His wounds, it seemed, were all part of some elaborate ruse. “I’m going to kill every last one of you! I’m going to torture you, slice you, burn you, dismember you! You’ll wish you’d never been...”

The dull thud of the arrow and the cracking of bone could not be heard from where Faylore stood. Realising his madness, she had decided his fate. Her bow still raised, she watched as Xarran stood momentarily, his lips still moving but uttering no words. She blinked, the rain dripping from her long lashes as she witnessed him fall, grateful for the downpour that disguised her tears.

The companions charge their remaining foe!

***

Karrak, seated on the throne in Merrsdan, pondered over what he had seen through Alex’s eyes. Xarran had acted impetuously and with less composure than a petulant child, thereby sealing his own fate. Perhaps his death was a release for them both? What concerned him was the ease with which his enemies had despatched his forces. The rage of the swordsman, the ferocity of the dergon, the speed of the Gerrowliens and the swift accuracy of the Thedarian were things that only a fool would ignore. But why had the wizards not taken part? Did they believe that they were not needed to defeat such a small force?

Karrak rose from the throne and swept across the room. Staring through the doorway, he watched as his undead guards shuffled aimlessly around the halls. They would obviously not be enough of a distraction when the time came to face his greatest adversary. Karrak knew that his only real nemesis was Prince Jared. He had sensed his power long before Xarran had made his fatal mistake. He was unsure of how Jared had achieved his new strength. He ran his hand over the Elixian Soul. He must have found something, an ancient relic or artefact to rival his own, he thought. Drifting back and forth, he considered his options. Should he have done with it, and face Jared sooner rather than later? No, that was the mistake the boy had made. He would bide his time and strike only when he was ready. “I need more,” he whispered to himself.

***

The green flames of the funeral pyre dissipated as the companions began to disperse. They instinctively headed toward the village. For whatever reason, Drake and Harley, their arms around one another’s shoulders, ambled away in the opposite direction. Hannock was about to call them back, but Emnor placed his hand on the captain’s arm and shook his head. Hannock nodded in understanding. He, having served in the military for so long, was used to losing people close to him. He sighed as he watched the two yound wizards, knowing that no words would comfort them.

Reaching the village, they entered the tavern. Hannock headed straight for the bar. "We leave at first light," he growled.

"For where?" asked Emnor. "We still have no idea where Karrak is."

"Exactly!" growled Hannock. "But we aren't going to find him sitting on our arses in here!"

"Charles, please!" exclaimed Faylore, "There's no need for crudity."

Hannock snorted, "And tell me, why did we bring back the body of that sorcerer? We should have left his mangy carcass for the beasts to tear apart."

"In his defence…" said Jared, quietly, "… Darooq did save Emnor's life."

"According to you!" exclaimed Hannock. "None of us witnessed it."

"Do you doubt my word, Hannock? Do you think I would defend a guilty man?"

"I don't know what to think anymore!" snapped Hannock, turning to face him. "You've been gone for days, yet somehow you manage to be right there when you were needed! And what about that thing in the woods, the ball of light that knocked me off my feet when I tried to reach you?"

Jared lowered his head, "Hannock, you are my dearest friend. I could never harm you, I could never harm any of you."

"How sincere you sound… a bit like your brother to be honest. He tends to plead innocence, right up until he stabs you in the back!"

"Hannock, that's enough!" roared Emnor. "How dare you accuse your prince! Apologise at once!"

"Apologise! Give me some answers, at least I'll understand what the apology is for. We don't know where he's been or what he's been doing. Look at his eyes, Emnor! Does the light behind them seem natural to you? Oh, we'll just ignore it, shall we? What if Karrak got to him? Imagine that, we come face to face with a homicidal maniac, only to discover that we're harbouring another one within our own ranks!"

"Mr Captain, sir. You can't say things like that about Prince Jared. He's been as good as..."

Jared held up his hand, "Lodren... he's right," he sighed. "The last few days have been our greatest test and I don't blame him for his suspicions. But it was not by choice that I abandoned you for those few days."

"So you would have us believe that you were a prisoner, that you were held captive within that ball of light? That, despite the powers you now hold, you were unable to escape its grasp and return to us?" asked Hannock.

"In a way, yes. However, I was not being held entirely against my will," replied Jared. "The light was the Heart of Ziniphar. It knew that I would be vulnerable once I went into a trance and generated that wall merely to protect me."

"What'd ye have to go in a trance for, was it showing ye somethin', somethin' that can help ye beat Karrak?"

"Yes, Grubb... and no, not specifically," replied Jared.

"Oh, that'll help then," scoffed Grubb. "Teaches ye somethin', but doesn't! Makes perfect sense, that!"

Jared gave him a sideways glance, “The Heart is ancient,” he began, “it pre-dates every scroll and tome in existence. It wanted to show me everything, and that takes time. Forgotten magic of how to fight pure evil now resides within me, Grubb. The Heart of Ziniphar has no desires, it has no specific destiny to destroy a person or thing that would do harm. It is pure, it wants all evil to be eradicated from the world.”

“So, it has taught you something that will help us beat Karrak then, Mr Jared?”

Jared smiled at Lodren, “It has taught me far more than that, my friend. It has shown me how to destroy that which possesses him. I know how to destroy the Elixian Soul!”

***

The door to the tavern opened quietly. All eyes turned to see Poom and Lawton looking a little sheepish.

“Sorry to interrupt,” said Poom. “It’s just that… well, we thought you might want this.” He produced Yello’s staff from behind his back. “We don’t mean to be indelicate but, even if you don’t want it, it shouldn’t be left out in the open for anyone else to tamper with.”

Emnor stared at the staff. Memories of his friend flooded his mind as he fought to contain his grief. “Quite right,” he said, his false confidence visible to all. “Give it… erm, just put it over by the bar, there’s a good chap. I’ll decide what must be done with it later.”

“Your friend died for a cause he believed in, and you should take both pride and solace in that,” said Lawton.

"He would not want you to grieve over him until your task is done, and the greatest honour you could do him would be to use his own staff to avenge his death," he added as he headed for the door.

"Thank you, my friend," Emnor called after him, "I know that Yello would have appreciated those kind words."

"Before you go," said Hannock, "could you do me a favour? See if you can find that bloody blacksmith and get me my sword back, would you? I feel naked without it."

Drake and Harley had followed the Gerrowliens into the tavern. Drake shuddered at Hannock's last statement, "Not a pleasant thought," he mumbled. "Ooh, is that Yello's staff?" he asked excitedly.

Emnor looked suspiciously at him, "Yes, it is," he replied slowly. "Why?"

"Well if you're going to use it, Master Emnor, it'll have to be tested first. Who knows what kind of curses and hexes he put on it to keep it safe! And let's face it, I'm the best tester there is."

"And the luckiest!" added Harley. "You should've been splattered to the four winds so many times but you're still standing here, being as annoying as ever."

"There you go, a rousing affirmation by my colleague, I've survived every explosion, burn... annoying?"

"The boy has spirit," announced Poom. "Admittedly it's mixed with insanity, but he does have spirit."

Drake frowned, it was the kind of compliment he could do without.

"There'll be no testing," announced Jared. "No explosions, no burns, nothing. So, you won't be getting your hands on that staff, Drake," he added, wrapping his arm around the boy's shoulders. "Something tells me you should stick to using that fabulous wand you created."

"So, what did the Heart teach you? How do you hope to destroy the Elixian Soul?" asked Emnor, backtracking on their conversation.

"That's not important now," replied Jared. "Just know that, when the time comes, I will succeed."

"What happened to Xarran?" asked Harley, quietly.

"He must have fallen under Karrak's spell, when he…."

"I mean, his body," said Harley, raising his voice as he interrupted Emnor.

Emnor paused momentarily, "We… we're not sure, Harley. Our intention was to deal with him in exactly the same way as Yello." His voice cracked as he mentioned his friend's name.

"We don't know!" Hannock announced loudly. "We went to retrieve it, but it had vanished. There were drag marks on the ground. It seems that we didn't get all of his ghoulish accomplices, they must have taken it amidst all the confusion."

Drake shuddered, "You don't think they'll turn him into one of them do you? I don't know if I could handle that. Imagine coming face to face with someone you knew looking like… that!"

“No… let’s not. We have quite enough to deal with without letting our imaginations run riot,” suggested Emnor.

“Nothin’ to worry about anyway,” mumbled Grubb. “They’re all dried up ain’t they? Ye can squash ‘em easy enough and ye wouldn’t need a hammer anywhere near as big as Lodren’s.”

The rest of the companions glared at him in disbelief.

“Oooh Grubb, how could you say such a thing?” exclaimed Lodren. “He was our friend.”

“No, it wasn’t!” snapped Grubb. “The lad you knew ‘ad been gone a long time. What ye saw out there weren’t no friend o’ yours, or mine. Ye saw the way ‘e behaved, the way ‘e spoke! If ye cast yer mind back it might remind ye of someone! Whoever he was, he would’ve ‘appily killed us all without a care. If Faylore wasn’t as good a shot as she is, the end could’ve been a lot worse!”

“So what’s the plan?” said Drake, loudly. “Do we set out after them?”

“Of course we do,” growled Hannock. “And we don’t stop until we’ve destroyed them all, and that includes Karrak.”

The last person anyone expected to offer an opinion was Faylore. Throughout many conversations during their time together and regardless of topic, she had remained silent, but this time was different. The guilt of having to kill what had once been a confident, caring young man, despite what he had become, was weighing heavily on her.

“Charles,” she said calmly, “it is unlike me, but I too yearn for revenge. The loss of our friends is a burden we shall not endure lightly, but I am afraid, for now, it is what we must do. Our minds are clouded and that could lead to any one of us making rash decisions or taking irrational, impulsive actions that could lead to further losses. For now, we shall bide our time and allow ourselves to grieve. Only once we are fully prepared, shall we seek out our enemy. Then, together, we shall strike a blow to end the madness that Karrak has brought to our world."

CHAPTER 13

The days that followed were a difficult time. Still residing at the inn, the companions would set out into the forest each morning to hone their skills as they saw fit.

Many posts met their end as Hannock, cursing aloud, hacked them into nothing more than wood shavings with his blade and peppered others with holes as he practiced with his crossbow.

Harley and Drake, at a safe distance of course, held their wands and froze their targets solid or incinerated them. Drake was beginning to act far more sensibly than he ever had before and would advise Harley occasionally on his technique. Harley was, of course, Harley. He looked upon Drake's advice as being constructive, although the desired effect was actually for his spells to be more de-structive.

Faylore preferred to train alone and would be gone for hours at a time; Jared would meditate; and poor Emnor would sit, quietly reminiscing. His thoughts were mostly of Yello and occasionally a faint smile would curl the corners of his lips. Other memories however would cause tears to well in his eyes before they trickled slowly down his wrinkled cheeks.

There was no practical way that Grubb could practice his transformation skills, choosing, most days, to change into a hawk and watch Lodren from above. The Nibby wielded his hammer as if it were as light as a feather, his tree-felling providing the many posts that Hannock required.

The Gerrowliens had to be very careful when selecting a bough in which to nap when Lodren was about.

Two more weeks passed, and the hunt began anew. The innkeeper gave a huge sigh of relief as the door closed behind the last of the companions and he began to dance a little jig, this due partly by their departure, but mostly to the large pile of gold coins Hannock had placed on the bar to cover any inconvenience they may have caused him. Rubbing his hands together briefly, he scooped them into his raised apron, "And don't bloody well come back!" he mumbled.

***

They had set camp at the end of their first day. The companions lowered themselves wearily around the campfire, except Lodren, who scampered about eager to cater for his friends.

"I must say," began Emnor, "I do believe that village life has softened me up a little, I'm exhausted."

"Either that, or the million years you've been alive is starting to catch up with you," laughed Drake.

"Ignore the runt!" growled Grubb. "Ye don't look a day over half a million," he added with a grin.

Emnor gave Grubb a look of disdain, "I believe Maddleton can be sufficiently obnoxious without your support, Grubb," he mumbled sleepily. "So, if you don't mind, keep…" His voice tailed off as he yawned loudly.

His mouth closed, as did his eyes, and he began to snore gently.

"Poor Mr Emnor," sighed Lodren, "he really was exhausted. Oh well, I'll keep his supper warm, he can have it later. It's an old trick I learned ages ago, you simply wrap the food in a scrap of glamoch hide and keep it close to the fire. The secret is not to put it too close because that would make it too dry…" Suddenly, Lodren also began yawning loudly.

What's wrong with you lot!" exclaimed Hannock. "A gentle stroll and you're all worn out! Imagine what you'd be like if I'd had you marching all day, at least you'd have a real reason to be tired." Nobody responded. Hannock glanced around for a few seconds, then his eyes closed, and he fell face first into the ground.

Jared was left alone. The others had not noticed the faint mist as it began to shroud each one of them in turn. Jared had realised immediately that it was no natural fog. It was a vapour that seemed to move with purpose, yet he felt no alarm. Something deep within compelled him to allow events to unfold, as to intervene could be far more dangerous.

A familiar voice came from the darkness beyond the camp, "They look so peaceful," it announced. "As safe as babes nestled in their mothers' arms."

Jared raised his eyebrows, "But are they?" he asked, calmly. "They are defenceless, their only protection lies with me. But that is one thing of which you are undoubtedly aware, are you not, Karrak?"

A sinister laugh echoed around the clearing. Karrak was still reticent to reveal himself. "Come now, Brother. If I had meant to harm them they would already be dead, you know that!"

"An elaborate snare," observed Jared. "But why? It is unlike you to be so gracious. Is it that you are wary of raising my ire? What reason requires the negation of any witnesses?"

"Strange that you should choose the word 'reason', my brother, for that is why I am here. I come here, not to confront nor challenge you, quite the opposite. I came here in a bid to put an end to this conflict. You obviously have something in your possession which enhances your powers, something that rivals my own. Many more will die should we play this out, Brother. Whereas, if we were to combine our powers we may yet bring about a peaceful resolution." Karrak had relented and approached Jared slowly. The light from the campfire cast ghostly shadows across his face. The person who stood before Jared was his brother, not the shadow lord.

Jared studied him for a moment. "Really?" he laughed mockingly. "You want me to join with you?" As he spoke, an aura had begun to glow gently around him. "I don't know who you are, but I must commend you for your audacity."

"My offer is sincere, I only wish to bring peace to this world," urged Karrak.

Jared wagged his finger, "Now that's where you've slipped up. You see, my brother is insane! He doesn't want peace, he never did. He thrives on the pain and suffering of others, bathes in chaos and would have the screams of his victims as a lullaby!"

"I am your brother! Join with me and allow me to show you that I am changed. Keep your trinket with you if you have mistrust in your heart… what is it that has corrupted you so? You should rid yourself of it before it consumes you, Brother. I could help you."

"At last!" exclaimed Jared. "That is the purpose behind your ruse! I have you scared, you want to know what you're up against! Well you're out of luck!" he announced, his voice getting louder. "You cannot win, and you know it. Well let me tell you this, whoever or whatever you are, you will face me! It will be at a time and in a place of my choosing. I swear, if you appear like a thief in the dead of night again, it will be the last time you appear anywhere! The answer is 'no', I will not join you, not now, not ever. Leave now while I allow it. Our final battle will come, but not yet!"

"I understand," replied Karrak, unphased by Jared's warning. "You need to consider my offer. After all, time is plentiful. But, however shall I find you again?" he asked, almost leering as the enquiry left his lips. With a nonchalant wave of a hand and an insipid grin, he dismissed his own question. "Not to worry, I'm sure it won't be too much of a problem. I know, I'll send a messenger!" Karrak paused as if in thought. "Yes, a messenger, a peaceful envoy in the hope that you have made the right decision. Until then farewell, Brother," Karrak bowed briefly as he backed away before vanishing into the darkness.

An ominous silence had befallen the camp during Karrak's impromptu visit, but now, the familiar night-time sounds returned; the hooting of an owl; the chirp of the insects; and the rustling of the undergrowth as small mammals searched for an evening meal.

Jared smiled. Was Karrak so concerned that he would expose himself so readily? He shook his head. Yes, he himself had become far more powerful, but he was unable to read minds. He lay down near the campfire and closed his eyes. It was clear that no answers would be forthcoming, he would discuss it with the others the following morning.

***

Jared watched his rousing companions. He should not have found the looks of confusion on their faces amusing, but did nonetheless.

The campfire was somewhat diminished to what it had been the night before. Lodren immediately went into a panic at not having prepared breakfast for everyone before they awoke. "I'm so terribly sorry!" he babbled, "I don't know what happened! I remember I was going to set some supper aside for Mr Emnor and then… well, nothing! I've never known anything like it! Mr Jared, can you forgive me? I promise it will never happen again."

Jared assured him that it had been no fault of his own and, after much persuasion, convinced him to sit with the others and listen to what he had to say. As he told them of the events of the previous night, they quickly found themselves fully awake as they listened intently.

"Bloomin' 'eck, Jared! Why didn't ye wake us up? We could've 'ad 'im!" growled Grubb.

"You weren't asleep, Grubb," said Emnor, "you were somehow enchanted, as were we all. Only two things can awaken you from a forced sleep. Either the caster has to reverse it or you have to wait for it to wear off."

"Well 'e could've at least tried," argued Grubb.

"You're not helping, Grubb. Please be quiet."

Grubb looked sheepishly at Faylore, "I… I was just sayin', Your Majesty," he mumbled, before adding in a whisper, "'e could've tried."

"It's no use worrying about it now," said Drake, loudly. "But… we could change what happens next."

"Come on then, clever clogs, you've obviously got something rattling around inside that mental head of yours. We can't see into the future… or do you possess a skill you haven't informed us of?" asked Hannock.

"We don't have to see into the future, Captain Crabby, Karrak has already told us what's going to happen," replied Drake, tersely. "He's going to send a messenger, he said that to you, right, Jared?"

Jared nodded, knowing where Drake's train of thought was headed.

"So," continued Drake, "we capture the messenger and find out where Karrak's hiding. If we're lucky, the messenger may even know what his plans are."

Hannock rubbed his hands together, "I like it!" he announced. "You're a devious little git, Drake, but I like it."

Emnor sat forward and peered at Jared, "Don't suppose he said when we should expect this messenger did he, or perhaps hinted at where he would appear?"

"Unfortunately not, Emnor. He was very cryptic. He emphasised that it would be peaceful, and hoped I would make the right decision."

"My word, Mr Jared, you have got him scared!" Lodren said suddenly as he hurried away. "See, I listened, but it's time for breakfast. I can't let you start the day hungry."

***

The days passed, days that soon turned into weeks. There had been no sign of a message from Karrak and some found this a blessed relief. Others took it as a sign that, if and when the message did arrive, it would undoubtedly bode ill for them all. Each day was as tedious as the last. They would rise at daybreak, eat breakfast, search until dusk, camp, eat supper and sleep.

One such day was drawing to a close and, as was a typical event, Emnor had fallen some distance behind his fellow travellers. Jared, as usual, slowed his pace in order to stay with him. Emnor was not ill, he'd never felt healthier, but something was missing. The loss of Yello told on him more and more as time went by and he was finding it difficult to focus on anything.

"How are you doing, barmpot?" Jared asked him with a smile.

"I'm fine, Jared! Stop fussing over me as if I were at death's door!" replied Emnor.

"Well why don't you keep pace with the others then? Every day you do exactly the same thing. I've watched you. You slow down just enough to allow them to get ahead, but you then match their pace easily."

"Can't an old man be left alone with his thoughts?" Emnor asked quietly.

"There are times when that would be ill advised," suggested Jared.

"Well, they get on your bloody nerves after a while!" chuntered Emnor. "Prattling on as if we hadn't a care in the world. And Drake! I swear I could throttle that boy some days!"

"He is a bit of an acquired taste, I'll give you that," Jared laughed. "But he means no harm, it's just his way of dealing with what he's witnessed. He's not like you and I, Emnor. We've seen and done things he could never comprehend, not yet anyway. It's simply the inexperience of youth."

"That's as the case may be, Jared, but to top it all, I still can't get this poxy staff to work. It's useless! I tried to perform a simple inferno spell with it a few days ago, you could barely see the wisp of smoke it produced, let alone the hint of a spark or flame!"

Jared became a little evasive, "Maybe it just needs time, you know, getting used to its new master."

"Cobblers!" exclaimed Emnor, "Get used to its new master indeed! You know better than that, I taught you better than that! Perhaps I should hand it to Drake! I swear that lad could blow anything up with a bag of feathers and an old broomstick given half a chance!"

"No!" Jared replied hurriedly. "You must not hand the staff to Drake!" Realising he had allowed an air of panic to overtake him, he tried to play down his response, "As you said, he can't take anything seriously. He doesn't have the control to handle a staff as powerful as that."

Emnor studied Jared through squinted eyes, "Out with it!" he demanded, "There's something you're not telling me, Jared. Come on, tell me, why wouldn't you want me to hand this staff to Drake? And I want the truth."

Jared rubbed his face with both hands and sighed. Before I begin, I want you to understand that, after careful consideration, I know that it was the only proper decision to be made and that's why I did what I did."

"So glad you came straight to the point, it's so annoying when people beat around the bush," Emnor said quietly, before raising his voice to a bellow. "WHAT DID YOU DO?"

"Drake has the entire knowledge that once belonged to Yello," Jared replied through gritted teeth. This was not said angrily, more… begrudgingly, realising how Emnor would react.

"HE HAS WHAT? JARED, HOW COULD YOU?" roared Emnor. "Knowledge and power of that magnitude could tear the boy apart! It could rip his very soul from his body! What were you thinking?"

Jared held his hands in front of him to repel Emnor's verbal attack. "Emnor, if I thought for one second that he would be harmed, in any way, I would never have considered it. The Heart of Ziniphar assured me that he was strong enough to receive it and that it was his destiny to become a wizard of legend."

"Have you gone mad? The Heart told you? That artefact is nothing more than an enhancement, Jared! It simply hones powers and only if the recipient allows it! There are few things as perilous."

"You're wrong, Emnor. The Heart is alive. It has its own sense of purpose, its own thoughts, beliefs and feelings," Jared argued. Suddenly, he frowned, "What was that about it being perilous?"

"What?" replied Emnor, raising his eyebrows and attempting to look innocent. "Oh, that! Nothing, it's not important, put it out of your mind."

"So, I'm not the only one who has made omissions when relaying information by the sound of things."

"A minor detail," Emnor assured him, patting him gently on the back. "A minor detail… or two," he added.

Jared peered at him, "You're a crafty old sod, has anyone ever told you that?" he grinned.

"Well… it may have been suggested in the past… a couple of… dozen times, perhaps."

Jared put his arm around his mentor's shoulders. "Shall we catch up?" he asked.

"Perhaps, shortly," replied Emnor. "First, tell me, what's the significance of the staff?"

"Ah yes, the staff," replied Jared. "It's the final link in the chain. Once that staff is handed to Drake, the chain will be completed. Everything that Yello knew, will begin to seep into Drake's mind. It'll take a couple of days," he tilted his head to the side, "… perhaps a week, but when the process is complete, Drake will possess the accumulated knowledge of your best friend."

Emnor had a look of dread on his face, "Will he have… his memories?" he asked, tentatively.

"No, of course not! It doesn't work like that, it's only his magical knowledge that will be transferred. Why do you ask?"

Emnor wiped away the few beads of sweat that had appeared on his brow, "Oh, no reason," he replied with a nervous laugh. "Just wondered, that's all," he added, turning his head and rolling his eyes in relief. "Let's pick up the pace," he urged. "They'll be setting camp shortly and Lodren will be livid if we're late for supper."

"We could catch up with them quite easily, Emnor, if you wanted to, of course," replied Jared.

"My legs work perfectly fine, thank you," he lied, craftily taking the opportunity to rest them momentarily. "One should never use magic simply because one can, Jared. That's the road to becoming fat and lazy." He paused, mulling over a question that seemed to be weighing heavily on his mind, "So, when do you think…" he held up Yello's staff, "we should hand this over to Drake?"

"Ooh, difficult question that one. I'm not sure, I thought perhaps a hundred years or so, give or take a decade or two," Jared laughed, "just to be on the safe side."

Emnor chuckled, "You're procrastinating, Jared. Most unlike you I must say. On a serious note, however, I think that sooner rather than later would be the best idea. I propose we give it to him tonight, after supper. We can all move away from the camp, lessens the risk to our other companions."

Jared shrugged his shoulders, "Tonight it is then," he agreed. Turning, he looked ahead and found that he could barely see the rest of their party as he and Emnor had fallen so far behind. "But right now, it's time to be fat and lazy." He placed his hand on Emnor's shoulder, and they both vanished.

***

"Why?" Drake asked, suspiciously. "Why do you want me to follow you away from a nice, well-lit, warm camp, into the dark ominous forest where who knows what could be watching us? There could be anything lurking in those trees, sizing us up for dinner."

"Oh, don't be so melodramatic, Drake," sighed Emnor. "Just do as we ask, there's a good fellow."

Drake's eyes widened, "I know what it is!" he exclaimed. "I've crossed the line again, haven't I? I've crossed the line and you've had enough! You're taking me into the forest so you can top me without the others seeing, aren't you? Look, you don't have to kill me. I'll leave right now, you'll never see me again, promise."

"Nobody wants to kill you," urged Jared. He pursed his lips, "Well, perhaps some days..." he admitted, "... but not today." With Emnor leading the way, Jared nudged Drake roughly, crooking his finger for Drake to follow.

A reasonable distance from the camp, Emnor and Jared lit torches and turned to face Drake, who was looking decidedly nervous.

Emnor looked him up and down, "Will you relax, boy," he instructed, "no-one's going to harm you," he assured him with a fake smile. "Well... it may sting a bit, but..."

"What Emnor is trying to say is that we're only here to give you something, Drake," said Jared, quick to interrupt. "That something, will benefit you greatly in the future."

"Yeah, a bloody good hiding no doubt! That's what all parents say to their kids when they're knocking the living daylights out of them, isn't it? I don't want to do this, but it's for your own good."

"I swear, if you don't shut your face that might…"

Jared interrupted Emnor for the second time, "We simply want to present you with this," he said, raising his voice slightly. He held out the staff.

Drake frowned, "Why?" he asked slowly. "That's Yello's staff. At least, it was. It belongs to Emnor now." He shook his head, "No, I can't, I can't take that, it's not right," he muttered, his voice beginning to crack as a solitary tear trickled down his cheek. "If I take that it'll mean… it'll mean he's not… coming back. I thought there might be a chance… you know… somehow."

Emnor lowered his head, "I hoped the same, Maddleton, I really did. But the only way he could return to us would involve the use of necromancy, a vile and despicable black magic that has been outlawed for centuries. All but the foulest of our kind would never condone its use. No, my friend, I'm afraid Yello is lost to us. We must be brave, for as long as we have our memories of him, he will never truly be gone."

Drake smiled unexpectedly, "He was a good old stick he was. I liked him a lot. How can anyone be as old as him but still act like a big kid?"

"Growing older is something that Yello could not prevent," smiled Emnor. "But the old sod fought tooth and nail against growing up."

"It's time," Jared said, offering the staff once more. He nodded at Drake, "Take it, he'd want you to have it."

Drake took a deep breath and stepped forward. Reaching out with both hands, he grasped the staff, closing his eyes and ducking slightly. Exactly what this was supposed to prevent his elders were unsure, but if it made him feel more comfortable, who were they to argue.

Drake opened one eye, the other still screwed tightly shut. Nothing happened, "Cor, that's a relief," he sighed, "I thought I might get blown up or frozen solid. I'm surprised though, I thought I might feel something. It's much lighter than it looks."

But Drake could not see what was happening behind him.

A blue mist was beginning to form, a mist that within seconds resembled a miniature storm cloud as it swirled and flashed. It began to take shape, appearing as a shrouded figure whose arms reached out to the young wizard briefly, before wrapping him in a macabre embrace.

Drake stopped talking, all expression leaving his face as he was lifted from the ground.

He dangled limply and remained silent for some time, the ghostly arms the only thing keeping him suspended in mid-air, but then he began to twitch.

It was quite amusing initially, Emnor and Jared watching as Drake's head flopped from one side to the other, not appearing dissimilar to someone who had dozed off in the back of a cart as it travelled down a bumpy road. But the amusement ceased as Drake began to convulse violently. He went rigid, as if he had been struck by lightning, his eyes growing wide as a look of terrified desperation swept across his face. His body thrashed around like a marionette controlled by an overzealous child, as his mouth opened and archaic spells unused for centuries spewed from his lips. The words were clear as was the voice that spoke them, it was Yello!

Emnor gasped and stepped forward but Jared grabbed his shoulder and dragged him back roughly. The old wizard could not be allowed to interfere.

They watched in horror as Drake's features changed, his skin contorting as if it were being kneaded by cruel, invisible fingers. Within seconds his face had changed. He was no longer the young man they had brought to the clearing, they were now looking upon the features of someone far older, Drake now wore Yello's face!

Emnor looked searchingly at Jared, hoping to find an explanation to calm the confusion in his mind. But the prince had no explanation to give. Looking back at Drake, he watched as his features became his own once more.

Only then did he notice the tempestuous winds and thunderous noise that had commenced with Drake's inexplicable transformation.

Emnor grabbed Jared, "WE MUST STOP THIS!" he bellowed. "IT'S KILLING HIM!"

Jared held his arms, "If we interfere, we might kill him," he shouted. "We have to wait!"

Without warning, Drake was suddenly thrown through the air, his limp body hitting the ground and tumbling over and over before coming to an abrupt halt at the foot of a tree.

The howling wind and flashes of light faded, and a serenity descended on the clearing, leaving them in inky blackness.

Jared and Emnor scrambled around, re-lighting the torches before rushing over to check on Drake. He lay motionless, eyes closed, but looking none the worse for wear.

Jared dropped to his knees and cradled the boy's head in his lap. Reaching for his belt, he ripped the waterskin from it and began to trickle some onto Drake's lips. His eyes still closed, the young man raised his hand to brush Jared away, "What are you trying to do, drown me?" he muttered. It was still Yello's voice that they could hear, but his tone soon changed to the lighter, smoother voice of Drake. "I have bathed this morning I'll have you know. Now tell me, what… erm… how am I on the… what the bloody hell did you do to me? I knew you were trying to kill me! Who threw me on the floor? Look at me, I'm filthy!"

Drake had survived, and all seemed well. However, unbeknownst to them all, they were being watched!

In the darkness, shrouded eyes flickered as they reflected the flames from the wizard's torches. Eyes furious at the peril in which Drake had seemingly just been placed.

Hannock's mind had been consumed of late with dark forebodings of what they were about to face. Jared seemed distant, they barely spoke to one another, and when they did, their conversations were always regarding Karrak and his deeds. He had begun to doubt his friend, and complete mistrust in Emnor was embedded in his darkest thoughts.

For some reason Hannock had taken to Drake, regarding him as the son he had never had. The wizard's decision to place the boy in danger did not sit well with him. He must be the one to protect Drake, it seemed.

Gritting his teeth and with one last glance, he backed away into the shadows, convinced that he had remained unseen.

But he was wrong!

High above him, two figures watched suspiciously.

"Well, what do you make of that then?" whispered Poom.

"It's obvious, isn't it?" replied Lawton.

"Go on then, clever clogs. What's obvious?" Poom asked.

"They're teaching the boy some kind of new magic they think he might find useful," Lawton snorted.

"No, I mean old one-eye. Why is he spying on them?"

"You know what Hannock's like, he always wants to know what's going on. It's the soldier in him, he's always sticking his nose into other people's business."

"Really?" chuckled Poom. "That's the best you can come up with? He's nosy."

"Well what else could it be?"

"Far worse than that. He doesn't trust 'em! And to be honest, I can understand why. All the sneaking about and hushed conversations, it'd make anyone suspicious."

"Whatever it is, it's none of our business. We're here for one simple reason, your favourite reason, we're here for a scrap. Come on, let's get back to camp."

CHAPTER 14

The companions began to look differently upon Drake. He was acting… strangely. Most of the time he was his usual carefree self, but occasionally he would say the most profound and intelligent things, things that were quite unlike him. This in itself was not alarming. His change of voice, however, was. It elicited different responses from various members; Grubb thought it was hilarious and would roll about laughing, begging for him to do it again; Emnor, understandably, found it a little upsetting; Faylore found it tiresome; but Lodren didn't like it at all. He would yelp as if he had been scalded and hide behind the nearest tree, that's if he didn't disappear into the woods completely. Luckily for Lodren, someone always volunteered to retrieve him.

One such occurrence had taken place just after breakfast one morning, but as everything was packed, and they were ready to leave anyway, they all followed him.

"Oh well," laughed Emnor, "at least he's fleeing in the right direction."

They caught up with him much sooner than they had expected. He was crouching behind a tree and turned to face them as they approached. He held his finger up to his lips, "Keep the noise down," he hissed, pointing frantically ahead of them. "Bears," he added, "loads of them."

Hannock marched forward, drawing his sword, "You just cower there, Lodren and protect that tree. I'll make the nasty bears go away," he sniggered.

"You don't have to say it like that," pouted Lodren. "And anyway, you won't get them all before they have you for breakfast, there are far too many of them. It looks like there's a pack of wolves with them as well!"

"Of course there is," chuckled Hannock, "and a couple of unicorns, and a dragon just for good measure."

"Don't make fun of me, Mr Hannock," snapped Lodren, frowning, "I know what I saw! There's at least ten bears and two wolves for definite."

Hannock craned his neck, perhaps he should give the Nibby the benefit of the doubt. Sure enough, he saw movement up ahead. Lodren was right, it was a bear! No… wait, two bears, three, four, five. He backed away. "He's bloody right you know!" he sighed. "They're everywhere. I can't see any wolves but there are definitely half a dozen bears or more."

"We'll have to retrace our steps and go around them," suggested Lodren.

"What!" protested Grubb, "I could bag at least three of 'em an' the wizards can kill the rest with their magic. It won't take five minutes."

"We are not going to kill any of them!" snapped Lodren. "They have more right to be here than we do! We go around them, alright?" he added, gripping his hammer a little tighter as he glared at Grubb.

"Alright, alright!" replied Grubb, his voice getting a little higher. "I was only kiddin', we'll go around 'em if it keeps you 'appy."

Their discovery of the bears added at least five miles onto their journey, but Lodren would not hear of them risking a second encounter, insisting that they were the ones who shouldn't really be there.

Despite their detour, it seemed that they had in fact been quite fortunate. Within minutes they found a well-worn track, allowing them much swifter progress. Winding their way through the forest was actually quite pleasant and the daylight even seemed a little brighter than it had been of late.

"'ere, Lodren," called Grubb, "Got anythin' I can munch on? I'm a bit 'ungry."

"Just be patient," said Hannock. "There's a clearing up ahead. We'll take a break there."

"Okay," Grubb sighed. "I suppose I can wait."

As they approached the clearing, there was much rustling of branches within the thickets beyond. They paused, weapons drawn, fearing the worst. The branches of a hedgerow parted, and through them, came the first bear. It glanced at them, tilting its head to one side. Looking completely disinterested, it stretched out and tumbled onto its side. It was quickly, well, comparatively quickly, followed by another, and another, and another, until their path was blocked by twenty or more very large bears. Each bear was as relaxed as the next as they lay there stretching and scratching themselves, but one had decided to approach them. It stopped a few yards ahead of them and sat down. Wrapping its arms across its chest it looked at them in turn, and almost appeared to be smiling.

Grubb's sudden outburst startled everyone but the bear, "Ignore 'em," he yelled. "Just ignore 'em. Don't make eye contact, just walk past 'em as if they weren't even there. We don't need their sort taggin' along with us. Come on, follow me." Grabbing Buster's reins, he proceeded to march ahead.

"Grubb get back here!" urged Lodren, "They're bears, if you startle them they might attack you."

Grubb was now standing next to the bear that had sat before them. Curling his lip, he looked it up and down, "No," he said slowly, "they're somethin' far more dangerous. Trust me you lot, just follow me and ignore 'em. You'll regret it if ye don't."

"What are you on about?" exclaimed Drake. "We're not blind, Grubb, they're bears! Admittedly, they're very strangely behaved bears, but they're bears nonetheless."

The bear turned and stared, wide-eyed at Drake, "You'll have to forgive him," it growled, "manners never were his strong suit."

***

The companions stood there open-mouthed, aghast at what they had just heard. Lodren began tugging at Jared's sleeve, "Mr Jared, that bear just spoke!" he exclaimed. "Did you hear me? It's a talking bear!"

Grubb looked back at him, "No it ain't," he groaned.

"I'm not deaf, Grubb!" shrieked Lodren, "I know what I heard, he was talking."

"Yes, he was talking, true enough. But 'e ain't no bear!"

Lodren looked puzzled, "Of course it is… I mean, he is. I'm not blind either."

Faylore smiled, "He's one of your kin, isn't he, Grubb?"

Grubb sighed, "Yeah, he's one o' my cousins. This is Lorzic," he announced.

The bear smiled, at least it appeared to be a smile, "Nice to meet you all," he said quietly. "Despite my cousin's disapproval of our meeting."

"But why are you all disguised as bears?" asked Lodren as politely as possible.

"It's what they always do," barked Grubb. "When they're scared of somethin' that is. Bunch o' lily-livered…"

"Grubb! Don't be rude," snapped Faylore.

"It's the truth, it's what they've always done! They make 'emselves look as big as possible to scare anybody as might want to hurt 'em, and bears is the best they can do."

As he said it, a pack of wolves began to creep out from behind the trees and headed straight toward the bears.

"Oh," added Grubb, "I forgot about the kids. Wolves is the best they can manage."

"So all the bears are adults, and the wolves are all their children?" asked Drake, flabbergasted.

"Yeah… 'orrible ain't it," replied Grubb, shuddering at the thought.

Jared stepped forward, "So if this is a defence mechanism, what was it that you were defending yourselves from?" he asked slowly.

"No offence, Mr…?"

“Dunbar,” interjected Hannock, “Prince Jared Dunbar.”

Lorzic rubbed his head, “Ooh my word,” he sighed. “Forgive me, Your Highness, only… you don’t appear to be at your best… not exactly… regal,” he continued nervously, pointing at Jared’s worn apparel and tarnished armour.

“Watch your tongue,” snapped Hannock, “I may be forced to cut it out for you, as a bear or whatever else you care to turn into.”

“Don’t worry, Hannock,” called Grubb, “’e ain’t bein’ disrespectful… ’e’s just a bit thick in the head.”

“I’m the mayor, Grubb. You can’t say things like that about me,” protested Lorzic.

“You’re forgetting somethin’, Lorzic. I don’t live in your poxy village anymore, and furthermore, we ain’t even in it!”

Lorzic seemed a little flustered, “No, sadly not,” he said softly. “But we hope to get back there one day.”

“Something drove you out of your own village?” asked Drake. “What could possibly drive a complete township from…” He paused, “I think we need to sit down and discuss this.”

Grubb fell to his knees and began pleading with Jared, “Please,” he begged, “don’t get involved. They’ll be fine out here, no-one will bother ‘em. Trust me, Jared, they’ll drive ye mental within a week. They’re all nuts! Let’s just go.”

As they all settled at the treeline, the Vikkery began to transform. It appeared that there were more females than males, which was obvious by their lack of horns.

But the children, the children were adorable. Their tiny faces were covered with downy hair, and they were constantly giggling as they chased one another around. Even Hannock smiled at one point.

Lorzic and two other Vikkery huddled together with the companions so that their conversation would not scare the youngsters.

“Let me guess,” whispered Jared, “A shadow lord, no real face just features present in black smoke.”

Lorzic, now as himself, smiled, “Who’s that then?” he asked.

“The shadow lord, the one who drove you out of your village,” replied Jared.

Lorzic frowned and shuffled closer to Jared, “Have you been drinking?” he asked, seeming genuinely concerned. “Don’t get me wrong, there’s nothing wrong with the occasional tipple, but you have to be careful. It’s barely midday and if you feel you need a bit of something to get you through the day, well… just saying.”

Jared was speechless and sat there agog at Lorzic’s suggestion. “No, I have not been drinking!” he protested.

“See?” mumbled Grubb, “I warned ye… mental within a week.”

“Prince Jared merely thought that your problem may be the same as ours,” suggested Emnor.

“Oh no sir, definitely not,” replied Lorzic shaking his head vigorously, I don’t drink at all.”

“That’s not what I meant,” urged Emnor.

"I'm not condemning you," Lorzic re-assured him. "We're all different. Just letting you know I'm here if you ever need someone to confide in. Don't worry, your secret's safe with me."

"But I don't have a drinking problem!" hissed Jared, trying to keep his temper in check.

"That's it, my boy, keep telling yourself that and eventually it'll become fact," smiled Lorzic.

Grubb was sucking in his cheeks and biting his lower lip, "I've got to feed Buster," he squeaked, and dashed off, Lodren in hot pursuit.

Out of earshot, Grubb roared with laughter. Through his tears of joy, he saw Lodren chasing after him, "Did ye hear that?" he asked, barely able to breathe.

"Well I'm glad you think it's funny!" Lodren replied, glaring at him. "Jared's taken to drink, and you think it's hilarious."

Grubb paused in disbelief as he looked at Lodren, then fell to pieces again.

"Grubb, stop it! What if Jared's in danger and doesn't realise it because he's squiffy?"

Grubb wiped the tears from his face with his sleeve, "Don't be so daft," he shouted, "There's nothin' wrong with 'im! Can't ye see? This is what most Vikkery are like. They get an idea in their heads and straight away, they believe it! Go on, test it. Go an' 'ave a chat with one of 'em, I dare ye. It only took 'alf a minute before Jared was ready to strangle Lorzic, but you're far more patient. I'd say that you could stand the full minute before ye squashed someone's head with that hammer o' yours."

"Well, if they're all that daft, how do they ever get anything done?"

"Oh, they're not daft with everythin', you'll find that out soon enough. It was the look on Hannock's face that got me though, I just 'ad to move away. What a picture!"

"So, we're going back to them then?" asked Lodren, dubiously.

"Too bloody right!" replied Grubb with glee, "I ain't 'ad this much fun for ages."

After quickly feeding Buster, his excuse to dash off not being a complete untruth, Grubb and Lodren re-joined the others.

"What did he look like?" Emnor asked Lorzic.

"He was really weird looking," Lorzic replied. "Young, pale skin, bony gangly arms and legs. You know… ugly, straggly hair. Looked like him, actually," Lorzic pointed at Drake. "Well, he looked a lot like all of you really. Apart from you," he added, pointing at Emnor, "He wasn't quite as ugly as you, not wrinkled, no horrible matted, smelly beard."

Drake blinked slowly, "Tell me, Lorzic," he enquired, "do you make friends easily?" He made no attempt to hide his sarcastic tone.

"Strange that you should mention that, young man," replied Lorzic, with a smile. "Yes, I do actually. Then again, with good looks like mine it's hardly surprising."

Grubb was sucking in his cheeks again.

"This… ugly youngster, did he speak to you?" asked Hannock.

"Oh yes, he was very polite in fact, until he started threatening to roast my people alive. That's when I started going off him."

"Funny how the threat of incineration can turn you off a person," grinned Hannock.

"But you say he wasn't alone?" asked Emnor, trying to regain a little focus.

Lorzic pretended to wretch, "No, he had those horrible snake things with him."

"Snake things?" enquired Emnor.

"Big heads like snakes, slid around like them too. Blowing dart-things at stuff and melting it."

Jared passed knowing glances with the other companions. "Why did they attack you?" he asked.

"Said he wanted us to work for him, but we didn't like the terms, so we told him we weren't interested. That's when it all turned nasty."

"What did you do next?" asked Faylore.

The Vikkery directly behind Lorzic sat bolt upright and puffed out his chest. "We did what any sensible Vikkery would do," he announced. "We scarpered."

"Didn't you try to defend your village?" asked Faylore. "Surely there were more of you than there were of them?"

"Probably the case, Faylore," suggested Grubb. "But they ain't the kind o' numbers a true Vikkery cares about, are they Lorzic?"

Lorzic looked more uncomfortable with Grubb's question than he had with any other, "The village was no longer worth defending, Grubb. Those snake things had already taken the amulet, the helm and the hammer. There was no point, I tell you! The sacred relics had been stolen, would you have us all lose our lives as well?"

"No…" Grubb replied slowly, "… but at least ye could've put up a bit of a fight."

"Do you have any idea where they went, Lorzic?" asked Faylore. "We are searching for someone and they may know where he is."

"I don't know where the young one went…" Lorzic took a deep breath, "… but I do know where those snake things headed off to."

"Where?" asked Grubb with a stern look on his face.

Lorzic glanced up, fear in his eyes, "Mallorkan caverns," he replied. "They went into Mallorkan caverns. A couple of us followed them. We thought they might stop somewhere along the road, so we could slip into their camp and get the relics back. They never even paused, they headed straight in and haven't been seen since."

"These relics you speak of, Lorzic, do they possess some type of power?" asked Emnor, far more interested in the conversation since they were mentioned.

"Oh, that they do!" laughed Grubb, "Well… a power this lot can't resist anyway."

"And what exactly is the secret that they hold?" asked Drake, his voice once again not sounding like his own.

Lodren immediately disappeared behind Jared, "He's doing it again, Mr Jared! Tell him to stop doing it, please tell him to stop doing it," he implored.

Drake frowned, "Doing what?" he asked, completely oblivious to the changes in his voice.

Jared ignored Lodren, "You were saying, Grubb?"

"The only power that could ever influence a true Vikkery," replied Grubb, "... greed!"

Hannock was becoming impatient, "Well get on with it," he sighed.

"The relics have been in the main village hall for centuries. They've been there so long that nobody even remembers where they came from. We Vikkery are not very good at keeping tomes and scrolls like Faylore's people, but we do know when something's valuable. You see, the relics are made from pure silver and gold. A king's ransom wouldn't be enough to buy 'em."

Jared drummed his fingers on his knee. Leaning forwards, he looked Lorzic dead in the eye, "Perhaps we could be of some help to one another," he suggested.

Lorzic shrugged his shoulders, "I know we could be of some help to you, Prince Jared," he smiled. "We could help you with your drinking problem for a start, but how could you possibly help us? And what's more, what sort of remuneration would we be talking, gold or barter?"

"I do not have a..." Jared paused and took a deep breath. "What I'm suggesting, is that we could retrieve your priceless relics for you if, in turn, you could do something for us."

Lorzic eyed him suspiciously, "What sort of thing? It wouldn't be anything... dangerous, would it?"

"No Jared, please don't," pleaded Grubb yet again. "These lot think getting out of the tub is too dangerous to do by yourself. Always best to have someone to hold yer 'and in case ye slip."

Jared rolled his eyes.

"Well one can't be too careful," said Lorzic. "Many accidents take place in the home you know."

"See! And you probably thought I was making that up," exclaimed Grubb.

Lorzic turned to face Grubb, "I know you've always been unhappy with the way you are, Grubb. Who and what you chose to be are your own affair. But, those of us without psychological problems and a very short temper are apt to tread far more carefully as we make our way through life. And, we don't squash our cousin's heads."

"Now you listen 'ere you pompous old git…" bawled Grubb, "… just 'cause I don't change into normal beasts as boring as you do, doesn't mean there's somethin' wrong with me. And I haven't got a short temper neither, I didn't mean to squash 'im, but at least it ended the feud!"

"And that's why we reversed the judgement and said you could stay, but you wouldn't! I still say you should have taken your father's advice and joined the family business. You could have remained with the ones you love instead of going off into the wilds to live as a hermit. I mean, healing sick animals and people, where's the profit in that?"

Grubb suddenly became very calm, "That's it with you, isn't it? It's all down to coin! If it doesn't pay, don't do it. Well I've got news for ye, this…" he said pointing at his friends, "… is what life is really about. Having people around ye that ye care for, and care about you.

People you'd give yer life for and would put their lives at risk to protect you. I'll tell ye something, Lorzic, I'm richer than you'll ever be. I wouldn't give one moment of my time with any o' my friends for a hundred times what those relics o' yours are worth." He turned his back and began to walk away, "Good luck findin' 'em," he called, "'cause you'll get no 'elp from me."

Lorzic raised his eyebrows, "See what I mean?" he sighed, "Totally unstable."

Lodren was shaking with rage. Storming forward, he grabbed Lorzic and hoisted him into the air with one hand, "You…" he hissed, "… are the most unpleasant and the rudest person I have ever met. If there weren't ladies present, I assure you I would tell you exactly what I thought of you. Grubb is my best friend, and nobody talks to him like that. Do you understand?"

Lorzic nodded frantically.

"Now you go after him and apologise. When you come back, and I'll just add that if Grubb's not with you, don't bother coming back, we'll have a civil discussion on how we can help one another. Am I making myself quite clear, you nasty little Vikkery?"

Lorzic nodded again.

"Good," said Lodren, forcing a smile as he lowered Lorzic to the ground. "We'll see you shortly then. Pardon the pun." He tugged down his tunic, a habit he had picked up from Hannock, and sat back down.

"Impressive," said Hannock with admiration. "Ever thought of becoming a diplomat?"

The companions watched as Lorzic ran as fast as his short legs could carry him, in pursuit of Grubb.

"I wonder what it was?" asked Drake, curiously.

"What what was?" replied Hannock.

"Lorzic said that Grubb should have joined the family business. Just wondering what sort of business it was."

"Something to do with making money, I suppose. You heard what Grubb said, the Vikkery are obsessed with anything that earns coin."

"Perhaps that's why he doesn't like shiny things. That's why he chose Buster when King Tamor offered him a reward," suggested Lodren.

"I'll ask him when he comes back."

"You'll do no such thing, Mr Hannock!" exclaimed Lodren. "It's to do with his family, and that's private."

"Speaking of family, Jared," said Hannock, "When are we going to rescue His Majesty? I'm not happy with him being trapped as he is."

"Neither am I, Hannock. But we know that he's safe, for now at least. I'm just a little concerned as to how we're going to bring him out of the enchantment. You know, with Yello…" his voice tailed off.

"Don't worry yourself about that, dear boy. It'll only take five minutes once we get back to Reiggan."

Lodren's eyes grew wide as he stared sideways at Drake, "Mr Jared…"

Drake looked up, realising how quiet it had gone, "What?"

***

It didn't take long for Grubb to calm down. He and Lorzic re-joined the companions, although Grubb still didn't seem to be completely happy. Lorzic on the other hand wore a smile that would suggest that nothing untoward had taken place.

"Everything alright?" asked Hannock, an air of humour apparent in his voice.

"Fine, why shouldn't it be?" asked Lorzic, oblivious.

Closing his eyes and shaking his head slightly, Jared spoke to Lorzic, "We have decided that the first thing we should do is escort you all back to your village."

"Why would you want to do that?" asked Lorzic, curling his lip.

"So that you can return safely to your own homes," replied Jared.

"What homes?" asked Lorzic.

"Your homes of course! Your homes in your village." He's so infuriating, thought Jared.

Lorzic laughed, "What's the point in that? There's nothing left now. It's all flat. It would cost far too much to rebuild it, we may as well start afresh somewhere new, somewhere safer."

Grubb frowned, "What do ye mean, there's nothin' left?"

"Well..." replied Lorzic, "... as we were leaving..."

"Ye mean, as ye were running away, don't ye?"

"Alright, Grubb," replied Lorzic. "As we were fleeing for our lives... a few of us looked back. We could see the buildings being torn to pieces! Whole roofs were being thrown as if they were paper and walls were being smashed until they were nought but pebbles flying through the air."

"But the hissthaar, that's what those snake-like beings are by the way, don't have the strength to smash buildings like that!" exclaimed Drake. "They can melt things with those poison darts they use, but not throw a roof off a building."

"Maybe they've made friends with their new neighbours in Mallorkan caverns," suggested Grubb.

Hannock sighed loudly and dropped his chin to his chest, "Go on then, what lives in the caverns?" he asked, slowly.

"Zingaard," mumbled Grubb.

"A zingaard, is that it?" laughed Drake. "Are you forgetting what Lodren did to the first you told me about?"

"No, I'm not!" growled Grubb. "And I ain't forgettin' what it did to Queen Faylore neither."

Faylore hurried to him. Leaning down, she gave him a huge hug, "Oh, you big sweetie, how lovely of you," she cooed.

"Alright, alright," protested Grubb, "Stop makin' a fuss," he moaned, trying unsuccessfully to pry her arms from around him, "And I didn't say a zingaard, I said zingaard."

"So, you think there are more than one in there?" asked Emnor.

Grubb laughed, "I don't think, Emnor. I know. Mallorkan caverns is… well… how can I put this?" he blushed, turning his head so as not to make eye contact with Faylore. "It's erm… oh dear. It's their… erm, breeding ground," he mumbled.

"What!" shouted Hannock. "You mean there are loads of those hairy, smelly, ferocious beasts in there, and they're looking for a date?"

"Not quite," replied Lorzic, "they're looking for a mate."

Hannock stared wide-eyed at Jared, "And you're suggesting that we go in there to retrieve a couple of bits of old tat that they want back simply because it's made of gold?"

Jared smiled nervously at Lorzic before grabbing Hannock's arm and marching him away from the others, "No…" he whispered, "I'm suggesting that we rescue a few bits of old tat so that we can get them to trust us and make them our allies."

"What use would they be? They're scared of their own shadows for goodness sake. They aren't like Grubb! He'd fight half a dozen of those horrible hairys by himself if he had to, but this lot would scarper if you showed them a picture!" Hannock placed his hands on his hips, sighed and tapped his foot on the ground, "If they aren't prepared to fight, what could we use them for?" he asked, patiently.

"They could be our spies," replied Jared. "Imagine. Any agents of Karrak would ignore a bear or a wolf if they saw one. They could get into places virtually unnoticed and eavesdrop on conversations. They could inform us of anything they think might be of help to us quicker than any other messenger, by turning into a bird and flying to us, wherever we are."

Hannock raised his eyebrows and nodded, “Could prove useful, I suppose. Now all you have to do is convince Lorzic.” He smiled and slapped Jared on the shoulder. Gesturing to the others, he gave a slight bow, “After you, Your Highness.”

“How many zingaard are we talking about, Grubb?” Jared asked as he approached.

“I’d say at least a couple…”

“A couple?” laughed Drake, “No problem, we’ll wipe them out before they even know we’re there.”

“I hadn’t finished,” said Grubb, giving Drake a disdainful glance, “A couple of dozen, at least.”

Drake gulped, “Couple of dozen! How the hell are we supposed to get past that lot? And there’s the hissthaar to consider! Jared, it’d be suicide!”

Jared gave the young wizard a stern look, “We’d better have a really good plan then, hadn’t we? Because, like it or not, we’re going to get those relics back for Lorzic.”

Lorzic’s smile grew wider than ever as he nudged Grubb, “Very brave, your friends, aren’t they!” He paused, “Or, of course, they could just be terribly stupid.”

***

Jared had convinced Lorzic that checking on the condition of the village was a good idea and, as they made their way toward it, Lodren’s head was full of screaming questions. However, he managed to contain himself long enough to begin his probing politely, "You never mentioned your village to us in all the time we've known each other, Grubb. What's it called?"

Grubb sighed. He had left behind all that he was ashamed of, barely giving distant memories a thought. He knew that Lodren's insatiable appetite for other people's business would not be easily sated and resigned himself to the inquisition that was about to commence, "Pellandrin," he groaned.

"Ooh, what a lovely name!" exclaimed Lodren, "Is it named after anyone?"

"Probably," mumbled Grubb. "But before ye go on, I have no idea who it was!"

"Is it a big village?" persisted Lodren.

"Not any more, I don't think!" said Lorzic from behind him. "Not from what we witnessed anyway."

"Oh, dear. That doesn't sound promising," sighed Lodren.

"No, it doesn't," one of the Vikkery agreed. "It sounds expensive!"

Grubb rolled his eyes, "Well at least you're alive to worry about yer precious coin, ye should be grateful for that at least."

As they approached Pellandrin, the true devastation became apparent. Before they actually reached it, they could see the black smoke billowing into the air and blocking out what little daylight there was.

"I told you it was going to be expensive," groaned the Vikkery.

They entered what little remained of the village. Not a single building was left standing. The footings of a few corners were dotted around where they had been, but nothing was left intact. The entire village had been razed to the ground.

Many of the Vikkery could be heard sobbing, tears rolled down their tiny cheeks as they surveyed the wreckage of their lives. However, on the faces of the companions, only rage could be seen.

Lorzic suddenly went into a panic, “Oh, no… no, no, no, the bank!” he exclaimed, running toward the centre of the debris-filled landscape. “The gold!” he added, as he began to dig frantically where a building had obviously stood.

Many of the male Vikkery ran to join him in his efforts, the dust from their digging almost as choking as the black smoke that poured from smouldering timbers around them.

“Never mind yer poxy gold!” bellowed Grubb, “It’s not safe here, Lorzic! We have to go!”

Lorzic stood and turned to face him, a look of dread on his face, “Go? Go where? We have nothing, Grubb. How can we make a home elsewhere? How do we pay for it? Nobody will want us. We’ll be outcasts, beggars, vagabonds to be mocked and ridiculed. We may as well wait here and hope that our enemies return, at least we shall die with our dignity intact,” he said mournfully.

Grubb began to shake with rage. He tried to control himself, tried with all his might to remain calm, but it was no use. His transformation came upon him even before he could think of what he was to become. His arms thickened, as did his legs. His fingers fused together and became huge, scaled claws. His face stretched outwards, his tiny horns elongating, huge teeth sprouting from his jaws. He arched his back as massive leathery wings sprouted from it. He opened his mouth and roared, flames mingling with his bellowed words, "None of my kin will die today."

Everyone stopped what they were doing and stared in awe at what stood before them.

Grubb had transformed into a dragon.

The reactions of the onlookers were mixed, to say the least. The children bounced up and down with glee. Admittedly Grubb wasn't as large as a real dragon, but he had grown to around twenty feet in height and that was more than enough to impress them. The adult Vikkery however, responded quite differently. Their disapproval was apparent, and they made no attempt to hide their head shaking, tutting and frowns.

Lorzic scowled at Grubb's transformation and began yelling at him, "Grubb!" he screamed loudly, "How could you? Of all the things… and you, you choose this? I swear, if your mother and father were here, they'd be ashamed! They'd disown you! To turn into the very thing that…" his voice tailed off. Turning away and seeming much calmer, he began to usher the children away, "Come on now, don't look at it," he urged. "Nasty things they are, if ever you see a real one, hide as quickly as you can before it chases you down and eats you."

The companions were at a loss. Not only did they not understand why the Vikkery had reacted the way they did, they were completely confused by Lorzic's statement that dragons were nasty man-eaters.

Lodren gazed up at his friend, "You look fantastic!" he exclaimed, "Just like a real dragon. A bit shorter, I must say, but every bit as magnificent." He frowned, "Why did Lorzic say that dragons eat people?"

The rest of the companions were relieved that, in his innocent child-like way, he had been able to ask the very question to which they all wanted an answer.

Grubb began to shrink, the flubbering sound of his quivering skin amusing his friends. He now stood before them at his normal height, shaking his head. "Ah, ye don't want to take any notice o' what 'e said. Mad as a fremble 'e is! That lot 'ave been on about dragons for years, and not one of 'em 'as ever even seen one!"

"But they must have the idea in their heads for a reason, Grubb," suggested Faylore. "Grubb…" she asked slowly, "… is there something you're not telling us?"

"O' course not!" snapped Grubb, "I don't know what that wally-head is on about, why would I keep secrets from you?"

"So why would he think your parents would be ashamed of you transforming into a dragon?" asked Drake. "It really seemed to hit a raw nerve with the rest of the Vikkery, alright, not the kids, but the adults didn't seem too happy about it."

"Now you keep yer nose out, Drake!" Grubb answered, angrily, "I don't go pokin' my nose into your family, do I? I'll thank you not to involve yourself with mine!"

Drake held his hands up, "Alright, I get it! Sorry, just wondering, that's all."

"Well next time wander off a cliff, ye nosy git!"

Faylore put her arm around Grubb, "Come on Mr Grumpy, cheer up, what's done is done. We still need to help Jared. And that means all of us, you especially."

Jared smiled at the Vikkery as he tried to free himself from Faylore's grasp, "Are you up for a bit of cavern exploring, Grubb? Come on, it'll be just like old times."

Grubb had never been able to resist delving into any cave or cavern. With a mischievous grin, he ran over to Buster and started to gather what he thought he might need.

"So we're going now?" asked Drake, nervously, "I mean, right now?"

"What's the matter, young 'un?" laughed Grubb, "Do ye think we should wait until the sun comes out so we can see where we're goin' in the caves?"

"Shut your face," mumbled Drake.

CHAPTER 15

It would take them at least two days to reach Mallorkan caverns. Leaving the other villagers to fend for themselves, Lorzic had set off with the companions. Grubb was not the only one who did not relish the thought of his prolonged, solitary company. Whilst his kin were around there were always distractions that took him away from them, but they knew that there would be no relief from his judgemental attitude for at least the next four days, and that alone seemed more daunting than facing an entire cavern full of zingaard.

Not surprisingly each companion was given a reason to glare at him as they travelled, but Grubb was the only one who wondered whether any of his kin would be at all concerned if, by accident, he was eaten by one of the zingaard.

It took a little longer than expected to reach Mallorkan. On the morning of the third day, they approached the entrance to the ominous-looking caverns. Moving stealthily, they were watchful for the slightest movement. Whispered plans passed between them, but the companions were quite taken aback when Lorzic announced that he would be going with them.

They were far less surprised however, when Grubb explained why, "It's only 'cos he thinks we might steal the relics for ourselves!"

The heat as they entered the mouth of Mallorkan caverns surprised them all, however the rancid, foul stench that was carried on the warm air soon made them forget it.

"By all wars…" hissed Hannock, grabbing his nose, "… I don't remember it being this bad the first time!"

"That's because there was only one zingaard the first time," whispered Jared, "There's a whole pack of them down here, and I don't suppose the hissthaar will smell too sweet when you get up close either."

"I have no intention of getting up close," replied Hannock, "That's why I have this," he added, holding up his crossbow.

Faylore leaned on their shoulders, "Wait here…" she advised, "… I'll scout ahead."

Lodren grabbed her hand, "You just be careful, Your Majesty," he urged, "We don't want a repeat of last time." He vaguely saw her nodding in the dim light before she disappeared.

They could do nothing else now but wait. Emnor glanced around, studying the walls of the cavern, "This is the same moss that we've seen too many times before," he whispered, peering at the spores.

"Bennemfud," whispered Lorzic.

"Sorry, what?" asked Emnor.

"The fungus on the walls, it's called bennemfud. We use it inside our houses, put it in the children's rooms so they aren't in complete darkness at night."

"How fascinating!" exclaimed Lodren. "How come you never told us about that, Grubb?"

Grubb scowled, although nobody could see, "I don't know, I just didn't," he chuntered.

"I don't know if you lot have forgotten…" hissed Hannock, "… but we're in the lair of two of the most dangerous species we've ever encountered! So, if you don't mind, will you shut up and save your bloody botany lesson for another time!"

It was silent for the next few minutes, but a sudden sound made Jared's ear twitch. Faint at first, but getting louder, Jared could hear rasping breath as something unidentified approached. They cowered as low as they could. To be discovered before their mission had even begun would be disastrous. A silhouette grew nearer, the light from the bennemfud revealing its large, hooded head. It was undoubtedly a hissthaar. Jared slowly reached for the hilt of his sword. Yes, his staff would destroy the beast in an instant, but it would also alert others nearby of their presence. Hannock had also seen it and raised his crossbow. Caught completely off guard, it recoiled, alarmed by its discovery. Its claws reached for the blue leather belt around its body, but it made no sound. Before Jared had drawn his sword or Hannock had even had time to pull the trigger, there was a sharp crack followed by a gruesome squelching noise. The hissthaar's arms dropped and its body went limp. The scraping noise of the blade as it left the hissthaar's skull was almost melodic as it hummed in the darkness. Placing her foot against its back, Faylore pushed the carcass away. "I suggest…" she said quietly, "… that from now on, we keep volume to a minimum. Follow me, we're leaving… now."

Departing the cavern, Faylore spoke openly, "I have no idea what has happened in there," she began, "Getting your relics back, Lorzic, is going to be far easier than we thought."

"Oh, happy days!" exclaimed Grubb, "We still might be ripped to shreds but at least ye get your trinkets back!"

"Not exactly," said Faylore, "I did say easier, not easy."

"What, there aren't as many as we thought there would be?" asked Lodren, hopefully.

"Well, to be fair, there are probably far more than we anticipated," she replied, "The thing that makes the difference is that they are all caged!"

"Caged!" cried Lorzic, "That's wonderful news, I'll just go and fetch the relics then. I won't be needing your help after all. That means there'll be no need for me to compensate you."

"See what I mean!" exclaimed Grubb, "All 'e cares about is that 'e ain't got to pay anyone! Go on then, in ye go! Go and fetch your flamin' relics, I 'ope there's still somethin' left in there that eats ye!"

"Oh, there is," said Faylore, "Hissthaar, fifty or more I'd estimate."

"But you, you said it wasn't dangerous!"

"No, Lorzic, I said no such thing. Weren't you listening?"

Lorzic flopped to the ground, "That's it then," he moaned, "All hope is lost! Our last chance to retrieve the only thing that could save us has gone. We could have secured a loan, begun rebuilding our homes using the artefacts as collateral and worked off our debt somehow. But alas, it seems the fates are against us once more."

"Oh, do be quiet!" exclaimed Faylore, "I grow tired of your incessant whining, you horrible little beast." It seemed that even Faylore's patience had a limit. Unfortunately for Lorzic, it had just been reached.

"Well that's not very nice, is it?" protested Lorzic, "Who are you calling a beast?"

"Enough!" ordered Jared. "This isn't helping. Faylore, do you have a plan?"

Faylore glanced at Lorzic and shook her head in disbelief, "As a matter of fact, I do," she replied. "Only, why we are prepared to put ourselves in danger for this nasty…"

"Can we just hear the plan?"

Faylore turned her attention to Jared, "We're going back in, but before we do, I need you all to keep an open mind."

There were questioning looks from all of the companions. Hannock, as always, needed to know more, "We're not going to like this plan of yours, are we?" he asked, "Come on, out with it."

"It will be far easier to show you," she suggested.

"Ladies first," chuckled Grubb, bowing and gesturing toward the cavern.

***

Once inside, they allowed their eyesight to adjust to the dim light once more. Faylore assured them that they would be quite safe for some time, but still advised that they should take care and move as stealthily as possible.

The illumination allowed them to avoid the obvious perils of venturing through unknown caves. Jagged edges and small crevices in which one could easily turn an ankle could be seen quite clearly once their eyes became accustomed to the pale glow of the bennemfud. They had seen it many times now, but none of them had ever considered touching it.

Poor Lodren was the first to have the pleasure of its nasty surprise! He giggled as it squelched beneath his palm as he reached out to steady himself, and didn't even mind the fact that it was freezing cold to the touch. But then the smell hit him! It was faint at first, and he couldn't help but to look at his companions suspiciously. How rude, he thought. But the pungent odour lingered far too long. He waved his hand gingerly in front of his face and sniffed gently. He was horrified. He began to wretch, frantically searching his pockets for anything he could wipe his hand with, a handkerchief, a rag, anything to free himself from the awful whiff!

Grubb had seen it happen and, although slightly amused, grabbed Lodren's arm, "Don't touch nothin'!" he urged, "The stink'll never go away! 'ere, rub this on it, it's the only thing that works."

"What is it?" asked Lodren, quietly, heaving and trying not to vomit.

"Onion," replied Grubb. "Suppose I should've warned ye about this stuff before."

"That might have been a good idea!" hissed Lodren. "Just a minute… an onion? Where did you get an onion from? You've been in my supplies again haven't you, Grubb?"

"I was hungry. Ye wouldn't want your best friend to starve to death now, would ye?"

“No, I wouldn’t, but next time, ask. You don’t have to steal.”

“Oh, shut it, stinky,” Grubb sniggered. “Come on, we’ve fallen behind.”

They seemed to travel for an age before Faylore eventually called them to a halt. The light ahead was slightly brighter, but all it showed was more bare rock. She gathered everyone close to her, “You probably noticed we came a different way,” she said, “But it was for good reason.”

“To avoid the caged zingaard?” suggested Hannock.

“Yes, and no,” she replied. “We needed to avoid those ones but… oh, never mind, just follow me. There’s someone I’d like you to meet but keep quiet.”

Although her behaviour was mysterious, they followed. As they moved deeper into the cavern, they could distinctly see that the light was being produced by flames, causing faint shadows to dance on the damp walls. Their route suddenly took a sharp turn, unveiling far more than they had expected. The cavern was huge, seemingly endless as it stretched into the distance and at least a thousand yards wide. Torches burned, driven into the ground on tall poles and sconces adorned the walls, revealing the shocking scene before them. They were horrified. There were massive cages everywhere, each one housing a single zingaard. Some lay dormant on prison floors that were barely wide enough to hold them. Others, more recently captured they suspected, roared and shook the bars believing they had strength enough to break free. It was obvious to the companions that they were wrong.

Faylore again beckoned for them to follow as she moved closer to one of the cages.

"Faylore, move away!" hissed Lodren, "A few more steps and that thing will be able to reach you through the bars! Move back!"

Faylore placed her index finger to her lips and smiled, "It's alright," she whispered. "Come and say 'hello'." As she reached the cage, the zingaard did indeed put its arm through the bars, but it showed no sign of aggression. In fact, it looked sad.

Leaning its head against the bars, it gazed deep into Faylore's eyes, "Bogg… good," it said wearily, "Bogg… no hurt. You… me out?"

Not one member of the companions could believe what they had just witnessed. One of the most ferocious beasts they had ever encountered, had asked them for help!

Faylore held Bogg's hand, a hand that was actually three times the size of her head. "He's just a child," she informed them. "They learn their savagery from one another as they mature. Bogg has been in this cage for as long as he can remember, he has never been outside nor seen daylight. He needs our help to escape."

"Are you forgetting, Your Majesty…" snorted Lodren, "… that one of those things nearly killed you, and would have if it hadn't been for Grubb?"

"Perhaps," replied Faylore. "But it wasn't this one."

"If it's never been outside…" asked Hannock, dubiously, "… how did it learn to speak? I mean, speak our native tongue."

"Well, in all fairness, Captain," said Emnor, "it does seem to have a somewhat limited vocabulary."

"I understand that," replied Hannock. "But how did it learn the words that it does know?"

Bogg pushed his face to the bars, "Learn words from man… pretty man in pretty things. Man get new shiny things. Bogg show… show you. You… me out?"

Lorzic's ears pricked up, "New shiny things?" he exclaimed. "It must mean the relics! Set it free immediately! No time to waste if it can show us where they are."

Bogg heard every word and began to plead with Faylore, "Yes, yes! You… me out. Bogg no be dead thing…" he pointed through the other side of his cage, "… like they."

They all looked passed Bogg's cage. They had not noticed it before… the body pile. Dismembered carcasses of dozens of zingaard were piled high against the cavern wall. Arms, legs and torsos were strewn about, lying on a thick oozing carpet comprising their own blood and offal. Many of the bodies were still intact, but they appeared to be the results of deranged experiments. They were twisted, misshapen and disfigured, whilst others had been burnt to a crisp or desiccated.

"Who did this, Bogg?" exclaimed Faylore, pointing at the gruesome scene.

"Pretty man," replied Bogg. "You… me out?"

Faylore looked pleadingly into Jared's eyes. He approached the cage and leaned forward, staring at Bogg, "I warn you now, beast," he snarled, "one wrong move and I swear it will be your last." He held out his hand and conjured a fireball. "Do you understand?"

Bogg reeled back as far as the bars would allow him, "Bogg… good, Bogg… good. Bogg no… dead thing!"

Faylore reached into the cage and took his hand, "Bogg, where are the other things? Things not like you, snake things," she made a motion across his hand, trying her best to imitate the writhing movement of the hissthaar.

Bogg nodded in understanding, "With shiny things," he replied, pointing into the distance, "Bogg show, you… me out?"

"We don't have time for this," said Hannock, tersely. "This is all very noble, but how are we supposed to remain hidden whilst we have this hulking great beast leading the way? That is of course if it doesn't turn on us as soon as that cage door is open."

Emnor smiled, "There are eight of us, Captain! How did you think we would remain hidden? It's a good thing Poom and Lawton elected to remain on guard at the entrance, at least we know nothing will attack us from the rear."

"I know I'll probably regret this," sighed Jared, stretching out his hand. Strange that the blue flame that appeared to free the incarcerated zingaard was last seen torturing another. It sliced through the lock in seconds. The cage door swung open slowly and noisily, the grinding of the hinges a clue to how long it had been since the door was first closed.

Bogg stretched out his arm, stroking the air in disbelief. His whole life, or what he could remember of it, had been spent within the confines of the cage. Unsure of what to do next, he crept warily through the open door. He stood upright, something he had never been able to do before, and the companions cringed as they heard his bones cracking as he stretched to his full height. Hannock instinctively reached for his sword, and the flame in Jared's hand had not yet been extinguished. Bogg faced Jared and Faylore and lowered himself to his knees, "You… good things," he said gently. "You… me out," he continued, glancing back at the cage. "Bogg… good thing. Bogg… show shiny things. You… with me," he finished, turning and heading away. Pausing briefly to check that they were following, he moved rapidly, but surprisingly quietly, ahead.

***

Cautiously, the companions hurried after him. Occasionally, Bogg would stop and hide behind one of the many cages. The first time he hid, it confused the companions, but they knew it was probably for good reason. He had spotted a lone hissthaar. Luckily however, it had not seen him. All it saw was a mass of iron cages and matted fur. Bogg, hiding directly behind another zingaard who lay sleeping in its cage, had discovered the perfect camouflage.

Hannock could not believe what he had just witnessed, the beast was five times the size of the hissthaar above it, but it was hiding like a frightened child. It could have torn the guard to pieces but instead crouched quivering in terror. He sneaked as closely as he could to Bogg's hiding place and raised the crossbow. Seconds later, the hissthaar was dead, sliding from the craggy outcropping that had been its vantage point and hitting the ground with a dull thud. Hannock moved closer to Bogg. He recoiled slightly, "My word!" he exclaimed. "Has anyone ever told you your name really suits you? You stink!"

They eventually reached the end of the cages and, studying the scene ahead, realised just what they were up against. The hissthaar camp was not as well lit as the area in which the zingaard were caged. Being nocturnal, they had no real need of illumination.

The companions suspected that they may be nearing the exit. The floor rose gently, the walls smattered with many tiered ledges, all of which held varying numbers of hissthaar who slithered about aimlessly.

"How are we supposed to get past that lot?" hissed Drake, "Let alone find his precious artefacts," he added, flicking his thumb at Lorzic.

Fortunately, the solution to their problem was presented to them quite by accident. They watched the hissthaar, each companion trying to formulate a favourable solution to their predicament. It was then that they noticed that two of their foe seemed to be having a heated disagreement. It was only seconds before their petty squabble escalated and they began writhing around on the ledge above them, slashing with their claws, snapping their fangs and hissing loudly. Their battle became frantic, neither feeling any sense of danger other than that of their opponent. Thrashing around they rolled off the edge, still snapping at one another as they tumbled down the sloping wall.

The flaming sconce exploded as they smashed through it, sparks and embers showering them as they crashed through the barrels stacked on the level below. They screeched as the barrels split, the powdery contents suddenly strewn around them. Multi-coloured sparks flew in all directions, a veritable rainbow illuminating the cavern until it was as bright as a mid-summer's day. Every hissthaar now joined the chorus of screeching, attempting unsuccessfully to shield their eyes from the blinding light as they fled in terror. Within moments, the hissthaar were gone. The impromptu light-show continued, the sound of popping and fizzing echoing around the cavern. The companions were unsure of how long their good fortune would last, realising they must quickly make the most of this opportunity!

"Scatter," urged Jared, "Find the artefacts, but hurry."

They scampered in various directions, hunting fervently but making sure to stay in the light.

"Here!" called Emnor, suddenly. "They're over here," The others joined him. He had already snatched up the amulet and the helm. The hammer, however, was proving to be a little more difficult. "I can't lift it!" he panted. "Lodren, I think this calls for your strength."

Lodren pushed his way through and reached down without thinking… then he saw it. A hammer even larger than his own lay at his feet. It shimmered as he gazed upon its magnificence and he shuddered slightly when it hummed melodiously at his slightest touch. Made from solid silver with gold inlays, its oak handle seeming to mould to his grip as he raised it. It was undoubtedly the most glorious weapon he had ever seen. He stroked it, caressing it as if it were a long-lost friend. The voices of his companions were muffled, background noise to the hammer's song.

"Lodren… Lodren," begged Faylore. "We have to go, come on now, hurry!"

Lodren blinked and smiled up at her, "What?" he asked, dreamily, "Oh, oh yes. Let's go! Lead the way, Your Majesty."

Faylore looked about frantically, "Where's Bogg?"

"Who cares?" growled Hannock. "Let's run before the light show stops!"

Charging forward, they followed the slope uphill. They did not look back but, after twenty minutes and still finding no exit, decided that it would be safe to lessen their pace.

They walked in silence for the next few minutes. Some were breathless, others trying to understand how something had gone right for a change.

"When this is all over…" chuckled Drake, "… I'll have to find out what was in those barrels. That was brilliant!"

"Well at least we all made it out in one piece," said Emnor. "Although some of us aren't as enthusiastic about explosions as you are, Master Drake."

"None of us have escaped yet," Faylore corrected him, "And we aren't all here, we have no idea what happened to Bogg."

"He probably ran the other way when the commotion started," suggested Grubb. "He'll just keep goin' until he finds the way out. Same way as we came in."

"Oh dear!" said Faylore, "That means that he'll have to pass our Gerrowlien friends."

"Give 'em some credit, Faylore! It's not as if they're goin' to attack a zingaard when there's only the two of 'em!"

Faylore looked down at Grubb, “We’re talking about Poom, Grubb. Lawton would simply ignore Bogg, but Poom wouldn’t hesitate at the chance to battle a zingaard.”

Grubb raised his eyebrows. He knew, as did everyone else, that she was right.

“Well, there’s nothing we can do about that now, we’ll just have to hope for the best,” smiled Emnor. “Would anyone mind if we take a minute? I’m not as young as the rest of you. Let’s have a look at these artefacts,” he suggested.

“Now you, you b-be careful with those!” spluttered Lorzic, “They’re very valuable… and they’re mine!”

Grubb tilted his head to the side as he studied his cousin, “Yours?” he asked, quizzically, “I thought they belonged to the whole village.”

“You know what I mean, Grubb,” spat Lorzic, “I am responsible for them. They’re in my care.”

“Oh really?” said Grubb, “Well, as far as I can see, they’re in our care now! If it wasn’t for us they’d still be back there, covered in snake slime or whatever else.”

The companions sniggered.

“Lodren,” called Emnor, “Let’s have a look at that hammer. It looks most impressive.”

Lodren looked across at him nervously, “Yes, okay… erm, in a minute. I just wanted to… you know, hold it a bit longer…” His voice tailed off. There was a gleam in his eye that had never existed before. He held the hammer closer to him than he ever had his own, nursing it, stroking its head like a new-born’s cheek.”

Emnor squinted as he watched the Nibby, "Lodren?" he said gently, "Lodren?"

The Nibby looked up, "Hm?" he said.

"The hammer?" said Emnor.

"Magnificent, isn't it," answered Lodren.

Emnor smiled again, "Yes, it is. But it doesn't belong to you, you must give it back to its rightful owner."

"Mr Emnor!" protested Lodren, "I do hope you're not suggesting that I would steal it!"

"Of course not," replied Emnor. "Now bring it over here and let me have a look at it."

Lodren idled his way toward Emnor, shuffling his feet like a child who knew they were about to be scolded. With arms outstretched, he held the hammer in front of Emnor's intrigued eyes.

"I must say, the craftsmanship is beautiful... in a blunt, violent way of course. Whomever crafted this weapon definitely had a passion for their art." Emnor glanced up at Lodren, "It looks incredibly heavy." Lodren shrugged. "As heavy as yours?" he asked.

"No," replied Lodren, quietly. "It's a lot lighter actually, even though it's a bit bigger."

"Curious," said Emnor, "Probably due to the density of the metal," he suggested. "But who would forge such a thing? And more so, why?"

Lodren shrugged again.

"I think we should move," suggested Hannock. "The hissthaar move quietly, remember. I'm not sure that they're actually giving chase, but let's not run the risk, eh?"

Following his recommendation, they moved quickly on. It was far darker as they proceeded, an issue that was easily dealt with as Emnor conjured a ball of light to illuminate their path. The cavern floor was a lot smoother than it had been, a blessing for Emnor's weary old legs. Although they remained in the cave for far longer than they had anticipated, their passing through yielded no more surprises. Leaving the caverns, they lowered themselves onto the moss-covered rocky ground, taking a moment to enjoy the pale sunlight.

Lodren nursed the hammer as Lorzic insisted on reminding him that he would eventually have to return it. They squabbled like children over a favourite toy, under the concerned, watchful eye of Emnor. Why had Lodren become so possessive of it? He wasn't the type to covet another's property. Something didn't fit in this tale. Emnor was unsure of what it was, but he intended to find out. On discovering the artefacts, Emnor had hurriedly concealed both the helm and the amulet within his robes. Unseen, he ran his hand over the, still hidden, helm. Far larger than one would expect, he thought. He cast his eyes to Lodren once more. Best keep that hidden for now. He drew out the amulet, holding it close to his face and peering at it. Runes! And ancient ones, he thought as he studied it. He seemed to remember having seen something similar before, but he couldn't bring to mind when, or where. Having lived as long as he had, it was hardly surprising that he would forget things occasionally.

"What does it say?" Emnor gave a start. He was so deep in thought that he had not even noticed Faylore as she sat next to him. “Oh, I’m so terribly sorry, I didn’t mean to make you jump,” she giggled.

“That’s alright,” laughed Emnor, “My fault. My mind had drifted somewhat, I was miles away.”

“The amulet?” Faylore repeated, “What does it say?”

“I have no idea,” replied Emnor. “I’ve seen runes like these before, but for the life of me I cannot place them.”

“May I see?” asked Faylore, politely.

“Of course,” replied Emnor, handing it to her.

She looked at it briefly, rubbing her thumb across it before lowering her voice and leaning over to Emnor, “You have never visited my homelands have you, Emnor?” she asked.

“Strangely enough, no,” he replied, “I’ve never had that pleasure.”

“I thought not,” she continued, “You would have recognised the speech on the amulet if you had.”

Emnor shook his head questioningly.

“It is an ancient form, I’ll admit that, but this amulet… hails from Thedar. It was made by my people.”

“Are you sure?” he whispered, “Oh what am I saying? Of course you’re sure. Can you read it?”

“There are words I have never seen before, unfortunately. However, it hints at a tale involving fire, doom… oh, dear. It is the tale of the dragon rider!” As they looked to Lodren, they were interrupted by Hannock.

"Grubb's going to lead Poom and Lawton back to us," he informed them. "Calculating the route we came underground, well a rough calculation anyway, we think they could be with us in an hour or so. We're going to carry on anyway, so, when you're ready," he added rubbing his hands together.

"Are your hands cold?" asked Faylore.

Hannock looked at his palms, "No, why?"

"Why are you rubbing them together then? Is there a circulation problem? Is there something I can do to help?"

Hannock looked at her, baffled, "No, it's… well it's…" Faylore had reverted to typical Thedarian mode. "Oh no, I'm not getting wound up in that nonsense again," he winced.

Faylore smiled at Emnor, "Stops all the silly questions," she whispered.

***

"You shouldn't do it," protested Lorzic, "It's not natural!"

"And turning into a bear is, I suppose?" laughed Hannock.

"This is not your concern! You wouldn't understand, you're far too large and stupid!"

Jared nudged his friend, "And there I was thinking that they were always wrong," he sniggered.

“Ye can’t tell me what’s right and what ain’t anymore, Lorzic,” argued Grubb. “I’ll do what I want, and if I choose to turn into a hawk and fly it’s my business alone!”

“We do not turn into anything that flies!” continued Lorzic.

“No, you don’t turn into anything that flies. I, on the other ‘and, do it all the time.”

Hannock nodded, “He does you know, I’ve seen him do it,” he said, smirking.

“But…”

“The reason none of the villagers turn into birds… is ‘cause you banned them from doin’ it!” bawled Grubb, “An’ why? ‘cause you’re scared o’ heights, ye chicken.”

“That is not true!” exclaimed Lorzic, “I outlawed it to keep our people safe! All it takes is a momentary lack of concentration and someone could plummet to their death.”

Grubb waved his hand dismissively at Lorzic, “Just shove it, ye whinin’ little creep. I’m done wasting my time with ye.” Turning to the companions, he smiled. “See you lot later.” He transformed into an eagle and flew away.

***

It wasn’t long before he was soaring above the entrance to the caverns they had used many hours before. His piercing raptor eyes scanned the ground and within seconds he spied the Gerrowliens. They were in exactly the same place as when they had parted from them, but they were not alone. Close by, lying perfectly still on the ground, was Bogg. Grubb began his descent. Landing close to Poom and Lodren, he transformed. Poom made the slightest twitch to reach for his spear but, realising it was their friend, relaxed once more. Grubb could find no words, he pointed at Bogg.

"Yes," said Poom, thoughtfully, "Most strange. It came hurtling out of the caverns a few hours ago. We had no idea what to make of it."

Grubb sighed, "Is he… dead?" he asked slowly.

"Not sure," replied Lawton, "It hasn't moved for quite a while, so I suppose it's possible. Hang on, you said he. Don't you mean it?"

"No, I mean he. He helped us find the artefacts for Lorzic. I suppose ye could say he's a friend."

"Well, you lot have a strange choice in friends, if you don't mind me saying so," said Poom, lazily.

Lawton shook his head, "Do you even realise what you just said, Poom?"

"He knows what I mean."

"How badly did ye wound 'im?" asked Grubb, "Do ye think I could fix 'im?"

"We never wounded it at all, we never even touched it!" Lawton assured him. "It saw us when it emerged and started talking to us. Kept on about being a good thing and not wanting to be a dead thing."

"Yes," added Poom, "and that he helped a nice thing find a shiny thing."

Lawton began his snarling laughter, "Seems like things are what they always were, or not."

"Yes," continued Poom, "Why make some-thing out of no-thing." The Gerrowliens were back to their usual, childish selves, which was most annoying for Grubb.

"Will you two pack it in!" he cried, "If you didn't hurt 'im, why's 'e lyin' on the ground like that?"

Lawton padded gently toward Grubb and lay down to look him in the eye, "That'll be because it's asleep," he whispered, "Shhh!"

"Shut it, Lawton! I'm not in the mood for your mucking about, nor his," said Grubb, nodding toward Poom, who just grinned.

"I'm presuming you came to give us directions?" asked Lawton.

"Yeah, but I've half a mind not to tell ye."

"Well, one part of your statement is correct at least. It's not as if you could outrun us when you leave, is it?" sniggered Poom.

Grubb gave Poom a filthy look, "Up yours!" he snapped. "Question is, 'ow do we get 'im back?"

"You're not suggesting we take it with us?!"

"Yes, Lawton, we're taking him with us," replied Grubb. "We can't leave 'im out here on his own, he'd never survive."

"Look at it, it's huge! Massive claws, fangs bigger than my spearhead, what more would it need to defend itself? Then of course, it has its secret weapon. The smell! That alone could kill you from fifty feet!"

“He’s a child, Lawton. He’s got no idea ‘ow to defend ‘imself. He can’t remember anything other than bein’ in a cage ‘e couldn’t even stand up in all his life!”

“But, it’s a zingaard, it’ll learn. In a couple of weeks it’ll be tearing lumps out of anything that gets close, just like the rest of them,” argued Poom. “It’s their nature.”

“Well that’s where you’re wrong, see. Bogg isn’t like that. He…” said Grubb, emphasising the word deliberately, “… is very calm. I suppose you could even say ‘e’s a bit of a coward.”

The Gerrowliens guffawed with laughter, “Bogg?” roared Poom, “You couldn’t make it up, could you? Bogg! That’s hilarious.”

It took a while, but eventually the Gerrowliens managed to compose themselves. Grubb roused Bogg and, transforming back into an eagle without the slightest reaction from the zingaard, they set off. Poom and Lawton soon disappeared into the distance, but Grubb was kind enough to circle back a few times so that Bogg would not get left behind.

CHAPTER 16

"Oh, my days, you're serious!" exclaimed Lorzic.

"It makes perfect sense to me," replied Jared.

It had been three days since their encounter with the hissthaar and now, many miles from Mallorkan caverns, in a very large, makeshift camp, they were debating exactly what they should do with the Vikkery.

"You can't expect us to give up our home just like that, we've been here for generations!"

"Have you forgotten, Lorzic, your home no longer exists? There's nothing but rubble and a few charred timbers to show that you were ever there," said Hannock.

"Perhaps!" snapped Lorzic, "But once we find a village and show them our artefacts, they'll be more than happy to help us out. We'll be able to borrow money and make a fresh start."

Jared sighed, "Lorzic, there are very few villages left, and the ones that remain have no coin to invest in the redevelopment of yours."

"We'll find one, don't you worry about that," snorted Lorzic, "True, we may have to travel a little bit farther afield, but we'll find one."

Faylore stared Lorzic in the eye, it was a look he could not ignore, "There are no villages," she said angrily. “They have suffered the same fate as yours, or worse. The buildings have been razed to the ground and their occupants slain or enslaved by Karrak! Jared is offering you a haven and you throw it back in his face! You should be ashamed of yourself! Or do you prefer that your people become nothing but starving refugees wandering the lands so that you can hold on to an imaginary status and your precious trinkets?”

Lorzic looked around nervously. A few of the Vikkery had overheard their conversation and began chuntering amongst themselves. It seemed that they were not entirely happy with the way Lorzic had been running things in Pellandrin. They felt that he only had his own best interests at heart, not theirs.

“Don’t we have a say in this?” called one.

“What about the children?” shouted another, “Are we expected to raise them in the wilds?”

“The kingdom is empty,” said Jared, sympathetically. “From the citadel to the outlying farms, Borell is silent. There are market places, shops, stables and dwellings for you all, if you so wish. You will have a place to call home, all you need do is make the journey.”

Lorzic became agitated and began pacing, “Yes, it all sounds very nice. But once you’ve got us there, you’ll start imposing taxes! You’ll want more and more in payment for your precious kingdom until we are penniless, whilst you get fat from our labours!”

Drake shook his head, “You just can’t help some people, can you?” he said, exasperated at Lorzic’s outburst.

Lodren strolled slowly toward Lorzic, his own hammer in one hand and the silver one in the other. He allowed them to swing like pendulums as he walked, not once taking his eyes from the tiny figure of the Vikkery until he stood directly in front of him. The onlookers were silent, intrigued by the Nibby's sudden approach. Lodren gripped the two hammers firmly in his muscular hands. He studied them for a second, first his own, then the other. Slowly, he raised them high into the air, then with a deafening crash, drove them both deep into the ground. He leaned down to Lorzic, "Say… you're… sorry!" he whispered. Terror gripped Lorzic. He stared at the hammers that Lodren had driven a yard into the earth and then to Lodren's rage-filled eyes, "Say you're sorry, or I'll do it again! Only next time, you'll be underneath them."

The other Vikkery began to cheer. It seemed that Lorzic had abused his power for far longer than the companions had thought. They swarmed around Lodren, jumping up to pat him on the shoulder.

The children hugged his legs, although his thighs were far too thick for any of them to wrap their arms around, and started chanting, "We're going to live in a castle, we're going to live in a castle."

Hannock smiled at Jared, "It seems…" he said, "… that the people have spoken."

***

There was much excitement over the next few days. Although the companions had suggested that the Vikkery return to Borell, they knew what an arduous journey they would have to face. They addressed the entire village and explained the possible dangers that may lie ahead. The hardy Vikkery remained undaunted, well, all but one.

"You'll never make it!" shouted Lorzic, "You'll all be dead within a couple o' days, you mark my words."

They all tried their best to ignore him as he wobbled through the crowd. It seemed he had a stash of wine somewhere and had deemed it appropriate to consume it by himself. "You'd rather believe some pretend prince in rusty armour than one of your own. Well go on then, push off! Get lost the lot o' you. And you!" he shouted, waggling his finger at Lodren, "You… you, with your big muscles and that stupid fat head o' yours… you can give me my things back. I want 'em…" he lost his train of thought momentarily as he stared bleary-eyed at the spectators, "… What was I saying... Oh, my things… yes, my things, NOWWW," he continued, belching out the last word.

Lodren pursed his lips as he glanced around. Without a word, he lifted the silver hammer and marched up to Lorzic. The companions screwed up their eyes, Lodren did not take insults well, especially from someone who was drunk. To their surprise, he placed it on the ground at Lorzic's feet. "There you go," he said politely, "One hammer. But there is a catch. If you can manage to lift it by yourself, you can take it. And there'll be no cheating. Transformation is not allowed."

Lorzic swayed back and forth, trying to focus on the Nibby's blurred features, "Pffft, easy!" he replied. After his third attempt, he eventually managed to take hold of the handle. "Blasted thing keeps moving," he mumbled. Then the fun began. He pulled, pushed, yanked and tugged as hard as he could, cursing the one who forged it for making it so heavy. “You won’t beat me!” he panted. “I’m leaving and you’re coming with me!”

The crowd was in hysterics as they watched their former mayor making such a fool of himself. His pomposity and arrogance were gone, all that remained was his avarice as he tried in vain to lift the hammer. With a final grunt he fell face first into the dirt and began to snore loudly.

Lodren was never one to bear a grudge. Grabbing Lorzic by his belt with one hand and the hammer with the other, he shrugged as he smiled at the crowd, “Maybe I should put these two to bed.”

The crowd applauded. It seemed that they liked the performances that Lodren put on for them, as impromptu as they were. As he passed Jared, he paused, “I don’t think this will be the last we hear from this one,” he chuckled. “But at least he’s quiet for now.”

“I’m sure you’re right, Lodren,” agreed Jared, “He’ll be back with his tales of doom as soon as the drink wears off.”

Lodren looked thoughtful, “Here, Drake,” he called, “you couldn’t just…” Holding the hammer with just his thumb, he wiggled his fingers and tilted his head toward Lorzic, “You know, just for a while? A few days, perhaps a week.”

“No, he can not, Lodren! How could you even contemplate such a thing?” called Emnor in mock disgust, “That is not the discerning behaviour we have come to expect from such an admirable Nibby.”

Lodren shrugged, “Just a thought,” he grinned, “I must be picking up bad habits from you lot.”

***

It took far longer than Jared had hoped for the Vikkery to prepare for their journey. He felt a little guilty, but he was losing patience with them. He understood the hardships they were about to face, but they were so annoyingly precise in their needs that they sometimes made the Thedarians seem slipshod! Insisting on taking far more than seemed necessary, they had spent two days building handcarts. This was time the companions did not have, each realising that the longer it took to send the Vikkery on their way, the greater the chance that Karrak would slip from their grasp. "Lorzic," he called as the disgruntled Vikkery passed him, "How much longer is this going to take? They've been at it for days!"

Lorzic curled his lip as he glared at Jared, "What are you asking me for?" he growled. "I don't run things around here anymore, you saw to that. Try asking Tambly, it seems the people prefer her advice to mine."

Jared was about to ask Lorzic where he could find Tambly, but the former mayor of Pellandrin simply turned his back and walked away. Charming, thought Jared.

"Me!" came a voice from the crowd ahead, "That was what ye were about to ask, I take it? I'm Tambly."

A very plump Vikkery approached Jared, smiling. "Bit of a chill in the air this morning," she chirped, "Oh well, we'll just have to work a bit harder to keep warm."

"Yes, quite," replied Jared, slightly taken aback by her chipper attitude. "Tambly, I don't want to push you, but we are a little short on time here. How much longer before you're ready to leave?"

Tambly placed her hands on her hips and stared at the ground. Her head wobbled from side to side as she thought out loud, "Couple more handcarts, no, make that three and then there's the food, we'll need to hunt a bit more game. If I get a good fire going tonight, that Nibby fella can make some more o' those honey cakes, everyone likes those. Oh, hang on, have we got enough honey? Best be on the safe side, we'll find some beehives sometime tomorrow, might be able to scrape the last dregs before it gets too cold. Then there's the…"

"Tambly! How long?" pleaded Jared.

"Couple o' days… maybe three, not much longer than that," she replied, grinning.

"We don't have three days!" exclaimed Jared. "We don't even have two. Tambly, I'm very sorry but you must leave at first light tomorrow. Whatever you don't have by then you'll have to survive without, alright?"

Tambly pouted, "Alright your princeship, if you say so," she replied pleasantly. "Shame though, we really like those honey cakes."

Jared smiled as Tambly returned to her kin.

"Bit different to Lorzic, isn't she?"

Jared turned to Drake, "I hadn't noticed," he chuckled.

"They're a funny lot aren't they? I mean, it's one thing having to deal with Grubb, but to have a whole village full of them around you… it's exhausting! I'm going to miss them when they leave."

“Ah, yes…” said Jared, taking a deep breath, “… I’ve been meaning to talk to you about that.”

“What about it?” asked Drake, suspiciously.

“About them leaving. You see, Drake, they’ve been here for so long, I don’t think they’ll ever find Borell if we allow them to go alone.”

A look of horror swept across Drake’s face, “No!” he groaned, “You’re not suggesting…?”

“They’ll need protection! You’ve seen what they’re like, the slightest noise and they’ll scamper off into the hills never to be heard from again!”

“But Jared, why me?” asked Drake, almost pleading with him. “Send Emnor, he’s old and tired… or send Grubb, they are his people after all.”

“Who said anything about you?” frowned Jared. “I’m talking about Harley! I don’t want him in the thick of things if we should happen to run into Karrak. He’s not like you, you think on your feet, you react to things far more quickly, it’s instinctive!” Jared lowered his voice, “If Harley goes with us, I fear he may not survive. No, I need you with me, Drake. After all, you’re the man who’s going to save my father.”

Drake’s eyes widened, “Me! How can I save the king? Tamor is protected by a seclusion spell, I wouldn’t have the slightest notion of how to find him. I wouldn’t even know where to begin!”

“Yes, Drake, you would,” Jared assured him. “Or should I say, you do.”

“No, I don’t! You probably could Jared, with the powers you have. I’m just a novice!”

"You're far more than that, Drake," Jared smiled. "Come here, let me show you."

Drake stepped forward nervously.

Jared placed his palms gently on the sides of Drake's head and stared into his eyes. "Trust me," he said quietly. "Close your eyes."

Drake followed Jared's instructions and closed them. Initially all was as it should be, nothing but darkness. However, it took only a few seconds before he began to see brilliant flashes of light. He saw flames, giants and other beasts he had never seen before. He heard the roar of battle cries and felt pulses of energy deep within his chest. One voice seemed much louder than the rest. He turned toward it and recognised the wizard beside him, it was Emnor! His beard was much shorter than Drake had ever seen it, and both it and his billowing hair, were as black as a raven's wings. They were in the throes of battle, but where, and when? A huge boulder suddenly flew past his head, missing him by inches. He threw up his hands… he was holding a staff, an ancient, gnarled, wooden staff. He felt its power and that it was part of him, but somehow not. Emnor charged headlong toward their foe, passing him as the vision began to fade. Drake blinked slowly but as his eyes opened the only man standing before him was Jared.

Drake looked horrified as he realised what had just happened. He raised his arm, gazing at the familiar wooden staff clutched tightly in his fist. His expression cleared as the truth dawned on him. "What the f…?"

"Calm yourself, Drake," Jared said reassuringly. "You were quite safe, it was merely a memory," Jared cooed.

"Yeah, a memory!" yelled Drake, "But it wasn't my bloody memory, was it!"

"No, it wasn't," replied Jared.

"Jared, how could you do this to me? I've always done what you asked, but this!"

Jared held his shoulders, "I'm sorry, Drake. It was the only way. If I hadn't, not only would we have lost Yello, we'd have risked losing my father as well! I had to do it!"

Drake pulled away, "You could have done it to someone else, or at least asked me if I was okay with it!"

"Drake, it had to be you, please understand," Jared implored.

"Just… leave me alone!" hissed Drake as he turned. He paused without looking back, "I thought I could trust you."

"Don't worry, he'll come around," said Emnor, who had been watching closely.

Jared sighed, "I'm not so sure this time," he admitted.

"It's difficult for him, Jared. He's far from being a boy, but even farther from being a man," sighed Emnor. "That's enough of a struggle for anyone. If he was to discover the power he now holds, it could be his undoing. The last thing we need is for him to doubt our aims, it could turn him against us."

"Do you believe that could happen? Would he join Karrak if the temptation were strong enough?"

"It doesn't matter what I believe, Jared," replied Emnor, as he watched Drake vanish amongst the trees.

"He may have the occasional tantrum, but that's to be expected at his age. Fear not, he knows right from wrong."

***

Drake flopped to the ground. Confused and angry, he kicked his heel into the dirt in frustration. In the past he had always pushed ahead of the others if there was a ridiculous test to be performed, never once considering the consequences. But to have the decision made for him felt wrong somehow!

"He was very much like you in his youth, you know." Drake was startled. He hadn't seen or heard Emnor approach, "Yello I mean. Always at the front when there was a risk to be taken. And his temper! Honestly, I'd rather face a herd of stampeding glamoch than be in the same room with him when he was in one of his moods."

Drake scowled at him, "Is that supposed to make me feel better?" he asked. "Because it doesn't! I'll never be by myself again, not now that I've got your old pal stuck inside my head. I'll never know whether a decision I make is my own!"

Emnor smiled, "Trust me, my young friend, whatever mistakes you make will be entirely your own." He lowered himself slowly and sat near to Drake, using a tree as a backrest. "On the other hand, every unique discovery you make, every miracle you perform and every person that you choose to aid will be entirely of your own volition."

"But how could I be sure?"

“All your mind contains is a selection of Yello’s memories. His conscious mind no longer exists, it can have no control over the choices you make.”

“But that vision I just had, Master Emnor, it was so vivid! I actually felt like I was there.”

“Why…” asked Emnor, frowning slightly, “… what did you see?”

“I was in the middle of a huge battle. There were giants, you could barely see anything there was so much smoke,” he turned and grinned at Emnor, “and you were there. You don’t half look different with black hair and a black beard,” he sniggered.

Emnor searched his memories, “Oh, yes!” he exclaimed. “The Battle of Herraldim Tor! Oh, that was a good one, that was!” He began to laugh. “You see, what had happened was that one of the giants had charged into a nearby village a few weeks before, grabbed a couple of prize horses, and then scarpered. Well, by chance, Yello and I turned up and every person we passed was simply bursting to tell us their tale of woe. The thing is, it hadn’t been the first time it had happened, apparently. They’d been losing livestock for months. Cows, sheep, goats, the lot, but they thought they had just wandered off, until they saw the giant grabbing the horses. I mean, how did they not notice a giant in the middle of the village before? Anyway, later that day, Yello and I went into the tavern. Now Yello did enjoy his wine but, as a younger man, he also liked to have a fair bit of coin in his purse. The locals, realising that we were wizards, started offering bounties if we were to clear the area of the giants. Well of course, Yello’s eyes lit up when he saw how much gold they were piling on the table in front of us. He came up with this scheme to enrol some of our fellow wizards…"

***

Jared peeked at Drake from behind a tree. He and Hannock had followed Emnor after he had said he would speak to Drake and try to calm him down.

"Do you think he'll be alright?" asked Hannock.

"I wouldn't have asked him if I didn't think he could do it," Jared whispered.

They heard raucous laughter coming from their two friends as Emnor related one of his tales of adventure, "I tell you, Drake, if Yellodious hadn't been there, that giant would have squashed me flat. He saved my life that day, although his methods were a little… below the belt."

CHAPTER 17

It was just before dawn when the companions gathered. All but a few of the Vikkery were still sleeping. Jared's concerns regarding Drake had been addressed the night before by Emnor who had simply stated, "He's fine," as he passed him.

Drake himself looked confident, now feeling quite honoured that he was to be entrusted with the task of returning the king to his rightful place, the throne of Borell. Emnor had eased his mind and a sense of duty had replaced all his self-doubts. Ready to face his fears, he had vowed to Emnor that he would do his best.

The companions would continue to escort the Vikkery for some time yet, something that Jared was thankful for. He had not as yet informed Harley that he would be the one solely responsible for them when it was time for he and the others to depart for Reiggan in a bid to retrieve King Tamor. Drake had been sworn to secrecy, Harley would be told when Jared felt the time was right.

"He can't do it by himself, Jared."

Jared looked up to see Lawton lounging in the trees above him, "Sorry?" he said.

"Harley," replied Lawton, "He'd need eyes in the back of his head to keep track of that lot," he added, nodding toward the slumbering Vikkery.

"Keep your voice down!" Jared urged. "He'll hear you. Anyway, how do you know about the plan?"

"I may be getting a little plump and Poom may resemble a half-plucked chicken, but there's nothing wrong with our hearing!"

"They're scars!" protested Poom.

"I have little choice," explained Jared. "Someone has to lead them, and Harley is the most suitable."

"If you send him off alone, that lot'll drive him mad within a few days! He'll probably end up killing them himself," chuckled Lawton.

"Well, do you have a better idea?"

"Yes, Jared, I do," said Lawton, smugly. "We'll go with him!"

Jared could not hide his surprise, "You'd do that?" he asked.

"Don't get me wrong," said Lawton, "If there were any other way, I'd gladly take it!"

Jared smiled, "You're a good friend," he said quietly. "You too, Poom."

"I know," said Poom, snorting. "One of the best."

"This is another reason why I got away from this lot," growled Grubb as he sauntered toward Jared. "Look at 'em. They'd sleep 'alfway through the day if ye let 'em. Lazy, good for nothin's."

Hannock smiled, "It's not even light yet, Grubb. Give them a bit of credit, for goodness sake."

"Goodness?" snorted Grubb. "They don't know what it means, unless you're givin' them somethin' for nothin'. Like a free home, and free businesses, and free food like Jared's givin' 'em!"

"They'll pay for them in one way or another, Grubb," laughed Jared.

"Yeah? Well just make sure they do, they'll 'ave the shirt off yer back if you ain't careful!"

***

Lodren squinted and rubbed his eyes as he stared at the horizon, "Bit early for sunrise isn't it?" he asked quietly.

"It is indeed," agreed Hannock, "And since when did the sun rise in the north?"

"That's a lot of light," said Poom, sounding a little concerned. "Want me to go and have a look?"

Jared shook his head, "No," he replied, "That's the way we're headed anyway. We'll find out soon enough what's causing it, and I think it best that we investigate it together."

Dawn broke and it was as chaotic as the companions had feared it would be. It was bad enough that the Vikkery wouldn't be rushed. Worse still, was that wherever you turned there seemed to be another child screaming and giggling, just waiting to be trodden underfoot. But the most infuriating thing was the bombardment of inane questions and statements:

Are there any villages at all?

Do they have wells in the villages or a stream nearby? Only we must have fresh water. We're clean living folk, we bathe every week without fail.

Will there be a dress shop? Only my daughter insists on having a new dress every Thursday.

These shoes, will they be okay? Or do I need something a bit sturdier?

It seemed endless.

Drake leaned on Jared's shoulder, "I don't know about bringing King Tamor out of his sleep…" he groaned, "… after spending time with this lot, I'll probably join him."

Eventually, they set off. The rattling of the cartwheels on the barren earth seemed rather soothing as they made their way ahead of the tiny villagers. The buzz of the Vikkery in the background quietened as they travelled, perhaps they don't have that much to complain about for a change, thought Jared.

The Gerrowliens would cause an occasional dust cloud as they skidded to a halt after scouting ahead, each time having nothing to report.

For some unknown reason Jared felt anxious. He paused, tilting his head to the side. Something was wrong, he just didn't know what.

"Everything alright, Mr Jared?" asked Lodren.

"I'm not sure," he replied.

"Do you hear something?" asked Hannock.

"No, old friend," Jared replied slowly, "That's what's so strange… I don't hear anything! Remember Cheadleford when there was nothing but the wind in the trees? There was no birdsong nor insects buzzing and this is exactly the same."

"Well we can be sure there ain't no hissthaar hidin' in the bushes, that's for sure," laughed Grubb, "There ain't no bushes!"

"Jared, there's nothing there," said Faylore, "Poom and Lawton would have seen."

"Perhaps you're right," Jared sighed, "Maybe I'm becoming paranoid, only…"

There was a sudden commotion amongst the Vikkery. Some screamed in terror whilst others just gasped in amazement.

A hundred yards ahead of them a black shrouded figure had appeared.

The Gerrowliens roared, their reaction taking longer than it did for Faylore to ready an arrow on her bowstring and aim it at the intruder, "Perhaps you're not so paranoid after all," she mumbled.

Jared raised an eyebrow to her, then began to approach the stranger.

With both hands raised, their visitor stepped forward and spoke, "I believe you have been expecting me?" he said.

Hannock drew his sword, "Who are you? What do you want?" he asked, brusquely.

"I am the messenger," he answered politely. "You were clearly informed of my imminent arrival."

"That's not what I asked, give me your name!"

"A name? Tell me Captain Hannock, would it change matters if you were to have my name? My name is not important, whereas, the message I bear, is."

"So, you're just another one of Karrak's lapdogs?" growled Grubb.

"Prince Jared," began the man politely, "Do you think it appropriate to allow one of your companions to insult a guest? Surely not?"

Jared remained silent.

"Very well," continued the stranger, slowly raising his hand. "If you will not chastise him, perhaps I should."

"One move and I put an arrow through your hooded brow," threatened Faylore.

A slow, menacing laugh came from beneath the hood, "Ah, Queen Faylore, how you love your little pointed sticks. A word of warning, Your Majesty. You aren't as good an aim as you believe you are." He lowered his arm, "Very well, as a show of good faith, I'll allow Grubb to live. For the time being at least."

Lodren was becoming agitated and started rhythmically slamming his hammer into the ground, "How do you know our names? Come on, start talking, or do I have to start bashing?"

"Oh, my friends, you wound me," said the stranger mockingly, "And I thought we were all so close?" He pointed at Drake, "Studying together," he announced, his voice taking an aggressive tone. Turning his finger to Emnor, "Being lectured by. And of course, let's not forget…" he turned to Faylore, "… having an arrow put through your skull by."

As he drew back his hood, he glared at Jared, "But worst of all…" he bellowed, "… being banished by."

Faylore's eyes widened as they filled with tears, "Xarran," she mouthed. "But you… you're…"

"Dead?" screamed Xarran, "Is that what you were going to say? That I'm dead because you murdered me?"

Tears streamed down Faylore's cheeks, "I never wanted to," she said, her voice hardly more than a breath, "You gave me no choice, I had to, you…"

"See what you did to me!" he roared, his voice now shrill and rasping as he turned and swept his hair aside to reveal his scars. One side of his face was as it had always been with handsome young features and smooth skin. The other showed hideous scarring, twisted and discoloured. His voice became calmer, "If not for Lord Karrak, I may not have survived your cowardly attack. My father saved a life that was left hanging by a thread. If I had not been at one with the black arts, you would have broken that thread, Thedarian. Had the arrowhead been forged of pure gold, you would have surely severed it." He paused, "Oh dear… you look shocked. Have I given away a secret? Why do you think that half-faced freak always carries his beloved crossbow and golden bolts?"

"This half-faced freak is warning you, errand boy, deliver your message and leave!" snarled Hannock as he twirled a golden bolt between his fingers.

"Put it through his eye, Hannock, it'll be quicker than Lodren shoving 'is 'ammer up his…"

"Threats, threats, threats!" exclaimed Xarran, "I come here to deliver a message and all I receive in return, is threats."

“Well bleedin’ get on with it then,” screamed Grubb.

“My dear Uncle Jared… you don’t mind if I call you that, do you? After all, I am your nephew.”

“Whatever!” Jared sighed, in frustration, “Just deliver your message and go!”

“Well, Uncle Jared, it seems that things between you and my father have become a little… tense.”

“That may have something to do with him being a deranged psychopath who murders innocents indiscriminately,” barked Hannock.

“He can be a little… impulsive, shall we say. You may not agree with his methods, but his intentions are noble. He aims to bring an end to all conflict. Imagine, Uncle, no more battles, no more wars, all pain and suffering, gone.”

“Yeah, no pain an’ sufferin’ if you’re dead is there?” snapped Grubb. “Jared, can’t we just kill this git an’ be on our way?”

Xarran tutted a few times, “Any attempt to harm me, Grubb, would be most unwise.”

“Your magic is no match for mine, Xarran,” Jared warned him. “Add to that the fact that you are hopelessly outnumbered, and you will see that you are in no position to make threats.”

“Not a threat, dear Uncle,” said Xarran quietly, “simply a statement of fact.”

A sudden howling gale began as Xarran slowly raised his arms. The sky darkened as black clouds formed high above them and forked lightning struck the ground, splintering any rocks that lay there.

Jared raised his staff, “Xarran cease immediately or I will end your life,” he warned.

“No need for concern, Uncle,” shouted Xarran as the wind grew stronger, “I believe it only fair that you witness the true power I wield. You doubt my word, but will you doubt your own eyes?”

“Jared, just give the word,” bellowed Hannock as he raised his crossbow.

“No, wait!” Jared shouted, “Xarran, last warning!”

A gargantuan shape emerged from the clouds, its leathery wings causing a tremendous gust as it hovered above them. The lightning flashes illuminated its ruby-red scales making its entrance even more terrifying. Xarran laughed manically, “Now do you see?” he bellowed, “Your attempts to thwart my father are futile, Uncle. You will bow down or be destroyed!” He turned his back and looked up, “To me,” he roared.

The dragon landed with a crash and immediately lowered its head to the ground. Xarran approached its outstretched wing and grinned wryly as he used it as a stepping stone with which to mount his steed.

Lodren was agog, “No!” he gasped, “It can’t be! Jared, that’s Fireweigh. Why is he helping Karrak?”

Now astride the dragon’s neck, Xarran took great pleasure in continuing his taunting, “It appears the tides have turned, Uncle. It is now you who are hopelessly outmatched. You seem shocked!” he laughed. “But not as shocked as those two dergon eh, Charles?”

Jared studied Hannock, a questioning expression on his face. Hannock avoided his gaze, glaring at Xarran and hoping that the subject would pass.

"Oh dear," laughed Xarran, "Now I have let a secret slip, haven't I, Captain? He never told you did he, Uncle? Have you never questioned what happened to them the day that Faylore left me with this little memento?" he asked, pointing to his face.

"What's he talking about, Hannock? What happened to the dergon?"

"Take no notice of him, Jared," Hannock growled. "He's just trying to goad us into a fight."

"Come now, you're far too modest, Charles," laughed Xarran. "Tell him… tell him how you butchered them!"

Hannock was shaking with rage.

"I'd be careful of that one," smiled Xarran, pointing at Hannock, "He professes to be so noble and upstanding. He calls my father a psychopath and a murderer, when he is no better. At least Lord Karrak has honour enough not to hide his deeds! You see, Uncle, Charles here just couldn't forget the past. He never forgave the dergon for what they did to the people of Borell so he exacted his revenge on the two that had so gallantly come to your aid. Now, I know that they were your sworn enemies and to face them in combat would have been an honourable way for them to die, but that wasn't the case. This coward stabbed them in the back, waited until they had sheathed their swords and hacked them to pieces. They didn't even see it coming."

"One good deed could never outweigh the atrocities they were guilty of in the past!" roared Hannock. "They deserved to die! I'm just glad that I was the one fortunate enough to carry out their execution!"

Jared, although taken aback, knew that he could not allow himself to be distracted from their current situation, “What’s done is done,” he bellowed above the tempestuous wind.

Lodren could contain himself no longer, “What have you done to Fireweigh?” he roared. “He’s my friend, you let him go!”

Xarran patted the dragon’s neck, “I don’t think so,” he answered, slowly. “This beast belongs to me now, it obeys my every command.”

“Fireweigh is not an it!” snarled Lodren, “And he’s a good dragon, you must have done something for him to behave like this.”

Fireweigh arched his neck, spewing a gout of fire into the air. “It…” emphasised Xarran, “… will do as it is bid, and I am the only one who will be doing the bidding.”

“Well that’s where you’re wrong, the dragons will obey my word above yours. I’m the…”

“Yes, yes, we know,” Xarran interrupted him, “You’re the dragon rider!”

Lodren’s mouth stayed open.

“However, there is something you may not know. You see, Lord Karrak discovered something that was far more interesting. He heard a rumour of a legendary artefact that contained the soul of the most powerful dragon that ever lived.”

Faylore shook her head, “No!” she exclaimed quietly as the word stuck in her throat.

“Ah, Faylore,” said Xarran, “Was there something you wanted to say? No? Oh well, as I was saying. The artefact of legend was, in fact, a crown! I mean, of all things! Why would anyone seal the soul of a dragon in a crown?" He reached inside his robes. Drawing out the crown, he placed it on his head. "It's a bit ugly I must say, however, I was delighted to find that it actually works! Whoever possesses the crown controls all dragons." He leered at Faylore, "Your mother says 'hello'… well, I'm sure she would have if she'd lived long enough."

Faylore collapsed to the ground. To lose her father was devastating, but the news of her mother's passing was too much for her to bear.

"Anyway…" continued Xarran, "… time is pressing and we all have better things to do. You, obviously, are taking these horrible vermin back to Borell in the vain hope of protecting them. As for any other plans you may have, I'd rethink them if I were you. Of course, we could attempt to settle our differences now and you may kill me, but how many of your tiny friends are you willing to sacrifice, Uncle? Swallow your pride, Jared, make the right decision."

Jared glanced at his friends. Not one would hesitate to follow his lead should he choose to do battle with Xarran and the dragon. His heart sank, he had no choice. As fearless as his companions were, he knew that some would not survive such an encounter. The added concern of the Vikkery also had to be addressed. He found it hard to admit it to himself, but Xarran, the young man that he thought he knew, was right. A battle now would be catastrophic.

With hatred in his eyes, he faced Xarran, "What happens now?" he asked.

“Nothing,” replied Xarran. “Nothing at all. You take your little rats wherever you like, I watch you leave and nobody gets hurt.”

“And Karrak?” asked Jared.

“Will send for you,” replied Xarran. “When the time is right. I have to be honest, he won’t be pleased when I return. He was hoping that you would join him, today.”

“His pleasure is not in the forefront of my mind,” replied Jared. “But, as you are playing the part of the messenger, you can carry one to my brother for me. Tell him that the next time we meet, I’m going to kill him.”

Xarran lowered his head, a wry grin parting his lips, “Off you go then,” he said, mockingly.

The Gerrowliens began herding the Vikkery past Fireweigh, making sure to give him a very wide berth. Once they were clear the companions followed single file, each glaring at Xarran as they passed.

At the rear, was Lodren. The turmoil in his mind was obvious for all to see as he dragged his feet. Pausing at Fireweigh’s side, he raised his hammer, pointing it at Xarran, “If you hurt one scale of any dragon, I swear I’ll flatten you,” he whispered.

“Why would I hurt them?” Xarran laughed, “I love my new pets. I would have wasted so much time destroying that rats-nest of a village, but with the help of this beast…” he said, slapping Fireweigh’s neck, “… it took but a few minutes.”

Lodren’s grip tightened on his hammer’s handle.

“Oh, but I’m forgetting!” exclaimed Xarran. “Where are my manners? I never thanked you properly, did I?” he said, looking toward Grubb.

Grubb looked as puzzled as the rest, "Me?" he asked, "Ye ain't got me to thank for nothin'," he growled.

Xarran shook his head, "No, not you," he replied, dismissively, "Your shy little friend, the one hiding behind that scrag-end of a pony you drag around with you."

Cowering behind Buster and trying unsuccessfully to remain hidden from Xarran's eye, was Lorzic.

Grubb knew that Lorzic was there but had paid him no mind, believing that he was simply terrified of the dragon. "Lorzic?" he asked, suspiciously, "What's 'e talkin' about?"

"No idea," replied Lorzic, far too quickly and nervously for it to be convincing.

"Oh, come now, Lorzic!" protested Xarran, "You're far too modest! I mean, allowing me to use your trinkets as a distraction for my uncle was a stroke of genius. You said he wouldn't be able to resist a cry for help, and you were right. It gave us just enough time to get what we actually wanted," he added, stroking the Thedarian crown.

Grubb transformed in an instant and grabbed Lorzic with all four hands, "Is that true?" he roared.

"I had no choice!" screamed Lorzic, struggling to breathe. "He said he'd kill everyone if I didn't help!"

"Grubb!" bellowed Faylore, from far ahead, "Put him down… NOW!"

Lorzic babbled incoherently, his eyes fixed on Grubb's bared fangs. Grubb knew that the fate of the snivelling wretch he longed to tear apart, was not his to decide. The traitor would be judged by another, he would be judged by the Thedarian Queen. He threw Lorzic to the ground. Shrinking, he took hold of Buster's reins and marched away. As he reached the other Vikkery, Jared noticed the astounded looks they were giving him. There were many sounds of tutting and visible shaking of heads. Were they disappointed that Grubb hadn't given in to his anger and torn Lorzic apart?

CHAPTER 18

"Well it scares the life out of me."

"Why? It never even comes close to us when we camp."

"I don't care! I just know it's out there somewhere watching us."

"How? Come on, how do you know? I mean, I've not seen it since we managed to escape that loony and his dragon."

"Trust me, it's out there! Wait 'til the wind changes, then you'll know. Bloody thing stinks."

The Vikkery sitting around one of many campfires were obviously discussing Bogg. The zingaard had developed an attachment to Grubb and had been following them for weeks. Grubb in turn, felt responsible for Bogg and would sneak off under cover of darkness every night to feed him. He understood that there was no way he could bring the beast amongst the companions and Vikkery, but he wasn't prepared to abandon him and just hope that he could fend for himself either.

Jared watched him through half-closed eyes as he crept back into camp one night. He was completely unlike any of his kin. Grubb was caring, loyal and good natured, traits it seemed that were complete mysteries to the rest of the Vikkery. Jared smiled, his face hidden by the coarse blanket he had drawn tightly about him as he lay pretending to sleep. He felt no guilt at spying on his friend, he had no suspicions of ill deeds where Grubb was concerned, only a deep admiration for his most honourable convictions. But one question burned in his mind, a question that had arisen from an offhand comment made by Lorzic. His investigations would begin the following morning.

***

As dawn came a faint mist drifted through the camp, a sure sign that winter was fast approaching. The Vikkery were a total enigma to the Nibby. They never ate breakfast, and that was something that Lodren simply could not comprehend. He would scurry around before daybreak every morning, tutting and shaking his head as he prepared a veritable feast for the companions. It was his duty to ensure that they were heartily fed before they had to endure the rigours of the day, at least, that's what he believed.

"Good morning," he said cheerily as Jared approached, "What can I tempt you with, Your Highness?"

Jared seemed distracted, "Oh… erm, nothing, I'm fine thank you."

Lodren was horrified. What an insult, he thought. He frowned, "You can't go all morning without at least something, Mr Jared, you'll make yourself ill," he warned. His eyes widened, that was it, Jared must already be ill. Why else would anyone decline his delicious food? "Oh, Mr Jared, I'm so sorry!" he exclaimed, "What are your symptoms? Stomach ache?

Nausea? Maybe Mr Drake has some of Yello's potion left, that… Abigails Mercy that he swore by."

"Lodren, I'm fine," Jared insisted, "I'm simply not hungry, and besides, I have something I need to do." He patted Lodren on the shoulder, "See you later." As he drifted between the Vikkery he would pause occasionally, lean down and make enquiries.

One of them gestured toward the woods, "Went to the stream to bathe, I think," she said. He thanked her and headed toward the trees. He could hear the trickling of the water as he neared it, but there was no sign of his quarry.

"Tambly," he called, "Are you out there?" There was no reply, "Tambly, I need to speak with you." Still there was nothing.

He continued until he reached the stream. Tambly wasn't there. Perhaps she's gone back to the camp he thought, but as he turned he saw a tiny blanket on the ground. He picked it up, perhaps she had dropped it? Then, he saw the blood. Raising his staff, he began to call her frantically, his voice getting louder each time he called her name, "Tambly…" no response, "… Tambly!" still nothing, "… TAMBLY!"

Then, he saw Bogg. The zingaard stood, its head tilted to one side, staring at him. Cradled in one of his huge hands lay the limp figure of Tambly. Jared, fearing the worst, conjured a fireball. He desperately wanted to disintegrate the beast but, if by some miracle Tambly were still alive, he could not risk harming her.

"Put her down!" Jared called, "Gently."

Bogg tilted his head to the opposite side, then looked down at Tambly. Jared's heart skipped a beat as the beast suddenly clutched Tambly closer to him, but his panic turned to confusion as Bogg suddenly stretched his arm out as if to show him what he held, “Nice thing,” he grunted, “Good thing.”

“That’s it,” said Jared, trying to remain as calm as possible. He did not want to alarm the creature in any way.

Bogg began to approach him a little quicker than he would have liked, “Good thing,” he kept repeating. He stopped directly in front of Jared, handing Tambly carefully to him, “Good thing… no dead thing.”

She was alive!

Bogg backed away. Jared was unsure exactly what to make of the situation. Had the zingaard done this, by accident or intention? It was an answer that would have to come later. He turned and sprinted back to camp. Frantically he began to call for Grubb. Tambly was gravely hurt and Jared knew that Grubb was her only hope.

“What happened to her, Jared?” he asked as he rushed across to him.

Jared had placed her near to one of the dwindling campfires that remained. He held up his hand, causing it to flare up once more. “I’m not sure,” he replied, “The zingaard from Mallorkan… it… oh, never mind that! Will she be alright!?”

“Give me a second to ‘ave a proper look at ‘er,” urged Grubb. “Yeah… well, that cut’s a nasty one, don’t think there’s any bones broken or nothin’ though. She’s froze’ to the bone, must’ve been out there a good while.”

Various Vikkery were offering blankets to cover poor Tambly but Grubb, more intent on healing her wound, ignored them. Faylore swept through them, taking a blanket or two and leaning down to cover Grubb's patient.

"She'll be fine shortly," announced Grubb as he rose, "Mind you, she's going to 'ave one cracker of a headache. Some o' that stuff that Yello used to swig might help," he said thoughtfully, "Drake, is there any of it left?"

Drake smiled apologetically as he shook his head.

"Well don't none of yer know 'ow to make some more, you are supposed to be wizards!"

"Potion making was something that never came into conversation I'm afraid, Grubb," said Emnor, "I have no idea of its ingredients."

"Penellerim leaves, simfax petals, pollum and gibbonite hair," muttered the voice, "Simple process really, everything we need is in my bag."

The companions stared at Drake. They saw his lips moving, but none of them heard his voice. Once again, they heard Yello.

Lodren shuddered, "Mr Jared, I'm begging you, please tell him to stop doing that!"

Drake glanced around at the amazed looks on the faces of his friends. His head dropped, "Did our old friend just pop in to say hello again?" he sighed. It seemed he was getting used to his situation.

"Right!" announced Hannock, "Now that we know the little one's going to be alright you'll have to excuse me!" he announced.

Taking up his crossbow, he marched briskly toward the trees.

"Where are you going?" called Jared.

Hannock paused briefly as he answered, "I believe I may need a new rug, and I know exactly where to find a pelt that has outlived its usefulness!"

"Now you just 'ang on a minute, Captain carve up!" yelled Grubb as he chased after him, "You don't know that Bogg did this," he added, grabbing Hannock by the sleeve. "We'll wait for Tambly to come 'round before we do anythin', and not before! If it turns out that Bogg is guilty…" he struggled to finish his sentence, taking a deep breath before he could, "… then, I'll do it!"

Hannock folded his arms, deliberately resting the crossbow on his shoulder, "You'll do what exactly?" he asked.

"You know what I mean!" snapped Grubb, "I'll…" he twitched his head to the side a few times.

"Kill it," said Hannock, finishing the sentence.

Grubb scowled, "Yes!"

It seemed they were destined to encounter delays as it was a few hours before Tambly regained consciousness.

Grubb had not left her side, although he was diligent enough to keep an eye on Hannock as he tended to her, "'ow ye feelin' sweetie?" he asked as she opened her eyes.

"Ooh, my head," she answered, raising her hand to her brow but managing a weak laugh, "It feels like a tree fell on it."

"It looked like it had, when I first saw ye, but you're alright now," he said smiling, "Yer as pretty as ye always were." He blushed, realising what he'd just said.

“Are you flirting with me, Grubb, or are you like this with all your patients? I’m a married woman…”

“No ye ain’t!” laughed Grubb, “Ye just tell everyone that so they don’t give ye funny looks.”

“Oh really!” Tambly protested, “And how would you know?”

“’cause if ye had a husband he wouldn’t ‘ave let ye wander off to find water on your own, would ‘e? And he’d be ‘ere with ye now.”

“Terribly sorry to interrupt,” Jared crouched as he reached them. He had overheard their conversation as he approached. He didn’t even attempt to hide the knowing smile. It wasn’t in mockery, it was that he’d never seen Grubb acting so tenderly. He actually thought it was quite romantic in a strange, miniature way, of course.

Grubb quickly became his normal self, “What do ye want?” he grunted.

“I need to speak with Tambly,” replied Jared, still smiling.

“Alright, but you go easy on ‘er,” warned Grubb, “An’ take that stupid look off yer face, ye look like an idiot!”

Jared watched as Grubb shuffled away mumbling to himself, then turned his attention to Tambly, “You gave us quite a scare,” he said. “If it wasn’t for Grubb you may not have survived.”

“He’s lovely, isn’t he?” said Tambly with a glint in her eye.

“Yes, well…” Jared felt a little uncomfortable, “… erm, lovely. Tambly, what happened to you?” he asked, wanting to change the subject as quickly as possible.

"Did the zingaard attack you? If it did, we shall have to destroy it."

"Oh, no!" she exclaimed, a clear note of panic in her voice as she grabbed Jared's hand, "He didn't mean it, honestly, he didn't do anything wrong! Please sir, don't hurt him!"

"Calm down, Tambly," said Jared, soothingly. "But he is responsible for this?"

"No, and yes," she replied, "It was my own fault, see."

Jared frowned, "Go on," he urged.

"Well, I was by the stream having a wash and fetching some fresh water, as you do. Now, at first, I didn't realise that the beast was there watching me. It gave me a start when I saw him out of the corner of my eye, I thought he was going to attack but he didn't, he waved to me! I was taken aback, I must say! Anyway, he never moved any closer, just sat there watching me. He was rocking from side to side, I think he liked the feel of the morning sun on his fur. He started rocking faster but the sun was melting some of the frost. He either didn't notice it or had never seen frost before, because suddenly he slipped and fell flat on his face. Well I know I shouldn't have, but I thought it was one of the funniest things I'd ever seen and couldn't stop laughing. He must have known, because he started to pretend to fall again and again. I was so busy laughing that I wasn't paying attention. That's when I slipped. I remember hitting my head on a jagged rock and seeing the blood… and the beast picking me up, but after that, nothing."

"So, it was simply an accident?"

"Yes, sir," replied Tambly, "Just my stupid clumsiness. You won't hurt the poor beast will you, sir? I'm sure he was only trying to help."

Jared patted her on the leg, "We won't lay a finger on a single, smelly hair, promise," he smiled. His expression changed, "Tambly…" he began tentatively, "… I wondered if you could answer a few questions for me?"

Tambly looked puzzled, "Well I don't know how a Vikkery like me could possibly know anything that you don't," she smiled. "But I'll help if I can."

"I think you'll know far more than I do. You see, it's about Grubb."

"What about him?" she replied, blushing a little.

"Do you know anything about his family? It's what Lorzic said about them being ashamed of him. Why would they be ashamed that he transformed into a dragon?"

Tambly scowled, "That Lorzic's a fool, always has been!" she said curtly, "If it doesn't line his pocket, he's not interested. Everything else to him is wrong, so he picks on everyone to get them on his side and make him more coin. He's not fit to even speak of Grubb's family, let alone say anything about what they'd think."

Jared was intrigued and leaned forward, eager to learn more.

"They're a legend amongst our people, especially his father," continued Tambly, "He could change into things the rest of us could only dream about! Look at our normal size," she said, spreading her arms. "But it wasn't a problem for Grubb's dad, he could change into things thirty feet tall and it didn't even weaken his skin!"

Jared shook his head slightly, “I don’t follow your meaning,” he said apologetically.

Tambly thought for a moment, working out the best way to explain it to him, “Imagine a water skin,” she suggested, “Once it’s full, it’s full, but if you keep trying, it’ll stretch a bit, so you can fit more in. But if you try to put too much water in it, it splits when the hide gets too thin.”

“So the bigger the form you Vikkery take, the thinner your skin becomes?”

“Exactly!” replied Tambly. “And the easier we can be wounded. But not Grubb’s dad, his skin actually got thicker. The bigger the form he took the stronger he got, it was the only way he survived as long as he did. He wouldn’t have lasted a day otherwise! I suppose that’s why he was as successful as he was when he had to do what he’d promised.”

Jared leaned even closer to Tambly, “Which was?” he asked, inquisitively.

Tambly suddenly looked a little uncomfortable. She hadn’t meant to say as much as she had but realised that it was too late to do anything but answer the question that had been posed to her. She took a deep breath, “He was a dragonslayer!” she whispered.

Jared’s mouth fell open. Had he misheard what Tambly had just said? “Forgive me, Tambly,” he said, laughing gently, “I could have sworn you said he was a dragonslayer.”

Tambly frowned, “That’s because it is what I said!” she replied. “Why do you think we were all staring at Grubb when we met that scarred sorcerer? We were all expecting him to change into something huge and attack the dragon, not just walk past like there was nothing he could do about it. He has the same strength as his dad, you saw him turn into a dragon the same as we did, or had you forgotten about that?"

"Sorry, Tambly," replied Jared, "It's just a bit of a shock to discover that my friend's father was a dragonslayer."

"Not just his father," Tambly corrected him, "His mum, his brothers and both of his uncles were too."

"Brothers?"

"All three of 'em," replied Tambly, nodding her head. It was so horrible for Grubb, losing 'em all at the same time. His whole family gone in a flash, literally. Broke his heart it did."

"How?" asked Jared, exasperated by what he had just been told.

Tambly shook her head, "Sorry," she said abruptly, "I've said too much already. Now, if you'll excuse me I'm feeling a bit queer, I need to sleep. If you want to know anything else, you'll have to ask Grubb yourself."

Shuffling down, she pulled her shawl tightly around her and closed her eyes.

Jared watched her for a few moments, then rose and quietly strolled away.

"So now ye know," came a voice from the bushes. It was, of course, Grubb. He hadn't gone as far as Jared had thought and had heard every word that had passed between him and Tambly. He didn't seem angry, or even slightly annoyed, more… disappointed. "My terrible family secret," he snorted. Looking up at Jared, he sighed. "All ye had to do was ask," he muttered.

"Grubb, I'm terribly sorry," Jared said, apologetically, "I didn't mean to pry. It's just…"

"Yes ye did," chuckled Grubb, interrupting him, "Ye wouldn't 'ave been asking so many questions if ye didn't."

"But…"

"It's alright, Jared. Don't worry about it, you were bound to find out sooner or later. Tell ye what, you get everyone together and I'll tell ye everything ye want to know, 'cause I'm only sayin' it once and after that… ye can all stuff yer questions!"

***

A few minutes later every companion was seated in a circle around one of the campfires, eager to hear Grubb's tale.

Grubb himself felt easier walking around it as he began, "It all started before I was born," he said. "My old dad used to tell me some fantastic tales when I was a lad, made my hair stand on end sometimes it did. At bedtime I used to stare out into the darkness, terrified that a fire-breathing dragon would suddenly come charging out of it and roast us all alive. We hadn't built the village then, see, it was decades before we got around to that. Then I'd realise I had my dad there to protect us so as I stared into the flames of the campfire, I'd doze off feeling safe."

"But you said it started before you were born," urged Lodren with excitement, "Tell us about that."

"And do be quick about it," yawned Poom. "I have a very nice tree branch picked out for a nap, and I'd rather not keep it waiting."

Grubb scowled, "Well…" he continued, glaring at Poom, "… years before, there weren't many Vikkery and as we aren't the largest of folk, we tended to hide out in forest areas as much as possible for safety. There were far more wolves and bears around apparently when my dad was young," he paused, making sure that he had everyone's undivided attention.

"My dad was kind of the leader of the Vikkery. They always asked his advice and looked to 'im for guidance with most things, but then the rumours started. One of the youngsters said he'd been playing in the woods and lost track of time. It was getting dark before he realised how late it was and how far he'd wandered. He started heading back and got the shock of his life. Because the light was failing he couldn't make out exactly what it was that was ahead of him, only that it was very large and seemed to have small flames coming from its mouth."

"So it was a dragon then!" whispered Lodren, his eyes wide.

Grubb sighed, "Well, yes it was. But he didn't know that! He'd never seen one before! Now, do you mind if I carry on? Or was there anything else?"

Lodren looked suitably embarrassed, "Sorry," he said quietly.

"As you can imagine, the poor lad was terrified. He hid behind a tree for ages, even after the dragon had gone. Thought he'd be gobbled up for supper if he so much as moved an inch. That's where my dad and the others found ‘im the following morning, shaking and cryin’ with fear.”

“From what you’re saying, the elders didn’t believe his story,” suggested Hannock.

“No, unfortunately not. They thought that because he was alone in the dark he’d just imagined it. After a few days the boy seemed fine and everyone started to forget all about his fanciful tale. It would prove fatal!”

“But dragons aren’t dangerous!” protested Lodren, “They’re our friends, they wouldn’t deliberately hurt anyone.”

“Not now,” agreed Grubb, “But I’ve watched them over the years, Lodren, they’re not the same as they were. The last thing you’d have as a friend back then was a dragon!”

“Pleeaaase,” urged Poom. “My lovely tree! Get on with it!”

“Anyway, a few weeks passed, and more and more tales were being told of sightings of the huge beast that roamed the forest. My dad decided to investigate. He was the most seasoned hunter of them all and set out to see if ‘e could discover any tracks that might give ‘em a clue of what might be causing the rumours. It didn’t take ‘im long. He found massive clawed footprints everywhere! Normally you’d find ‘em on soft damp ground, but these were all over the place. When ‘e got back to the camp ‘e told everyone that they had to move on ‘cause they weren’t safe. It was late in the day, so they agreed that they’d leave the very next morning,” Grubb suddenly looked very solemn, “That delay cost ‘em dearly.”

“The dragon attacked?” asked Jared.

"In the middle o' the night while most of 'em were asleep," sighed Grubb. "They never stood a chance! Some of 'em were roasted alive before they knew what 'appened and others were chomped up as they tried to escape the flames. My family were some of the lucky ones. As they ran for their lives the way they went led to a ravine. They all went over the edge, figured that they might survive the fall. The odds were much better than facing a raging dragon."

"And did they all survive?" asked Emnor.

"Yeah..." sighed Grubb, "... not so much as a scratch between 'em. Well, my family anyway. Some o' the others weren't so lucky. Them that was, hid wherever they could and waited 'til morning. My dad and a few others scrambled back up the ravine to check the camp. There was nothing left but charred trees and earth, the dragon had killed 'em all!"

"So your father didn't have his special powers at that point?" asked Emnor, "He was the same as all the other Vikkery."

"Nobody had any special powers!" laughed Grubb, "We weren't shapeshifters back then. That didn't 'appen until years later!"

"How did you become shapeshifters then?" asked Drake, now totally engrossed.

"Well if you'd all shut yer faces for five minutes, I'll tell ye," snorted Grubb.

There were mumblings of apologies from the companions. Grubb was enjoying being the centre of attention for a change. He cleared his throat and continued.

"As ye can imagine, such a disaster completely changed the behaviour of my ancestors. Once they'd just huddle together and follow a path that was clear enough with no real destination in mind. They'd stop when they needed rest and pitch a camp, life was simple. However, now that they were aware of the existence of dragons they were cautious of everywhere, and everyone. They moved more like a military unit than simple folk seeking a peaceful life. Scouts would be despatched to make sure the way was safe, and the slightest hint of danger would cause them to change course. One night, they found a place that seemed safe, a small cave set into a rock face that was difficult to reach without careful climbing. Better to take a risk clambering up a rock face than tackling an unknown beast or two."

Poom fell onto his back and rolled his eyes. It was obvious that Grubb was now in full storyteller mode. This was going to take some time, but all he could think about was his nap.

"That night..." whispered Grubb, "... whilst everyone slept, my dad was keeping watch. It had been a hard day, one of many, and my dad hadn't slept properly for over a week. He tried his best but fatigue took hold of 'im and, despite fighting it as hard as he could, he nodded off! He started to topple forward and jolted 'imself awake. His sight was blurry, but he was sure he'd only nodded off for a minute. Then he saw the man! Sitting as bold as brass warming 'is 'ands by the fire was a young chap dressed in black robes. He turned and smiled at my dad as if it was completely normal! 'I hope you don't mind?' he said, 'This night air has chilled me to the bone'!"

"Who was he?" asked Lodren, unable to contain himself.

Grubb frowned at his friend but carried on with his tale, "That was the strangest thing, he never gave his name. My dad asked him, of course, but he said it wasn't important. It made my dad a bit suspicious of the stranger but as he continued to talk, my dad started to relax a bit. The rest o' the family, having been woken up by their talk, huddled together behind my dad just in case things got nasty. Turns out there was nothing to worry about, the stranger was really friendly. He asked why they were in such a desolate place and seemed very interested when he was told about the dragon that had murdered so many Vikkery a few years before."

Drake opened his mouth but Hannock, not wanting Grubb to be interrupted yet again, shook his head and clamped his hand over it before he had time to speak.

"Deep into their conversation, this young chap revealed that he was a wizard! He said he could help my people protect themselves, but that there would be a price!"

"How much!" blurted out Lodren, clamping his own hands over his mouth before anyone else did.

"He didn't want coin," replied Grubb, slowly, "He said that they must make a solemn vow and keep it until their dying day! If he bestowed a gift upon them they would have to swear that they would hunt down every dragon they so much as heard a whisper of and slay it!"

Lodren gasped.

"My old dad could still hear the screams from the folk the dragon slaughtered years before and had 'orrible nightmares about the attack every night. Without so much as a pause, he agreed! The wizard explained how the spell would work, adding that once done it could not be reversed and would be passed down through every descendant of those present! It took about an hour apparently, but when the spell was completed every Vikkery was exhausted and fell into a deep sleep. When they woke the following morning, the wizard was gone! Not a trace of how he left, or arrived for that matter. Less than an hour later, my people began their very first dragon hunt. Their prey? The one dragon my father wanted his revenge on!"

"I take it they found it?" asked Jared.

"Oh yes, they found it alright. It took 'em months to get back to where it all happened. They didn't know if it would still be there, but it was. It was the very first trophy my dad ever collected. Back in the village, in my family home, there was a whole collection of 'em. Dragon teeth, scales, even a few bones, only small ones, but dragon bones nonetheless."

"I apologise in advance for this, Grubb, but…"

"How did they die?" said Grubb, pre-empting Hannock's question. Hannock pursed his lips and nodded.

"As dragonslayers, my family had hunted every type of dragon you can imagine. There were fire-breathers, frost dragons, even dragons that could shatter rocks with a roar, but they were all doomed once they were discovered by my family. Until one day. There were whispers of a dragon far more powerful than any that had been mentioned before, a black dragon whose scales were like polished iron. Rumour suggested that it could summon the lightning from the sky and disintegrate anyone who so much as set foot near it. That was a challenge my old dad just couldn't resist! He was fascinated by the myth of the black dragon and before long my whole family ventured out to hunt it down…"

Grubb cleared his throat and turned his back to them, "... none of them returned."

"What happened to them?" Lodren screwed up his eyes, he had not meant to say it aloud. He glanced to his right, even in the failing light he could see Faylore glaring at him.

Grubb never turned around, "Nobody could say for sure," he replied quietly. "They went looking for my family but all they found was a few pieces of scorched armour. I was told when I was much older that the ground was just ash, as if a huge fire had burned all the vegetation. But it couldn't have been a fire because it would have spread further, and it formed a perfect circle. But all around, there were tracks... tracks made by a very large dragon."

"Have you any idea why they changed so much over the years?" asked Lodren, deciding he may as well keep asking questions for as long as Grubb was willing to answer them.

"No idea," he replied, "But the strangest thing was, the black dragon was never seen again. There were stories of all sorts of different coloured ones, but never a single mention of the black one!"

Lodren pondered for a while, wondering what he could ask next. Before he could, Grubb spoke again, "Which reminds me..." he muttered as he began to march away.

Jared nodded to Hannock, who promptly rose and followed the storyteller.

It didn't take long for Hannock to discover what was playing on Grubb's mind. Within minutes, Grubb had found his quarry... Lorzic. As he stormed toward him, his arm transformed. Grabbing Lorzic by the throat, he hoisted him into the air, “Me an’ you need to ‘ave a little chat,” he said, menacingly.

“Grubb,” called Hannock, questioningly, “… you’re not going to kill him, are you? Only you know how tetchy Faylore can be regarding such matters.”

Grubb sniffed loudly, “Don’t know!” he replied abruptly, “Ain’t made me mind up yet.”

Lorzic began pleading with his attacker, “Don’t kill me, Grubb,” he whined, “I’ll do anything you ask, anything, but please let me live!”

“Give me one good reason why I should?” asked Grubb. “You didn’t care about anybody else when ye sold ‘em out to that sorcerer and ‘is pet dragon, did ye? They could ‘ave all been killed, but it didn’t matter to you as long as ye got to line your own pockets.”

“No, Grubb!” exclaimed Lorzic. “It wasn’t like that at all. He said if I told anyone, he’d slaughter everyone in the village, even the children! I wasn’t paid, I swear to you!”

Grubb pulled him close, “Ye didn’t, not for one minute, think that a dragon could kill anyone by accident when it was rippin’ buildings apart?”

“I didn’t know about the dragon, just that he was a sorcerer. He grabbed me one night after dark and magicked me into the middle of a forest somewhere. He started setting fire to the trees and bushes with a wave of his hand. He said he’d do the same to every villager if I didn’t agree to help him…” Lorzic looked more terrified than ever as he finished his sentence, “… distract you.”

"So he knew where we were," Grubb mumbled thoughtfully. "How?" he shouted, shaking Lorzic roughly.

"I have no idea!" wept Lorzic. "You must believe me!"

"Grubb, put him down," sighed Hannock. "A horrible little money-grabber he may be, but he's telling the truth."

Grubb frowned, "How can ye be sure?"

"I'm a soldier, Grubb. I've interrogated enough men in the past to know when someone's lying."

Grubb snorted and released his grip.

Lorzic fell heavily to the ground but didn't try to flee, he just lay there, weeping and feeling sorry for himself.

CHAPTER 19

"So, how long before we reach this place then?" asked Tambly.

"Not really sure?" replied Grubb, "I don't take much notice of time. I just follow the others. All I care about is Buster, as long as he's alright, I'm alright."

Tambly laughed, "You have all these lovely friends but all you care about is your pony?"

Grubb smiled, "I never said I don't care about 'em, but they're big enough to look after 'emselves. Buster's only got me to take care of 'im."

"He earns his keep though, doesn't he!"

"Course 'e does!" exclaimed Grubb, "Carries all my stuff for me does my Buster. But, when the ground gets a bit too slippery I carry 'im and all the stuff, in case 'e hurts 'imself."

Two more weeks had passed since Lorzic had been questioned by Grubb. Their journey was blissfully uneventful, apart from Lorzic receiving the occasional scolding for being annoyingly helpful to everyone and the occasional pungent whiff when Bogg was brave enough to venture a little closer to the camp at night.

"Ooh look," said Tambly suddenly, "The prince is calling a halt. Looks like we're setting camp here tonight."

"Good!" replied Grubb, "I can give Buster a good rub down, 'e must be exhausted."

"I hope that's not directed at me!" exclaimed Tambly, "It was your idea for me to ride on his back."

"No!" exclaimed Grubb, "No… I didn't mean that… what I meant was, well we found those fruit trees and he's got loads …"

Tambly began to laugh again, "Oh do shut up, Grubb, I'm only teasing."

Grubb blushed, "I know, I know!" he replied looking flustered, "I was just going along with your little joke, is all."

***

Now completely dark, save the light from the fires, the camp was peaceful. The companions as always were together discussing provisions and other mundane topics, when a small voice hissed to them from the shadows.

"Excuse me."

They looked around. Faylore peered into the darkness. Her eyesight, being far superior to her friends, allowed her to see a tiny vikkery child waving to her.

"I'm sorry to bother you," she whispered, "I just thought you'd like to know…" she pointed toward the forest, "… there's somebody out there watching us."

The companions stared into the darkness, most now clutching weapons.

Faylore beckoned the child toward her, “Where?” she whispered.

“Everywhere,” she replied, “There are quite a lot of them.”

“Did you see what they look like?” asked Jared, “Were they big like us, or small like you?”

“As big as the lady,” replied the child, “But you can’t see them because they aren’t there.”

“Do you mean… they’re ghosts?” asked Lodren, nervously.

“I don’t know,” whispered the tiny girl, “They could be.”

“Charming!” came a female voice from the darkness. “We travel all this way to offer our help and what thanks do we receive? A mutant child comparing us to the dead!”

Faylore tilted her head slightly. She knew the voice, knew it very well indeed, “Jendilomin, is that you?” she asked.

“Were you expecting someone else?” replied her sister, suddenly shimmering into view.

Faylore hurried forward and embraced her sister enthusiastically, “What are you doing here?” she asked.

Jendilomin was not used to such shows of emotion and gently pushed her sister away, “Well, if I’m not welcome,” she said curtly.

Jared smiled. The tone in her voice was identical to that of her sister’s when they had first met… patronising and dismissive.

"Of course you are welcome, I'm simply surprised by your appearance," replied Faylore.

Jendilomin looked herself up and down, "What's wrong with my appearance?" she asked, "Do I have mud on me, or do you not like my clothing?"

"I meant that I am surprised to see you here," laughed Faylore.

Jendilomin looked puzzled, "Well why didn't you just say that?" she asked. "You've been around these people far too long Faylore, you're picking up dreadful habits."

Faylore glanced at her friends briefly, raising her eyebrows apologetically. Jared wondered if she realised how alike they were, or at least, were once. "How many are with you?" asked Faylore, keen to change the subject.

"Our ten best," replied Jendilomin, "But I'm afraid I have some bad news for you, Sister. News concerning our mother."

Faylore lowered her head, "I already know," she said quietly.

"How?" asked Jendilomin.

"That's not important," Faylore replied, "I just know that our mother is dead."

"Dead!" exclaimed Jendilomin, "When, how?" she screeched.

Faylore stood back confused, "Well, to be honest, I thought you might be able to tell me what happened."

"She was fine when I left her yesterday!" exclaimed Jendolim. "Did something happen?"

"No… at least, I don't think so. I mean, I don't know!"

"A dragon-riding sorcerer told us he'd attacked your home and your mother had been killed, but it was weeks ago," blurted out Lodren.

"So, Mother was not killed?" Faylore asked excitedly.

"No!" replied Jendilomin, becoming tetchy, "She's not dead, it's far worse than that!"

Grubb screwed up his face in disbelief, "How can somethin' be worse than bein' dead?"

Jendilomin craned her neck and studied him, "She's gone completely mad!" she stated abruptly.

"What do you mean, she's gone mad?" asked Hannock.

Jendilomin glared at him, "Family business," she said slowly, her way of telling him to be quiet.

Lodren sensed that it was all becoming a little confusing, "Why don't you all make yourselves comfortable by the fire?" he suggested, "I'll get some refreshments and you can discuss your business a little more calmly."

"At last!" Jendilomin sighed, "Someone with manners."

They were soon settled by the fire, eager to hear Jendilomin's news. Insisting that there be no interruptions, she began, "There was no attack," she informed them. "All was as it had always been, apart from a sense of unease when we ventured too far from our home. It was as if something were casting a permanent shadow across the lands, but we encountered no strangers nor beasts. However, we realised that all was not well. Late one afternoon some of our scouts reported that they had seen dragons on the wing. That concerned our mother greatly…" she said, glancing at Faylore, "… and she immediately ordered an escort to accompany her to the hall of history. Imagine our surprise when, on her return, she informed us that your crown had been stolen!"

"That much I do already know," Faylore informed her, "That young sorcerer has it, it has given him control over the dragons."

"Rotten stinker!" exclaimed Lodren. "We will get it back for you, Faylore! Perhaps the other dragons will help us?"

Faylore smiled at him, "I know you want to help," she said, "however, I'm afraid that there will be no aid from any dragons whilst Xarran has possession of the crown. It does not simply give the one who holds it the power to command a single dragon, it gives them the power to command them all."

Lodren's shoulders dropped, "Oh dear," he said quietly, "that's not good."

Faylore turned her attention back to her sister, "And what of Mother?" she asked. "What makes you think she has lost her mind?"

"The fact that she's only a day behind us and has every able-bodied Thedarian following her, armed to the teeth and is ready to go to war against the dragons!" exclaimed Jendilomin.

A huge grin spread across Grubb's face, "I always liked your mum," he said loudly.

"We can't wage a war against the dragons!" screeched Lodren. "They aren't evil! We can't hurt them, they don't know what they're doing!"

"We are not going to war with the dragons, Lodren," Faylore assured him.

"Speak for yourself," huffed Jendilomin, "If one of those things comes near me, I'll put an arrow through its eye."

"I thought you cared about all beasts, Sister?" asked Faylore.

"I do," replied Jendilomin, "But not ones that are intent on burning me to a cinder!"

"Now, now, they aren't all like that," protested Grubb, "Some of 'em will just turn ye into a big ice block," he added, roaring with laughter.

Before he could blink, Lodren's hammer appeared right in front of his face, "You're not helping, Grubb," hissed the Nibby.

"I don't want to interrupt," came a dreamy voice from above them, "But as you're not going to allow me to sleep in peace, would you like me to inform the rest of your people of your location? I'd be happy to guide them, providing they aren't too slow of course."

They looked up to see Poom hanging by his feet from a branch with Lawton close by, nodding in agreement.

"They are quite capable of…"

"That would be very kind of you," said Faylore, quickly interrupting her sister, "I'm sure you'll have no difficulty finding them with your superior night vision."

"Did you hear that, Lawton? Superior. That's what we are you know, superior." Laughing raucously, the Gerrowliens sprinted away.

Jendilomin turned to Faylore, "Why have you sent them to find Mother?" she asked, "Our people have no problem with following a trail."

"They are our friends, it would be rude to refuse their offer of aid whether it is needed or not," replied Faylore, smugly.

"Can we get back to the subject of the dragons?" Lodren asked, the concern obvious in his voice.

"Be serious for a minute, Lodren!" exclaimed Hannock. "Do you honestly think that any one of us is physically capable of doing harm to a dragon?"

"Ah, so you're saying you would if you thought you could?" shouted Lodren.

"That's not what I meant, stupid. But if it was a choice between any one of you or a dragon being hurt, I'd at least have to try!"

Lodren pouted, "Yeah…" he said slowly, "… I suppose you're right."

"We don't want to hurt them, Lodren," said Jared, "But we must learn how to defend ourselves against them. More importantly, we need to devise a plan to retrieve the Thedarian crown."

"Aren't we forgetting what our ultimate goal is here?"

All eyes turned to Drake, "Whilst we have to consider the threat, dragons are not our main concern." He looked around slowly at his friends, "Neither is Xarran, who seems to be controlling them with the power of the Thedarian crown," he added. "We need to concentrate on the heart of the problem, the very root that needs to be destroyed. Karrak is behind it all, we must find him and finish him, everything else is secondary!"

"And by finish, you mean…?"

"Yes, Hannock," said Drake, "I mean kill him!"

The companions stared at the young wizard. He was no longer the foolish adolescent that they had learned to tolerate so very long ago, he seemed to be more than he at first appeared. He rarely spoke, but when he did, what he said seemed very carefully thought out. Even his voice had changed. Mostly it was his own, but occasionally a phrase or comment would sound identical to the way Yello would have said it. In the past his opinions on virtually everything were ignored by the rest of the companions, but that was no longer the case.

There were a few moments silence before Jared spoke, "He's right, of course," he said quietly, "But for now at least, we stick to the plans we have made. We escort the Vikkery to Borell, retrieving my father on the way."

"Yeah," said Grubb slowly, "You sure you can get 'im back, Drake? Only it's one heck of a detour if ye ain't."

Emnor smiled as he patted Grubb on the back, "Don't you worry about that," he said quietly, "He's been doing this for centuries."

Grubb looked puzzled, "No he ain't!" he exclaimed, "He ain't even been alive for a quarter o' one!"

"I trust him, Grubb," Jared assured him, "That's all you need to know. Let's all get some rest," he suggested.

"The Thedarians should be here with Poom and Lawton at first light and we'll need to be ready to leave shortly after."

***

The following morning everything went as expected, with the Thedarians arriving before sunrise. Seeing over a hundred shimmering into view at once thoroughly impressed Lodren, who immediately began charging between them offering them a breakfast of honey cakes. Introductions were made and pleasantries exchanged, but it was quite clear that they were all of the same mind. They must proceed without delay if they were to have any hope of retrieving King Tamor, settling the Vikkery and finally defeating Karrak.

The only decision to be made was who was going to take the lead. The Thedarian's pompous nature naturally meant that they believed that no other could follow a trail better than they, something that didn't sit well with the Gerrowliens. Hannock also felt a little put out, having lead many a mission through the wilds. In the interest of co-operation, it was decided that two Thedarians would accompany Poom and Lawton as scouts, although this left a slight tension between them.

Faylore along with Jared, explained to Erenthas the events that had brought them to where they now stood, a process that took far longer than necessary due to her mother's constant interruptions and questions. Two days passed and still she would need something clarifying.

"So you say this boy, Sarrap, was a friend of yours?"

“Yes, Mother, and his name is Xarran,” replied Faylore, being as patient as she could.

“Why did you not simply kill him when you had the chance?” her mother continued.

Faylore sighed, “I thought I had,” she said, “I shot an arrow through his head, but somehow Karrak brought him back.”

Erenthas shook her head, “No dear,” she said almost sympathetically, “That’s not possible. You must have missed him.”

“Missed him!” exclaimed Faylore, “Mother, I never miss my target.”

Her mother patted the back of her hand, “I know,” she cooed. “Not usually, but no-one can bring back the dead my sweet, so you must have.”

Faylore gritted her teeth, “Karrak studies necromancy,” she said.

“It doesn’t concern me what his hobbies are,” snorted her mother, “You should tell me more about the type of magic he uses, that would be far more useful.”

Jared and Hannock were walking directly behind them, both struggling to keep their faces straight.

“Faylore,” said Jared, half biting his lip, “Terribly sorry to interrupt, but there’s something I could use your help with.”

Erenthas turned briefly and looked him up and down, “You run along dear,” she said quietly. “By the looks of them they’ll definitely need our help if they are to survive.”

Hannock quickened his pace slightly and strolled next to Erenthas, "Perhaps I could keep you company for a while?" he suggested.

She paused momentarily, inspecting her would-be companion, "No!" she said abruptly, and briskly walked away.

Hannock turned to Faylore, a huge grin on his face. Raising his arms out to his sides, he laughed, "Well I tried!"

Things got easier as the days passed. The Thedarians had learned to tolerate their new-found friends but still recoiled every time one of the Vikkery children came anywhere near them. One Thedarian even grabbed a branch to steer away a child who was playing nearby as if it were a stray animal, something its parents did not appreciate. Faylore calmed the situation down as quickly as she could and discovered that the branch-wielding Thedarian was concerned that if the child touched him he would be transformed into one of them, or something far worse. Faylore knew it to be nonsense but couldn't help noticing that throughout their conversation, not once did he take his eyes off Bogg. She did her best to allay his fears, laughing to make light of the situation. A typical Thedarian however, has no sense of humour and Faylore's attempts proved to be a fruitless gesture. Eventually, as queen, she simply ordered him not to be so ridiculous and, surprisingly, that worked.

And so it was, that after many weeks, the strangely populated caravan of refugees now had the measure of one another. Their co-existence had become peaceful, bar the occasional petty squabble, which was always caused by one of the Vikkery taking offence at nothing.

The Borellians, having travelled this way before, recognised a large clearing ahead. They paused, it seemed different somehow… dark and ominous.

The carcasses of small animals were strewn around, undoubtedly killed and devoured by larger predators. Jared, Hannock and a handful of Thedarians crept forward, wary of what they might encounter. All but Hannock carried bows, he clutched his crossbow. Every one a seasoned hunter, they could be trusted not to fire at the slightest movement of branch or twig. They would hold their nerve until it was absolutely necessary to release arrow or bolt. Standing stock-still, they waited. One by one the beasts were revealing their hiding places. Some wolf-like, others slightly larger, but all ferocious predators with saliva dripping from large canine teeth. Their would-be prey looked almost as dangerous, their evolution resulting in defensive horns and razor-sharp scales.

A sudden roar startled them all.

Bows were turned in all directions waiting for a charging attack. The carnivores howled and bayed in terror, their prey squealing like wild boar in unison. Where was the attack to come from? it was a split second before all became clear.

So intent were they on what may lie ahead, not one of them had considered what was behind. They had been followed.

Bogg had watched them with interest, why were they sneaking like that, what were they doing? He had seen weapons before and knew that they were only used for one purpose, making dead things. He studied them, saw their weapons raised and then beasts ahead. His mind was filled with confusion and panic. He remembered the horrors he had witnessed when trapped in his tiny cage. He roared as loud as he could and charged forward.

"No," he bellowed, "No! No! No make dead thing, no make dead thing!"

One by one, he chased every beast from the clearing. He wanted, needed them to be alive. The weapons were going to kill them, he couldn't allow it even if it meant he himself would perish. Satisfied that every animal had fled, he turned to Jared. Squatting on the floor, he gazed up at the prince, "Me, good thing. You, me out," he said solemnly. "Me, no dead thing. No more dead thing," he added, looking over his shoulder to where the wild animals had been.

Jared smiled at him, "No Bogg," he whispered gently, "No more dead thing."

Hannock was flabbergasted, "Well I never!" he exclaimed. "He chased them all off in case we killed any of them!"

"It certainly seems that way," agreed Jared.

"Right then," sighed Hannock, "I think it's time we made camp."

Jared watched as the Vikkery and Thedarians proceeded to settle for the evening. Walking across to Harley, he placed his arm around the young man's shoulder, "I need to speak with you," he said quietly.

"Oh, you mean about me taking care of the Vikkery while you and the others go off to fetch the king?"

Jared was lost for words and smiled.

"I'm not an idiot, Jared. I know you're just trying to protect me," said Harley, "I'm not as good in a fight as the rest of you, the last thing you need is to have to keep an eye on me if you get into a scrape."

"It's only for a few days," Jared assured him, "and you won't be alone, you'll have Poom, Lawton and the Thedarians with you, so they'll always be an excuse for you to escape if they start rattling your brain."

"I'll be fne," laughed Harley, waving his wand, "if it gets too bad, I can just send them to sleep with this."

"Just so you know, Harley," said Jared, "We're leaving tonight. We thought it would be easier if we waited until the Vikkery were asleep."

"You mean, so that you didn't have to spend hours and hours answering questions?"

"Precisely!" replied Jared. "If we planned to leave tomorrow morning it would undoubtedly be tomorrow evening before we escaped the dreaded Vikkery Inquisition," he laughed.

***

It was still dark when they appeared in Reiggan. Not knowing what to expect they were on their guard immediately, but there was nothing to guard against. The eerie silence was the same as it had been when last they stood within the ruins of the once great wizard fortress. Now, with only the six of them, it seemed more desolate than ever.

"Do not worry my friends," said Emnor quietly, "we shall restore it to its former glory in time."

Drake sighed, "Perhaps," he said, "but it'll never be the same without our friends."

***

Drake opened his eyes. Despite protesting that he was fine, Emnor had insisted that he rest before even addressing the recovery of the king. He felt a little embarrassed as he looked at his friends, it seemed that they either hadn't slept at all or had already been awake for some time.

"Ah, good morning," Emnor said, smiling.

"Only just," sighed Lodren. "You do realise your breakfast's ruined!" he groaned.

"Sorry," said Drake, instinctively, "Why didn't you wake me?"

"Ha!" laughed Grubb, "If Lodren had brought the walls down around ye, ye wouldn't 'ave stirred! You were dead to the world!"

"I wish you'd have tried harder," said Drake, frowning, "I was having terrible nightmares! At least, I think they were nightmares," he added quietly.

Emnor glanced at Jared, "You don't remember do you, Drake?"

Drake looked up at him, "Remember what?"

"What happened before you went to sleep," replied Emnor.

"Of course I do," smiled Drake, "You told me to get some rest and..." His voice tailed off.

Emnor smiled at him again, “There’s nothing to panic about, Maddleton. Something extraordinary happened, but it may take some time for you to recall it.”

Grubb suddenly burst out laughing, “It was one o’ the funniest things I’ve ever seen!” he roared. “If Lodren hadn’t caught ye, I’m certain you would’ve snapped in two! Solid as a rock you were. We couldn’t even bend yer arms and legs!”

Drake looked confused, “Would someone please explain what’s going on!” he asked.

“You’ve been accepted!” Emnor said excitedly.

“Accepted for what?”

“By Reiggan,” replied Emnor, now beaming.

“Did I bang my head or something when I had this fall, or am I right in thinking you’ve all gone barmy?”

“Neither,” said Emnor, chuckling, “The Fortress has recognised you as a master,” he squeaked, “I’m so proud of you!”

Drake looked horrified, “But I’m not old enough… oh dear!” He began running his hands over his face fearing that he had suddenly aged hundreds of years, “I knew there’d be something!” he exclaimed. “How bad is it? Will I start growing a huge white beard? Tell me, Emnor, I’m old, aren’t I?”

“Oh shut up, Maddleton,” snapped Hannock, “There’s nothing wrong with you. You haven’t changed a bit!”

***

Later that afternoon they gathered in the room where Tamor had been secluded. Drake was concerned, but not overly. He knew that Jared and Emnor would step in if anything seemed to be going awry.

"Now, Maddleton, relax," said Emnor, soothingly. "It will come to you naturally if you allow it. Simply empty your mind…"

"Shouldn't take long," mumbled Hannock. Jared glared at him, "The king," Hannock added hurriedly, "I meant for him to retrieve King Tamor!"

They watched as Drake slowly tilted his head to one side and then the other. Pictures formed in his mind as he followed a corridor off which lead many doors. He reached for the doorknob of the first one he came to but snatched it back as a familiar voice warned him of the danger behind it.

"Ha! You crafty old devil," he said aloud.

Emnor began to chuckle, "You didn't think he was going to leave you alone in there did you, Drake? I knew he'd help you."

Grubb nudged Lodren, "What's 'e on about?" he whispered.

"Well," replied Lodren, "when Yello… you know… died, Jared somehow gave all his magical powers to Drake. Now Drake not only knows his own magic, he knows all of Yello's as well."

"Ahhh," said Grubb slowly, "so Yello's alive but he's inside the boy?"

Lodren shook his head, "No!" he hissed, "Yello died, but his magic… oh do be quiet, Grubb, I'm trying to listen!"

Drake opened his eyes, “Wow!” he exclaimed, “I knew Yello was a bit cracked, but you wouldn’t believe some of the traps for anyone trying to find the king! Sorry Emnor, I didn’t mean to say he was cracked. What I should have said is that he was an absolute barmpot, and a spiteful and sadistic one to boot! Do you have any idea what could happen to you if you went the wrong way in that place?”

“He did have a flair for the dramatic, I’ll admit,” laughed Emnor.

“Perhaps,” agreed Drake, “but to have bits of you explode…” he added, squirming, “it’s positively barbaric!”

“But you found him?” asked Jared, “He’s safe?”

“Oh yes, but he’s not where we left him. He’s moved.”

“Moved! What do you mean he’s moved? How could he have moved?”

“Captain,” said Emnor, quietly, “the magical world is a very delicate one and it would take far too long to explain how this particular spell works. Now if you’d be so kind as to erm… how does Prince Jared put it? Ah, yes. Shut your face!”

Jared grabbed Drake’s shoulders, “But you can find him?” he asked, almost pleading. “You can bring him back?”

Drake embraced the prince, “Oh yes,” he smiled, “but not yet, not until my third visit.”

“Third visit!” exclaimed Hannock.

“Something wrong with yer ears, Hannock?” snorted Grubb.

Drake held up his hands, “It’s to keep King Tamor safe,” he assured them. “Anyone attempting to harm him would obviously try it immediately and, if unsuccessful, may try again. Only a fool would try a third attempt.”

“Can you go straight away?” asked Lodren.

“I’m afraid not,” replied Drake. “The visits have to be at least a day apart.”

***

They waited. Drake’s second attempt to find Tamor was far more eventful than his first, but only because he chose it to be. Fascinated by the traps that had been laid by Yello, he spent hours studying the intricacies of the ancient spells that had been used to create them. The companions watched with interest as his unconscious body would stretch out an arm or lean to one side as if investigating unseen hazards.

Lodren was most uncomfortable with the strange way that Drake was behaving. He tolerated it for as long as he could, but when the questions began, he ran out of the room as fast as his legs would allow.

Grubb, as usual, followed him, “What’s wrong?” he asked.

“It’s not right, it’s just not right!” exclaimed Lodren. “What if he falls for one of the traps? He shouldn’t be doing this, he’s only a boy!”

“So, Jared should abandon his father then?”

Lodren was flustered, “No, no, of course not,” he said, “but Jared or Emnor should be doing this, not poor Drake.”

“They can’t though can they. Drake is the only one who knows how Yello’s magic works!” Grubb paused, “Mind you,” he added, “it’s probably not Yello’s magic any more, it’s Drake’s.”

“Well I don’t like it!” flapped Lodren. “He’s going to get hurt. I just know he’s going to get hurt!”

Fortunately, Lodren was wrong and Drake returned unscathed, but far more enthusiastic than he had been prior to his two visits.

Day three came.

Lodren flatly refused to attend, “My nerves won’t take it!” he exclaimed. “I’ll be in the courtyard if you want me, I’m not coming down there again until you’ve finished.”

Entering the room for what they hoped would be the final time, they wished Drake well, and fell silent.

The air ahead of Drake shimmered as he began to chant, murmuring incoherent words that could not be understood by any other. Drake smiled as a gentle breeze fluttered his robes. His voice became louder as a swirling, rainbow-coloured vortex engulfed him, “Got you,” he sighed, “Your Majesty, time to wake up!” King Tamor shimmered into view.

Jared was about to run to his father but was grabbed by the shoulder as he passed Emnor, “I wouldn’t do that if I were you,” he chuckled. “If you interrupt before the reclamation is complete, we may have nothing but three piles of ash to accompany us on the rest of our journey.

Jared smiled at his friend, "Apologies," he said. "It's just..."

"No need for apologies, Jared. Your father is safe, as you can see, but it will take a little longer before you are able to speak with him."

As agonising as it was, Jared waited. His father was roused and now stood conversing with Drake. It lightened his heart to see Tamor safe and well, but the swirling light still surrounded them. Should he ask Emnor why? He thought back to Emnor reprimanding Hannock and decided against it. He stared at the staff he held in his grasp. It housed the Heart of Ziniphar, why did he not understand the magical process that was being performed before his very eyes?

Emnor was watching him, studying his expression, knowing the question that had just entered his mind.

"It does not hold every answer, Jared," he called slowly. "It is meant to carry the burden of far greater magic than this," he added, gesturing toward Drake.

"Strange choice of word, my friend," said Jared, thoughtfully. "Burden."

"Indeed," replied Emnor. "The magic we use is for good and it helps us in our everyday lives. The Heart, however, has a much greater responsibility. It exists to protect our entire world. Petty magic such as ours is far beneath it."

"Jared... Jared."

The prince looked up. Drake smiled as he stood beside the king and beckoned Jared, who immediately rushed to greet his father, "You are returned to us!" he exclaimed with joy.

"Yes," replied Tamor, looking him up and down. "And you are?"

A look of concern swept across Jared's face, "I… I'm Jared," he replied slowly.

Tamor slapped his thigh, "Of course you are," he laughed. "I remember you now, Jared. You're Pullim the farrier's boy aren't you? Wouldn't trust my stables to anyone else."

"No, Your Majesty! I'm Jared, I'm your son!"

Tamor stroked his chin, "No my boy, you're mistaken. I have no children. I'm not even married." He placed his hand over his mouth and leaned over to Drake, his attempt at a whisper totally ineffective, "I think this one's been out in the sun too long," he hissed. "He thinks I'm his father!"

Drake held up his hands, "He'll be fine, Jared," he said. "Give it time, his memory will return."

CHAPTER 20

Seated in a large, padded chair, Jared studied the comfortable surroundings of his chambers. That they had remained intact, as had the rest of the castle, perplexed him. He had wandered the halls and courtyards many times and all were empty. Every citizen of Borell had been taken by Karrak. How cruel his brother had been to enslave an entire kingdom but not leave the slightest trace of battle nor skirmish. His heart was heavy, and he despaired at the thought of what may come next.

The companions, Thedarians and Vikkery had reached the castle many months before and, although all seemed serene, Jared had not been able to shake the feeling of dread that dwelt within him. Each day he would stare at the Heart of Ziniphar, longing for it to impart news or somehow give a warning that danger approached, but it never did. It was simply a jewel that adorned the magnificent staff that he was now never seen without.

The Thedarians had stayed and helped the Vikkery settle for a few weeks before their departure, leaving only Faylore and a select few that she had chosen personally. Her mother had protested profusely, so much so that Faylore eventually had to exert her authority as queen and order them to leave. Little did they realise that it was Jared himself who had requested that Faylore order her people to return home, in order to keep them out of harm's way.

The Vikkery had settled into their new home and resumed as normal a life as they could. They adapted quickly to their new surroundings, which was no mean feat considering all that had happened. They were respectful of Jared's royal status and kept their word, offering various wares as remuneration in exchange for their dwellings, businesses and apparent security.

Jared did his best not to mingle with his new subjects. Each time one of them thanked him for bringing them to safety, his heart skipped a beat. Deep inside he felt that he had not. He had given them a roof over their heads and something to focus on in order to carry on, but safety was the one thing he could not guarantee. It troubled his mind greatly.

Then there was the issue with his father. King Tamor's memory had returned, to a degree, but he was no longer the strong ruler he once was. Occasionally in mid-conversation, his mind would wander, and he would completely forget the subject that was being discussed.

But the nights were the worst time for Tamor. He would retire in good spirits, but Jared knew it would only be a matter of time before the screaming started. During the day his memories were not a problem as there were many distractions to occupy him, but the terrors of Tamor's torture at the hands of Karrak came flooding back to him as nightmares each time he slept.

Whenever Jared would race to his father's side to reassure him, Hannock was always by his side.

***

As Jared stood on the ramparts, Hannock approached him. Bathed in sweat, he bowed briefly, “Your Majesty,” he said, before leaning his head forward and thrusting it into a water barrel. “Oh, that’s better.”

“How’s the training coming along?” asked Jared.

“Awful… terrible… crap! Take your pick, they all fit,” sighed Hannock.

“They can’t be all that bad!” exclaimed Jared, “You’ve been training them for two months, well, longer than two months as memory serves.”

“There’s not one bloody soldier amongst them, Jared! They’re farmers, millers, blacksmiths, what use are they?”

“They’re all we have, Hannock! You should be grateful.”

“They’re refugees, Jared. No two of them come from the same village! They couldn’t agree on the colour blue if you showed them a famper’s nose!”

“So, they have some fight in them then?”

“Yes, Your Majesty, they do. But all they want to do is fight each other!”

“Perhaps you’re going about it the wrong way, Hannock.”

“Jared, I’m a soldier… I am used to training other men who want to be soldiers. I’m not used to turning a man into something he doesn’t want to be!”

“Oh really?” said Jared, raising his eyebrows. “You turned me into a king. I didn’t want to be the king, but somehow you talked me into it.”

Hannock frowned, "That's different and you know it. Your father was no longer well enough to perform the duties of a king. I know it isn't his fault and before you say it, I love him as much as you do but it was for his own good."

"You believe it was for his own good?" asked Jared, smiling.

"He still thinks he's the king! He doesn't even realise that you now sit on the throne of Borell, he's completely oblivious to it all!"

"Let me get this right, you can make a king, but you can't make a soldier?"

"Well… what… what are you talking about?"

Jared laughed, "One soldier is useless, correct?"

Hannock nodded.

"We need them to need each other," Jared said slyly, "I have an idea, Hannock. Come with me."

***

Jared began to walk briskly ahead of Hannock, but even as he took his first steps he began to feel strange. His vision blurred and a dizziness caused him to stagger sideways slightly. He turned to face Hannock and was astounded at what he saw. Jared had stumbled at least two yards before he had regained his footing, but Hannock was still looking at where he had been. With his arm outstretched, Hannock was motionless. Jared placed a hand on his shoulder, "Are you alright, Hannock?" he asked, "Can you hear me?"

Not surprisingly, Hannock did not respond. Jared hurried to the edge of the ramparts and looked down into the courtyard. There were a few of the would-be guards there but none were moving. Returning to Hannock, he tried again, "Hannock! Hannock! Speak to me!"

"He cannot hear you."

Jared lowered his head, "So, at last you have chosen to face me."

Karrak drifted closer toward him.

Jared raised his staff, "Release Hannock!" he ordered.

"I have no hold over your friend, mortal. It is you who is changed."

"Mortal?" ask Jared, confused. "Who are you? What do you want?"

"Exactly the same as you, for there to be peace," replied Karrak.

"Then leave."

"As you wish," replied Karrak. "But you must come with me if we are to put an end to this. It is our destiny."

"What does that mean? What destiny?" His question remained unanswered as he and Karrak vanished.

***

"Jared!" Hannock began to panic. His king had vanished before his eyes. It could mean only one thing… Karrak. He whirled around hoping that Jared was still nearby and began charging across the ramparts calling his name. Then the screaming began.

Hannock scanned around, trying to ascertain what could be causing such panic. He saw one of the farmers glance to the heavens briefly, before screaming and fleeing for his life. Hannock peered into the sky and saw them. Descending slowly, their fiery breath seeming to ignite the clouds and set them ablaze, came three dragons. Their intent soon became apparent as their viscid expectorants rained down, adhering to the highest towers of the castle and engulfing them in flames.

They were here to destroy the last remnants of Borell!

Hannock watched in horror as the stone towers began to melt, such was the intensity of dragon fire. There was nothing he could do to defend against the ferocity of the dragons, he was as helpless as the rest. He slumped to the ground as despair took hold of him, Borell would surely fall this day! He was resigned to his fate, he would not flee and closed his eyes, waiting for death to take him. But he was premature in his assumption. Suddenly there was a loud crash. Opening his eyes he saw that a ruby dragon had landed in the courtyard and sat high on its neck… was Xarran!

“So, this is my home,” he shouted. “This is the birthright that was taken from me even before I was born. This is the luxury in which I should have been raised had my dear uncle not seen me as an embarrassment to the Dunbar name. I’m surprised he didn’t kill me whilst I was in the womb and have done with it!”

Hannock rose quickly and glared down into the courtyard, “Xarran, what have you done with Jared?” he bellowed.

“Ah, Captain Hannock!” exclaimed Xarran with glee. “How nice to see you again. We really should stay in touch, it’s been almost a year since last we met.”

“Answer the bloody question!”

“Ooh, you should be careful, Charles, or you may force me to change my plans. Now Uncle Jared…” he said thoughtfully, “Oh yes, he’s taken a little trip with my father. Don’t bother waiting, he won’t be coming back!” he added with a sneer.

“Where is he?” repeated Hannock.

“I think you may want to focus on your own predicament before you start worrying about anyone else’s,” growled Xarran.

“I already am! You want the castle and everything in it! Well you can have it.”

“Oh, you really don’t understand, do you? I don’t want it, I’m going to destroy it! Every stone and beam will be nought but molten rock and ash when I’m finished. As for you and your little friends,” he added, “by all means, run. It won’t make any difference. I’m going to destroy this castle and then, when I’m done with that, I’m going to kill you and everyone else in this pompous cesspit.”

Hannock shook his head in disbelief, “You’re insane!” he hissed.

Xarran shrugged and tilted his head slightly, “I know,” he sighed. “But it’s so much fun!”

As he raised his hand, Fireweigh stretched to his full height. Opening his jaws he roared, a gout of fire erupting from them toward Hannock. Hannock dived to the side as the flames narrowly missed him. He watched as the stone where he had stood began to melt. Fire that could melt stone? He had never heard of such a thing. It seemed retreat was his only option if he wished to remain alive. Half scrambling, half falling down the nearest staircase, he hugged the wall to avoid detection by Xarran or Fireweigh. Picking his moments, he dodged from one hiding place to another. Glancing up, he saw Lodren, and was horrified.

***

The Nibby was out in the open. He was not only choosing not to hide, he was walking straight toward Fireweigh, tears in his eyes. “Why are you doing this, Fireweigh?” he shouted. “You’re a good dragon, you don’t want to hurt anyone!”

Xarran frowned at him, pausing the dragon’s attack, “It does as I command, shrimp,” he roared. He took a deep breath, “Sorry,” he said, quietly, “Forgive me, I do have a bit of a temper and it’s hard to control at times. Listen to me, Lodren. I always liked you, you’re a bit annoying at times to be honest, but I do like you. If you run along now and stop bothering me, I’ll make you a promise… I’ll kill you last! Does that sound fair?”

As Xarran burst into maniacal laughter, Fireweigh leaned down to Lodren, struggling to speak, “He has the crown, I must obey his commands.”

“You have to try!” pleaded Lodren.

"Don't beg the dragon to help you, Lodren, it cannot. In fact, no-one can," he said mockingly. "Just go. Go on, see how far you can get before I catch up with you."

Lodren's shoulders dropped as he turned and shuffled away. It seemed all hope was gone. As he passed a cart, Hannock grabbed his shoulder and dragged him behind it. Lodren looked at him with big, doleful eyes. "Hello Mr Captain sir," he said woefully.

"What were you thinking?" hissed Hannock, "You could have been killed!"

"Looks like I'm going to be anyway, might as well get it out of the way."

"You are not going to die, Lodren. Not if I have anything to do with it anyway. I know the layout of this castle like the back of my hand. There are tunnels we can use to escape, follow me and you'll be fine."

"But what about everyone else?" exclaimed Lodren. "They don't know about the tunnels, how do they get out?"

"We'll take any we meet with us, but many more will perish if we ourselves don't get out of here. The safest place is the forest. Once we're out of the castle we'll head there."

"The forest?" exclaimed Lodren, "It's full of wild beasts."

"Exactly!" replied Hannock, "So we have to head that way in case anyone else has the same idea. We are the only ones left to protect them."

***

They gathered every terrified Vikkery as they went and eventually reached one of the concealed entrances to the tunnels. Hannock ushered them in one-by-one before instructing Lodren to follow them. He shuffled in. It was a bit of a tight squeeze for him, but the tunnels had not been dug for comfort. They were to give anyone unfortunate enough to be under siege, the chance to survive.

"Hannock," hissed Lodren, "it's pitch black in here! How will we find our way?"

"I may be able to help with that," came a voice from behind them.

Suddenly a flame erupted, blinding them briefly. Their sight cleared, and they were relieved to see the smiling face of Drake.

"Where did you come from?" exclaimed Lodren.

"Powerful wizard now, you know," sniggered Drake, "And I'm not alone."

Faylore shimmered into view, "Quite an eventful afternoon," she announced.

"Did you see anything?" Hannock asked them. "What were our casualties, how many did we lose?"

Drake shrugged, "None, so far as we could tell," he replied.

"But, the dragons?" asked Hannock, puzzled by the answer.

"The two that landed outside the walls aren't doing anything!" said Faylore. "They're just lying there."

"So, as long as they stay out there, we'll only have to deal with one," said Hannock thoughtfully.

"Oh good!" replied Drake, "We'll only have to fight one dragon!"

The journey through the tunnels took hours. When Tamor had ordered them to be dug he had made sure that they would lead whoever used them as far from harm as possible before they ventured back out into the open.

"There's daylight up ahead," whispered Drake.

"I'll exit first," Hannock replied.

In the torchlight, Hannock saw Drake smile as he placed his hand on the captain's chest. Holding up his staff, he disagreed, "Not this time," he whispered. "A sword won't offer much protection against a dragon's breath."

Hannock looked at the young wizard. Once he would have argued the point, but no longer. The inept young man that he had become so fond of no longer existed, before him stood a fully grown, competent wizard. "After you, Master Drake," he said, gesturing with his hand and bowing.

Drake shook his head and smiled, "Barmpot!"

They were concerned that the grinding of the metal door would alert anyone nearby of their presence, but they had no need to fear. As they stood, bathed in the glow of the setting sun, Lodren began to cry.

Faylore hugged him, "Lodren, what's wrong?" she cooed.

"Fireweigh and the others," he wept, "Xarran's got them doing things they never would, and they can't stop him!"

"Oh dear!" sighed Faylore, "Don't worry, Lodren. We'll stop him."

"And I haven't seen my best friend yet! Where's Grubb? I know something horrible has happened to him… I just know it!"

"He'll be fine, Lodren," Hannock assured him. "You know Grubb, he's as tough as old boots. A simple thing like a dragon can't hurt him!"

Lodren wiped the huge tears from his eyes with his sleeve, "I suppose you're right," he sobbed. "But if they've hurt him, I'll give that Xarran a good bashing with my hammer." His expression changed, "Oh, no!" he exclaimed, "My hammer… I forgot my hammer!"

"Oh yeah," said Drake, "how forgetful of me. Here you go, I picked it up for you. You really should be more careful with your things, Lodren." As he held out his hand, Lodren saw a tiny hammer resting in his palm.

Lodren looked confused, "My hammer…" he said, shaking his head. "It's a lot bigger than that, Drake."

Drake laughed, "Oh sorry." He passed his staff over the hammer which immediately grew to its proper size. It fell to the ground with a heavy thud as Drake danced around rubbing his shoulder. "Silly arse!" he exclaimed. "I should have put it down first, nearly pulled my bloody arm out of the socket!"

Faylore scowled at him, "Your magical prowess may be increasing, Drake. But your manners are suffering as a result!"

Drake looked sheepish, "I apologise, Your Majesty," he said, "Won't happen again."

"Make sure it doesn't!" Hannock warned him as he slapped him on the back of his head.

Some things weren't ready for change just yet.

"Oh yeah," added Drake, "I brought this as well. I just had a feeling it might come in useful."

Reaching inside his robes he produced another tiny hammer, only this one was silver.

***

Treading carefully, they reached a large pile of boulders and concealed themselves behind them. Most of the Vikkery were exhausted and collapsed on the soft grass, many falling asleep immediately.

Lodren leaned back on the large round boulder at the foot of the pile and was quickly joined by Hannock, Drake and Faylore. "Bit like old times," he sighed, "Out in the open at dusk, nowhere in mind as a destination. Feels free somehow."

The warm breath on their backs petrified them. Their hard cushion shivered as the deep growling voice spoke, "Going somewhere?" it asked. Their eyes darted from side to side. It was inevitable that they must turn to see what was behind them, although each suspected the same. They rose slowly before turning to face the inquisitor. The dragon blinked slowly, its huge fiery eyes studying them in turn. "Nothing to say?" it asked.

Lodren brandished his hammer, "Don't you move!" he warned, "Or you'll get a bashing you won't forget in a hurry!"

The dragon's eyes widened, "Really?" it asked. "Do you think you could crush my 'ead as easily as you could a zingaard's?"

Drake held up his staff, "He'd have a damned good try, and I'd help him."

"How?" continued the dragon, "You're just a boy with a stick. Ye ain't scaring me ye know!"

Lodren eyed the dragon with suspicion, "You don't sound like any dragon I've met before," he said slowly. "There's something… different about you."

"No there ain't!" protested the dragon, "I'm just an ordinary dragon, there ain't nothin' different about me!"

"You don't speak the same as they do." Lodren ventured nearer to the dragon, studying his scales and colouration. He was a magnificent specimen, that could not be denied, although he was slightly smaller than the dragons they had encountered before. Well, all but one. Lodren cautiously stretched out his hand, "Grubb… is that you?"

The dragon began to laugh, but as it did, the familiar squelching sound could be heard as Grubb shrank back to his normal self, "Had ye goin' for a while though, didn't I?"

"What were you thinking, we could have attacked you, you stupid Vikkery!" exclaimed Lodren. "You could have just waited until we got here and just shown us what you could do!"

"I had to be sure that it was convincin' though," argued Grubb. "You'd 'ave said it was brilliant even if it weren't… and that would've jeapordised my plan. Anyway, swords and arrows and stuff couldn't do me any harm, it'd be like any one o' you tryin' to run yourself through with a bit o' straw!"

"Perhaps," said Drake, "but a bolt of ice up your jacksey may have stung a bit!"

"I could have taken your leg off with the use of my wand," added Harley.

"But ye didn't!" sniffed Grubb. "So everythin's alright."

"Faylore had been listening a bit more closely than the others, "What plan?" she suddenly asked.

Grubb looked up, "What? Oh yes, my plan," he smiled, "We're going to get your crown back for you, Your Majesty."

"Oh really!" exclaimed Faylore, sounding dubious. "And how are you going to manage that?"

"Me and Lodren are going back into the castle, and we're goin' to take it right off Xarran's head! Well, knock it off to be more precise… the crown that is. Then again, maybe we'll knock 'is 'ead off and just pick the crown up after. Either way, you'll get it back," Grubb smiled broadly.

"You're going to march in there and just… take it off him?" asked Hannock, a rather bemused look on his face. "Forgive me for pointing out the obvious here, Grubb, but he is a powerful sorcerer and, now what was the other thing? Oh yes… he's riding a fifty-foot dragon whose breath is hot enough to melt solid stone!"

"I know that!" said Grubb haughtily, "And if you noticed, he's having a great deal of fun destroying the castle! He doesn't care what's goin' on around 'im. That's his weak spot ye see, overconfidence. He won't turn a hair if another dragon comes in behind him, but by that time… it'll be too late!"

"And when were you going to tell me about this brilliant plan to put me in mortal danger?" asked Lodren, scowling.

"I just did," answered Grubb, screwing up his face and shaking his head. "Would ye like me to tell ye again?"

Hannock exhaled loudly, "Oh my days!" he exclaimed, "He's serious."

"Too bloody right I'm serious!" yelled Grubb. "If we don't hurry up there'll be nothin' left of the castle and Xarran will be comin' after us. We need to do this NOW."

Hannock shook his head as he stared at the ground, "It's such a simple plan," he said quietly. "Do you know something?" he asked rhetorically, "It might just work."

"Nonsense!" exclaimed Faylore. "You may ignore a dragon, but as soon as Xarran sees Lodren he'll fry his bones."

"Then we'll just have to make sure that he doesn't see him," said Drake with a wily expression. He glanced over at Emnor, "Know any invisibility spells?"

CHAPTER 21

Soon after, a small dragon approached the remnants of the castle gates. Astride his neck was the invisible Lodren who clutched the silver hammer tightly to his chest, "Are you sure nobody can see me?" he asked sounding slightly alarmed.

"There'd only be a strange shimmer if you jumped about in front o' someone, so if ye keep as still as ye can you'll be fine," answered the dragon quietly.

"Before we go in," whispered Lodren, "I'd like you to know that you're the best friend I've ever had."

"I know," growled the dragon, "and you're mine, now shut yer face or you'll get us both roasted."

Xarran turned, eyeing the new arrival suspiciously. He had arrived with three dragons and this one was unfamiliar to him. He slid from Fireweigh's back and approached Grubb with caution, "What are you doing here?" he asked slowly.

"I was nearby," replied the dragon, "Somethin' was callin' me, so I came."

Xarran raised his hand and ran his finger along the crown. Did it summon dragons by its own volition? He thought. If that was the case he would never be alone, protection would always be close at hand. He stared hard at the dragon, desperately wanted to believe his own thought. But deep inside something did not ring true. Xarran began to back away, “Destroy it!” he roared.

Fireweigh immediately began to turn, a fiery glow appearing as his huge jaws began to open. Grubb recoiled, spilling Lodren from his back. Climbing to his feet as quickly as he could Lodren was just in time to see the flames that erupted from Fireweigh’s gaping mouth. Instinctively, he held the silver hammer in front of him. He was unsure why he did this, surely nothing would protect him from dragon fire? But he was wrong. The flames were somehow diverted around him as if he was protected by a magical, invisible shield. Those crafty wizards, he thought. But it was a thought on which he had little time to ponder.

Xarran had smiled sadistically as the flames engulfed Grubb, but he had also noticed the anomalous re-direction of them at his side. It seemed that there were two intruders. His spell pierced the fiery wall, a pulse of energy that struck its target and sent it skidding across the floor. However, and luckily for Lodren, Xarran still could not see his hidden foe who lay dazed amongst the rubble strewn across the courtyard.

“I will find you!” screamed Xarran.

Grubb had his own problems. Surprisingly, he had not been incinerated, his dragon scales had protected him. However, realising that his demise was not imminent but also a little confused, it took him a few seconds to react. He charged forward, headbutting Fireweigh as hard as he could. The larger dragon stumbled, bumping into Xarran and knocking him to the ground. Rolling away to avoid being crushed by the wrestling dragons, he was unaware of the invisibly Nibby bearing down on him.

Lodren raised the silver hammer as he approached, he tired of the tyranny of the sorcerers and one less would be a blessing. He closed his eyes ready to strike the fatal blow to Xarran. But his plan too, was about to be thwarted.

The dragons with their slashing claws, were writhing on the ground trying to best one another. Grubb, being slightly smaller, had the advantage of speed and managed to get to his feet. Clamping his teeth into Fireweigh's throat, he shook him as hard as he could. He was unused to being in the guise of a dragon and had not learned how to control all of his body parts at once, this was the issue that would affect the Nibby. Grubb's tail lashed about wildly, catching the Nibby full in the chest and flinging him high into the air. To be fair to Grubb it wasn't entirely his fault, Lodren was invisible after all.

Then, good fortune came their way! As Lodren was launched, he lost his grip on the hammer and it sailed almost as high as he did. Once he had let go, it became visible and he watched it as it fell. As if in slow motion, it plummeted to where Xarran sat in a daze and struck the side of his head. The Thedarian crown was dislodged and fell to the floor with a loud 'clang' before rolling away. Lodren however, landed with a thump. He scrambled across the ground as fast as he could, snatching up the crown and raising it high into the air.

"DESIST!" he bellowed.

Fireweigh immediately pulled away from Grubb. His head snapped to the side, fire in his eyes as he saw Xarran. Two steps was all it took for Fireweigh to be upon him. Raising his mighty, clawed hand into the air momentarily, he roared before slamming it down where Xarran lay.

Lodren had lowered his head. He knew that the sorcerers were evil and had been willing to end the life of this particular one. To bear witness to it being done by another was somehow far more difficult. He approached Fireweigh, preparing to apologise for attacking him and being responsible for him having to take a life.

Fireweigh spoke first, "What will you do with him now?" he asked.

To Lodren's amazement, Xarran was alive!

Fireweigh had him held down firmly, a large claw embedded deep into the ground on either side of him.

Grubb shrank, "Ye should kill 'im, Lodren," he growled, "Face it, he was going to kill you."

Lodren sighed as he walked over and picked up the silver hammer, "I just wish there was another way," he said.

Standing over Xarran, he raised the hammer, "But I don't think there is."

***

Lodren was not the type to hide his feelings, especially if anyone had the audacity to criticise his culinary skills, but they had never seen him like this before. His expression surpassed rage. He was red in the face and gripped his hammer so tightly, they half-expected the handle to splinter at any moment. He stormed past them, Grubb hurrying to stay on his heels.

"Well?" asked Hannock. "What happened?"

Grubb looked up at him in disbelief, "Ain't it obvious?" he asked. "We were killed! We're ghosts!"

"So your plan worked?"

"O' course it worked!" exclaimed Grubb. "We wouldn't be standin' 'ere if it 'adn't would we?"

"What about Xarran, did he escape again, or did you manage to defeat him?" asked Harley, eagerly.

"No, 'e didn't get away this time," sighed Grubb. "We got 'im."

"So he's dead?" asked Faylore.

"You'd better ask him," Grubb suggested, pointing at Lodren.

Lodren couldn't bring himself to face his friends, "I know I shouldn't have," he said quietly. "After everything he did, he deserved to die. He even said he was coming after us once he'd finished destroying the castle. I don't know what came over me. I'm so sorry."

Faylore put her arm around his shoulders, "It's alright, Lodren. Any one of us would have done the same, you had a responsibility to kill him if you had the chance."

"That's the thing," sighed Lodren, "I didn't! I had him, he was lying on the floor defenceless, but I just couldn't do it!"

"You had the chance to end him, yet you let him live!" exclaimed Hannock.

"Yes!" bellowed Lodren. "And for good reason! We might need him to bargain with!"

"Well done," said Faylore. "Do you have any idea of their plans?"

Lodren looked surprised, “Oh dear,” he replied blushing, “I never thought to ask.”

“I’m sure Xarran will tell us with a little… persuasion,” said Hannock, raising his sword menacingly. “Where is he?”

“Fireweigh’s keepin an eye on him, well… a couple of claws to be precise. Which reminds me,” He held up Xarran’s wand, “Anybody want this?”

“Hang on a minute!” Harley suddenly yelled, “Where are the kings? Where are Tamor and Jared?”

“Well…” sighed Grubb, “… Tamor’s in the castle takin’ a nap!”

“What!” replied his friends in unison.

“Yeah… strangest thing I’ve ever seen,” continued Grubb. “Just after Lodren decided not to squash Xarran’s head, King Tamor appeared from the far end o’ the courtyard. Gave us a right royal roastin’ for disturbin’ ‘im ‘e did. He took one look at all the mess and told us to get it cleaned up by the time ‘e came back or he’d ‘ave us put in the stocks!”

The companions laughed at the thought of Tamor in a confused temper, but Harley didn’t find it as amusing as the others, “And what about King Jared, where’s he?”

“He disappeared,” said Hannock quietly.

“Disappeared?” asked Drake.

“We were on the ramparts when he suddenly felt dizzy. I reached out to steady him, but he vanished before I could get to him.”

“Did you see anything else?” asked Emnor with grave concern. “Was there anything unusual?”

"More unusual than him vanishing into thin air!"

"Sorry, Hannock. What I meant to ask was, did you see anyone else, Karrak perhaps?"

Hannock shook his head.

"We could send out search parties," suggested Harley. "He can't be far away."

"Search parties?" said Hannock raising an eyebrow. "We have no idea where he might be, he could be a thousand miles away!"

"We can at least try!" protested Harley.

"It would be pointless!" argued Hannock. "Even if we searched from dawn 'til dusk, we'd never cover enough ground."

"Unless…" said Lodren, thoughtfully. Reaching inside his tunic, he produced the Thedarian crown, "… We had a few friends who could help us cover more of that ground."

"Finding him won't be the issue, I can do that easily," laughed Drake. Realising he had suddenly become the centre of attention, he continued, "We'll use the Tallarans Eye! All we need is a piece of his clothing and it'll tell us where he is. However, if we locate him, Karrak might have hidden him another way and we may not know when he is."

"When he is what?" asked Grubb, seriously.

"When he is, in time," replied Drake.

"In time for what?" asked the confused Vikkery.

Drake sighed and closed his eyes, "Will someone please explain it to him. I must prepare."

Grubb was getting tetchy, “When he’s in time for what?” he exclaimed. “Faylore, what’s he on about?”

CHAPTER 22

Jared had appeared in an immense cavern and marvelled at the beauty of his unfamiliar surroundings. Jewels, embedded deep in the walls and roof, danced like a thousand blazing stars as they reflected the firelight from the braziers that surrounded him. The river of lava was also something to behold, and he approached it with interest as he once more glanced up at the fiery gems above.

"Fascinating aren't they," echoed Karrak's voice. "Dull, lifeless stones, but add a little light and they transform with a magnificence mere words cannot describe."

"Is that why you have brought me here, Karrak?" asked Jared, "To show me the pretty lights."

"No, Jared, I have brought you here so that you may join me or die," replied Karrak.

"Oh, I think you already know that I would never join you, Karrak. However…" Jared said calmly, "… I have no intention of dying either."

"There are only two options, Jared. Your survival having not chosen the first will inevitably mean that it will be the second."

Jared smiled, "If it were that easy, you would have already tried," he said, "Now why don't you face me and reveal your true identity? I know that you appear as my brother, but we both know that he would never have the ability to hold his temper for this long."

A shadowy figure drifted from the gloom, Jared could see the light from the Elixian Soul as it throbbed in its chest, "I am here," it said calmly, the voice no longer holding the familiar tone of his brother. "Does it make a difference now that you see me?"

Jared stared at the entity before him. There were no features, no eyes, nothing discernible for him to focus on. "Who are you?" he asked.

"I am the beginning," it replied. "And I shall be so again."

"The beginning?"

"I have existed since the dawn of this world. From its birth until now, I have watched over it. Once, there was peace and silence, that peace must return."

"Is it that it must return, or simply that you yearn for it?" asked Jared.

"That is none of your concern," replied the entity, becoming agitated, "You have something that belongs to me, return it and I may provide you with the answers you seek. I may even allow you to leave this place."

Jared held on to his staff a little tighter as he glanced at the Heart of Ziniphar. "How do I know that I can trust your word?" he asked, turning his back.

"You do not," it replied. "I would have already killed you and taken what is rightfully mine if that were my intention."

Jared had noticed that the Elixian Soul was beginning to pulsate quickly and far more brightly than it had before. He laughed again, a new confidence building inside him, "From experience, I know that you have no qualms with murdering any who stand in your way. If I am to take you at your word, you must first prove your sincerity."

"You waste my time, Jared Dunbar. You should not test me!" warned the figure, tersely.

"But you have been here since the beginning of time! Surely a few more moments are as insignificant to you as I am?"

The entity floated closer, "Very well," it hissed, "What is it that you want?".

"Release my brother!" snapped Jared. "Free him and then we shall discuss your request."

"You demand payment for what is mine!?"

"Perhaps," replied Jared, nonchalantly, "but I did not steal it as you stole my brother."

The entity studied Jared, circling around him as it pondered over his demand. "As you wish, I shall release him, then you must return my belongings to me."

"As I said before," repeated Jared, "we shall discuss it."

"I warn you, do not try to trick me. Your own life is not the only one at risk here."

"I understand that," replied Jared.

"I do not refer to your brother," said the entity, menacingly. "There is another. Follow me."

Jared followed at a sedate pace as his foe drifted ahead. To show concern would be perceived as a sign of weakness and, regardless of who was being held captive, he could not allow that.

To strike his enemy with its back turned would be the logical choice, but what of the other life of which his enemy spoke? Although presented with such an easy target, Jared knew that he must bide his time. Deliberately slowing his pace even more, he stared at the cavern walls. Who could possibly exist in such a place? Despite its beauty, there would be no comfort to be had from bare rock. The answers to his questions came all at once as he saw it… In the distance, tethered to the ground with magical bindings, lay a golden dragon!

Jared recalled the descriptions he had been given by Faylore, Lodren and Grubb as they related their story of their time with the dragons, and all became clear.

As he grew nearer, a rage began to burn inside him. The pitiful sight of such a magnificent creature imprisoned as it was, was almost more than he could bear. He longed to free him, longed to blast his bindings apart but could not allow himself to fall into such an obvious trap. He must be more cunning than that.

"Ha!" he scoffed, "Is this it? This is the life with which you seek to influence me? A beast?"

"A beast it may be, but it is also your most powerful ally. A fact you know to be true," it sneered. "Shall I kill it now?" it asked, menacingly.

"It matters not to me," scoffed Jared, convincingly. "Kill it, don't kill it, it is of no consequence." He paused and held up a finger, "However…" he continued, "… death is something that you obviously enjoy, and to deprive you of that would give me great pleasure."

Thelwynn spoke for the first time, "I am of no import!" he whispered, "Let the thing do as it will, do not allow it to use my life as leverage, Dunbar."

Jared could not let his feelings show now. "Do be quiet, beast," he said, dismissively, waving his hand to further prove his disinterest. "I have enough to contend with without your interruptions."

Turning his attention back to his enemy, his expression changed to a snarl, "Now, return my brother to me."

His enemy began to quiver. Black smoke poured from it, drifting across the floor and forming a murky pool. Thelwynn took the opportunity to speak again, "The boy…" he whispered hoarsely, "… he has the crown. I can offer no aid, I must obey its commands!"

Jared shook his head and held up his hand to both silence, and reassure Thelwynn. The entity began to look more and more like his brother as the pool took a form of its own. Jared stared hard. A face was forming, slightly disfigured, but somehow familiar to him. He could now see Karrak clearly as he fell heavily to the ground. He took a step toward him, but the entity moved swiftly between them.

"I have delivered my side of the bargain, mortal," it hissed. "Now, return what is mine," it ordered, stretching out an ethereal arm.

"Jared don't give it to her!" Karrak pleaded urgently. "She is Felludar! Her purpose is to bring silence, once she has the Heart and Soul she will destroy all life to bring peace to the world!"

Felludar let out a scream of outrage as she turned to face Karrak. Jared backed away and raised his staff. "Face me!" he roared.

She paused momentarily and turned slowly, "You agreed," she said slowly.

“She cannot take it from you, Jared. It must be given willingly, to take it by force would destroy it,” added Karrak.

Jared smiled, almost leering at Felludar, “It seems we have reached an impass, Felludar. You cannot take the Heart from me and I am unwilling to hand it to you. What would you suggest we do now?”

Felludar retreated slightly, “You will give it to me,” she said calmly. “Or do I have to take something of yours?” She whirled around, her manic gaze falling on Karrak. There was a flash. Karrak had expected it, but in his weakened state his attempt at a protection spell proved mostly ineffective. He was blasted twenty feet across the cave floor, rolling many times before his body lay motionless.

Jared roared and thrust his staff forward. Fireballs and bolts of ice flew from it, a few managing to strike Felludar before she could defend herself. Reeling back and finding her balance, she began to fight back. She was not allowed to attack Jared in order to take the Heart of Ziniphar, however, she was allowed to defend herself from his attacks.

Their battle continued, but neither could gain the upper hand. Spells that were cast were either deflected or completely nullified. Suddenly it dawned on Jared that, only when he cast a spell, was Felludar able to retaliate. Testing his theory, he lowered his staff. His heart leapt as, in the distance, Karrak was starting to stir. He was still alive! If he could somehow instruct his brother without Felludar realising, they may gain the upper hand if they were to attack her simultaneously.

“You have strong magic, Felludar,” he said, feigning admiration. “Perhaps if there were two of me, I could defeat you. It seems we are destined to be here some time."

"You cannot defeat me," said Felludar, confidently. "The outcome will be the same, whatever steps you take. It has been foretold since the beginning of time."

"Foretold!" said Jared, questioningly. "By whom? You were the first, were you not? Why would it take another to prophesy the outcome of your endeavours?"

Karrak was now on his feet, stealthily approaching Felludar from the rear. He was a little unsteady but nodded at Jared to let him know he was ready to play his part in Felludar's annihilation.

Jared raised his staff slowly, admiring the Heart of Ziniphar that Felludar so yearned for as her prize. He smiled at her, "Shall we try again?" he asked.

"Do you not feel anything for me, Jared?" asked Felludar, her voice taking on a pleading tone, "I brought you into this world, as I did your brother. We should stand together."

Jared paused, "What do you mean, you brought us into this world?"

The entity lowered its arms. Its appearance altered as it took a solid form.

Jared's expression changed, as a look of horrified confusion swept across his face, "No!" he said quietly, "You can't be! It's not possible."

Felludar smiled at him, "No, Jared, you are wrong… I am your mother!

Jared fell to his knees. Faint memories of his mother flashed through his mind as he fought to hold back the tears.

"I have missed you both, my sons," continued Felludar, "To bring peace to the world is the reason why I brought you into it."

Jared weakly held up his staff, "That is a lie," he whispered, "Our mother was a gentle soul, she could never commit the atrocities that you are guilty of."

"The person whose body I occupied died long before you were born, Jared. I gave birth to both you and Karrak. Every childhood memory you hold dear is a memory of our time together."

Jared's mind was in turmoil. He looked from the face of his mother to his limping brother. Did Felludar speak the truth, or was it just another ploy to get him to lower his guard? He couldn't decide as he knelt there shaking his head in disbelief. Furthermore, regardless of the answer, could he destroy the one who now wore his mother's features?

Felludar walked slowly toward him, "Give me the Heart, Jared," she cooed softly, "End this torment, end your pain and join with me."

Jared lowered the staff and ran his thumb across the Heart of Ziniphar. He was tired. So many had died, friends had been lost, perhaps it was time for the turmoil to cease. He sighed as he wrapped his hand around the Heart. He would tear it from its setting and hand it to Felludar, believing that it was the only way that it could end.

"No, Dunbar," roared Thelwynn, "You cannot, she will kill you all."

Jared smiled at him, "I know," he said quietly, "But at least we will be at peace."

Thelwynn began to struggle against his magical bindings. Felludar laughed loudly as he writhed in a bid to free himself. But her laughter stopped abruptly as suddenly one of the tethers snapped!

Thelwynn had found a new strength. Bit by bit he was breaking free!

“No!” screeched Felludar, “This cannot be!”

Jared shook his head as if waking from a dream. He saw the golden dragon tearing free and climbing to its feet, its breath illuminating the cavern.

Huge chunks of rock fell from the roof as a thunderous booming began. Daylight shone through as large cracks appeared and through them could be seen Thelwynn’s kin.

The dragons had come home!

Jared rose to his feet, shaking off the enchantment with which Felludar had been so cleverly ensnaring him. Deep inside, he knew that Felludar had been telling the truth about being their mother, he also knew that she was inherently evil and must be destroyed!

Fireballs flew once more. Felludar defended herself easily with an invisible forcefield that nothing seemed able to pierce, but her confidence was to be her downfall. She had paid no mind to Karrak as she focussed on the Heart of Ziniphar. His hands raised, he conjured an ice spike in mid-air. Biding his time, he released it. As it struck Felludar, her shield fell, allowing the last few fireballs to strike her full force.

“It seems that you can defeat me after all,” she said quietly. There was no anger or disappointment in her voice, just resignation that she had lost the battle. She swayed slightly as life left her, the Elixian Soul falling from her chest and rolling across the floor toward Jared. Then, she too, collapsed to the floor.

Dragons began to land heavily all around them and familiar voices could be heard.

"'e alright?"

"Just wait a minute… honestly!" exclaimed another.

Gentle arms wrapped around him, "Are you hurt?" asked Faylore urgently.

"I'm fine," sighed Jared. "Is Karrak alright?"

"Yes!" exclaimed Hannock as he loaded a golden bolt into his crossbow, "But not for long."

"No!" cried Jared, "You don't understand. It wasn't him!"

Jared hurried to his brother and crouched beside him. Taking his hand, he looked into his eyes lovingly, "Brother, you are free," he assured him. "Evil no longer has a hold on you, you can return home with Father and I and we can rebuild Borell together. All of this will fade, and we can revert to our old lives."

Karrak smiled, "Well, we can't have that, can we?" he said, his expression changing.

Without warning, Jared was hit full in the chest by a spell. He flew into the air, only stopping when he struck the cave wall. Karrak grabbed his staff from the ground and blasted the companions. They were still mid-flight as he snatched up the Elixian Soul. Throwing up his arms, a forcefield similar to Felludar's now protected him. Two dragons roared and open their jaws, but neither fire nor ice could penetrate the shield. Faylore's arrows and Hannock's bolt bounced off and even Lodren's hammer was ineffective.

“I warned you, Brother!” screamed Karrak, “If you had only listened to me once, just once, you wouldn’t be lying there about to die! You look confused, let me explain. I told you about Felludar, I told you that she had to be given things willingly, and that includes fealty. She could never have possessed me if I hadn’t allowed her to. Unfortunately, that meant that I had to follow her agenda, whereas now, I am free to do as I please, now that I have the Heart and the Soul.”

Jared was still slightly stunned as he stared at Karrak, “You surrendered yourself to her? Why?”

“Because, just for once, I wanted to have all the best toys. You have no idea what it’s like to always be second best. But, we’ve had this conversation before so, if you don’t mind, I’m going to kill you now,” Karrak raised the staff.

“So you’re still a coward then,” laughed Hannock.

Karrak glared at him.

“You say you are the most powerful sorcerer to ever live, but you hide inside your bubble, too afraid to face anyone without the aid of your magic.”

“Well, what can I say, Hannock?” replied Karrak, “What’s the use of possessing the power if I have no intention of using it?”

Moments before, Karrak had not witnessed the subtle signal that Hannock had given to Lodren. The Nibby had indeed tried to break through the invisible barrier, but with his own hammer. Edging back, he now held the silver hammer. With Hannock playing for time, Lodren sneaked around behind Karrak. He could not recall having used as much force before as he struck the shield with all his might.

Karrak was startled as the shield began to spark and flicker, unsure of what had caused it, but the momentary glitch was all the time Jared needed to act. Knowing that his own magic would be enough to protect him, he launched himself at his brother, his fist striking him full in the face.

The companions sprang forward in a bid to follow their friend but were immediately repelled by the shield.

The sound of Karrak's nose breaking echoed off the cave walls as he fell back in a heap, dropping both the Soul, and the staff. Jared dived on him, his fist raised for a knockout blow, but Karrak was quicker than he had expected and parried the blow. Clambering to their feet, they wrestled one another but, as he was much bigger, and far stronger, Karrak easily threw Jared to the ground once more, following up with a kick that caught Jared squarely in the jaw. Jared rolled away, feeling as if he had been kicked by a carthorse. He had only moments to compose himself. Glancing up he saw that Karrak was looking for the staff. He charged at his brother, thrusting his shoulder into Karrak's midriff. They tustled on the ground but Karrak got the upper hand again, this time by headbutting Jared and returning the favour by breaking his nose. Ineffective punches were exchanged as they rolled around on the floor, covered in blood and trying to gain an advantage. Karrak caught Jared with an elbow to the temple and, while his older brother was disorientated, rolled away from him and made a grab for the staff.

Jared had to act quickly. The staff lay in a pool of blood, a pool to which both he and Karrak had contributed. The Elixian Soul was at his feet and, remembering the words from the Scroll, he kicked it perfectly and it came to rest next to the staff.

Karrak leered at him as he took both blood-soaked relics in his hands. “And now, Brother, it ends. You could never have defeated me.” He pointed the staff at Jared and jerked it slightly. Nothing happened! Karrak stared at it in disbelief as it began to shudder. Sparks suddenly erupted and began to arc between the staff and the Elixian Soul. Karrak shook as if he were being electrocuted and he let out a scream. The explosion that destroyed the staff threw him to the ground and he lay there, convulsing. The shield dropped, and Jared stepped forward, stooping to pick up the dull, black stone that lay on the ground.

The companions watched as he approached Karrak. Leaning forward he grabbed the front of his robes. “It looks as if you were wrong,” he snarled.

Karrak’s rasping breath could not hide his venom as he answered, “That is where you are wrong,” he hissed.

Jared’s eyes widened. He looked down as his brother grinned. The knife embedded in his chest was buried to the hilt, his blood already beginning to drip from the handle. Even in defeat, Karrak would not submit.

Jared rocked back and fell cross-legged, still trying to fathom how he had allowed himself to be so easily duped. As he stared at his brother, his eyes remained open long enough to witness the golden bolt pierce the sorcerer’s temple.

He fell backwards, and all went black.

EPILOGUE

Hannock admired himself in the mirror. His uniform was pressed, his armour was gleaming and he was most impressed with his new haircut. "I must say, Lodren, there's nothing like a clean uniform to make a man feel new again."

"You virtually are a new man!" exclaimed Lodren, "Although, what you did was a bit of a cheek, if you ask me. No pun intended."

"You're just jealous," snorted Hannock, finding it hard to leave the mirror.

"Jealous? I don't think so," laughed Lodren. "Don't you think it's about time you went and saw the king?"

"There's no rush, he won't have woken up yet."

"I still think you should go and check," Lodren said, pushing Hannock toward the door.

"Alright, alright, I'm going. Don't crease the tunic," he said, tugging at it.

Making his way through the castle, he passed Grubb, "Good morning, Grubb," he said cheerily. "Back to our old smiling self, are we?"

Grubb looked him up and down briefly, "Ye look like a bloody peacock with them feathers in yer 'at," he mumbled. "Oh, and get stuffed ye sarky git."

Entering the king's chambers, Hannock stood to attention, "Time to rise, Your Majesty. Things to do and all that."

The king opened his eyes, "Hannock!" he exclaimed, "What happened to your face?"

"Nothing sire," replied Hannock with a smile, "Just as handsome as ever."

"But, your eye, your cheek? Just a minute, how the hell did I get here?"

"Take a breath, Sire, I'll explain."

"Explain!" came the shrieked response. "I was dead! Karrak killed me! I know he did!"

"Calm down, Jared. You weren't dead! You were only… nearly dead. You're fine now, good as new, well better than new."

"I was in a cave, Karrak…" he paused, trying to remember, "… the bolt! You killed Karrak!"

"Yes, Jared, I know. But not before he seriously wounded you. Luckily, the dragon saved you."

"But that's the thing, Hannock, it didn't!"

"It did!" exclaimed Hannock, "Well, it didn't stop you from being wounded, but it did stop you from dying."

"Necromancy! Hannock… did the dragon…"

"No, Jared it did not use necromancy," sighed Hannock, "It's a bit like what Grubb can do when he heals someone, only far stronger. It's called The Dragon's Sigh. Even if the subject is on death's doorstep they can bring them back by breathing on them. Oh, and it can be used to heal old injuries as well," he added stroking his cheek.

"So they saved my life and then you asked them to heal you as well?"

"No, not really. I just happened to be holding you at the time," replied Hannock.

"Yeah, and that weren't no accident was it?" said Grubb as he barged into the room. "Cryin' like a big babby 'e was. Thought ye might like some breakfast, Jared," he added, placing a tray next to the king. "The others are lookin' forward to seeing ye, they're all waitin' downstairs." He scowled at Hannock as he left the room.

"Everyone is here?" asked Jared, tentatively.

"Except for the wizards," replied Hannock. "They took the Darkness to hide it. They don't think it's wise to keep it around, far too much temptation."

"The Darkness?"

"That stone you picked up after your battle with Karrak," replied Hannock, "Before it was split, it was called The Darkness."

"I might regret asking this," said Jared, "But why is it called The Darkness?"

"From what I can gather," replied Hannock, "It's because that is its purpose, to bring Darkness. Without light there's no life and ultimately, peace."

Jared nodded, "And Karrak?" he asked, solemnly.

"Bullseye!" replied Hannock. "Strangely though, his body vanished!"

Jared sighed, “We’ve seen some awful things, Hannock, let us hope that we can now live in peace.”

“Absolutely,” agreed Hannock. “However, there is still one thing I don’t understand. I mean not fully anyway.”

Jared raised his eyebrows, “Which is?” he asked.

“What exactly, is a Nibrilsiem?”

Printed in Great Britain
by Amazon